Finding Forever: Falling for the Rebel

ANNE FRASER

ALISON ROBERTS

KATE HARDY

MILLS & BOON

First Published in Great Britain 2022
by Mills & Boon, an imprint of HarperCollins*Publishers* Ltd,
1 London Bridge Street, London, SE1 9GF

www.harpercollins.co.uk

HarperCollins*Publishers*
1st Floor, Watermarque Building,
Ringsend Road, Dublin 4, Ireland

FINDING FOREVER: FALLING FOR THE REBEL
© 2022 Harlequin Books S.A.

St Piran's: Daredevil, Doctor...Dad! © 2012 Harlequin Books S.A.
St Piran's: The Brooding Heart Surgeon © 2011 Harlequin Books S.A.
St Piran's: The Fireman and Nurse Loveday © 2011 Harlequin Books S.A.

Special thanks and acknowledgement are given to Anne Fraser for her contribution to the *St. Piran's Hospital* series
Special thanks and acknowledgement are given to Alison Roberts for her contribution to the *St. Piran's Hospital* series
Special thanks and acknowledgement are given to Pamela Brooks for her contribution to the *St. Piran's Hospital* series.

ISBN: 978-0-263-30404-6

MIX
Paper from
responsible sources
FSC™ C007454

This book is produced from independently certified FSC™ paper to ensure responsible forest management.

For more information visit: www.harpercollins.co.uk/green

Printed and Bound in Spain using 100% Renewable electricity at CPI Black Print, Barcelona

An... ...ned that one day she would be writing for a living. She started life as a nurse a... .... m... ...al romances, is married to a hospital doctor! ...e and husband have lived and worked all over the ...id, including South Africa, Canada and Australia ...d many of their experiences as well as the settings find their way into her books. Anne lives in Glasgow with her husband and two children.

New Zealander **Alison Roberts** has written more than eighty romance novels for Mills & Boon. She has also worked as a primary school teacher, a cardiology research technician and a paramedic. Currently, she is living her dream of living – and writing – in a gorgeous village in the south of France.

Kate Hardy has been a bookworm since she was a toddler. When she isn't writing Kate enjoys reading, theatre, live music, ballet and the gym. She lives with her husband, student children and their spaniel in Norwich, England. You can contact her via her website: www.katehardy.com

Finding Forever

ST PIRAN'S: DAREDEVIL, DOCTOR...DAD!

ANNE FRASER

To my lovely editor, Joanne, with heartfelt thanks
for her support and guidance.

CHAPTER ONE

ABBY sank onto the sofa transfixed by what was happening on the TV screen. At the end of a rope, a man was being lowered out of a Royal Navy helicopter. Abby held her breath as the figure swirled precariously in the buffeting wind. She had put on the TV to catch the weather report but now she couldn't tear her eyes away from the drama unfolding in front of her.

Beneath the helicopter a boat was listing dangerously to one side, obviously in serious trouble. The reporter covering the story was telling the viewers that the Royal Navy rescue service had been called out to the stricken vessel. 'The family of four were on a sailing trip when they got into trouble off the Cornish coast. Heavy seas pushed their boat onto rocks and it is now taking on water rapidly. We have heard that the helmsman took a heavy blow to his head and is unconscious. His wife, who radioed for help, and their two young children, are still on board.'

Although the newscaster's expression was calm, Abby could detect suppressed tension in her voice. 'The helicopter crew has only a short time to get everyone off before the boat sinks. We understand that there is a doctor helping from the Royal Cornwall Air Ambulance Service.'

The man at the end of the winch dropped onto the listing boat, unhooked himself from the line and slithered his way across the deck. Within minutes he was being lifted back on board the helicopter, with two small figures attached to him like clams.

He swiftly dropped down to the boat again, retrieving another person from the stricken yacht. Heart in her mouth, Abby leaned forward. The injured skipper was still on the boat! Could he be rescued before the yacht sank, taking him and his rescuer along with it? If he had a head injury, as the newscaster was suggesting, then it would be dangerous to move him. But what other option was there? To leave him would be unthinkable.

The downdraught from the helicopter whipped the sea into a frenzy. Nearby, a coastguard rescue boat was making valiant attempts to approach the yacht but the heavy waves were preventing it from getting anywhere close. Abby squeezed her eyes closed. She could hardly bear to watch.

'A second man is being lowered onto the boat.' The newscaster's voice dropped to a whisper. 'We understand he's a doctor.'

Abby opened her eyes. Sure enough, she could just make out the letters on the fluorescent jacket of the second man.

The line attached to the helicopter was swinging wildly as the pilot struggled to keep the aircraft level. The small boat rose up to meet the man on the end of the winch then dropped away again. The figure swung first to the right then to the left as the deck kept veering away. Abby knew there was a real possibility that the rescuers might lose their own lives in the attempt to reach the injured skipper.

Suddenly the doctor was on the deck. Quickly he

released himself from the harness and the line was reeled back into the helicopter.

Almost unable to breathe, Abby watched him pick his way across the slippery deck, almost losing his balance as the boat shifted wildly in the heavy seas. Moments later another man dropped down from the helicopter, this one with a stretcher. Abby lost sight of the first man as he disappeared from view. Had he slipped overboard?

While she'd been watching, Emma had come into the room. Seeing Abby staring at the screen, she unplugged herself from her MP3 player and sat down next to her.

'Is that what you're going to be doing?' Emma asked. 'In your new job?'

'Sometimes,' Abby admitted. Although she hoped to hell she wouldn't be involved in anything quite as dangerous as what was going on in front of her. It was one thing being trained to be winched up and down from a helicopter in calm conditions—this was something altogether different.

Emma looked at her wide-eyed. 'Cool,' she said.

Thankfully her daughter didn't seem to appreciate the danger the men were in. That was good: Abby didn't want Emma worrying about her.

It seemed like hours but it could only have been a few minutes before the stretcher, now loaded with the injured skipper, was being attached to the winch. Abby knew the danger was far from over. The yacht was sinking rapidly. She was amazed that it had managed to stay afloat as long as it had.

Then the men with the stretcher were being lifted back onto the helicopter. As soon as they were on board the aircraft swung away. Seconds later the boat tipped up and with a final surge was engulfed by the waves. Any sooner and it would have taken the three men with it.

'I understand the mother and two children have been taken to hospital where they are being treated for hypothermia and shock,' the reporter continued. 'At this time we have no details about the condition of the skipper except that he is stable. But right now we can give you a live interview with some of the men involved in the daring rescue.'

The drama over, Emma went back to her music and left the room. Before Abby could switch the television off, the camera panned out slightly, revealing two men. One, a man in his fifties, was wearing the jumpsuit of the Royal Navy, the other the fluorescent jacket of a rescue doctor. Both men were smiling broadly, as if what they had just done had been exhilarating—and no more dangerous than a routine training exercise.

But as the camera zoomed closer, it was the younger man, the doctor, that made Abby's heart leap in her chest. Underneath his five-o'clock shadow there was something disturbingly familiar about his hooked nose and wide grin. But before Abby could get a better look at him the camera, frustratingly, focussed solely on his colleague.

'I have Sergeant Lightbody with me, who was the winchman involved in the rescue,' the reporter said.

The older man shifted slightly, looking uncomfortable to find himself on TV.

'Sergeant Lightbody,' the newscaster continued, 'can you tell the viewers at home what it was like out there today? From what I could see, it seemed that you just managed to get the victims off the boat in the nick of time.'

Sergeant Lightbody looked even more ill at ease. 'It was certainly a little breezy out there. I guess it was one of the more difficult situations we've been involved in for a while.'

'A little breezy? A bit of an understatement, surely? If you and your men hadn't been able to get these people off, it could've ended in tragedy. That all the family members survived is testament to the skill and courage of your team.'

'It's what we do.' Sergeant Lightbody shrugged. 'Anyway, if it hadn't been for Dr MacNeil here, we might not have got the skipper off without further injury—if at all.'

The camera shifted to the younger man. He was shaking his head. Despite the hat pulled low on his brow, shadowing his eyes, Abby realised with a jolt that she did recognise him. She didn't need to check the photograph she had kept for all these years to know that Dr MacNeil was Mac—her dead sister's lover and Emma's father!

Her legs shaking, Abby got up and retrieved the remote then froze the screen. She was breathing rapidly as she studied the fuzzy picture. It was him! He was older, yes; there were faint smile lines on either side of his mouth and radiating from the corners of his ice-blue eyes. He had filled out a little, and his hair was shorter, although still sun-bleached at the tips. Still, she would know that wide smile and glinting, expressive gaze anywhere.

She pressed the remote and the picture moved again.

'Dr MacNeil, could you tell us what happened back there? I understand you work with the Royal Cornwall Air Ambulance team. Is this just another typical day for you?'

Abby's heart was pounding so hard she could almost

hear it. She had found Mac! And not just found him, she was actually going to be working with him. She sank back down on the sofa as her legs threatened to give way beneath her. Thank God Emma had left the room. She would have known immediately that something was wrong, and right now Abby needed to make sense of what she was seeing.

Mac grinned into the camera. Unlike Sergeant Lightbody, he seemed completely at ease. 'Not exactly a typical day but, yes, the Royal Cornwall Air Ambulance teams up with other rescue services when required. We believe that having immediate medical attention on the scene can often make the difference between life and death.'

'Even if it means putting your own life at risk?' The stunning blonde reporter was almost whimpering with admiration.

'I'm pretty certain the Royal Navy wouldn't let anything happen to me,' Mac replied lightly. 'Besides, they are the real heroes. They do this sort of thing day after day. If it wasn't for the pilot of the helicopter and his team, we would have never been able to get to the casualties.'

Abby still couldn't believe what she was seeing. It was ironic, really. Abby had tried desperately to find this man years before without any success, and now he was here, in Penhally, and she'd be working with him!

Incredible to think that the reason they were here in the first place was because Emma didn't have a father.

A few months ago, just before Emma's eleventh birthday, Abby had asked her whether she wanted to invite her schoolfriends over for a party. To Abby's horror, Emma had burst into tears. When she'd eventually managed to calm her down, Emma had admitted that the children at the school had been ostracising her for the last couple of weeks. Only her best friend had still talked to her.

'But why, darling? Has something happened? You used to have loads of friends.'

Between tears and sobs of anguish Emma had explained that one of the girls had started taunting her about not having a dad.

'I told them that of course I had a dad,' Emma had said, indignant. 'So they asked where he was. When I told them I didn't know, they made fun of me. They said that I was lying or else I must be a rubbish daughter that my dad didn't want to know me. I tried to ignore them but they kept coming after me, saying these horrible things.' She'd looked up at Abby, her blue eyes swimming with tears. 'I know you're not my real mum, Mum.' She'd smiled, realising what she'd said. 'I mean, you're my real mum, but not my birth mum. But you've never told me who my father is. Why doesn't he care about me? Why *hasn't* he ever come to see me?'

Abby's heart had ached for her child. Although, as Emma had put it, *she* wasn't her biological mother, Emma was hers in every way that counted. She couldn't love her more had she given birth to her, and Emma being her twin sister Sara's child simply made the bond closer.

'I want to know who my dad is,' Emma had continued quietly. 'All the other girls at school know who their dad is, so why can't I?'

Abby had looked into the stormy blue eyes that were so like Sara's and a lump had formed in her throat. She'd known only too well how Emma had felt.

'My darling, he probably doesn't even know you exist.'

'How can he not know? How could my real mum not have told him?'

Abby winced before she'd begun speaking. 'Sara was very happy you were going to be born. I guess she didn't want to share you.'

The truth was that Sara hadn't wanted Emma's father to know about the pregnancy. At least not until she discovered that she was going to die. It was only then that she told Abby that Emma's father was Mac, the windsurfing instructor they had met while on holiday in Mykonos. When Emma was just three months old Abby went back to the Greek island to try to track him down, but it was hopeless. The summer season was over, and the visitors as well as the instructors had long since packed up and left. No one could tell her anything about Mac. Who he was or where he'd gone.

Before Sara died, Abby promised she would raise her daughter as her own. She had kept that promise and even though it hadn't always been easy, Abby had no regrets. Emma brought such joy to her life.

'I don't want to stay at that school, Mum. Please. Can't I go to a different school when I go to secondary?'

'It's not that easy, sweetie. Here in London it's difficult to find a good school within walking distance. Let me try and sort things out with the school first.'

But despite several visits to the school, the bullying continued. It both angered and saddened Abby to see Emma withdraw more and more into herself, so when Abby saw an ad for an experienced paramedic for the Royal Cornwall Air Ambulance Service, after talking it over with Emma, she decided to apply. Cornwall would be perfect for them. It was near the sea and would suit Emma's love of the outdoors much better. They were both thrilled to leave London and its sad memories behind. Abby had promised Emma that as soon as they were settled in their new home and she in her job she would continue the search for her father. Little did Abby know then that fate was going to throw them directly in his path, sooner than either of them could possibly have imagined.

Abby retrieved the tattered holiday snap from the sideboard drawer. It had been taken on the last night of her and Sara's holiday on Mykonos and Abby studied it for what must have been the hundredth time. It was a group photograph, taken on the beach. Mac had his arm draped around Sara, who was laughing up at him. She herself was at the end, a solemn figure with mid-length hair, her eyes hidden behind sunglasses. She doubted if Mac had even been aware that she was there. They had been introduced, of course, but his glance had slid almost immediately straight past Abby to her much more glamorous and fun-loving sister.

She turned to stare at the TV again, almost expecting him to reappear. She still had a week of training to complete before she started her job, so she had some time to think before she came face to face with Dr William MacNeil.

What was she going to tell Emma?

What was she going to say to Mac when they met?

What the hell was she going to do?

CHAPTER TWO

ABBY'S stomach fluttered nervously as she stepped into the base of the Royal Cornwall Air Ambulance Service. Although she had been a trained paramedic for almost twelve years, this would be an altogether different experience. She would be *flying* to rescues and despite the intensive training she had just undergone, she worried how she would cope with being lowered from a helicopter, particularly in gusty weather. But she was here now and those concerns paled into insignificance in comparison to her anxiety about meeting Mac again.

Ever since she'd seen him on television she'd been agonising over what to do. What if he was married and had a family of his own? What if Mac didn't want to know about his daughter? That hurt would be too great for the little girl. In which case should she even tell Emma that Mac was here? Did she have the right to keep the truth from Emma?

In the end she decided she wouldn't say anything to Emma until she'd had a chance to suss Mac out for herself. After all, a bad father was worse than no father at all.

The air ambulance leader, who had interviewed Abby when she'd applied for the job, met her at the door. Paul was in his early fifties with an easy smile and a relaxed and welcoming manner.

'Abby, we've been looking forward to you joining us,' he said. 'Did you enjoy your training? The course leader spoke highly of you.'

The course leader might have spoken highly of her, but that meant zilch. How she would cope in a real-life rescue would be what counted.

'What do think of Penhally Bay?' Paul continued.

'It's lovely. I haven't had too much time to explore yet—what with the course, getting my daughter settled into school and all the unpacking. But I promised Emma that on my first day off we'll have a proper look around.'

'It's a great place for a child to grow up,' Paul said. 'My kids have long since flown the coop, but they come back whenever they can. Is Emma liking Penhally High? Mine went there and they loved it. I can't imagine it's changed too much.'

Abby nodded, managing a small smile. If nothing else, their move here had been the right thing for Emma, at least as far as her new school went. Although her daughter had only been at Penhally High for a short while, she had quickly made new friends and already seemed much happier and settled.

So she was here to stay, and if life had thrown her a curve ball by flinging her directly in Mac's path, so be it. There was no going back. But until she decided what, if anything, to tell him, she would play her cards close to her chest.

Nevertheless her heart was pounding uncomfortably at the thought of meeting him again. Would he recognise her after all these years? It was unlikely. Her appearance had changed quite a bit and he hadn't paid her much attention twelve years ago. He had been far too caught up in her twin sister, the glamorous, effervescent Sara.

'Come up to the office and meet everyone,' Paul interrupted her thoughts. 'They're looking forward to meeting you.'

Her legs like jelly, Abby followed him up a steep flight of steps and into a large room where a number of people were chatting and drinking coffee.

Immediately her eyes were drawn to Mac. He was sitting, his long legs stretched out in front of him, his arms cradling the back of his head as he chatted to a colleague. Like most of the others in the room, he was dressed in an orange jumpsuit, but his was unzipped almost to the waist, revealing a dazzling white T-shirt underneath. There was no disguising his powerful build and Abby felt as if a bird were trapped in her chest.

'Everyone, I'd like you to meet our latest recruit, Abby Stevens,' Paul introduced her.

This was the moment she had been dreading. Would Mac remember her? Would he recall Sara's last name? Had he even known what it was? Although everyone turned to look at her, Abby was unable to stop herself from watching Mac's reaction. Blue eyes narrowed for a moment as if she had triggered a memory, but then he grinned and jumped to his feet. His eyes swept over her body.

'I'm Dr William MacNeil. But everyone calls me Mac.' His grip was firm and to her dismay it felt as if she had touched a live wire. Abby withdrew her hand quickly and turned to greet the other members of the team but not before she'd seen Mac's puzzled frown.

Abby forced herself to concentrate as she was

introduced to the others in the room. Apart from Paul, there were two paramedics, Mike and Jim, a pilot—an older man called Greg—as well as Lucy, another doctor, and Kirsten, whose job it was to take the calls and keep in touch with the ambulance throughout the rescue. They all smiled welcomingly.

Instinctively Abby knew she would enjoy working with this group of people—with one possible exception.

'Would you mind showing Abby around, Mac?' Paul asked. 'I have some paperwork to attend to and Lucy and Mike have just popped in to give us a report on yesterday's callout.' Paul turned to Abby. 'I'll see you all later.'

'A car accident on the coastal road,' Lucy explained as Paul left the room. She was small and plump with bright, intelligent eyes. 'The driver was going too fast for these roads and hit another car head on.'

'Any fatalities?' Abby asked.

'Surprisingly not. Luckily the oncoming car managed to swerve in time. The fire brigade had to use the jaws of life to get the driver out. It took hours and we had to keep him ventilated by hand. He's still on the critical list, but he's damned lucky to be alive.' Lucy glanced at her watch. 'Time for me to go!' She held out her hand again. 'It's good to have another woman on board, Abby. Kirsten and I get a little overwhelmed by all the testosterone around here, don't we, Kirsten?'

Kirsten grinned back. 'Don't let Lucy kid you—she's a match for the guys any time.'

Abby glanced across at Mac, who had remained silent throughout the exchange. He was studying Abby as if she puzzled him.

'Hey, have we met before?' he asked.

Abby's pulse beat even faster. Although she and Sara hadn't been identical twins there had been similarities between them—hazel eyes, straight noses and curvy mouths. But Sara had cropped her hair short and bleached it platinum blonde for their Greek holiday. In contrast, Abby had kept her shoulder length caramel hair tied back in a ponytail and at that time had worn glasses. The two sisters could hardly have looked more different and unsurprisingly Mac had barely glanced at Abby back then. Even if he did recognise her, this was hardly the time or place to tell him about Sara and Emma. Not that she had decided *what* to tell him.

She forced a smile. 'I don't think so.'

He lost the frown and grinned at her. 'You're right,' he said, lowering his voice. 'I would have remembered you. I don't tend to forget beautiful women.' He winked at her.

'And unless you're losing it, they don't tend to forget you either. That's what you mean,' chipped in Lucy. She turned to Abby, her eyes twinkling. 'Watch out for our Mac here. We love him to bits, but he's a heart-breaker. Luckily I'm too old for him and Kirsten's already taken.'

'You know I'd take you to dinner any day of the week, Lucy. Just say the word.' Mac grinned back.

'Ah, if only,' Lucy sighed theatrically. She picked up her handbag. 'I'm out of here.'

'Me too,' Kirsten said. 'I've got work to do around here!'

Left alone with Mac, Abby felt as if she had a coiled spring somewhere in her chest. He was still looking at her through half-closed eyes as if she puzzled him. 'Dr

MacNeil,' she said stiffly. 'I think we should get on with that tour, don't you?'

Again there was that heart-stopping grin. 'Call me Mac. Everyone else does.'

Mac stood back to let Abby go in front of him. He whistled under his breath as he watched the way her bottom swayed as she walked. On anyone else the orange uniform tunic top and matching trousers would have been unflattering, but it could have been tailor made for Abby. And, even apart from her figure which looked as if it had been designed with him in mind, she was a stunner. A man could drown in those eyes and as for the high cheekbones, emphasised by the hint of colour his remarks had brought to her cheeks, he had dated models who would scratch their eyes out for bone structure like that. Even the spattering of freckles over her nose didn't detract from her beauty—if anything, it made her cuter. He had already checked the third finger of her left hand. No wedding ring. Good. This was going to be interesting.

Mac had only just started showing Abby the little office where Kirsten and her small team fielded the calls when the telephone rang.

Kirsten held up a finger, asking for silence. They listened as she entered a few details into the computer.

'Try not to worry, love. We'll have someone there as soon as possible. Stay on the phone while I talk to the doctor.'

She swivelled around in her chair until she was facing Abby and Mac.

'I have a lady on the line. She's thirty-four weeks pregnant but thinks she's gone into early labour. She can't get herself to the hospital because she's on a farm and her husband is away with the car.' Kirsten covered the mouthpiece with her hand. 'She also tells me she has placenta praevia and was due to be admitted for a Caesarean section in a couple of weeks.'

'Where is the farm?' Mac asked. Gone was the laconic man of earlier. In his place was someone who was entirely focussed.

Kirsten pointed to a map. 'Over here.'

'What about the local road ambulance?' Abby asked.

Kirsten shook her head. 'It's at least an hour away on these roads and, besides, the woman—she's called Jenny Hargreaves—says the track to the farm is pretty impassable for anything except a four-by-four. We've had some heavy rain over the last fortnight.'

'We need to get her to the maternity unit as fast as possible,' Mac said. 'Okay, Kirsten, get Greg to fire the 'copter up and tell Jenny we're on our way. Is there anyone with her who can help? A friend? A neighbour?'

Kirsten shook her head. 'She's on her own, apart from her nine-year-old son.'

'Get him on the line and keep him there. Then phone St Piran's and bring them up to speed. Could you make sure we have an incubator for the baby on board, too? C'mon, Abby. I guess you're on. Let's go and get kitted up.'

As Abby raced after him down the steps and into the cloakroom where their gear was kept, she ran through what she knew about placenta praevia. And what she did know didn't make her feel any better.

'Not good news, is it?' she said as Mac passed her a jacket.

'Tell me what you know about the condition.'

'Placenta praevia is where the placenta is lying in front of the baby, blocking the birth canal. I know it can cause massive, even fatal bleeding if left untreated. If she's already in labour, we don't have much time.' Although they had covered complications of childbirth in their training, until Sara it hadn't crossed Abby's mind that it could really happen. Now she knew better. Please, God, don't let this first call end in disaster.

'Do we have an obstetrician on call?' she asked.

'At St Piran's. Kirsten will patch us through as soon as we're airborne. There's no time to wait, though.' Mac stopped for a moment and rested his hands on her shoulders. He looked directly into her eyes. 'Are you going to be okay?' His look was calm, reassuring. Everything about him radiated confidence and Abby relaxed a little.

'Sure.' She kept her voice light. 'All in a day's work.'

They piled into the helicopter and lifted off, heading towards the coast.

'ETA twenty minutes,' Greg's voice came over the radio. 'It's a bit breezy where we're heading so it might get a little bumpy.'

'Do you think we'll be able to put down?' Mac asked.

'There's a good-sized field behind the farmhouse, but I guess it depends on how soggy the ground is. We won't know until we get there.'

Abby and Mac shared a look.

'Have you ever done an emergency section before?' Abby asked. If they couldn't get mother and baby to hospital, it would be their only chance. But such a procedure would be tricky even for a qualified obstetrician in a fully equipped theatre. Her heart started pounding again. Confidence was one thing, but did Mac have the skill needed to back it up?

'I have.' He leaned across and flashed Abby another wicked grin. 'But don't worry, I have every intention of letting the obstetricians do it.' He held up a finger and listened intently.

A quiet voice came over the radio. 'Hello, Mac. Dr Gibson here. What do we have?'

'A thirty-four-weeker with placenta praevia who has gone into early labour. Control has her son on the phone. Mum tells him she thinks her contractions are coming about five minutes apart. The mother's name is Jenny Hargreaves. She tells us she was due to be delivered by section at St Piran's so you should have her case notes there.'

There was a short silence. Abby guessed Dr Gibson was bringing up Jenny's record on her computer screen.

'I'll make sure neonatal intensive care is standing by and that we have a theatre ready. How long d'you think before you'll have her here for us?'

'Another ten minutes until we land. If we can. Say another ten to examine our lady and get her loaded and twenty back. Do you think we'll make it?' Again there was that easy smile as if this was just another everyday callout.

'If anyone can, you can,' came back the reply. 'But if she's gone into active labour she could be bleeding massively and you may have to section her there and then. It won't be easy.'

'Hell, whoever said anything is easy in this job? But trust me.' He turned and winked at Abby. 'If I can get her to you without having to section her, I will.' He flexed long fingers. 'Been a long time since I did one of those.'

'Good luck,' Dr Gibson said calmly.

A short while later they reached the farm. To Abby's relief the pilot had been able to find a spot to land. The helicopter rotors had barely slowed when Mac hefted the large medical bag over his shoulder.

'Okay, we're on. Remember to keep your head down.' Abby took a deep breath, sent a silent prayer towards heaven, and followed him out of the helicopter.

Mac sprinted towards the farmhouse, carrying the medical case that weighed at least ten kilos as if it were nothing. Abby ran after him, doing her best to keep up.

A child with wide, frightened eyes was waiting for them by the doorway.

'Please hurry, my mum is bleeding,' the boy said.

This was the worst possible news. Jenny being in labour was one thing, but they had banked on having enough time to get her to hospital. If she had started bleeding it meant that the placenta was beginning to detach. As it did, the baby's life support system became compromised and the life of the mother was in jeopardy. It would have been dangerous enough in hospital, but all Abby and Mac had was some morphine and basic equipment. It wasn't good. Abby's heart jumped to her throat.

Mac paused by the doorway and hunkered down so that he was at eye level with the boy. He placed a hand on the child's shoulder.

'What's your name, son?'

'Tim.'

'It's going to be all right, Tim, I promise. Now, if you could take us to your mum, we'll look after her.'

Whatever Tim saw in Mac's eyes seemed to reassure him. He nodded and led them inside the farmhouse and into a bedroom. On the bed, a woman lay writhing with pain. She was pale and her eyes were stretched wide with fear.

Abby and Mac rushed to her side.

'Jenny, isn't it?' Mac said as he laid the medical case on the floor. 'I'm Dr MacNeil and this is Abby Stevens. We're going to do everything we can to look after you and your baby.'

Abby felt Jenny's pulse.

'Over one hundred and thready,' she told Mac as she unwrapped the stethoscope from around her neck.

'How long have you been bleeding? And when did the contractions start?' Mac asked.

'I just started bleeding a few minutes ago. The contractions started about an hour ago. I phoned the hospital and they said they would get an ambulance.' Jenny reached out a hand and squeezed Abby's fingers hard. 'You have to save my baby. Please. You've got to help us.'

'We are going to do everything possible,' Abby replied with what she hoped was a confident smile.

She checked Jenny's blood pressure. As expected, it was low. Jenny was already bleeding heavily.

'I'm just going to give you some fluids through a needle in your vein,' Mac explained as he swabbed a patch of skin near Jenny's elbow. 'Then we're going to get you onto a stretcher and into the air ambulance, okay?'

'What about Tim? I can't leave him here by himself. My husband isn't due back until tomorrow morning.'

'Is there a neighbour we could call for you?'

Jenny shook her head. 'We only moved here a couple of months ago. I don't know anyone yet. I've been so busy getting ready for the new baby.'

'In that case, Tim can come in the helicopter with us. How about it, Tim?' Mac turned to the little boy who had remained by the door, taking everything in with wide eyes.

'Wicked,' he said. Now adults were taking control, the colour had returned to his face.

Mac finished setting up the drip.

'Okay, Jenny. The helicopter's just outside waiting to take you to hospital. We're going to get you on board as quickly as we can.'

Jenny clutched her stomach as another contraction took hold. 'Just get me to the hospital,' she said through gritted teeth. Then she forced a smile and turned to her son. 'Tim will help, won't you, love?'

Tim's terror had disappeared. Whether it was because they were there helping his mother or whether it was the excitement of the helicopter ride, Abby didn't know or care. All that mattered was that the boy was calm. It would help Jenny and give them one less thing to worry about.

Abby draped a blanket round her patient before strapping her into the stretcher. As they carried her outside, Abby tried not to wince when a contraction gripped the mother and she squeezed Abby's fingers with ferocious strength.

Please let her hang in there, Abby prayed silently. At least until they got her to hospital. She slid a glance at Mac. Nothing in his demeanour indicated that at any time they could be dealing with a life-and-death scenario. Was he really as calm as he appeared?

Inside the helicopter they attached Jenny to the on-board monitoring equipment and pumped fluids into her. Abby checked the fetal heartbeat again. So far so good.

As soon as they had Jenny settled and the helicopter was heading towards St Piran's, Mac raised his thumb to Tim. Greg had given the boy a helmet and earmuffs to deaden the noise.

Tim returned the salute, unable to hide his excitement.

Abby slid a glance at Mac as he leaned over Jenny. He puzzled her. Everything about him contradicted the image of him she had held in her head for the last twelve years. Whenever she'd thought about him, she'd imagined an ageing Lothario chatting up young women on the beach under the pretext of teaching them how to windsurf, not this caring and utterly professional doctor.

Even if it was obvious from his behaviour when they'd met as well as Lucy's comments that he still was a blatant flirt she liked the way he had taken the time to reassure Tim.

Her thoughts were interrupted as the helicopter touched down on the hospital landing pad. Abby breathed a deep sigh of relief. They had made it!

'Stick close to me,' Mac said to Tim after removing the young lad's helmet.

The helicopter's rotors hadn't even stopped when the hospital staff were there to take charge of Jenny. The transfer was quick. Mac and Abby updated the hospital staff as they ran next to the trolley with Tim following closely behind.

'Thanks, guys. We'll take it from here,' the doctor Mac had addressed as Dr Gibson said.

They watched as Jenny disappeared from view.

'C'mon, Tim. Why don't we get you a drink or something?' Abby offered, knowing that now the excitement of the helicopter journey was over the boy would start fretting again. 'And in the meantime we can try and get your dad on the phone and either me or Dr MacNeil here will speak to him. How does that sound?'

'Sounds okay. When can I see Mum?'

'Not for a little while,' Abby said. 'But while Dr MacNeil is speaking to your father, I'll find somewhere where you can wait.'

Tim's face crumpled. 'I don't want to stay on my own. I want my dad.'

Abby felt terrible for the little boy. If something happened to her, she'd hate for Emma to be left alone. But what could they do? They had to get back to the air ambulance base. There could be another call at any time.

But Mac seemed to have his own ideas. 'Tell you what,' he said. 'When I speak to your dad, I'll suggest you come back with Abby and me to the air ambulance headquarters. How about it? You could have a look around see all the stuff we use. We have some cool things we can do with our computers. I'll let the staff here know where we are and as soon as they have any news about your mum they can let us know. What do you say?'

Tim's face brightened. 'Could I? No one will mind? I promise I won't get in the way.'

Once more, Abby was pleasantly surprised. Mac could easily have left the child here. After all they had done their job and Tim wasn't their responsibility. She really had underestimated him. Nothing about him made sense. Her head was beginning to ache. Right now she would have given anything for some time on her own to think, but she had promised Tim a drink while they waited for Mac to speak to his father and do the handover.

Spotting a vending machine against the wall inside the A & E department, Abby scrabbled in her pocket for some change and fed it into the slot. To no avail—the wretched machine stubbornly refused to part with its goods. Banging with the flat of her hand against the side had no effect either.

'Here, let me help.' A woman who looked as if she had stepped out of a magazine came across. She fiddled with the machine and a can rolled out.

'It just takes a certain knack.' She held out a mani-cured hand. 'You must be new. I'm Rebecca O'Hara, my husband Josh is one of the A & E consultants.'

'Abby Stevens. First day with the Air Ambulance Service.'

'Pleased to meet you, Abby. Where are you from? I can tell by your accent that you're not from here.'

'I've been living in London for the last few years.'

'London?' Rebecca looked wistful. 'Don't you miss it?'

'I love it here,' Abby said honestly. She glanced across the room to where an anxious Tim was wait-ing for her. Although she had the distinct impression Rebecca wanted to chat, Abby didn't like to leave the boy any longer than she had to.

Just then Mac appeared. 'Oh, hello, Rebecca.' He smiled. 'If you're waiting to see Josh, I'm afraid he's up to his neck with patients at the moment.'

Rebecca looked dejected. 'I'll have a cup of coffee with the nurses while I'm waiting.'

She turned back to Abby. 'Lovely to meet you.

Perhaps we could have a coffee some time?' And then with a flutter of slim fingers she headed towards the staffroom.

Back at base, no one seemed particularly surprised to see Tim. Mac gave him the promised tour after which he settled Tim in front of the computers and started explaining how the system worked.

A little while later, Dr Gibson phoned to say that they had sectioned Jenny and although she had lost a great deal of blood, she and her new baby son were going to be fine. Tim was ecstatic about having a brother, but as it was going to be a couple of hours before Jenny would come around properly from the anaesthetic, they decided to keep him with them a bit longer. Tim's father was on his way to the hospital.

'I'll drop Tim back at the hospital later,' Mac said to Abby. 'I'm due to do some teaching there this afternoon.'

Abby raised an eyebrow.

'I keep my hand in at the hospital when we're not busy. It helps keep me up to date and it only takes me a couple of minutes to get back here if we get a call-out.' He smiled. 'You don't fancy a drink later, by any chance? I can tell you all about Penhally.' His expression was teasing, his eyes glinting.

Abby was horrified to feel a tingle run down her spine. Damn it! Why did she have to find him so damn sexy? Even sexier and better looking than twelve years ago. And the fact that he had a caring side made him all the more attractive. What was she thinking? There was no way she could be attracted to her dead sister's ex-lover; it was too weird. What was more, she had to remember that Mac was the type of man for whom flirting was as natural as breathing. It didn't mean anything. Wasn't the way he'd treated Sara evidence of that?

He was looking at her, waiting for her reply, certain she would say yes. He was so supremely confident she would love to turn him down. And she would have, if it wasn't for Emma. Her antennae, honed by years of being let down by men just like him, were on red alert. Of all the men in all the world, why did she have to be working with him?

Despite every nerve cell in her brain telling her to keep her distance from this man, for her daughter's sake, she needed to learn more about him. Emma was going to a friend's after school and wouldn't be home until seven. Abby made up her mind.

'I'll tell you what,' she said. 'I like to go for a walk after work. You can join me if you want.' She shrugged. 'It's up to you.' Smiling to herself as she saw the look of surprise in his eyes, she whirled on her heel, ignoring the feeling that two blue eyes were watching her speculatively.

Mac watched Abby's retreating back until she was out of sight. He would have bet a hundred bucks she had been about to turn him down, and her acceptance had taken him by surprise. Not that a walk was what he had in mind and not that he would have let one refusal put him off. In fact, it would have heightened the excitement of the chase. He tried to ignore the unpleasant feeling lurking somewhere deep down that felt uncomfortably like shame. Should he really be going after Abby? Although she intrigued and excited him, there was a certain wariness about her that suggested she had been hurt before, perhaps badly. And then there was the odd way she had kept looking at him during the callout. For someone as experienced as she was supposed to be there was an edginess about her that, while not quite alarming him, concerned him a little.

There was something else about Abby that was niggling him. He could have sworn he had met her before, but he had to be mistaken. He might have been with a lot of women in his life, but he would never have forgotten someone like her.

What was her story anyway? Not that it really mattered. He liked women, enjoyed their company and had a lot of respect for them, but he had no intention of having a long-term relationship with one. Once they made demands on him, he couldn't help but lose interest. But he was getting way ahead of himself. This was simply a walk with a colleague, albeit a beautiful one. What was the harm in that? Nevertheless, however much he tried to dismiss the feeling of unease, he couldn't quite shake it. A sixth sense he had relied on all his life was telling him that something extraordinary had arrived in the form of Abby Stevens and he wasn't sure he liked the feeling one little bit.

CHAPTER THREE

MAC was leaning against the side of a four-by-four, look-ing relaxed, when Abby eventually emerged at the end of her shift. After changing out of her jumpsuit, she had taken a few moments to put on some lipstick and brush her hair. She told herself that she wasn't preening herself for Mac, it was simply that she needed the confidence of make-up as well as the time to get her thumping heart rate under control. But she knew deep down that wasn't the whole truth. Wasn't there just a tiny part of her that liked it that he had made it clear he was attracted to her? She dismissed the thought immediately. This wasn't about her. It was about Emma.

Mac was wearing a pair of faded jeans and a white T-shirt under a well-worn leather jacket. His teeth flashed in a wide grin when he saw her. Surely it was anxiety over what she had to tell him that made her stomach flip?

He opened the passenger door of the Jeep with a flourish.

'There's an interesting cliff walk about ten minutes' drive from here. There's a fantastic fish restaurant nearby. We could have something to eat after our walk and I'll drive you back here so you can collect your car.' He paused. 'Unless you want to leave your car at your house? I could follow you home and we could leave from there. Where is it you live, anyway?'

Something in the way his eyes were glittering made Abby wonder if he was imagining an ending to the evening that included him and her in bed together. Little did he know there was a greater chance of hell freezing over.

'I'm renting a cottage in Penhally Bay while I look around for a place to buy. But I'd rather follow you in my own car. And as for supper...' she shook her head '...sorry, I have other plans.' A walk was one thing, a meal *à deux* quite another.

Mac frowned and Abby felt a small stab of triumph. He was clearly a man who was used to getting his own way. Well, he'd find out soon enough that she liked having her way, too.

She followed his four-by-four, uncomfortably aware of the anxiety that was coiling in her chest. He had no idea about the bombshell she was soon going to be dropping into his life. For a second she felt sorry for him, but only for a second. Emma was the only person who mattered in this whole sorry mess.

The sun was slipping lower, streaking the sky with gold, but it would be light for another hour or two. There was still a hint of warmth in the air, and the earlier wind had subsided. It was a perfect October evening, with just a hint of summer still.

The hordes of tourists had long since left and there was only one other car in the car park as they parked their cars side by side.

'The walk I had in mind is a couple of miles each way,' Mac said. 'That's not too far for you, is it?'

'I like walking,' Abby said. 'As long as I'm home for seven.'

She had to walk rapidly to keep up with Mac's long strides. He glanced down and checked his pace so it matched hers.

'How are Jenny and the baby doing?' she asked. As promised, Mac had taken Tim back to the hospital where his father had been waiting for him.

Mac frowned. 'Last I knew, mother and baby were doing fine. Why, did you hear something?' There was no mistaking the concern in his eyes.

'No, I haven't heard anything.' Abby said. 'I just thought you might have popped in to see her when you were at the hospital.'

Mac looked puzzled. 'Why would I do that?'

'Don't you follow up on your patients? Aren't you curious to know how everything turned out?'

He shook his head. 'I treat them, look after them as best I can, then let the hospital staff do their bit. All I care about is giving the best treatment I am capable of. I don't see the point in getting too involved with patients. We have to know when to let go, so we can move on to the next one.'

Abby was dismayed. Once again it seemed she had got this man wrong. Could he really be as disinterested in his patients as he seemed? Abby couldn't imagine not following up on her patients. Most of the time, out there on a rescue, she formed a strong bond with the people whose lives depended on her. It was part of who she was.

'So tell me, what brings you here, to Cornwall and Penhally Bay in particular?' Mac changed the subject. 'Someone mentioned you'd been working with the London ambulance service for the last eleven years. What happened? Did you get tired of the big city?'

Anxiety raced along her spine. It was the perfect

moment to tell him about Emma, but she wasn't ready. Not yet. Not until she knew more about him. Once she told him there would be no going back.

'My daughter needed a change of air,' Abby said evasively. 'And I needed a change of scenery.'

'You have a daughter? I didn't know.' He sounded surprised…and regretful.

Abby suspected he wouldn't have been so keen to ask her out if he'd known she had a child. Most of the men she had dated in the past had reacted the same way. They all backed off when she told them and if they didn't, her refusal to put them before Emma usually made them give up on her sooner or later. And that was fine. She didn't need or want a man in her life who couldn't accept Emma. Not even this one. *Particularly* not this one.

He flicked his eyes to her left hand again. 'You don't wear a ring so I'm guessing you're not married.'

'I'm a single mum.' Let him make of that what he would. He would know the truth soon enough. First she had some questions of her own.

'What about you? I assume you're not married?'

'Nope. Not the marrying kind, I guess.'

'Children?' Abby held her breath as she waited for his reply.

'No, none of them either. Not the father kind.'

Little did he know.

'How long have you worked for the air ambulance?' Abby asked.

'Two years. I completed my specialist training in anaesthesia, then I did a course in medical emergency retrieval in Glasgow. But unfortunately the surfing conditions aren't great there, so when I found they were looking for a rescue medic here, I jumped at the chance. It means I can kite board when I'm not working.'

So his sport was as important as his job. Maybe more so. Abby was disappointed. Minute by minute she was having to revise her opinion of the man who was Emma's father.

'Although I can tell you're Scottish from your accent, it doesn't sound very Glaswegian,' Abby probed. The more she knew about this man, the better.

'I was brought up on Tiree. It's an island off the west coast of Scotland. I lived there until I went to medical school in Glasgow when I was eighteen. I don't go back to Tiree very often.' His mouth tightened and as Abby glanced at him she could have sworn she saw anger behind his eyes, but it disappeared so quickly she couldn't be sure. Did Mac have secrets of his own?

She was about to question him further when he stopped in his tracks. She followed his gaze to see what had caught his attention. To their left, close to the edge, a man was pacing frantically up and down, shouting a boy's name.

'Something's wrong,' Mac said. 'I'm going to take a look-see.'

As Mac called out, the man turned to them, relief evident under his panic.

'It's my son,' he said. 'I can't find him! One minute he was here, and then the next he was gone. I only meant to close my eyes for a minute, but I must have dropped off. You've got to help me find him. He's only eight.' The man's eyes were darting around while he was speaking.

Mac placed a hand on his shoulder. 'Stay calm and tell me everything. What's your name?'

'Dave. My son's called Luke.'

'Where did you last see Luke?'

'He was over there.' The man pointed behind him.

'He wanted to go down to the beach but I told him there was no path. I said I'd take him there tomorrow. Oh, my God. What if he tried to go down by himself and fell?'

'Have you phoned for help?'

'No, I haven't had time. I've been too busy looking for him.'

Mac's eyes raked the side of the cliff. Something caught his attention and he stopped and sucked in a breath. Abby followed his gaze. Near the edge, a piece of the cliff had broken away. From the look of it, it had only happened very recently. Seeing the troubled look in Mac's eyes, she knew he was thinking the same thing. There was a good chance the boy had got too close to the edge and slipped over. If they were right and the boy had fallen, he could be badly hurt, or worse.

'Abby. Phone 999 and get them to alert the coastguard and the rescue services. Dave, I'm just going to have a look over this cliff and see if I can see him. You stay back, okay?'

Abby touched Dave's shoulder reassuringly as she used her mobile. It was still possible the boy had wandered off and was nowhere near the cliff but they couldn't take the chance.

Mac walked close to the cliff then dropped to his stomach to peer over the edge. 'I think I can see him,' he called. 'Is he wearing a red jacket?'

Luke's father rushed forward. Mac jumped to his feet and barred his way.

'You have to stay back,' Mac warned. 'The edge here is already unstable. If you come any closer you could slip or a bit of the cliff could crumble and fall on your son.

'I'm going to climb down there and see how he is, okay?' Mac added quietly.

'Shouldn't we wait for the rescue services?' Abby said. 'The operator said they shouldn't be more than ten minutes. If you go down there, you could fall, too.'

Mac dug in his pocket and pulled out his car keys. He tossed them to Dave. 'Dave, go back to the car park. My car is the Jeep. In the boot you'll find a red medical case, a rope and a yellow jacket. Could you fetch them?'

Dave hesitated and Mac gave him a gentle push. 'Go! It's the best way to help Luke. Be as quick as you can.'

As soon as Dave had set off at a run, Mac turned back to Abby. 'We don't have time to wait for help.' While he was talking he had removed his jacket. 'I'm going to go down. When Dave returns I might need you to lower my medical bag on the end of the rope. Okay?' He moved towards the cliff.

'Shouldn't you at least wait for the rope?' If Mac fell they would have two victims to rescue. Even in her anxiety, the irony wasn't completely lost on her. She had just found Emma's father. If he fell now, Emma might never get to know him.

Mac turned around and grinned. 'Hey, I was brought up near cliffs. Never met one yet I couldn't beat. I'll be okay. As soon as you hear the rescue 'copter, let off a flare. Keep Dave occupied by telling him to search for a good place for the helicopter to land.'

Before she could protest further, he disappeared over the edge.

Abby's heart banged against her ribs. What was Mac thinking? Although if it had been Emma down there, she would have gone herself. Fear of heights or not.

She tiptoed over to the edge, following Mac's earlier

example, and lay flat on her stomach and peered over. Although Mac was picking his way carefully down the cliff he was moving faster than she would have thought was safe. From this vantage point she could see that although the cliff was steep, it didn't fall away as sharply as she'd thought. Relief swept through her. Perhaps Luke had a chance.

As Dave returned with the bag, rope and Mac's fluorescent jacket she became aware of a whooping sound in the distance. Shielding her eyes against the sinking sun, she could just about make out the large yellow shape of a Sea King helicopter. Thank God! They would have proper equipment and hopefully a way to get both Mac and Luke up.

'Come on.' She jumped up and shouted across to Dave. 'We need to find a decent landing place to direct the pilot to land.'

'How is my son? Could you see him? Is he okay?'

Abby moved towards open ground and yelled back over her shoulder. 'Mac will be with him in a few minutes. He's a doctor. He'll do everything he can to help Luke.'

Without waiting to see whether Dave was following or not, she raced over to the flat piece of ground. It was just about big enough for the helicopter to land and thankfully the previous days' rain had run away, leaving it solid underfoot.

Abby waved Mac's jacket and immediately the helicopter headed in their direction. Dave was standing behind her, looking lost and terrified. She summoned up a smile. 'I promise you, your son is in good hands.' And she believed it. 'Stay back until they land, then tell them everything. Okay? I'm going to lower the medical bag down to Mac.'

She ran back to the cliff edge and dropped on to her front again. Mac was at the bottom now and kneeling next to the prone figure of the boy. At least he had made it down in one piece. But Mac couldn't risk moving the child on his own. If Luke had survived the fall, there was every chance he had serious neck and head injuries and any movement could mean the difference between a full recovery and life in a wheelchair.

Mac glanced up and gave her a thumbs-up. Luke must still be alive. She tied the medical bag to the rope and lowered it down but it snagged on the jagged rock face. The incline may have helped Mac reach the boy, but it was hampering her efforts to get the bag down to him. Almost crying with frustration, she was only vaguely aware of a hand touching her shoulder. She looked up into calm green eyes of a crew member from the helicopter.

'Miss, you have to stand away from the edge.' Before she could protest, the man took her arm and raised her to her feet. 'We'll take it from here.'

'Mac—Dr MacNeil—is down there with the boy. Mac's a doctor with the air ambulance. He needs his bag.'

'Mac, as in Daredevil Mac?' A broad smile spread across the man's craggy face. 'Well I'll be bug—blown. We know him well, and if he's onto it, everything will be A-okay. Don't worry, I'll get the bag down to him.'

Pulling the case back up, the man, whose name badge said Roberts, took it and ran back to the helicopter. Seconds later the Sea King took off again.

Abby joined Dave, knowing that for the time being there was little she or the anxious father could do. She hooked her arm in his as they watched the helicopter hover over the cliff. A couple of tense minutes passed

before a figure, clutching a stretcher and the medical
bag, was lowered from the side of the helicopter. Abby's
heart thudded painfully. In many ways she would have
preferred to be down there helping. This waiting was
worse than anything.

Minutes crawled like hours. Then suddenly the crew-
man came back into view. He was holding onto the
stretcher, which now contained a figure. Immediately
after the winchman and the stretcher were pulled on
board, the helicopter lowered the rope again and after
a few moments Mac appeared above the top of the cliff.
He, too, was pulled into the waiting Sea King.

Instead of flying off, the helicopter landed again.
Abby grabbed Dave's hand and ran towards it. Roberts
had barely pulled her and Dave in before the helicopter
banked away. Roberts passed her a helmet with a radio
attached.

With a brief word to Dave to stay where he was, Abby
hurried over to Mac, who was bent over the stretcher.

'He has a compound fracture of the femur. I can't rule
out internal injuries and of course we have to suspect
head and spinal injuries. I've given him IV morphine
for the pain.'

Mac attached his patient to the pulse oximeter while
Abby checked Luke's vital signs.

Although Luke's blood pressure was low and his
pulse elevated, and he wasn't out of the woods yet, he
was a very lucky boy. His leg would take time to heal
and would have hurt like crazy before the morphine took
effect, but as long as he didn't have internal injuries he'd
probably be able to leave hospital in a week or two. Abby
shuddered when she thought what might have happened
if she and Mac hadn't come across Dave when they had.
She was even more confused about Mac than ever. He

had risked his life for Luke, he had been thoughtful with Tim, yet he had made it clear that he didn't believe in getting involved with patients. Which one was the real Mac?

Luke tried to sit up, but Abby pushed him gently back down.

'Dad?' he asked. 'Where's my dad?'

Abby beckoned to Dave to come forward. Anything to help the child stay calm was good.

'He's right here,' Abby said gently. She moved away slightly so Luke could see his father. Both father and son started to cry. 'Dave, you need to move away again so we can work on your son, okay? Try not to worry, I'm sure he's going to be okay.'

When they touched down at St Piran's the staff from A & E were waiting for them.

'Status update?' the A & E consultant, bearing the name badge Dr Josh O'Hara, asked. Abby had only the briefest impression of dark hair and deep blue eyes before Luke was rushed inside.

Abby, her part in the drama over, went in search of Dave. He would be desperate for news of his injured child. She found him sitting outside Resus, his head in his hands.

She tapped him gently on his shoulder. 'Dave.'

He looked at her with red-rimmed eyes. He tried to speak, but couldn't. He shook his head, almost as if he were too scared to ask after his son.

'How is he?' he managed after clearing his throat.

Abby sat next to him and took his hand in hers.

'I think he'll be fine, Dave. It was good we found him when we did, and that we were able to start giving him medical treatment straight away. All that will make a big difference to his recovery.'

They sat in silence for a moment. 'Is there anyone I can call for you? Luke's mother? She'll need to know he's in hospital.'

Dave took a deep shuddering breath. 'She's dead.' He buried his face in his hands. 'She died from breast cancer six months ago.'

'I'm so sorry,' Abby said.

Dave's eyes were bleak. 'She'd never forgive me if I let something happen to our child. I promised her I'd look after him and I fell asleep. What kind of father am I?'

'You're human. It can be difficult, bringing up a child on your own. You can't watch them all the time.'

Dave raked a hand through his hair. 'But I fell asleep! I've been working overtime so I could afford to take Luke away on holiday. So he and I could spend more time together. He needs something to cheer him up. The loss of his mum was a terrible blow. To both of us.' Abby was only dimly aware of Mac coming to stand next to them. 'And I could have lost him, too.'

'You've not lost him,' Mac said quietly. 'He's got to go to Theatre to get his leg pinned where it was broken, but he's going to be fine.'

'He's going to be okay?' Dave said almost as if he didn't dare allow himself to believe what Mac was telling him. The relief in Dave's eyes brought a lump to Abby's throat.

'Yes, he is. I promise you,' Mac said firmly. 'You can see him for a few moments before he goes to Theatre, if you like.'

Dave sprang to his feet. He clasped Mac's hands in his. 'How can I ever thank you? I know you put your own life in danger and I'll never forget you for that.

Either of you.' Without giving them a chance to reply, he rushed away to see his son.

'Another satisfied customer,' Mac said wryly. 'Perhaps he'll take better care of his son after this.' He rubbed a hand across his chin. 'What the hell was he thinking? Having a nap while his eight-year-old played near a dangerous cliff. Some people just shouldn't have children.'

Abby rounded on him. 'He's doing the best he can. Do you know he only fell asleep because he's been working all hours to give his son a holiday? Luke's mother died recently and Dave has been doing the best he can to care for him. Being a single parent isn't easy. We all make mistakes. It's just by the grace of God, most of the time, things turn out all right.' What the hell did Mac know about being a parent, the demands, the worry?

Mac held up his hands as if to ward off her words. He looked stunned and contrite. 'Hey, I had no idea.'

'You shouldn't be so quick to judge, Mac. As the saying goes, you don't know what a person's life is like until you've walked in their shoes.'

Mac narrowed his eyes, his expression unreadable. 'I have no intention of ever walking in his shoes, as you put it.' The clouds cleared from his face. 'But I didn't know his circumstances,' he said. 'If I had, I wouldn't have been so quick to make assumptions.' He smiled ruefully. 'I stand corrected.'

Their eyes locked and Abby's heart somersaulted. She had the strangest feeling that he knew every thought that was rattling around her confused brain. Dismayed, she pulled her eyes away from his searching gaze and glanced at her watch. She had to get back for Emma, but her car was still miles away where she had left it when she and Mac had set out on their walk.

Mac caught her look of alarm. 'What is it?'

'I need to get home,' she said. 'Like now. But my car's on the other side of Penhally, still in the car park.'

'Mine, too,' Mac glanced up as Josh emerged from Resus.

'Know where I could borrow a car, mate?' Mac asked.

Josh dug in his pocket and fished out a set of keys. He tossed them at Mac, who caught them.

'Take mine,' Josh said. 'Just make sure you bring it back in one piece.'

'Hey.' Mac pretended to look offended. 'Don't I always?'

Josh raised an eyebrow. 'You know it's only a matter of time if you continue to drive like the devil.'

'I only drive fast when I'm on my own. And when the road allows. Your car will be perfectly safe.' Mac turned to Abby. 'I'll drop you off at your house then collect your car.'

Abby wasn't at all sure she wanted to be in a car with Mac after hearing Josh's comments, but she did have to get home. Emma was too young to be left on her own, even for a short while. 'What about yours?' Abby protested.

'Don't worry about mine. It's not a problem. I can get it any time.'

Inside Josh's car, Abby glanced at her watch again. She should make it before Emma. With a bit of luck.

'You did a brave thing back there,' she said as they drove down the narrow lanes in the direction of Penhally Bay.

Mac grinned at her and her pulse scrambled. He was having the strangest effect on her. As if she didn't have enough to contend with. Leftover adrenaline, she told herself.

'As I said before, it was a piece of cake. Where is your house?'

Abby gave him the address and he nodded. 'I think I know where you are.'

'But don't you think you were a little reckless?' Abby persisted. 'You could have been killed, or fallen and then we would have had two bodies to rescue.' *And Emma wouldn't have a father, suitable or unsuitable.*

Mac slid her a glance. 'Where's the fun in life if you can't take risks?' he said. 'You might as well be dead if you don't. And, anyway, I knew I could climb down to him. Believe me, it wasn't nearly as dangerous as it looked. At least, not for me. Free climbing is one of my hobbies.'

Abby frowned. She didn't like the sound of this free climbing, whatever it was.

'Which means what exactly?'

'It's a form of climbing where you don't use ropes. Great fun.'

Oh, dear Lord. Emma's father was an adrenaline junkie who didn't seem to care whether he lived or died. Could it get any worse?

'Oh, and by the way,' Mac said, following her pointed finger, as he pulled up in front of the small two-up, two-down where she and Emma lived. 'You owe me a date. And one thing you should know about me is that I always collect my debts.' His diamond-coloured eyes locked onto hers and once again Abby had the strangest feeling he could see into her soul.

The blood rushed to her cheeks. It was as if someone had lit a fire just below her skin and it was smouldering away. Any minute now she'd go up in a puff of smoke.

She was out of the car almost before it had come to a complete stop. So far none of this was going the way she'd planned.

Shortly after Mac left, Emma came running into the cottage and flung herself down on the sofa. She beamed happily at Abby.

'Hey. I gather you had a good time?' Abby asked.

'It was great. A few of the other girls came over and we had the coolest time trying on each other's clothes and make-up. Not one of them asked me anything about my dad. I don't think they care at all.'

'Those girls in your other school were the exception, Emma. They just had to make themselves feel good by putting you down.' She ruffled her daughter's hair. Whatever happened with Mac, they had made the right decision coming here. In the last few weeks Emma had changed back from the subdued, under-confident girl she had become in London to the lively fun-loving kid she had always been before that.

Emma jumped up from the sofa and hugged Abby fiercely. 'You're the best mum in the world,' she said.

Abby's heart twisted. All she had ever wanted was to give Emma the security and love she and Sara had never experienced. There was nothing she wouldn't do for Emma. Not even risk losing her to her father. If that father could make her happy. What she was not prepared to do now that Emma was just getting back to her bright usual self was risk her daughter being rejected. Abby knew only too well how that felt.

'Sara loved you as much as I do. You'll never forget that, will you?'

'I know. You tell me that almost every day.' Emma looked sad for a moment. 'I really wish I could have known her.' But in the way kids did, her face brightened almost immediately. 'At least I have you to tell me all the stories about her. I love hearing the ones about how you both kept getting into trouble. They make me laugh.'

'Yes, but, remember, I only tell you some of these stories as a warning about how easily you can get into trouble.' Abby was stricken. What if Emma tried to copy some of the pranks she and Sara had got up to? It didn't bear thinking about.

Emma grinned. 'You are so easy to tease, Mum. I get you every time.'

'Why don't you have your shower while I get supper ready?' Abby suggested. 'Then afterwards there's a movie on TV we can watch together.' Mac would be back any minute with her car, and she wasn't ready for child and father to meet.

And that wasn't the only thing she wasn't prepared for, Abby admitted to herself as she set about preparing supper. She hadn't expected to find herself reacting to him the way she did. The way her heart kept misbehaving every time he was around wasn't just down to her anxiety about Emma and was an unwelcome complication in a situation that was already complicated enough. Damn it, why did he have to be so infuriatingly gorgeous?

As she'd hoped. Emma was still in the shower when Mac arrived with her car. In her haste to have him gone before Emma came downstairs, she practically grabbed her car keys from his hand. All this emotional turmoil was exhausting. She knew she couldn't keep father and daughter apart for ever. Sooner or later, she would have to tell them the truth.

CHAPTER FOUR

BACK at work, Mac didn't mention another date. Abby wasn't sure if she was relieved or offended. For her second shift, she worked with Lucy, attending a car accident as well as a child with breathing difficulties. Although she enjoyed working with Lucy, she had to admit she was disappointed that she wouldn't always be working with Mac. She told herself it was simply because she was trying to figure him out and nothing to do with the fact she felt alert, more alive somehow, when he was around.

Every now and again she would look up to find his eyes on her. He would grin as if he'd caught her out and she would look away quickly, terrified in case he noticed the blush stealing up her cheeks.

'What do you say we go for a walk down on the beach?' Abby suggested to Emma one day after work. Although it was after five, it was unseasonably warm for October.

'Great. Can I go swimming?' Emma asked, and before Abby could reply she was off upstairs to her small bedroom. Emma had to be constantly on the go.

Abby fetched her own costume from the bedroom opposite Emma's. She slipped into her bikini before pulling on a long, silky cardigan to cover her until they got to the beach. Their rented home was tiny, having once been a fisherman's cottage. It had a sitting room and a small kitchen downstairs and two bedrooms upstairs with a small bathroom separating them. Abby would have preferred something bigger, but her salary as a paramedic didn't stretch very far. After rent and food, anything left over went on clothes and outings for Emma. Sometimes it was a struggle to make ends meet, but if the alternative had been not having Emma in her life, Abby knew it was no contest. Over the years she had scrimped and saved until she had some savings in the bank. Enough to put a deposit down on a small house when they found the right place. At least here in Penhally they had a chance of getting on the housing ladder. In London, it had been impossible.

'I'm ready. Let's go,' Emma called to Abby.

The beach was a ten-minute walk from their house. Although the tourists were away, the sun still warmed the air and there were plenty of locals making the most of the last few warm evenings.

As they walked, Emma asked Abby about her job.

'I love it. The rest of the team seem really nice. I went on my first rescue on Monday with one of the doctors. We managed to get a woman to hospital so her baby could be born safely. We also had to rescue a boy who had fallen down a cliff. Being here has different dangers from those in London. Ones that you might not even think about. So, please, Emma, you need to be very careful when you're out with your friends.'

'You worry too much, Mum. Nothing will happen to me.'

Abby smiled at her daughter. 'I know it won't. And I know I'm a worry wart. But just promise me you'll always be careful.' She couldn't bear it if anything happened to her.

'I might be a pilot when I grow up,' Emma said, dismissing Abby's fears. 'I think I would like flying off to help people in trouble.'

Trust Emma to be drawn to that kind of career. The little girl loved nothing better than taking on anything that was exciting. It struck Abby that she shared at least one trait with Mac. The worst possible, in Abby's opinion. How many more would there be? 'You can be anything you like, darling. As long as you stick at school and do your best.'

Emma stuck out her tongue. 'C'mon, Mum. I'll race you to the sea.' And with that she was off, long legs flying across the sand and her blonde hair streaming behind her. Abby laughed and raced behind her daughter, her heart feeling as light as it had for as long as she could remember.

The shore was busy with people either walking their dogs, playing ball games or paddling. To one side, in an area cordoned off, were the surfers, windsurfers and kite boarders. Abby had watched them once or twice before, impressed at their skill.

The wind down at the shore was gustier than it had been at the cottage and the surfers were taking full advantage of the substantial waves. Further out, where the waves were even bigger, was a kite boarder. Abby and Emma stopped paddling to watch as the boarder let his parachute pull him into the air. There was a collective gasp from other people who had stopped to watch as he somersaulted in the air before landing perfectly on the water. He caught the wind in his parachute to propel him across the water, faster than Abby had ever seen anyone move without the use of an engine. Just as she thought he was going to crash onto the beach, he flipped in the air again, this time landing so he faced in the opposite direction. Abby had never seen anything quite as graceful before. Although the figure was tall, well over six feet, his movements in the air were almost balletic.

'I want to learn how to do that,' Emma said, her eyes wide with admiration. 'It looks so cool.'

Over my dead body, Abby thought grimly. It was far too dangerous. But she didn't say anything. Experience of her headstrong daughter had taught her that the more Emma was told not to do something, the more she wanted to do it. In that way she was very like Sara.

'I think you have to learn to surf or windsurf first, before you can move onto something like that,' Abby said mildly. With a bit of luck it would take Emma years to master the basics. And by that time she would have forgotten her interest in kite surfing.

The kite surfer was racing back towards the shore. When he was only a metre or so away, he turned his board sideways and jumped off. He seemed to have given up for the day.

As he walked up the beach, Abby's breath caught in her throat. It was Mac. He shook the water from his hair before peeling his suit down to his waist. Abby sucked in her breath. His chest was as muscled as she'd remembered, the six pack of his abdomen even more defined than twelve years earlier. All at once a memory of the first time she had seen him came flooding back.

It had been the first full day of their holiday on Mykonos and Abby had been looking forward to relaxing in the sun with Sara. The last few years had been tough. Since their mother had more or less evicted them from the family home, Sara's behaviour had become wilder and wilder. Although Abby had trained as a paramedic, Sara had not found a job she'd wanted to do for more than a few weeks. More interested in partying than working, Sara had lost more than one job for failing to turn up for work after a late night. Abby had hoped that their holiday would give her a chance to talk to Sara and make her see that sooner or later she had to settle down.

As they'd made themselves comfortable on their sunloungers, Abby's attention had been caught by a tall windsurfing instructor who had been giving lessons to a group of beginners on the beach close by. His height alone would have caught her attention, but his tanned and toned physique had made him stand out like some Greek god. His sun-bleached hair had reflected the sun and when he'd grinned, which had been often, his eyes glinted. Abby had never seen anyone whose presence had been so immediate before and her stomach had flipped. He must have felt the intensity of her gaze as he'd looked up from what he was doing and, catching her eye, had winked with a wide smile. Abby had blushed and dipped her head.

Sara had noticed and followed her gaze to where Mac had returned his attention to his class and had been demonstrating how to move the sail on the board in order to catch the wind.

'Now, that's what I call hot,' Sara said appreciatively. 'I think I've just signed up to windsurfing classes.' Not having a shy bone in her body, Sara sauntered over to join the group, and that was more or less the last Abby saw of her for the rest of the holiday. Instead of the girly chats Abby had envisaged, from that moment Sara spent every spare minute with Mac, leaving Abby to amuse herself.

* * *

Abby was forced back to the present as Mac noticed them standing on the beach and walked up to them. He smiled widely.

'Fancy meeting you here,' he said to Abby. His eyes glinted as they lingered on her bikini-clad figure and Abby resisted the impulse to wrap her arms around her body to shield herself from his appreciative gaze.

'We were watching you out there. Pretty impressive.' Abby's heart was in her throat. This wasn't how she'd planned father and daughter would meet.

'Yes. It was really wicked,' Emma piped up.

He turned his gaze to Emma and raised a quizzical eyebrow at Abby.

'This is my daughter, Emma. Emma, this is Dr William MacNeil, my colleague.' *And your father.*

'I'm pleased to meet you, Emma,' Mac said with a tip of his head.

'How did you learn to do that?' Emma said, unable to hide her admiration.

'Many, many years of practice.'

'Could you teach me?'

'Emma,' Abby said warningly. 'I don't think it's fair to ask.'

Mac caught Abby's eyes over the top of Emma's head.

'Why not? I'd have to teach you how to windsurf first. And I could teach Abby, too.' He raised a challenging eyebrow.

Emma's face lit up. 'Would you? That would be amazing! My dad was a windsurfer. Mum, would that be okay? Please say yes.'

Abby suppressed a groan. Emma's dad was a windsurfer right enough. This one standing in front of them. And here he was, offering to give lessons to the child he had no idea was his daughter. Under any other circumstances, Abby would have smiled. In many ways, this was exactly what she had hoped for. Daughter and father getting to know each other, but it was all happening too fast. Abby hated to refuse Emma anything, but she *had* to tell her and Mac the truth before they met again.

'We'll see. But the weather's going to start getting colder soon and then it will be winter. Perhaps it would be better to leave it until next year?' she hedged.

'But that's ages away,' Emma protested. 'I can wear a wetsuit. That'll keep me warm, won't it, Dr MacNeil?'

'Let's just see how we get on. You might decide you hate it after a go or two and that's okay. Not everyone sticks it out.'

'I will. Mum always says I stick to everything once I make up my mind, isn't that right?'

Abby ruffled her hair. 'It's true.'

'Okay, then. How about next Saturday? If the weather holds. I can pick you and your mum up.'

Emma squealed with delight before remembering she was trying to be cool these days. She clamped her hand over her mouth. 'Can I, Mum? Please say yes.'

Abby hated to refuse Emma anything and right now she couldn't think of a single reason to say no. She could always cancel the lesson later. If she had to. She shivered as the sun dropped below the horizon. 'Okay, but we'd better let Dr MacNeil get on. And I should be getting supper ready.'

'Why don't I take you girls out for something? My treat,' Mac suggested.

Behind Emma, Abby shook her head at him. The last thing she wanted right now was to have these two spending time together. At least, not until she had told them the truth.

Emma's face dropped. 'I said I would go round to Sally's house to watch a film. Her mother said she'd order pizza in for us.'

'In that case...' Mac grinned at Abby '...there's no reason why we can't go, is there?'

Abby wanted to refuse, but now that Emma and Mac had met she knew she had to speak to Mac. Putting it off would just make it harder.

'I'll have to drop Emma off at her friend's and get changed first,' she said.

'No problem. I need to go home, too. What about if I pick you up in an hour's time? We could go to the restaurant I mentioned the day we went for a walk.' Without waiting for a reply, he picked up his sailing gear and walked away, whistling.

CHAPTER FIVE

ABBY was breathing so fast that too much oxygen was making her knees weak. She would have to find the words to tell Mac that Emma was his daughter. And after that she would have to tell Emma. There was no way she could let this windsurfing lesson go ahead without both of them knowing who the other truly was.

Emma chatted about Mac and kite boarding all the way back to their little cottage. 'I can't wait to learn how he does that. How long do you think it will take me to learn? I can't believe you're working with someone as cool as him. Just wait until I tell my friends.'

Abby ached for her child. Even before knowing Mac was her father, Emma was clearly starstruck. And Abby couldn't blame her. But the very things that made him an exciting figure were the very things that could make him totally unsuitable as a father. For the umpteenth time, Abby wondered if she were about to make a dreadful mistake. Now Emma had met Mac, she'd be even more devastated if Mac wanted nothing to do with her. Whichever way Abby looked at the problem, there was no obvious right answer.

After dropping Emma off at her friend's, Abby jumped into the shower. Then she attacked her wardrobe, pulling out one outfit after another before discarding them on the floor. She told herself she wanted to look good because she needed the confidence to face Mac with her news.

Eventually she settled on a pair of dark trousers and a deep red silk blouse. A slick of dark eye shadow and the merest hint of lipstick completed her make-up. She brushed her hair until it shone and left it loose around her face, studying herself critically in the mirror. Her eyes were bright, and two spots of bright colour on her cheeks stood out against her pale skin. Suddenly she had to laugh. When Mac saw her, no doubt he would think it was the thought of going out with him that was making her look like an over-excited schoolgirl. She had to relax. Cool, calm and collected was what the occasion demanded and she knew only too well how to do cool, calm and collected. She must never let herself forget, not even for a second, that Mac was Emma's father. That fact alone made him totally out of bounds.

Hearing a knock on the door, she ran downstairs, grabbing her raincoat from the peg beside her door.

Mac smiled broadly at her when she opened the door. He had changed into dark jeans and a white shirt, which accentuated his tanned skin and the dazzling blue of his eyes. A shot of electricity ran up her spine. Despite the warning signals her brain was firing at her, her body clearly wasn't listening.

Tonight he was driving a low-slung sports car instead of the Jeep. Abby looked at him questioningly.

'The Jeep's my day car,' he said carelessly. 'This one I save for night-time. What?' He laughed, catching her look. 'I like cars. You know—boys' toys.'

He drove the same way he did everything else—fast, but with total concentration. Thankfully he slowed down on the narrow coastal roads where visibility was limited.

Nevertheless, Abby found herself gripping her seat and pumping an imaginary brake pedal as if she could slow him down.

He caught her doing it, and grinned wickedly, but he slowed the car down even further.

'Isn't it beautiful?' Abby pointed to the horizon where the sinking sun was turning the sea red. Despite the way her heart was hammering, the sight had a calming effect on her. Abby relaxed into her seat. Why *did* he have to be so attractive? She had thought he was the sexiest man she'd ever seen the first time she'd ever set eyes on him, and she still thought that. Boy, she should have got out more.

'I find everything about it beautiful,' Mac said slowly, turning his head to look at her. 'Quite stunning.'

She couldn't think of a reply, let alone force the words past a throat suddenly as dry as dust. Thankfully moments later they drew up outside a quaint-looking building. It was single storey with thick stone walls. It had been built close to the sea and as Abby stepped out of the car she gasped with pleasure. Stretching before her, as far as the eye could see, was the ocean. It was bluer than Mac's eyes and crests of white tipped the waves, which boomed like thunder as they crashed onto the shore.

Mac came to stand beside her. 'You like?' he asked, his ready smile back in place. 'See that little cove down there?' He pointed to a sandy area to Abby's left. 'That's one of my favourite places to go kite boarding.'

'You mean you surf out there? Where all those rocks are? Isn't it dangerous? Not to say foolhardy?'

Mac's grin got wider. 'Safe is boring.'

Abby craned her neck to see down to the bay. As far as she could tell, there was no path down.

'How do you get down there? I don't see a path.'

'There isn't one—that's part of the attraction. It means I always get the place to myself.'

'So how do you get to it? By boat?'

'Sometimes. Sometimes I climb down. It's more fun. It's not really that difficult—as long as you know what you're doing. One day I'll show you.'

Abby shivered at the promise behind the words. He was making it clear he found her attractive and that he expected to see more of her. Soon he would learn that it was probably going to happen, but not for the reasons he thought.

His daredevil attitude worried her. What if Emma found her father only to lose him in some reckless escapade? She was beginning to appreciate where her daughter had got her own love of risky sports from. She'd always assumed it was from Sara, but now she knew it was from both her parents. It didn't bode well for the future. She shivered again.

'You're cold. I'm sorry. Let's get inside.' He sniffed the air. Wood smoke mingled with the scent of the sea. 'Smells as if they have a fire going inside. We're early enough to grab a table that's near the fire and also has a view of the sea.'

Abby was glad he'd put her shiver down to the cold. She was already beginning to dread telling him about Emma. What if he refused to accept she was his daughter? If he did, at least this way Emma would never need know. At least, not until she was eighteen and perhaps by then she'd be able to deal with her father's rejection. But she was getting way ahead of herself. Unlikely though it seemed, perhaps he'd be pleased to find he had a child. He had been good with Tim and Luke. There was only one way to know for sure and no point in putting it off any longer.

Nevertheless, she waited until they had ordered. Mac was looking at her with the same air of puzzlement that he had shown when they'd been first introduced.

'I can't get it out of my head that we've met before. We haven't, have we? You know...' He had the grace to look embarrassed. 'No, of course we haven't. As I said, I would have remembered you.'

Abby took a deep breath. 'I lied that first day at work. We have met before. Almost twelve years ago. On Mykonos.'

Mac's frown deepened and he looked at her intently. 'Mykonos? I was there as a windsurfing instructor, but I don't... Wait a minute. I do remember you. Your hair was shorter and you wore glasses. But of course. You were there with your sister, Sara.' He leaned back in his chair and whistled. 'You've changed.'

To her fury, Abby blushed under his frank admiration. Of course he hadn't remembered her. Nobody had ever given her a second glance. Not when Sara had been around. Sara had been confident, keen to meet new people and to try out new experiences. She had thrown herself into life almost as if she'd known she wasn't long for the world. Abby had always taken on the big sister role, even though she'd only been the elder by a couple of minutes, and had never minded always being in Sara's shadow. All she'd ever wanted had been for Sara to be happy.

Abby opened her handbag and pulled out the photograph she'd put in it. She handed it to Mac. 'That's my twin, Sara. Non-identical, obviously. You have your arm around her shoulder. The one at the end is me.'

'I remember now. Hell, I haven't thought about that

summer in years. Imagine you carrying that photo around all this time' He looked at her, his dark brows drawing together. 'Why?' He half smiled. 'Don't tell me you had a crush on me and I didn't know. If so, I'm sorry. One thing's for sure, no one could fail to notice you now.'

Once again he sent her a look that gave her goose-bumps and infuriated her at the same time. Did the women he knew really fall for that kind of patter?

'How is Sara?' he continued, grinning. 'If I remember correctly, your sister knew how to have fun! Has she settled down? Sorry. That was a stupid question. Of course she has. She must be what, thirty—thirty-one?'

'Sara's dead,' Abby said bluntly.

There was no mistaking the shock on Mac's face. 'Dead! I am so sorry. When? What happened?'

'She died just over eleven years ago. About nine months after the holiday where you met.' It still sent a stab of pain through Abby whenever she had to say the words. Would she ever get used to it?

'I can't believe it! She was so full of life.' He pushed his half-eaten food away. 'I liked her very much. She was a lovely person.' Clearly he hadn't fully grasped the implication in her words.

'So fond of her you never tried getting in touch after she left?' Abby couldn't keep the bitterness from her voice. Mac had taken advantage of her sister. He had used her. Although they had both been young, he must have known that there had been a chance Sara could fall pregnant. Or had he simply not given a damn?

'Hey, I did try to get in touch, once or twice,' Mac said. 'But the phone number she left with me was never answered.' He leaned across the table, his eyes unfathomable. 'We were both young. We both accepted it was a holiday romance. Nothing more.' He placed his hand on top of Abby's. She snatched it away. Whether it was because she was still angry with him or whether it was because his touch sent little sparks of electricity shooting up her arm, she didn't want to think about.

'How did she die?' he asked softly. 'Was it an accident?'

This was the hard part. This was where she had to tell him about Emma. But suddenly she couldn't. Not yet.

'Could we talk about something else?' she asked softly. 'Even though it's been years, it still hurts too much.'

Mac was immediately contrite. 'Sure.' He leaned back in his chair and studied her intently. 'Tell me about you. How come you ended up here? Penhally is quite a change to London.'

How could she explain the change without mentioning Emma?

'I'd rather talk about you,' she said evasively. 'When we met back on Mykonos you were a windsurfing instructor. It was a bit of a shock to find you are a rescue medic.'

Mac grinned. 'Yeah, well. Back then I'd just graduated and I wanted one summer off before I started my first house job. I was fortunate. I managed to get an instructing job every summer while I was a medical student. It helped pay the bills.' For a moment his eyes darkened and he lost his ready smile. Then just as quickly the grin was back in place. 'If I couldn't be a doctor, I probably would have been a professional windsurfer. Luckily I got into medical school. Better pay and much more satisfying.'

He paused as a couple took a table close by. 'Tiree has an international reputation for some of the best surf in the world. I couldn't grow up there and not do a watersport of some description.'

'Don't tell me that's what brought you to Penhally Bay.' She didn't even attempt to hide her incredulity. What kind of doctor took a job because of the surfing conditions?

He looked amused. 'Partly. Glasgow is a great city, but I couldn't live in a place I can't kite board regularly. But I also came here because there was an opening for a medic in the air ambulance service. The job here is exactly what I always wanted.'

'You love it, don't you? The excitement and the danger. I saw the rescue you did with the family on the boat on television. You risked your life to save those people. Just as you did with Luke.'

Mac grinned again. 'It's part of the job. But you're right. I feel more alive when I battle the elements—beat the odds. But what about you? Do you think you'll cope? It must be different from what you've been used to.'

How deftly he had turned the conversation away from himself again.

'Some of it does frighten me. Especially the thought of being lowered by a winch in blustery conditions. I think it has something to do with being a mum. You know that you have a child waiting for you at home. Someone who needs you to be around for a long time, and it makes you think twice about taking risks.'

'I wouldn't know about that.' Although he smiled, a shadow crossed his eyes. 'One of the benefits about being single is that I don't have anyone who needs me. Luckily.' Abby suspected she was being warned. *Don't expect too much. I'm not in it for the long term.*

So far nothing Mac had said was what she wanted to hear.

Sensing that Mac was about to ask about Emma, Abby added quickly, 'What about your parents? Brothers? Sisters?' It wasn't just that she wanted to keep the conversation away from Emma for the time being at least, she was intensely curious. She told herself it was purely because Mac's family would be Emma's family, too.

It was as if the shutters had come down. Mac's blue eyes grew cold and distant.

'I'm an only child. I have no idea who or where my father is,' he said shortly. 'My mother still lives in Tiree. I see her when I can.'

Abby felt a tug of sympathy—and recognition. Whenever she was asked about her parents, she gave pretty much the same reply. Her father had disappeared after she and Sara had been born. He had never come back to see his daughters and the only contact they'd ever had with him had been the odd birthday card. He had died years ago, and their mother had only thought to tell Sara and Abby long after the funeral had taken place.

'But let's not talk about the past.' Mac leaned forward. 'It's the here and now that matters. I want to know more about you.'

'And the future?' Abby persisted. 'Doesn't that matter?'

Mac grinned and narrowed his eyes speculatively. 'The only thing about the future that interests me right now is when you're going to come out with me again.'

Abby returned his look coolly. Her brown eyes were reproving, almost accusing. Mac could have kicked himself. He should have known the usual direct approach wouldn't work with this woman. Instinctively he knew that Abby was someone who would expect to be courted slowly and seriously. But he didn't feel like taking things slowly with Abby. If he could have taken her home with him tonight and made love to her, he would have without a moment's hesitation.

And he didn't do serious. Abby was a woman with a child. A mother, and a protective one at that. Everything he had learned about her so far told him that she wasn't the kind of woman to have casual affairs. Why, then, was he ignoring the alarms bells that were jangling in his head?

The faint scent of her perfume drifted across at him and before he could stop himself he leaned across the table and took a lock of her thick caramel hair between his fingers. It was heavy and silky. He swallowed a groan as an image of Abby naked beside him, her hair touching his skin as she leaned over to kiss him, flashed into his head. He knew without a shadow of doubt he would never be satisfied until he had this woman in his bed.

A range of emotions he couldn't quite place crossed Abby's face. He would bet his life, though, that she felt the attraction, too.

'But the future does matter, Mac. So does the past.' She fiddled with her napkin. 'Emma...' she started. 'Sara...' She took a deep breath. Some of the colour had left her face.

'Sara died following childbirth. She developed an infection a few days after she delivered Emma. The doctors did everything they could but it was no use.' Her enormous brown eyes swam with unshed tears.

'After Emma was delivered?' Mac echoed. 'I thought Emma was your child.'

'She is. But I'm not her birth mother. Sara was. After she died, Emma came to live with me.'

Mac was puzzled. Why was she telling him this? It did explain, however, why there was no father in the picture. Despite everything he'd just told himself, he couldn't help feeling glad.

'Sara delivered Emma nine months after she returned from Mykonos.' Abby caught her bottom lip between her teeth.

Did she have any idea how cute she looked when she did that?

'Mac, Emma is your daughter.'

Emma? His daughter? At least he thought that was what Abby said. He must have misheard.

'Did I hear you correctly?' he said. He hoped to hell he hadn't.

'Yes. I didn't know at first. Sara wouldn't tell me who the father was, although, given the timing, I had my suspicions.'

'So she might not be mine?' He heard the relief in his voice.

'She didn't tell me it was you until she knew for certain she was going to die. Then she confirmed what I had suspected all along. You were the father.'

Mac felt as if he was in a nightmare. He couldn't have a daughter. It was impossible. God knew, he didn't want one. He would make a terrible father anyway. His mind was racing. Admittedly, Sara and he had spent almost the whole fortnight together and, yes, they'd had sex. Neither of them had ever pretended that what they'd shared had been anything more than a holiday romance. And he remembered he had asked about contraception. He hadn't been such an idiot as to have unprotected sex. Although Sara had insisted she was on the Pill, they had used condoms, too. In his twenty-one years he had hardly been a saint and he hadn't taken chances with anyone's sexual health. So how could she have fallen pregnant? But then it came back to him. There had been one evening after a beach party when they'd both had too much to drink and they hadn't used condoms. It had never crossed his mind that Sara could have become pregnant. He forced himself to focus on what Abby was saying.

'When Emma was three months old, I went back to Mykonos to try and find you, but it was no use. You were gone. All I knew was that you were called Mac. I asked around, but nobody could tell me anything that would help me trace you.'

'That summer was my last of teaching windsurfing. After that I was too busy doing my house jobs. I didn't need the money or, more to the point, have the time.' He still felt dazed. 'You can't be sure she's mine, whatever Sara told you.'

'Think about it, Mac. Sara had no reason to lie. If she had wanted to, she could have told you she was pregnant, but she didn't. It was only when she knew she was going to die that she told me. And that was only because she knew that one day Emma would want to know something about her father. Possibly find him.' She paused. 'But if you still have your doubts I'm sure we can arrange a DNA test.' Although that wasn't what she wanted. Emma would be hurt to find out that the father she so desperately wanted had needed proof that she was his daughter.

'I think that might be a good idea.' Mac stumbled to his feet. He had to get out of there. He needed time to think. He saw his life changing in front of his eyes. A father!

'Mac, I know this has been a shock to you. It was to me when I realised I would be working with you. At least, in my case, I've known about you for years.'

'Does Emma know? That I'm her father, I mean?'

'She knows that her father is out there somewhere. She doesn't know it's you. Not yet. I thought it was only fair to talk to you first.'

'Will you tell her?'

'Yes. She desperately wants to find her father.' Abby reached out and touched him on the hand. 'Mac, please sit down. I can't think with you standing over me like that.'

Reluctantly Mac did as she asked. He owed it to Abby to hear her out, however much he didn't want to believe what she was telling him.

'The reason I took the job here was because Emma was being bullied at her school in London. You know how cruel kids can be. When they found out that Em didn't know who her father was they started teasing her. They wouldn't even come to her eleventh birthday party. Things just got worse from there.'

Ouch. Mac remembered only too well how that felt. Growing up in a small community, as he had done, it had been exactly the same for him, but at least he'd had his windsurfing. Out on the waves he'd been able to forget everything. Besides, his skill on the board had made him a bit of a hero in the other children's eyes. But their teasing had still hurt. He felt a rush of sympathy towards Emma. And anger. How dared those children pick on a little girl about something that was out of her control? If he had them in front of them right now, he'd be tempted to bang their heads together.

'If it turns out I am Emma's father, I won't deny her,'

he said. 'I'll do what's right. Provide financial support, whatever you need.'

Abby's eyes flashed with anger. 'Financial support isn't what is needed, Mac. Emma and I manage fine. What Emma needs is far more complicated than that. As soon as she knows about you she is going to want a relationship. Can you give her that?'

Right now, Mac had no idea.

Mac got to his feet again. 'I'm sorry, Abby, I just don't know if I can do what you're asking. I never wanted to be a father. I don't have the first clue about being one. There's a good chance I'll be rubbish at it. Emma is probably better off without me.' He jammed his hands into his pockets. 'I need time to think about this. Decide what to do.'

'Don't think too long, Mac. I have to tell Emma that I've found you.' She got to her feet, too. 'You said you'd take her windsurfing next Saturday. Whether you show up or not is up to you.'

He could see the determination in her calm nut-brown eyes.

'But let me warn you. If you do decide to get involved with her, it's not something you can back out of later. You're in it for keeps. Make no mistake, Mac, if you hurt my child, you'll have me to reckon with.'

CHAPTER SIX

MAC let himself into his flat and flung his car keys on the table. He had dropped Abby back home and they had sat in silence the whole of the journey. He was still reeling from what Abby had told him. There he'd been thinking he had been doing nothing more than taking a beautiful woman out to dinner. Now it seemed as if he was father to that woman's daughter!

He thought back to when he had seen Emma on the beach. She was tall—like him. And she had blue eyes— like him. But was that enough to go on?

He crossed over to his full-length windows and stared out to sea. How could his life have changed so dramatically in just a matter of hours? The last thing he wanted, or needed, was an eleven-year-old daughter. Why hadn't Sara told him she was pregnant? He felt a grudging respect for the woman who had given birth to his child. She had known how much his medical career had meant to him. She had also probably known, he admitted ruefully, that back then he had not been up to being a father. But was he up to it now?

The wind had risen, whipping the sea against the rocks. He wished he was out there, challenging himself against the elements. It was so much easier than dealing with the bomb Abby had thrown at him.

He poured himself a whisky and swirled the amber liquid around the glass. Memories of his own childhood came rushing back. The endless stream of men his mother had brought home, insisting that he call them Dad. He had refused. And just as well; none of them, except Dougie, had lasted more than a couple of months. Mac had got on with him. It had been Dougie who had given him his first second-hand board and Mac would have considered calling him Dad, but eventually Dougie had left, too, driven away by his mother's excessive demands. She had blamed Mac. Told him that he had ruined her chances of finding happiness. No wonder he had learned to windsurf. The time on the waves had been his only relief from his bitter, resentful mother. That, and school. As soon as he'd been able to, he had left home, supporting himself through medical school by taking out loans and teaching windsurfing. It had been hard. There had been too many times when he'd had to choose between buying a textbook and eating. But he'd survived, learning to depend on only himself. No wonder he'd never let anyone get close to him and so far it had worked out exactly the way he wanted. He was living the perfect life. A job he loved, this flat, mountain biking, free climbing and kite boarding whenever he could, and dating the kind of women who seemed happy to fit in around his other pleasures.

Until now.

He took a swig of his whisky, letting the liquid roll around his tongue. His life was going to be turned upside down. But what if Sara had been wrong? What if Emma wasn't his child? He had to know for certain one way or another. If she was his, he wouldn't abandon her. He couldn't do the same thing to a child, his child, as his father had done to him. At least Emma had Abby. An image of hazel eyes and a warm smile floated in front of his eyes. She was the opposite of the women he normally went after. She was serious, warm, caring and fiercely protective. He knew instinctively she would be like a tigress when it came to protecting her daughter. Abby, he was sure, would never have told him he was Emma's father if she hadn't been certain of it herself. She had taken a risk telling him and she knew it. Sighing, he placed his empty glass on the table and reached for the phone. He had to see Abby and arrange the DNA test after she had a chance to tell Emma. The sooner he knew for sure that Emma was his, the better for all concerned. But deep down he was getting used to the idea. Already he felt something strange, a sense of protectiveness towards the young girl who Abby claimed was his child.

Abby finished tidying the kitchen while listening to Emma's excited chatter. It was so good to see the little girl back to her usual self.

'Emma, I need to talk to you about something,' Abby said when Emma drew breath. 'Why don't I make us a cup of cocoa and we can take it in to the sitting room and chat there?'

When they were settled, Abby turned to Emma.

'You know how we spoke about your dad? Remember I told you I tried to find him when you were very little?'

Emma nodded and waited for Abby to continue.

'Well, I've found him.'

'Where? Who is he? How did you find him? Did he come looking for me?' The hope in Emma's eyes made Abby's heart stumble.

'He couldn't look for you, sweetie, because he didn't

know about you. I kind of found him by accident.' Abby
took a deep breath. There was no going back now.

'You know Dr MacNeil? The man we met on the
beach? He's your father.'

Emma looked stunned. 'Dr MacNeil? I thought you
said my dad was a windsurfer.'

'Well, he is. We saw that down on the beach, but he's
also a doctor. He taught windsurfing as a way to put
himself through medical school.'

A slow smile crept across Emma's face. 'That's so
cool. Does he know? Did you tell him? What did he
say?'

Abby smiled at Emma's excitement. 'Yes, he knows.
I told him.' Abby leaned across and took Emma's hand
in hers. 'It was a bit of a surprise to him. He had no
idea that your mother had even been pregnant. I guess
it'll take him a little time to get used to the idea he has
a daughter.'

Emma's brow puckered. 'You mean he doesn't want
me.'

Abby took the mug from Emma and placed it on the
coffee table, before pulling her daughter into her arms.
'Of course he'll want you. He just needs time to get to
know you better. You and I have always known that you
had a dad out there somewhere, but this has all come as
a big surprise to him.'

'Is he still going to take me windsurfing?'

'I'm not sure. Em, don't get your hopes up too much.
Remember when we've spoken about this before, we
always said that even if we found your father, he might
not want to be as involved as you might hope.'

'I don't care,' Emma said fiercely. 'I know I've always
got you.' She sat up, her brows furrowing. 'This won't
make any difference to us, will it? I mean, you'll always

be my mum, won't you? He can't take me away from you, even if he wants to, right?'

Abby had wondered the same thing herself. When Sara had died, Abby had thought about adopting Emma officially, but it hadn't seem to be necessary. The social services had been more than happy to leave Emma in her care. Surely, and Abby thought this was unlikely, even if Mac did want to have Emma with him full time, no one would give him custody?

'I don't think that's going to happen. You're my daughter and no one is ever going to take you away from me. Look, let's take this one day at a time. You and Mac can get to know each other and we'll take it from there.'

Emma nodded. 'At least the kids won't be able to tease me about not having a father any more.' She hugged Abby. 'I can't wait to meet him properly. What's he like? Tell me everything you know.'

Emma was too excited to go to bed and she and Abby talked into the night. Abby brought out all her old photos of Sara and repeated the stories of their childhood that Emma could never get enough of. Finally she was able to persuade an exhausted but happy Emma to go to bed. Looking down at her sleeping child, Abby made a vow: Dr William MacNeil would not be allowed to cause her daughter so much as a moment's pain.

Early the next morning, there was a knock on the door. Abby opened it to find Mac standing there, an uncertain smile on his face.

'Can I come in?'

Abby was glad Emma was still in bed, catching up on sleep after their late night.

She stood back to let him in.

He brushed past her and started pacing her small

sitting room. He only managed a couple of strides in each direction before he had to turn round.

'Have you told her?' He hadn't even said hello.

'Yes. Last night.'

'How did she take the news?' He seemed nervous, uncharacteristically unsure of himself.

'She was thrilled. I warned her that I didn't know what you were going to do about it.'

'I'm not going to ask for a DNA test,' Mac said abruptly.

'Oh? Why not?' Had he made up his mind that regardless of whether it could be proven Emma was his child, he still didn't want to know? Abby's heart gave a sickening thud. It would be hard telling Emma, but perhaps it was for the best. In that case, either Mac or she and Emma would have to leave Cornwall. It would be too cruel for Emma to be reminded daily that she had a father who didn't want her.

'I don't want a DNA test because it's not fair to Emma. You say she's my child. The dates fit. She looks like me. If I insist on a DNA test, how will that make her feel? I know that if I were in her shoes, I would think that my father was trying to prove I wasn't his. No child deserves to be put through that.'

'So what are you saying, Mac? I'm afraid you're going to have to spell it out.'

'Look, I don't know what sort of father I'll make, but I'm going to give it my best shot. You and Emma will just have to be patient with me. Can you do that, Abby? Can you accept I can only do the best I can? That it might not be good enough?'

Abby was relieved he wasn't insisting on a DNA test. But as far as what kind of father he would be? Well, that was up to him. It wasn't as if she could go and pick him up a set of instructions from some kind of parent supermarket.

'Just promise me you'll do the best you can,' she said softly.

He sighed. 'You're going to have to help me here, Abby. As I said, I have no idea how to go about being a father. I mean, what do I do?'

He looked so different from his usual confident self that Abby's heart melted a little.

'I think taking her windsurfing is a good start,' she said. 'That way you and Emma can get to know each other without it seeming forced and unnatural.'

'I can do that. What else?'

'Let's just take it day by day, Mac. Learning to be a father takes time.'

'Tell Emma I'll see her on Saturday.' And with that he turned on his heel and was out the door as if the devil himself were after him.

CHAPTER SEVEN

MAC took a gulp of his beer as he waited for Josh to emerge from the changing room. It had been a good match, even if it had been closer than Mac would have liked. Shortly after Mac had started working on the air ambulance crew, Josh had invited him to join the five-a-side football team that many of the staff at the hospital played for. In the end, their team had just pulled the match out of the bag. Mac was pleased. He hated to lose.

'I got one in for you,' he told Josh when he appeared, gesturing towards the pint he had placed on the table.

After the match, the team would have a quick pint and usually talk about work. For various reasons tonight it was just him and Josh who'd stayed for a drink. Everyone else had had reasons to rush away, but although Josh was married he never seemed in a hurry to leave after the game.

Mac knew little about Josh's personal life. He had met his wife, Rebecca, once or twice when she had dropped into A & E to see her husband. Mac had got the impression that Rebecca was a little lonely. The life as a wife of a consultant could be like that, especially if, like Rebecca, she didn't work. Another reason to stay footloose and fancy-free, Mac decided—except he wasn't, not any more.

'How's Rebecca?' Mac asked. 'Does she like living here?'

Josh studied his pint glass as he twirled it around in his hand. 'I think Rebecca is more of a city girl. She misses being able to pop into the shops any time she pleases.'

'Yet she agreed to move here?' Mac said.

'It was too good an opportunity for me to miss. Hopefully in time Rebecca will make friends. Although it's difficult when she doesn't work. Not having children doesn't help either. If we had kids, she'd probably meet some mothers down at the school gates.'

'If you're planning on having some, I wouldn't leave it too long. How old is Rebecca? Thirty-three? Thirty-four?'

Josh frowned. 'Thirty-four. But we always agreed they weren't part of the plan.'

The expression on Josh's face darkened for a moment. What's going on here? Mac thought. But whatever it was, it was none of his business. Josh and Rebecca's private life had nothing to do with him.

'Anyway, what about you? I guess you're not the father type either. Or haven't you met the right woman yet?'

Mac shifted in his seat. Served him right. He had started this conversation. Besides, people were bound to find out sooner or later.

'Er… Actually, it turns out I am a father,' he said. The words sounded strange, still unbelievable.

Josh's eyebrows shot up. 'You kept that quiet. A bit of a dark horse, aren't you?'

'I only just found out myself.' If it were possible,

Josh looked even more astonished. But he said nothing, simply waited for Mac to continue.

'It's complicated,' Mac said. 'You know our new paramedic, Abby Stevens?'

'She's the mother of your child?' Josh's eyebrows couldn't go any higher.

'No. She's the aunt of my child. Emma, my daughter, is the result of a relationship I had with Abby's twin— years ago.'

'I think you're going to have to be more explicit,' Josh said, leaning back in his chair. 'Go on, I'm all ears.'

Mac wasn't used to talking about himself, but he had to tell someone. Perhaps thinking out loud would help. So, hesitantly, between sips of beer, he told Josh the whole story.

'And you had no idea Sara was pregnant?' A shadow crossed Josh's face, making Mac wonder, but he kept his thoughts to himself.

'None. It never crossed my mind.'

'And you believe Abby?'

'If you knew Abby better, you'd know that's a daft question. She's not the kind of woman to lie about something like this. She's totally upfront. With Abby, what you see is what you get.'

Josh raised an eyebrow again. There was a hint of a smile at the corner of his mouth. Mac wanted to tell him that he was mistaken, that there was nothing between him and Abby, but he knew his protests would only increase that amused look in Josh's eyes.

'Besides, it is entirely possible. The timing works out. And I was young at the time. Not always as responsible as I should have been.'

Josh's frown deepened. Did he disapprove? Surely Josh must have behaved in ways he now regretted when he had been a medical student. But perhaps Josh had been sensible enough always to take precautions. As medics, they knew better. Or, at least in his case, should have known better. But, damn it, he wasn't asking Josh for his approval. 'Shortly before she died, Sara told Abby I was the father and I can see no reason why Sara would lie. Besides, Emma has my eyes. I don't think there's much doubt.'

'So what are you going to do about it?'

'No idea, Josh. It's not as if I planned to be a father. I'm pretty sure I'll make a rotten one. But I can't turn away from my responsibilities. I told Abby that I'll spend time with Emma. I'm going to teach her to windsurf. At least I can do that.'

Josh looked thoughtful. He put his glass down on the table and leaned forward. 'You know, Mac, sometimes life deals us a hand we never wanted, or expected. We get one chance at grabbing what's in front of us. If we don't take it while we can, it might be a mistake we end up regretting for the rest of our lives.'

Something in his voice made Mac wonder if he was speaking from personal experience, but before he could decide whether to probe further, Josh went on. 'If I were you, I would think very carefully before you turn away from something that might turn out to be the best thing that's ever happened to you.'

'It sounds as if you know what you're talking about,' Mac said.

'Let's just say, if I had a particular time over in my life, I might have made different choices.' Josh picked up his and Mac's empty glasses. He nodded in the direction of the bar. 'Fancy a refill?' he asked.

On the way home Mac thought about what Josh had said. There was a mystery there, he was sure of it, but he respected his colleague too much to speculate on what it could be. If he wanted him to know, he'd tell him. As far as his advice about Abby and Emma went—that was different. He had promised Abby that he would get to know Emma and he had never gone back on his promise. But the thought still scared him witless. What did he know about being a father? He hadn't exactly had a good example himself. Unless it had been how not to be a father. His father had walked out on him and his mother without a backward glance. Walking out of the marriage had been one thing, but abandoning your only child had been quite another.

He swallowed his anger. It was no use thinking like that. What he did have to think about was *his* child. Whatever the future brought, however much he hadn't planned on having a child and however much disruption that might bring to the life he had carved out for himself, there was really no choice. He was Emma's father and he wouldn't—couldn't—abandon her.

CHAPTER EIGHT

THE next couple of days were busy, and Mac and Abby were seldom alone together, for which Mac was grateful.

He was still getting used to the fact that he had a daughter and almost as strange was that Abby was the mother of his child. For the first time in his life he was confused by his feelings for a woman.

He liked working with Abby. He admired the way she was with the patients; calm, assured but gentle, as if they really mattered to her.

They had the usual callouts to walkers with broken ankles that turned out to be badly twisted, and a couple of car accidents that thankfully turned out to be less serious than initially thought. When there wasn't a call-out, the team went over rescue procedures and updated each other with new medical developments. Mac was careful to treat Abby like simply another member of the team.

It wasn't easy. He'd come to recognise the habit she had of biting her lip whenever she was anxious, and more than once he had to stop himself from leaning across and brushing a lock of hair from her eyes. He could hardly keep his eyes off her. He loved the way her mouth curved and her eyes lit up when she was pleased about something and he resented the way he kept imagining what it would be like to feel her mouth on his. Okay, so she was beautiful and sexy and warm but now he knew about Emma, Abby was out of bounds. He already had one commitment he had never expected and he didn't need another.

It was just after lunch on Wednesday when they received a call to attend a woman who had been thrown off her horse and then trampled. The only information they had to go on was that the woman was unconscious and in a field with no road access. The call had been transferred to the RAF, which was sending out a Sea King so that the medics could be winched down to the casualty if necessary

Within minutes Abby and Mac were being flown towards the injured woman.

'This could be nasty,' Mac said into his radio. 'If she's unconscious, it'll be difficult for us to be sure just how badly injured she is.'

'In that case, don't we treat her as if she has a spinal injury?' Abby asked.

'The most important thing is to keep her breathing,' Mac agreed. 'And not to make things worse.'

Ten short minutes later they were hovering over the accident site. A man was standing next to the woman, waving a brightly coloured jacket to get their attention.

'As we thought, there's nowhere to put down, I'm afraid,' the pilot said. 'It's too marshy. You're going to have to be winched out.'

Mac glanced at Abby and was surprised to see a flash of fear in her eyes.

'Are you okay?'

Abby nibbled her lip. 'It's the first time other than

training that I've had to winch down. I'm just a little nervous.'

'Tell you what,' he said. 'Seeing there is someone on board that can lower us both, why don't we go down together? That way we can get down quicker.' It wouldn't really make much difference timewise, but going down in tandem would make Abby feel better. It was the first time she had revealed a less than certain side to her and it made him feel unusually protective. Whether it was because she was the mother of his child or because this woman engendered feelings he had never experienced before, he didn't want to think about. He much preferred to think it was the former.

Mac stood and attached the winch to the harness they always wore in the helicopter. Although she was determined not to show it, Abby was relieved he'd be going down with her. She was intensely aware of the touch of his hands on her legs and hips as he tested the buckles.

The last few days he had been polite but distant towards her. When she'd asked him whether he still intended to take Emma windsurfing, he'd looked surprised. 'I don't go back on promises, Abby,' he'd said. 'Especially not to a child.'

They were lowered over the side, pressed together, one of Mac's arms holding her close. This was almost worse than going down alone. Her fear disappeared under her awareness of his hard, muscular body touching every inch of hers. She raised her head to look at him and he winked. She wasn't sure whether she was glad or disappointed when they touched the ground and Mac released them from the winch. All she knew was that her body felt as if it was on fire and that the blood was whooshing in her ears.

Mac raced to the fallen woman, leaving Abby to follow in his wake.

He crouched down beside her, feeling for a pulse. Then he used the small torch they all carried in the top pockets of their jumpsuits to shine a light in her eyes. Abby's heart sank when she saw that only one pupil reacted to the light.

'How long since it happened?' Mac asked the man who had stayed with her.

'I don't know, but not long before I found her. She cantered past me a few minutes earlier. I lost sight of her but then I saw her horse galloping away without a rider, so I knew something had happened. I telephoned for help immediately.' He looked at his watch. 'About twenty-five minutes ago. So I would estimate it's been approximately half an hour since she fell.'

'Has she been conscious at all? Have you moved her, Mr...?'

'Fox. No, I know you're not supposed to. I had some medical training when I was in the army. I just checked that she was breathing.'

Abby slipped a neck brace out of her bag. Although the head injury was their primary concern, they had to assume until they knew otherwise that the victim had a spinal injury, too.

Mac nodded and working together they slipped the brace round the fallen woman's neck and an oxygen mask over her face.

Then they strapped the rider's legs together to make the transfer to the helicopter. With Mr Fox helping, they slipped the two halves of the stretcher underneath her.

Mac was winched into the helicopter with the stretcher and a short time later the line was dropped again. Her heart thudding, Abby attached herself and gave the thumbs-up signal to be lifted. She could hardly ask Mac to leave their patient and come back for her. But to her relief the upward lift was okay. Having done it on the way down with Mac had helped. Abby knew that from now on she would never again worry about that part of the rescue, and she had Mac's thoughtfulness to thank for that.

Back in the helicopter, Mac had already attached their patient to the onboard monitoring system and was gently feeling her abdomen. As he did so, Abby noted some swelling just below the woman's ribs. She glanced up at Mac, who was shaking his head and looking worried.

'Damage to the spleen?' she asked.

He nodded. 'The sooner we get her to hospital the better. If she has ruptured her spleen she'll need surgery as soon as possible. I'll radio ahead and let them know so they can have the surgeons and a theatre standing by.'

The next ten minutes were tense as Abby continued to monitor the woman's vital signs and neuro observations. Her pulse was rapid, making the possibility of a ruptured spleen more likely. Mac helped Abby put up a drip. Giving the injured woman fluids would help keep her stabilised in the short term.

Abby sighed with relief when the helicopter landed gently on the landing pad at the hospital. As before, they were met by the A & E team. There was no time for introductions as they wheeled the woman straight into Resus and Abby stepped back, allowing the A & E team to take over. As they carried out their own assessment, Mac relayed what he and Abby had done so far.

'I think you're right about the ruptured spleen, Mac,' the dark-haired emergency consultant who had loaned them his car told them. 'Could I have a portable ultrasound over here, please?' While the A & E consultant prepared to scan the victim's abdomen, Mac was checking her reflexes. 'Right pupil still blown,' he said. 'I suspect a subdural haematoma, Josh. We should get the neurosurgeons down here to have a look.'

'I'm here.'

Abby whirled around to see a Latin-looking man enter the room. He crossed over to the trolley and Mac stepped aside to allow him to examine the rider. By this time the resus room was crowded. Apart from Dr Corezzi, the neurosurgeon, and Josh, there were several other people in the room, all occupied with the patient.

Mac passed an endotracheal tube down the woman's throat.

'Okay, let's get her to Theatre. The spleen *is* ruptured so she's going to need that fixed, too,' Josh said quietly. Despite his calm voice, Abby knew they were worried. A few moments later the woman was being wheeled out of the room to Theatre.

The emergency over, Josh and Mac peeled off their gloves.

'That was close,' Josh said. 'It was a good thing you were there, Mac. It makes a difference knowing in advance what we might be dealing with. This is exactly the type of case where having a doctor attached to the ambulance service makes a difference.'

'You're right. But whether a few successful cases will persuade the powers that be that having a full-time doctor attached to the service makes financial sense is a different story. She still might not make it,' Mac replied. 'But at least she has a chance.'

Mac glanced over at Abby, seeming surprised to see her still standing there. 'I couldn't have done it without

Abby. Abby, this is Dr Josh O'Hara, one of the A & E consultants here. Josh, this is Abby, our new paramedic, who has joined us from the London service.'

Josh grinned. 'We're lucky to have you.'

Abby took in his dark hair and ready smile. He was very good-looking, but for some reason he did nothing to her pulse. Unlike Mac. Unfortunately.

'Have you had a chance to look around St Piran's, Abby?' Josh asked.

Abby smiled. 'Not yet. There hasn't really been time. But I'd really like to go to the special care nursery. I have a patient there I'd like to see.'

'I have to pop into ITU,' Mac said. 'Josh, if you're not busy, perhaps you could take Abby up to Special Care? I'll meet you there in five.'

'Sure. No probs. I'll just let the nursing staff know where I am. I can introduce you to whoever is on duty at the same time, Abby.'

There were too many faces for Abby to take in, but everyone welcomed her warmly. She couldn't help but notice that Josh caused quite a stir in the department. There were several wistful looks in his direction of which he seemed oblivious. After they left the department, Josh took Abby upstairs to the SCBU. A nurse met them as they entered.

Josh introduced Abby. 'Abby was the paramedic who helped Mrs Hargreaves when she went into labour. She wanted to say hello and see how the baby's getting on.'

'Mum is with the baby now and they are both doing fine. It would have been a different story if you and Dr MacNeil hadn't got them here so quickly.' She peered over Abby's shoulder, as if expecting to find Mac standing behind her. She looked disappointed to find he wasn't. The nurse pointed to a cot near the middle of the room. 'They're over there if you want to go over.'

'Is Dr Phillips on duty?' Josh asked.

'Megan? Yes. Isn't she always? She's in the staffroom, catching up on paperwork.'

Josh looked at Abby. 'That's where I'll be if you need me. Mac should be along shortly.'

Abby found Jenny sitting by the cot, gazing down at her baby. As soon as she noticed Abby, her face broke into an enormous smile.

'How's he doing?' Abby whispered, peering into the cot. A tiny infant lay in it, his nappy almost taking up half of his small body. There were a few lines snaking from his tiny hands and feet, but he was breathing on his own. That was a good sign.

'He's doing okay. They think I'll be able to take him home in a week or two. And it's all thanks to you and Dr MacNeil. The staff say that if I'd been any later getting to hospital I might have lost him—or died, too. I don't know how to thank you enough.' Her voice cracked slightly. She had been through a very stressful experience and was bound to still be worried.

'You don't have to thank us. It's our job. I'm just thrilled that it all worked out okay.' Abby held out her arms and Jenny passed her sleeping child to her. Abby breathed in the particular blissful scent of baby.

Jenny was looking at something over Abby's shoulder. Abby turned round to find Mac standing there, looking at them. Jenny smiled and waved him over.

Mac approached them slowly, looking as if he'd rather be anywhere else than there.

'Dr MacNeil, I'm so glad I caught you. I wanted to thank you personally for saving my baby. And for taking care of Tim. I know he had his brave face on, but he was truly terrified until you came along.'

Mac shuffled his feet, looking uncomfortable. 'As I'm sure Abby told you, it was nothing. All in a day's work. How is Tim anyway?'

'He's at school today. His dad will bring him up later. He's totally besotted with his little brother. He kind of feels that he almost helped deliver him. He was a bit embarrassed when he first heard I was pregnant—you know how young boys can be about that sort of stuff—but now he couldn't be prouder.'

Just then Josh approached them, accompanied by a woman with russet hair and fine, delicate features.

'Abby, this is Dr Megan Phillips—one of the paediatric registrars,' Josh introduced her.

'Hi, Abby. I've heard all about you from Mrs Hargreaves here. I understand that it's thanks to you our latest miracle baby is doing well,' Megan said.

'Would you like to hold him, Dr Phillips?' Jenny asked. 'And seeing as you're all here, I might take the opportunity to pop to the bathroom.'

But Abby was surprised when Megan blanched. Instead, Josh stepped forward and took the tiny infant in his arms, cradling him with practised ease.

'Hey, Josh,' Mac teased. 'Looks like you're a natural after all. Are you practising for when you and Rebecca have kids? The nurses in A & E tell me that's all she talks about when she visits the department. You'd better make the most of the next few months. One of these days you'll be up to your ears in nappies.'

'Not me, I'm afraid,' Josh said lightly.

Abby saw Josh and Megan exchange a look. It was brief, the merest glance, but the paediatric registrar's face went even whiter. If she hadn't known Josh was married to Rebecca, Abby would have sworn there was something between the two doctors. But perhaps her own situation was making her hypersensitive. That was all.

As soon as Jenny returned Megan made her excuses. 'I'll be back to check on this little one in a while,' she told the happy mother. 'But if you'll excuse me, right now I have other patients to look in on.' She smiled, but Abby could see it didn't quite reach her eyes. After a brief nod at the two men, she left the ward.

'I should be getting back to A & E,' Josh said, handing the baby back to his mother. 'So if you'll excuse me, too? Abby, it was good to meet you. I'm sure we'll meet again soon.'

'We should go, too, Abby,' Mac said.

'No problem. If someone could just point me in the direction of the bathroom first? It was lovely to see you again, Jenny. And your baby. We don't always get the chance to catch up with our patients, so when we do, it's a real pleasure.'

'Thank you both, again.' She gazed down at her sleeping child, who was just beginning to stir. 'Looks like he's ready for a feed.'

'The bathroom's just outside the swing doors, Abby,' Mac said. 'I'll meet you downstairs.'

Abby found the bathroom. To her surprise Megan was leaning against the basin, her face streaked with tears. Concerned, Abby moved towards her and touched her on the arm.

'Megan? What's wrong?'

Megan managed a wan smile and leaned over the sink to splash her face with water. 'Don't mind me. I'm just having one of those days.'

'Are you sure there's nothing I can do?'

Megan reached for a paper towel to pat her face dry. 'No, really. But I'd appreciate it if you kept this to yourself. It doesn't seem too professional for the doctor to be found crying in the bathroom.'

'We all have our moments,' Abby said, 'when stuff gets on top of us.' She paused. 'Look, I'm new here and I haven't really met many people yet, and I'm always up for a bit of adult female company. Why don't you come over for supper one night?'

Megan smiled. She really is beautiful, Abby thought. But her eyes are so sad. Something was bothering her and it was more than just an off day, Abby would have staked her life on it.

'I would like that,' Megan said.

Abby wrote down her address and mobile number and passed it to Megan.

'Phone me?'

'Sure,' Megan said, pocketing the number. But somehow Abby didn't think she would.

CHAPTER NINE

ABBY woke early on Saturday morning to find that Emma was up before her. That in itself was unusual. She normally had to call Em at least twice before she could get her out of bed. Even more unusual was the smell of toast drifting from the kitchen. Moments later Emma appeared by her bed, carrying a tray with tea and buttered toast.

'Hey, what's this?' Abby said, sitting up and taking the tray.

'I woke up really early. I couldn't stay in bed so I thought I'd make you breakfast for a change.'

Emma's eyes were bright with excitement and it worried Abby. Perhaps she shouldn't have told her about Mac? Maybe she should have waited to see how the relationship developed? What if after today Mac backed away from having anything to do with his daughter? Abby knew the rejection would break Emma's heart. But what was the alternative? Lying to Emma? One way or another her daughter would have found out about Mac. Maybe not straight away, but eventually. And then how would she have felt about Abby keeping the truth from her? That would have been worse. One of the things Abby had always promised Em was that she would never lie to her.

Emma was dressed, with her long blonde hair, so like Sara's, tied back in a ponytail. She crept into bed beside Abby. 'When do you think he'll be here?' she asked.

Abby glanced at her watch and groaned. It was only six-thirty.

'Not for a little while. I think he said eight.'

'What if he doesn't come?' Emma asked anxiously.

'He'll come,' Abby promised. Or he'll have me to answer to, she thought grimly. But somehow she knew that once Mac had made a decision he would stick to it.

'Are you coming, too?' Emma asked.

'Do you want me to?'

'I think so,' Emma said.

'Then I will.' Abby tossed the bedclothes aside and jumped out of bed. 'But there is no way I'm going to try windsurfing. The sea's far too cold for me.'

Emma grinned up at her. 'Don't be such a wuss. We'll be wearing wetsuits. Come on, Mum. You have to give it a go. It'll be fun.'

'We'll see,' Abby said evasively. 'Right now, I need a shower.'

Bang on eight o'clock there was a knock on the door. Abby opened it to find Mac standing there, looking almost as nervous as Emma. He had a bunch of flowers in his hand. 'I brought these for Emma,' he said. 'To be honest, I didn't know what the form was for meeting one's daughter officially for the first time.'

Abby smiled. 'She'll be delighted. I don't think anyone's given her flowers before.' She took the bouquet from him. 'Emma!' she called out. 'Mac's here.' As she stood aside to let Mac into the small hall she added, 'I think Mac is best at this stage, don't you?'

Mac nodded, craning his neck to look behind her.

'Hi, Mac,' Emma said from behind her.

'Mac brought these flowers for you. I'll put them in water before we go, shall I?'

Emma's smile lit up her face. 'Flowers. Wicked. Thank you, Mac.'

Mac bowed slightly in acknowledgement. 'It is my pleasure. Have you got your costume and something warm to put on after your lesson? We'll be warm enough while we're moving, but when we get out of the water, you might get cold.'

Emma nodded. 'Mum's already been through all that. She's coming, too. She said she might even try it herself.'

Mac raised an eyebrow. 'Good for her.' He paused. 'Did you know I taught Sara how to windsurf?'

Emma nodded again. 'Mum told me. She said that's how you and my real mum met. Was she good at it?'

Abby's heart cracked a little. Emma was so desperate for any titbits about Sara. Abby had told her as much as she could about her, leaving out the bits about Sara's wild side, concentrating on the warm, fun-loving side of Sara. The only reason Sara had taken windsurfing lessons had been to get to know Mac. As far as Abby knew, once Sara and Mac had become an item, Sara had given up windsurfing, preferring to sit on the beach and watch.

'She wasn't bad.' Mac grinned. 'But she didn't take the lessons for very long.' Abby was grateful to Mac for his tactful answer. 'I have a feeling you're going to take to it.'

Ten minutes later they were on the almost deserted beach, and only the real die-hard surfers were out on the waves. While Emma was getting changed, Mac popped into one of the surfing shops that hired out equipment and returned with a couple of wetsuits. 'I brought one for you,' he told Abby, 'in case you do give it a shot. 'I'm just going to get a beginner's board for Emma then we'll be set.'

Abby was getting the distinct impression she wasn't going to be allowed off the hook.

By the time Emma appeared, wrapped in her towel and shivering in the cool morning air, Mac had organised a board for her. He handed her a wetsuit and helped her into it.

'Okay, this first bit we do on land. Abby can join in without getting changed. All she needs to do is slip off her shoes.'

Just as she'd suspected, Abby thought ruefully. There was no getting out of it. She undid the laces of her trainers and removed her socks. The sand squirmed pleasantly between her toes.

'Okay, Emma. Pop onto the board. I'll show you how you lift the sail and how to balance yourself. Then we'll have a go on the water.'

Emma got the hang of the basics pretty quickly. 'It will be more difficult in the sea,' Mac warned, 'but so far I'm impressed. Now, Abby, how about you having a go?'

Reluctantly, Abby stepped on the board and, following Mac's instructions, tugged on the sail to try and lift it. It was harder than she had expected. Determined to do it, she pulled with all her strength and almost toppled over when the sail whooshed up towards her. But Mac had anticipated her losing her balance and she felt strong hands circle her waist, steadying her. The feel of his hands cupping her waist sent all kinds of sensations shooting through her body and she prayed neither he nor

Emma noticed the heat that rushed to her face. The last thing she wanted or needed was to have such a physical reaction to this man and, even worse, for either of them to notice.

Mac remained behind her, close enough for every cell in her body to be acutely aware of him. His breath tickled her neck as he placed his hands over hers, showing her how to hold the board. She was getting more and more flustered. Abruptly she let the sail fall back to the ground and stepped off the board. She knew she had to put some physical distance between her and this man.

'That's enough for me for the time being,' she said, trying to keep her voice light. 'I think Emma's dying to get out on the water.'

Mac looked at her and the way his eyes danced told her he knew exactly why she had jumped off the board. His mouth twitched. 'Okay, then. Let's go, Emma.'

Abby found a rock and watched as Emma clambered onto the board and valiantly tried to pull the sail from the water. It took several attempts, but with Mac helping her she eventually got the sail up and started to move out towards the open sea. She must have surprised herself as she immediately let go of the sail and fell into the water. Even from a distance, Abby could see the flash of Mac's white teeth as he threw his head back and laughed. In response, Emma splashed him. Relief coursed through Abby. It really was the perfect way for Emma and Mac to get to know each other. From what she could see, the initial awkwardness of earlier had passed. It was early days, of course, but at least it was the right start.

After an hour, Abby was getting chilled despite having a cup of coffee from the flask she had packed. Emma had managed to get up on the board and move a little distance before falling off. Abby knew she must be getting tired and, sure enough, a few minutes later Emma and Mac, both grinning widely, made their way to shore. Emma flopped down beside Abby, her cheeks flushed and her eyes sparkling. 'That was so good.' She looked up at Mac, who was detaching the sail from the board. 'Can we do it again? Soon? Please?'

'Sure thing. But I think you should get changed now. I don't want you to get cold.'

As Emma hurried away to get dressed, Abby looked up at Mac. He really was gorgeous. No wonder Sara had fallen for him hook, line and sinker. She found herself wondering about him. How come a man as cute and as eligible as he was hadn't been snapped up? But perhaps he had. For all she knew, he had been married at one time.

'I think she enjoyed that,' Abby said.

Mac looked after Emma's retreating back. 'She could be very good, you know. She has natural balance and, more importantly perhaps, seems hugely determined to succeed. Is she like that in everything?'

Abby didn't attempt to hide her pride. 'She's a wonderful girl, Mac. She gives everything she does her best shot. I know her drive and determination will take her far in life.'

'And a lot of that must be down to the way you brought her up.' Mac's eyes glittered and once again Abby felt her body tingle in response.

'I hope so. But she has a lot of her mother in her, too.'

When Mac raised an eyebrow, a shot of anger coursed through Abby. She would not have this man making judgements about Sara. Okay, so Sara had been pretty wild, but she'd also been kind and loyal.

'Sara was a good person, Mac,' Abby said quietly.

Mac opened his mouth as if to reply but Emma, dressed in jeans and a thick woollen jumper, arrived back.

'Can we have something to eat now? I'm starving!'

The tension disappeared as they all laughed. 'It's not even ten o'clock yet, Em,' Abby protested.

'But it's ages since I had breakfast.'

'I swear I don't know where she puts it all,' Abby told Mac. 'She eats like a horse but is as thin as a rake.'

'At least she eats,' Mac said mildly. 'And she's still growing.'

'Mum says I'm going to be tall.' Emma looked shyly at Mac. 'I must take after you. How tall are you anyway?'

'Six foot three, or something like that. I'm hungry, too. What do you say we grab a burger?'

Abby frowned. 'I don't really like Emma to have junk food,' she said primly.

'I don't think one will hurt,' Mac protested.

Abby felt her hackles rise. One day as a father and already he was interfering. But she swallowed the angry words that rose to her lips. She was being overly sensitive. Why spoil the day by falling out over something as ridiculous as a burger? Nevertheless, she would have to speak to him and make it clear that as far as Emma was concerned, it *was she* who made the decisions.

'On the other hand,' Mac went on smoothly, 'there is a café up the road a little that does great home-made soup and sandwiches. And they have the best hot chocolate, too. Why don't we go there?'

'Whatever,' Emma said. 'I don't mind.'

Inside the café, Mac and Emma tucked into their soup and sandwiches while Abby nursed a mug of coffee.

She listened as Emma fired questions at Mac, and Mac replied with much the same answers he had given Abby. Nevertheless, there was a reticence, a carefulness about his replies that made her think he wasn't being totally candid. But why should he? No doubt he was, quite sensibly, feeling the way with his new-found daughter.

'Can I meet my grandmother?' Emma asked.

'Tiree is a long way from here,' Mac said evasively. 'But maybe one day.'

'Have you got brothers and sisters?'

'Only me, I'm afraid.'

Emma looked glum for a moment. Abby knew that part of her fantasy about finding her father was the hope that she'd discover a whole load of aunts, uncles and cousins at the same time.

But it wasn't long before her natural cheerfulness re-emerged.

'Did you always want to be a doctor?'

'For as long as I can remember,' Mac replied. 'What do you want to be when you grow up, or haven't you decided yet?'

'Not really decided. I might be a pilot or a vet.' She looked thoughtful. 'Or a doctor like you who rescues people. It looks fun.'

'Yeah, it can be fun, but it can also be a little scary at times.'

Emma's eyebrows shot up. 'I don't think you find anything scary.'

Oh, dear, Abby thought. One day in and already Emma had found a hero in Mac.

Mac flicked a glance at Abby and smiled. 'I find lots of things scary,' he said. Then he changed the subject. 'One of the other things I like doing is mountain biking. How do you fancy coming with me one day?'

'Oh, I'm not sure about that,' Abby interrupted before she could help herself. 'Can't that be pretty dangerous?'

Mac narrowed his eyes at her. 'It can be dangerous crossing the road, if you're not looking where you are going,' he said mildly. 'The important thing is to weigh up the risks, decide how you can best protect yourself then go for it.' Abby had the uneasy feeling he wasn't just talking about mountain biking. 'It's good for kids to test themselves. I believe it stops them from taking risks in other ways. Anyway, I'll only take Emma on gentle slopes and make sure she's wearing all the right gear to protect her.'

Once again he was challenging her authority as a mother and Abby didn't like it one bit. Keeping her voice level, she stood up. 'I'll think about it. Emma, it's time for us to get back. We need to go shopping for groceries.'

'Oh, do we have to?' Emma said. 'Can't I stay with Mac?'

Before Mac could say anything, Abby shook her head. 'I'm sure Mac has something planned for the rest of the day, and I would really like your help with the shopping, Em.' It was a pretty poor excuse, but Abby wanted Emma to get to know Mac slowly. Give them both time to let the relationship develop.

Reluctantly Emma got to her feet. 'Thanks, Mac. It was great.'

'We'll do it again next weekend, if you like,' Mac promised. 'And I'll try and work on Abby about the mountain biking thing.'

Emma smiled happily and Abby knew she was too late. Emma had found exactly the kind of father she had always wanted.

CHAPTER TEN

THE next few weeks flew past. Abby looked at a couple of cottages that would have been perfect for her and Emma—if the price hadn't been out of her reach. Mac and Emma had developed a routine, seeing each other a couple of times a week—either to go windsurfing or mountain biking. Abby's heart still leaped every time she saw Mac, but she tried to make sure they were never alone. He didn't ask her out again either. She didn't know whether to be pleased or disappointed. All she did know was that it was better this way. Much, much safer.

As the weather became more unpredictable, Mac had agreed with Abby, much to Emma's disappointment, that the windsurfing had to stop—winter was on its way.

'I don't mind getting cold,' Emma had protested. 'And I'm just getting the hang of it.'

'You're doing more than getting the hang of it.' Mac had grinned. 'I've rarely had a pupil that's taken to it as quickly as you have. But it's not just the cold. The waves are getting bigger now, and neither your mother nor I want to risk anything happening to you.' He ruffled Emma's hair as the child glowed with pleasure at his praise.

Abby was relieved. Although she trusted Mac not to let Emma do anything outside her capabilities, there was a recklessness in both father and daughter that frightened her. They were both risk-takers.

'But we can carry on mountain biking?' Emma asked. 'I like that, too.' Abby reluctantly capitulated and agreed to let Mac take Emma.

'As long as it doesn't get too wet, yes. And as soon as spring arrives, we can go windsurfing again.'

Emma wasn't prepared to give up without a fight. 'Are *you* going to stop kite boarding?'

Mac laughed again. 'When you learned to windsurf in Tiree, as I did, a little cold and big waves don't put you off.'

Emma started to protest, but Mac cut her off. 'I promised Abby that I won't let you do anything dangerous and I'm sticking to that promise, okay?'

Seeing the easy way Mac dealt with Emma, Abby was pleased. Despite her concerns, Mac seemed to be developing a real bond with his daughter. Emma's confidence was growing by leaps and bounds. Abby had one concern, though. She knew how much Emma wanted to impress her newly found father and she wouldn't put it past her to do something outside her comfort zone to impress him. But there was little she could do about that. She would just have to trust Mac.

Over the last couple of weeks Abby had been on several callouts with Mac. He was always calm and very efficient. Every day she was learning to respect him more and more. But that wasn't all. Every day she was finding herself more and more attracted to him, and not just physically. She was learning that he had an easygoing nature and that nothing ever fazed him. She often found herself wondering why he had never married.

This morning Mac came in looking tired.

'Late night?' Kirsten teased. 'Some woman keeping you up?'

Abby caught her breath as an unfamiliar stab of jealousy hit her in the solar plexus.

Mac shook his head. 'I wish.' He smiled. 'No, I was called late yesterday afternoon. There was a nasty accident on one of the main roads. Two fatalities, I'm afraid.'

'But you saved one,' said Mike, who had walked in in time to hear the last of the conversation. 'I heard it was a real touch and go.'

Mac pulled his hand through his hair. 'I had to intubate at the scene. It wasn't easy, even with the fire brigade giving me some light to work with—and some shelter. The rain was pretty torrential. But, yes, the driver of the second car is going to be okay. I just wish we could have done something for the occupants of the other car, but it looks like they died on impact.'

Everyone hated hearing about death, even if they knew it came with the job. Abby was a little surprised to hear the sadness in Mac's voice. He usually gave away very little of himself.

'I ended up staying at the hospital until the small hours. I wanted to make sure before I left that the man pulled from the car was stable.'

He caught Abby's eye and smiled. 'I think it's important we follow up on our patients. Don't you, Abby?'

Abby smiled back. It seemed that Mac was breaking his no involvement rules in more ways than one.

Except with her, that was. He was always friendly when he collected and returned Emma.

'Anyway,' Mac said, 'back to work. Anything on the board?'

'Shouldn't you be at home, catching up on your sleep?' Abby asked.

Mac shrugged his shoulders. 'I'll be fine. We doctors learn very early on to do without sleep. A gallon of coffee and I'll be fine.' He must have noticed that Abby was far from convinced. 'Honest.' He held up two fingers. 'Scout's honour.'

While he'd been talking Abby had spooned some coffee into a mug and added water from the recently boiled kettle. 'Drink this,' she ordered.

As Mac sipped his coffee, the radio came to life and everyone stopped talking. They could only hear Kirsten's side of the conversation, but the look on her face told them it was a bad one.

'We have a pregnant woman who has gone off the road. The road ambulance and fire brigade are there, but they're requesting assistance from us. She's complaining of severe abdominal pain and they have no idea what they are dealing with. The fire brigade is cutting her out of her vehicle at the moment.'

Mac jumped to his feet, every trace of tiredness banished.

'Okay, Abby. Let's go.'

'Mac has called from the air ambulance. They are bringing in a pregnant woman from an RTA with severe abdominal pain,' Josh told the assembled A & E team. 'Would someone page the obstetric and paediatric registrar, please?'

'I'm on it,' the senior nurse said, turning away and picking up the phone.

Josh pulled a hand through his hair. He was tired. Spending so much time at the hospital, putting in extra hours, was taking its toll.

But you don't need to, an insistent voice whispered in the back of his mind. The department copes well when you're not there. He knew the real reason. It was more and more difficult to spend time at home with Rebecca, pretending. Some time soon he would have to face the reality of the situation, but for now it would have to wait.

Minutes later he was called to Resus to see his patient. Mac and Abby were by her side.

'Who have we got here?' he asked.

'Mrs Diane Clifford,' Mac replied calmly. 'Twenty-four weeks pregnant and has been having right-sided abdominal pain for the last six hours. She was driving herself to hospital when she blacked out and crashed. No obvious injury from the accident. We're going to have to leave you guys to it, I'm afraid. We have another call to go to.'

As Mac and Abby left, Josh smiled reassuringly as he palpated his anxious patient's abdomen. 'Don't worry, Diane. We'll get to the bottom of this.'

He glanced up as Megan swept into the room. As usual she looked every inch the calm professional, her dark hair neatly swept back from her face, her expressive eyes already taking in the scene.

'You called the paediatric registrar?' she said, acknowledging Josh with a faint smile before introducing herself to the woman on the bed. 'I'm Dr Phillips,' she said softly. 'We're going to get your baby attached to a monitor so we can monitor the heartbeat. Is that okay?'

Diane's frightened eyes darted from Josh to Megan.

'Do you think there's something wrong with my

baby?' She reached out and grabbed Megan's hand. 'Don't let me lose my baby.'

Pain flickered in Megan's eyes before she rearranged her expression into her usual professional mask. Anyone else would have missed it, but for Josh it was plain to see. Damn it. Why did it have to be Megan who was called to this particular case?

'Dr Phillips, could I have a word?' he said, indicating that Megan step outside the cubicle with him. 'Diane, the nurse is just going to get you attached to the monitor while I have a quick chat with Dr Phillips here. Is that okay?'

Diane nodded silently and Josh followed Megan outside the cubicle. They moved away so they weren't overheard by their patient.

'What are you thinking, Josh?' Megan's voice was calm and steady, but she couldn't quite hide the anxiety in her eyes. He knew her too well.

'It could be three or four things. Appendicitis, premature labour or an abruption. But I don't really believe it's appendicitis.'

Megan sucked in a breath.

'You could get someone else to take over,' Josh said gently.

Megan's eyes flashed. 'No, I couldn't. Josh, you have to stop treating me as if I were made of china. I'm here now and Diane is my case.'

'She's twenty-four weeks,' Josh continued. 'I hope to God we don't have to deliver her.'

Megan bit her lip. 'We both know a twenty-four-weeker doesn't have much of a chance. We'll give her steroids just in case. But if you need to deliver, we'll do the best for the baby.'

Josh wanted to reach out and touch her. The need

to comfort her was so strong he had to lock his hands behind his back.

'Okay. We'll do an ultrasound. See how the baby's doing when we get the CTG result. After that we'll make a decision. I'll give you a shout if we need you.'

But before he could turn away, Megan grabbed his arm.

'I'm staying,' she said. 'If she has an abruption you might have to deliver her without waiting for the obstetric team. But have a look at her ovaries. A cyst could present in much the same way.'

He nodded. He hoped she was right.

Everyone waited anxiously while Josh ran the ultrasound probe over the injured woman's abdomen. He looked up and smiled.

'There's a ten-centimetre cyst on the right where the pain is.' He caught Megan's eye. 'Good call, Dr Phillips. We were right to wait.'

They both knew they were far from out of the woods but at least it wasn't premature labour and it wasn't an abruption. It was still serious and Diane had to be taken to Theatre immediately. But at least this was one woman who wasn't going to lose her baby. Josh explained to Diane that the cyst had probably become twisted on its stalk, cutting off the blood supply to the ovary and resulting in severe pain.

Megan blinked rapidly. 'I better go and get changed. They'll need a paediatrician standing by in Theatre, just in case.'

Then she smiled. God, he loved her smile. It seemed to start somewhere deep inside her until her whole face lit up. Once more he felt a pang of regret so deep it hurt.

Why couldn't things have been different between them? How in God's name had he made such an almighty mess of his life?

CHAPTER ELEVEN

ABBY was surprised to find Mac waiting for her when she emerged from the building after changing into her civvies.

'Are you okay?' he asked, his eyes searching hers.

Abby nodded. 'I am now. It got a bit hairy there for a while. I always get really anxious when the victim is pregnant.'

Mac smiled slowly and his eyes creased at the corners. Abby's heart lurched. How could anyone look so cool and sexy after all they had just been through? She was sure she looked as if she'd done a couple of rounds in the boxing ring. It felt like it anyway.

For a moment Mac looked directly into her eyes and what she saw there made her heart start pounding again. The world started spinning around her.

'How about you and Emma coming out for dinner?' he asked.

Abby struggled to control her breathing. What she was feeling was nothing more than a delayed reaction to the rescue.

'Normally we'd love to, but Em is going around to a friend's after school. Maybe another time?' She was pleased to hear that her voice was steady, betraying nothing of her inner turmoil, and she thanked the years of practice she'd had of keeping her feelings hidden.

'We could go on our own.' He smiled at her. 'Go on, say yes. I don't know about you, but every time I go on a rescue, I get hungry.'

There wasn't any reason to refuse as far as she could see, except for her reluctance to be alone in his company a moment longer than she had to. Every time she was near him, her body kept behaving in the strangest way. On the other hand, what harm could it do? It wasn't as if she could avoid being alone with Mac for the rest of her life. Not when they worked together and not when they shared Emma. Emma would be having supper at her friend's and Abby had planned on warming up soup to have with a sandwich. She hardly saw her daughter these days. Emma was either going round to see friends, or staying on at school for hockey practice, or out with Mac. But although she missed spending time with her, she knew it meant her daughter was happy and settled. It was natural for Emma to want some independence, and it was a sign that she was continuing to develop her confidence, knowing that Mac and Abby were there if she needed them.

'Unless you'd like to have supper at my place?' she said. The moment the words were out of her mouth, she regretted them. Although the thought of an evening alone with Mac excited her, it unnerved her, too.

'Home cooking? How could I refuse?'

Too late. She could hardly retract the invitation now.

'It won't be very fancy, I'm afraid. You might regret it.'

'Let me tell you, Abby, for a man who lives on takeouts and microwave meals when I'm not eating out, the thought of home cooking is irresistible.'

'Okay, then, you're on. Why don't you come home with me now? It'll save you a trip to your flat and back.'

'Sure thing. I'll stop off on the way and pick us up some wine, shall I? Red or white?'

'White. Although I'm not much of a drinker, so you might be drinking most of it yourself.'

'Give me half an hour?'

By the time Mac knocked on the door, Abby had rummaged around in the fridge and found enough to make a stir-fry. As she'd told Mac, supper wouldn't be fancy, but with the soup it would be adequate. She hoped she had enough. A big man like Mac was bound to have a healthy appetite. Although there wasn't an inch of flab on his muscular frame, given all the exercise he did, he was bound to need calories.

'Wine—and some olives,' Mac said, proffering his purchases to Abby. 'I didn't know if you liked them, but I took a chance.'

'Love 'em. Why don't you pop the wine in the fridge? You don't fancy lighting the fire while I finish supper?' Abby gestured to the open fire with a nod of her head. 'You'll find everything you need there.'

By the time the meal was ready, the fire was burning cheerfully. There was no room in the tiny house for a kitchen table, so Abby set two places on the coffee table in front of the fire.

'Sorry,' she apologised. 'I guess it'll be slightly awkward for you, but as you can see there isn't a lot of space.'

Mac looked around the small sitting room-cum-kitchen.

'I don't know,' he said. 'It's kind of cosy. But you know, if you and Emma need something bigger, I'll be happy to chip in.'

'We manage fine,' Abby said, more sharply than she'd intended to. 'I'm looking for something bigger to buy once we're sure where we want to live.' She didn't add that it was nigh on impossible on her salary, but she guessed she didn't need to.

'It must have been a struggle sometimes, bringing up a child on your own,' Mac said quietly. 'I wish Sara had told me. I would have done something to help.'

Abby shrugged. 'If you knew Sara, you'd know she had her pride. I guess when she found out she was pregnant the baby was the first thing she'd ever had that was truly hers. All through her pregnancy she refused to tell me who the father was. She said it wasn't important. She only told me about you right at the end.' Despite her best efforts her voice cracked. Mac put his fork down and laid a hand over hers.

'Tell me about her. Although we spent those two weeks together, all I really knew about Sara was that she had a great sense of humour and a genuine love of life.'

Abby placed her knife and fork on her plate and leaned back on the sofa.

'To understand who Sara was you have to know something about our upbringing. Our mother—well, I guess you can say she wasn't the maternal type. When Sara and I were eighteen she told us it was time to leave home.'

'Go on,' Mac said quietly.

'I think my mother thought we got in the way of her

life. Men weren't that interested in a woman with two children.'

She sneaked a look at Mac and was surprised to see anger in his eyes.

He smiled but his eyes remained bleak. 'My mother was the same.'

'Sara and I set up home together, if you could call it that. We didn't have much money, but we got by.'

'What about your father?'

'We never really knew him. He left when we were three and didn't come back.'

'Like mine,' Mac muttered. 'Except he didn't wait until I was three. He was off the minute he knew my mother was pregnant.'

Abby's heart ached for him.

'Anyway, Sara went a little off the rails when we left home. It's like she thought she was unlovable, and who could blame her? If your own mother doesn't want you, what does that say about you?'

'And you? How did you feel?'

'I was different from Sara. I decided that it was my mother's problem and I would find a way of proving to her that I could make it on my own. All through our childhood, I was the responsible one.'

Abby picked up a cushion and clutched it to her chest. Despite her words she had been hurt by her mother's rejection. It still hurt. 'I trained as a paramedic. I discovered I was good at it. Sara, though, couldn't find anything she really wanted to do.' Abby blinked the tears away. She had tried everything to get her sister to believe in her own self-worth, but Sara just wouldn't—couldn't—believe it.

'When we were twenty-one I had saved up enough money to pay for a holiday in Mykonos for both of us.

I thought two weeks of sunshine, together, would bring us closer again. I had hoped that I could really talk to Sara. Convince her it was time she made something of her life.'

'And then she met me. I can't imagine you were best pleased.'

'Then she met you,' Abby said softly. 'I have never seen her so lit up. I think she fell in love with you the moment she set eyes on you.'

'She spent most of the holiday you had planned together with me,' Mac said.

'Yes. It wasn't exactly the way I had thought it was going to be. But I couldn't deny her her chance. It had been a long time since I had seen her so happy.'

Mac groaned. 'I had no idea. I was so wrapped up in myself then, all I knew was that there was this beautiful woman who wanted to be with me. And I guess meeting me then falling pregnant was the last thing Sara needed. But how come I never noticed you?' He touched Abby briefly on her cheek. 'You are just as beautiful.'

'I wasn't back then. I was so much shyer than Sara. Anyway, the holiday wasn't a total disaster. I left Sara to it and took a ferry to the Greek mainland. I visited the Temple of Poseidon, and the Acropolis in Athens. Even if Sara had not been...' she paused '...occupied, she wouldn't have come with me. So I guess she got the holiday she wanted and I did, too. It was just a shame we didn't have the time I wanted to get closer to each other again.'

Abby smiled. 'I was happy for her. Those two weeks were the happiest I'd ever seen her. Instead of that vague sadness and emptiness that seemed to have followed her most of her life, it was as if she'd found something.

Something that made her believe in herself.' Abby looked at Mac. 'I know I have you to thank for that.'

'When did she tell you she was pregnant?'

'About three months after we returned from Mykonos. After we came back she was quieter, almost serene. I don't know…as if she'd found peace. I asked her if something had changed, but she just smiled. Then for a bit she was different again. Anxious and withdrawn. After a while, when she started showing, she told me she was going to have a baby. She said she hadn't told me at first because she hadn't been sure she was going to keep it.

'As you can imagine, I was stunned. I guessed the father must be you, but when I asked her she wouldn't say. She said it wasn't important. I didn't know how the three of us were going to cope, but Sara was so happy.'

Mac was listening intently.

'I wanted her to tell the father, even if she wouldn't tell me. I thought whoever it was had a right to know. But she refused point blank. She said the baby was hers and nobody was going to have any say about how she brought up her child. During her pregnancy she started a degree with the Open University. I could see she was determined to make a future for herself and the child and she knew I would always be there for her. Our own mother, of course, wasn't the slightest bit interested.'

'But she did tell you that I was the father— eventually.'

Abby squeezed her eyes closed.

'When she knew that she wasn't going to live to look after Emma, yes, she gave in and told me.'

The memory of those last few days were burnt into Abby's mind. At first everything had gone as planned

and Sara's labour, although long, had resulted in a healthy
baby girl. When Abby had seen her sister holding her
child, it had been a moment of such joy Abby couldn't
have felt prouder even if she had been the mother instead
of Sara. Not even their mother's disinterest in the birth
had blighted those first few days. After all, she and Sara
had each other and however difficult and challenging the
next few years would be, together they would be there
for Emma, be their own little family. Then Sara had
developed an infection and had been admitted to ITU.
Even then, Abby had never suspected for one moment
her sister might die. But Sara had got steadily worse.
She hated thinking about it. Her sister, lying in ITU,
pale and listless, and for once Abby had been totally
unable to help her.

'Abby, I don't think I'm going to make it,' Sara had
whispered, her face flushed with fever.

'Don't say that. Of course you're going to be okay.'

Sara smiled wanly. 'Somehow I knew deep inside
that this was too good to last.'

Abby reached for her hand and squeezed it tight,
trying to transfer all her strength to her failing sister.

'You can't die, Sara,' Abby cried. 'Emma needs you.
I need you.'

'I'm not strong like you. You'll be okay.' For a
moment strength returned. 'Look after Emma for me,
promise. Don't let anything bad happen to her. I want
her to know she's cherished and loved.'

'I promise, Sara. But you mustn't talk like that. You're
going to be okay.'

'Hey, I thought I was the optimist.' Sara managed
a smile. She struggled to speak. 'Remember Mac?
Back on Mykonos? He's the father. I'll leave it to you

to decide whether you want to tell him or not. Whatever you decide to do is okay with me.'

Shortly after, with Abby holding her hand, Sara had slipped into a coma. She never came round and died a few days later.

Tears fell as Abby repeated the story to Mac. She was barely conscious of his arm slipping around her shoulder and pulling her close.

'I'm so sorry,' he said. 'You must miss her. If I had known, I could have helped.'

'I tried to find you when Em was a few months old. But I knew nothing except that you were called Mac and taught windsurfing. I took Emma with me back to Mykonos to try and find you but the season was over and the resort closed down. I phoned their main office, but they refused to give me any details of the staff who worked there.' She shrugged. 'There was nothing more I could do, so we just came home.'

Suddenly conscious that she was in his arms, Abby pulled away. Her heart aching, she crossed to the fire and added a log. A sudden flurry of sparks crackled in the hearth.

'So you brought Emma up on your own. It couldn't have been easy. What about your mother?'

'She wasn't even there when Sara died. She had gone on holiday. Said she needed the break.' Abby couldn't keep the bitterness from her voice. 'To be fair, she couldn't have known Sara was going to die.'

'But you must have warned her? When Sara was admitted to ITU?' The anger in Mac's voice was almost palpable. How could anyone understand how a mother could stay away from her child when she needed her?

'She came back in time for the funeral,' Abby said. 'Then, unbelievably, when she held Emma for the first time, it was almost as if Mum changed before my eyes. She became besotted with her grandchild, in a way she never had been with her own daughters. Maybe it was different. There was no responsibility involved. She could have all the good times with Em without the bad. And maybe it was guilt. Guilt that she hadn't been there for Sara when she'd needed her most. Who knows? But she does love her granddaughter. She helped with child care when Emma was little so I could work. So people can change. And I'm glad. I've always felt it was important Emma knows who her family is. She's had little enough of them—until now, that is.' She forced a smile. 'But enough about that. What about your parents?'

This time it was Mac who shifted uneasily. 'My family isn't any better than yours, I'm afraid. If anything, they could be worse.'

Abby looked at him. He was studying his feet as if he could find answers there. She waited for him to continue.

'My mother sounds very much like yours. I also never knew my father. I sometimes wonder if my mother did. I was an only child and she made it clear from early on I was nothing but a nuisance.' He looked up and Abby saw the pain in his eyes. 'I spent as much time away from her as I could. She made it clear she didn't expect much from me, but I knew I wanted more from life. When I wasn't outside in the sea or on the hills, I was in my room studying. I was damned if I was going to give her the satisfaction of turning out the way she expected me to. I was lucky, I won a scholarship to medical school, and the rest is, as they say, history.'

'Do you see her?'

'I go back to Tiree once a year. She's not getting any younger. Whatever she is, she's still my mother.' He sent her a half-smile. 'You and I have a lot in common after all.'

'Does she know about Emma?'

'I phoned her. I thought she'd like to know. Perhaps she's mellowed or perhaps she's lonely, but she's asked to meet her.'

'Have you mentioned it to Emma?'

'I thought I should run it past you first.'

'Maybe we could all go?' Abby suggested.

'I'd like that.'

There was silence for a moment. 'I don't want Emma to grow up without a father. I told myself I would never have children, but now I have, I want her to know I'll always be there for her. Don't ever take her from me, Abby.'

Abby walked across the room and crouched by his side. She touched his face lightly.

'What makes you think I will? I want her to know her father, too.'

He touched her lips with a finger. 'Emma is lucky to have you as a mother.'

For a moment their faces were only inches apart. Abby could feel his breath on her skin, almost feel the warmth radiating from him. He smelled of wood smoke and earth. His eyes, drilling into hers, were as blue as the sea. Her heart was thudding so loudly she thought he must be able to hear it. Gently he slid his hand behind her neck. The feel of his fingers on her skin sent tiny shots of electricity fizzing through her.

She didn't know if he pulled her towards him or whether she was the one to make the move, but suddenly they were kissing. Softly at first, almost exploring each other's mouths, and then, as desire lit a flame in her belly, she was in his arms and he was kissing her as if his need for her was all-encompassing. No, no, no, a voice was shouting in her head. Don't do this. Nothing good can come of this. But her body wasn't listening. She could no more pull away from him than she could have walked across the desert.

Without knowing how it happened, they were lying on the sofa, their bodies pressed along the length of each other.

'Abby,' Mac whispered into her hair. 'Beautiful, sweet Abby.'

What was she doing? What were they doing? Apart from anything else, Emma would be back any moment. Reluctantly, Abby disentangled herself from Mac's arms and slid out of his grasp. Her heart was beating like a train and her breath was coming in short gasps. Mac reached for her again but she stepped away from his outstretched arm.

'This is so not a good idea,' she said.

'Why not? I think it's a very good idea.' His eyes darkened like the sea before a storm.

'Emma could come back any minute. I don't want her finding us in a clinch.'

'In a clinch?' The smile was back. 'Is that what you call it?' Laughter rippled under his words.

'Whatever.' Abby smoothed her hair with her hands. 'Nevertheless, if Emma walked in now...'

'Call it what you will, I think it's a very good idea.' He sat up and before she could move, his hand shot out lightning fast and caught her by the wrist, pulling her down on his lap. He buried his face in her neck, his lips touching her in places she hadn't even known, until now, had nerve endings.

She moaned softly. Being here with him felt so right. It had been so long since she'd been held. But she forced herself to push him away. There was no way she could think with him nibbling her neck.

'No, Mac. We can't. We have Emma to think about.'

Mac frowned at her. 'Emma?'

'Yes. Can't you see? If we start something, it'll give Emma all the wrong ideas. Besides, what if we fall out?' She held up her hand to stop the words he was about to say. 'It could happen, you know it could. How will it be for Emma then?'

Mac's frown deepened. 'I wasn't really thinking of a relationship. Hell, Abby, I wasn't really thinking at all. You must know I find you attractive. What's wrong with two adults…er…enjoying each other's company?'

Abby had to laugh. He was doing such a good impersonation of a well-known, ageing movie star. 'Seriously. Mac. Think about it. Don't we have enough to be getting on with? Trying to work out a way to co-parent Emma?'

Mac drew his hand across his face in a gesture Abby was beginning to know well. He looked so disappointed Abby almost changed her mind. Almost.

Mac stood up. 'Perhaps you're right,' he said, reaching for his jacket. He stopped and looked at her intently. 'Right now, Abby, you're holding all the cards.'

And before she could ask him what he meant, the door closed behind him with a gentle click.

CHAPTER TWELVE

BACK at his own house, Mac paced the floor. He still couldn't believe how much his life had changed in the last few weeks. It had been a shock finding out that he had a daughter, and the last thing he had expected was to feel the way he did about Emma. He found he was looking forward to spending time with her. She was so like him with her love of adventure.

And like Abby, too.

Over the last few weeks he had found himself drawn to Abby in a way that he had never been drawn to a woman before. It wasn't just that she was sexy, in that way that only a woman who had no idea of her own beauty could be, but it was her loyalty, her strength of character, her kindness that drew him. It couldn't have been easy bringing up a child—his child—on her own, but she had done it without a second thought. And she had made a good job of it.

But it was different now; he could help. Be there for Emma and Abby. Help financially. He thought about the little house they were renting. It was barely big enough for one, let alone two of them. And here he was in this spacious flat with more space than he knew what to do with. Perhaps he should ask them to move in with him?

Immediately he dismissed the idea. It was crazy. Abby

would never agree. The thought of sharing his home with Abby made the blood rush to his head. Seeing her every day. Her sleeping just a short distance away would drive him crazy. He'd never be able to keep his hands off her. And that way lay madness. She was right. What if they started something and it didn't work out? Having a child was one thing, but having a permanent relationship with a woman quite another. He didn't do relationships. If he started something with Abby it would, like all his other relationships, end sooner or later. And when it did there would be hard feelings and recriminations. There always were. No matter how often he warned the women in his life that he wasn't in it for the long haul, they never really believed him. They always thought they would be the one to change him. And if he gave in to his need to have Abby, what then? When it came to an end she might stop him from seeing Emma. He was surprised at how much the prospect alarmed him. Now he had got to know his daughter, he couldn't imagine a life without her.

And what if Abby met someone else? He didn't want that either. The thought of her in another man's arms made his blood boil. But if she did, what if she moved away and took Emma away from him? As it stood, he could do nothing to stop her. And what if that man treated Emma like his mother's boyfriends had treated him? As if she was a nuisance they could do without?

He pulled a hand through his hair. Now he had found Emma he was damned if he was going to let anyone take her away from him again.

The days sped by as winter approached. Abby kept her eyes open for a house for Emma and herself, but so far nothing remotely affordable had come onto the market. Abby knew the only realistic option for her and Emma would be to buy something in serious need of refurbishment, and she didn't have the time for that, or a small modern flat, and she didn't have the heart for that.

Emma and Mac continued to spend time together and had developed an easy teasing camaraderie. Often they would gang up on Abby, once forcing her to join them mountain biking. Although she had gone along with them, one experience of being soaked to the skin and terrified out of her mind had been enough. She had refused point blank to go again. Some evenings Mac would drop in and they would play Scrabble or play games on Emma's computer console, the latter usually causing Mac and Emma to share a laugh at Abby's expense. Abby didn't care. She treasured those evenings. It was the family life she had never known.

One Saturday, Mac turned up at the cottage with a big smile on his face. Although it was cold, the rain had stopped and the sun was doing its best to cast some sunshine their way.

'You're looking pleased with yourself,' Abby said as she stood aside to let him in. 'But if you're looking for Emma, I'm afraid she's gone into the town with some friends from school.'

'It's not Emma I'm looking for. I have something I want *you* to see.' His eyes were sparkling with barely suppressed excitement.

'Oh, and what could that be?'

'I'm not saying. You have to come with me. Go on, grab a jacket.'

Mystified, Abby did as she was told. Mac was waiting for her in his Jeep.

'Where are we going? Come on, give me a clue.'

'No way. You're going to have to wait and see.'

They followed the road out of Penhally, heading in the general direction of St Piran's. But then Mac turned off and headed inland. A little while later, still refusing to answer Abby's questions, he turned up a steep track and came to a halt.

'We're here,' he said.

'Here? And where's here?' From where they were standing, Abby could see the coastline in the distance. Otherwise they were on a small bit of land surrounded by trees on the sides facing away from the sea.

'This little piece of land I'm standing on is for sale. Remember the boy we rescued from the bottom of the cliff? Dave, his father, came to see me. He wanted to thank us all personally. Anyway, to cut a long story short, it turns out he owns an estate agency here in Cornwall. I told him that I was looking for a small piece of land to buy and he mentioned that he knew of one that hadn't gone on the market yet. This one. Well, what do you think?'

'Think of what, exactly?'

'Of this as a place to build a house. As a home for you and Emma. You can't continue living where you are right now. And I know you haven't found somewhere to buy. So what about here? It's the perfect place to build a house.'

Abby touched him on the shoulder. She almost couldn't bear to destroy his excitement, but she had no choice.

'Mac, I couldn't possibly afford to buy this land, let alone build a house. It's a lovely idea, but completely out of the question.'

'I would bear the costs. After all, Emma is my daughter. You've met the financial costs of bringing her up on her own for years. Now it's my turn.'

Abby shook her head regretfully. 'I'm sorry, Mac. I couldn't possibly agree to it.'

His mouth tightened. 'Why not?'

'Don't you see? It's a wonderful, generous gesture, but I couldn't let us be beholden to you like that. It wouldn't be right.'

Mac's frown deepened. 'Beholden? Not right? Why don't you just come out with whatever it is you're trying to say?'

'Please understand, Mac. I've been independent all my life. I don't want to have to rely on anybody else. What happens if you meet someone you want to be with? Move away? Have a new family? What happens to us then? I'd never be able to meet the repayments on my own.' She shook her head. 'I'm sorry. I can't risk it.'

If it were possible, Mac's eyes turned an even darker blue. 'I have the right to make sure my daughter has as good a life as possible. You have no right to deny her because of some misplaced sense of pride. And what's more, I promise you, regardless of what happens in the future, I'll never abandon my child the way my father abandoned me.' His eyes narrowed. 'It is far more likely to be the other way around. You can up and leave with Emma any time you like, and I won't be able to stop you. How do you think that feels?'

Abby took a step towards him and touched him lightly on the arm. 'I wouldn't do that to Emma, or to you, Mac,' she said softly. 'Remember, I also know what it's like to grow up without a father. I would never deprive Emma of hers.'

Mac turned away and stood looking out to the horizon. This was a different side to Mac and her heart ached for him. But neither was she going to budge. He could be involved, she wanted him to be involved, but Emma was her responsibility and he had to understand that.

Mac swung around to face Abby. 'I want a DNA test,' he said abruptly.

Abby reeled. 'Why? I thought you believed me when I said you were Emma's father? Good grief, Mac, do you think I'm playing some kind of game here?'

He rubbed his face. 'I know you say now that you'll never take Em away from me, and I believe you mean it. But things change in life, Abby. I know that to my cost. People might mean to stick around, but in the end they don't.'

Abby started to protest but he cut her off. 'Besides, God forbid, what if something happened to you? What rights would I have then? At the moment, legally, you are her only blood relative. I wouldn't have a leg to stand on. A DNA test would prove I was the father to any court.'

What he was saying made sense, Abby admitted grudgingly. If she were in his shoes, would she take a chance that one day she might lose Emma? Absolutely not. She nodded.

'Okay. If, and only if, Emma agrees. The last thing I want is for her to think that you want the test for the wrong reasons. If you can persuade her, and if she's happy to have the test, I'll agree.'

The furrows between Mac's brow disappeared and he smiled. 'Thank you, Abby. That means a lot to me.'

They stood looking at each other for a long time. Mac took a step towards Abby, but before he could touch her, she turned away.

'Let's go home,' she said.

* * *

On the way back to her house, Abby thought about what Mac had said. Although she wanted Emma to have a relationship with a father who would be a permanent feature in her life, it felt as though everything was moving too fast. Mac wanted to be part of Emma's life and that was good. It would have broken Emma's heart if Mac had rejected her, but this... Wanting to have legal rights, wanting to contribute financially, it was more than Abby had anticipated. When she had told Mac about Emma, she had imagined a more casual relationship between father and daughter.

But now? He wanted more. And she couldn't blame him. And then there was this *thing* between her and Mac. Back then, she'd thought he was going to kiss her. And she'd wanted him to. But that would only make everything more complicated than it already was.

'Do you want to suggest the DNA test or shall I?' Mac asked.

'I think we should talk to her about it together,' Abby said. 'As soon as we get home.' She glanced across at him. 'She needs to know we're united about this, Mac.'

'At least we're agreed on something.' His expression was unreadable.

When they got back to the house, Mac suggested that they take a walk along the beach. Emma, as usual, was delighted to have any opportunity to spend time with her father. She particularly liked it when the three of them spent time together.

They stopped near some rocks and Abby poured hot chocolate from a flask she had brought.

'Em,' she started hesitantly. 'Mac and I have been talking.'

Emma looked at her warily. 'What about?'

'I think it's great that I've found you,' Mac said. 'As you know, I had no idea you existed until Abby told me. But now I want to make things more official.' He paused. 'I've got to kind of like having you as my daughter.'

A smile spread over Emma's face. 'And I kind of like having you as my father.' She threw herself at him and, wrapping her arms around him, squeezed him tightly.

The look in Mac's eyes made Abby catch her breath. The love for his daughter was there for anyone to see.

After a few minutes Emma released him and screwed up her eyes. 'How are things going to be more official? What do you mean?' She looked at Abby then at Mac. Her eyes lit up. 'Do you mean you two—?'

'No, Emma. You're way off there,' Abby interrupted quickly. Where on earth had Emma got that idea?

'I know it's not at all likely,' Mac said cautiously, 'but say anything happened to Abby, I'd want to have a legal claim on you. You know, make sure no one could take you away from me.'

Alarm flashed in Emma's eyes. 'There's nothing wrong with you, Mum, is there?' she said. 'You're not going to die or anything?'

Abby laughed. 'I have no intention of dying. At least, not for years and years. But, Emma, accidents do happen. What Mac is saying is that he's become very fond of you, and he wants everyone, particularly the courts, to recognise you as his daughter. Or rather him as your father. To do that you would both have to do a DNA test. Then if, and this is a big if, something happens to me, both Mac and I want to make sure you would get to stay with someone who loves you.'

Emma still looked anxious. Abby slid a glance at Mac. This was the last thing she wanted, Emma thinking they were hiding something from her.

Abby took Emma's hand in hers. 'I promise you, there is nothing wrong with me. If you don't want to have the test, that's fine. We'll find another way.'

'This test, is it like those they do in *CSI*?' Emma asked.

'Yes.'

'Will it hurt?'

'Not in the slightest. They'll take a swab from the inside of your mouth and do the same for Mac.'

Emma sat in silence for a little while.

'I don't mind, then. If you both think it's for the best.' She got to her feet and, finding a flat stone, turned to Mac. 'Can you make this skip on the water?' she asked. 'I can make it skip three times. Mum's record is four. Can you beat us?'

Abby and Mac shared a look of relief. Emma seemed reassured and what was even better, she was totally unconcerned about the test.

Mac took the stone from her hands. 'Four times, huh?' he said, grinning. 'I think I can do better than that.'

CHAPTER THIRTEEN

A FEW days later, Abby opened the door of her cottage to find Mac standing there. Her pulse stuttered disconcertingly. He was so damn good looking it just wasn't fair. But for once his easy confidence was absent. Instead, he looked ill at ease, almost embarrassed.

'Emma's out, I'm afraid,' she said. Anxiety rippled through her. He looked so serious. 'Is something wrong?'

'No,' Mac rushed to reassure her. 'It's just that I had an idea I wanted to run past you.'

Mac wanting to run something past her? That was a turn-up for the books.

'You'd better come in,' she said, standing aside to let him enter.

She signalled to him that he should sit, but Mac shook his head.

'Look, whatever it is, you'd better tell me.' Was this where he told her that the novelty of having a daughter was wearing off? Her heart rate upped another notch. If he let Emma down now, she'd throttle him.

'Remember you told me that Emma's birthday party had to be cancelled when nobody would come?'

Abby nodded. It had been almost the worst day of her life. It had been so cruel and so unbearable watching

Emma pretend it didn't matter. But Emma hadn't been able to hide the sobs coming from her bedroom later that evening. Abby had crept into bed with her daughter, holding her until the tears had subsided. That was when she had decided to leave London. She would never let her child be hurt like that again. Not as long as she had breath in her body.

'Well, I thought we should give her another party. Here. She's made friends now and perhaps it will take away some of the bad memories of London.'

Abby was so surprised she felt her jaw drop. It was the last thing she'd expected Mac to say. But she was touched and delighted and not a little ashamed. Once again, she had underestimated this man. As she looked at him her heart melted. He was a better man than he gave himself credit for.

'We could organise something really cool, like paint-ball or...I don't know...something else. We could arrange it all as a surprise.' Now that the words were out, there was no hiding his enthusiasm. 'I never had a party as a kid.' He smiled but he couldn't disguise the hurt in his eyes. 'I always wanted one, but my mother always refused. She said there was no way she was going to let a bunch of kids run riot in her house.'

'Me too,' Abby whispered. 'I would have given any-thing to be able to dress up in a party dress, just once. But my mum said parties weren't for the likes of us.'

They looked at each other and the world spun on its axis. Abby could hardly breathe. For a moment she thought he was going to pull her into his arms, but then he stepped back and let his arms to drop to his side.

What just happened there? Abby wondered. Her heart was racing as if she'd run up the highest hill in England. Every nerve cell in her body was zinging. Lord help her, she wanted him to have taken her in his arms. She wanted to lay her head against his chest, have his arms wrap around her, feel the pressure of his mouth against her. What was she thinking? Thinking that way spelled danger. He was so not the man for her. Why, then, did she feel this crushing sense of disappointment? Because she was in love with him. The realisation hit her like a ten-ton truck. She loved him and would do until the day she died.

'I think it's a great idea, Mac,' she said, turning away lest he read her discovery in her face. 'I can speak to the mums at the school, swear them to secrecy and get the invites out. We could organise it for the weekend. If we leave it any longer, someone's bound to give in to temptation and tell her. And I think the paintballing is a great idea. Emma's always wanted to have a go and the boys should enjoy it, too.' Hoping that she'd removed every trace of latent lust from her eyes, she turned back to him. 'I'm warning you, though, we'll both have to take part. You do know that, don't you?'

Mac grinned broadly. 'Why do you think I suggested it?' he said.

Emma was surprised but thrilled to find out about her party. Mac arrived before the partygoers and Emma flung herself at him, forgetting in her excitement to adopt the cool façade she had been trying to perfect lately.

'Isn't this the best idea?' she said. 'I can't wait for everyone to arrive so we can get started. Mum says she's going to join in, too.'

Mac looked at Abby over the top of Emma's head and grinned. 'I'm looking forward to seeing her moves,' he said.

Abby wagged a playful finger at him. 'Don't you underestimate me. I can run pretty fast when I have to.'

Emma's friends started to arrive, their laughter and shrieks of excitement filling the reception area. Mac had to shout above the clamour to make himself heard.

'Okay, guys. Before we get changed, we need to pick teams. Emma is captain of Team Arrows and, Simon, I believe you want to be captain of Team Blades. Since it's your party, Em, you get to pick first.'

Abby knew her daughter's every expression and she could see her hesitation as her eyes flicked between Abby and Mac. Abby's heart twisted painfully, sensing her torn loyalties. She wanted to choose Abby but also wanted to impress Mac. Was this how it was going to be from now on? She'd had her daughter all to herself for the past eleven years but now it was time to share her with someone else. Her father. Mac. The knot of jealousy felt alien to her but she had to remember this wasn't about her—it was about Emma.

Catching Emma's eye, she nodded her head slightly towards Mac. She caught the almost imperceptible flash of gratitude in her daughter's eyes as she selected Mac. Simon then chose Abby and the rest of the teams were quickly divided up.

Despite what she'd told Mac, Abby had no real idea what to expect. Obviously it had to do with firing balls of paint at each other and using various items around the course to hide behind to avoid being hit yourself. And taking the other team's flag.

When she emerged wearing her lurid green overall, she blushed under Mac's amused grin. She felt slightly ridiculous, holding her 'gun'. On the other hand, he looked the part in his blue overalls, like a dashing secret agent on a dangerous mission. The way he was looking at her warned her she was going to be his prime target. Abby felt a flutter of excitement—there was nothing she'd love better than to out-fox Mac. He was underestimating her if he thought she was Team Blade's weakest link! It was game on.

Fifteen minutes later Abby had to keep reminding herself it was only a game. The darkness, lit only sporadically by flashing lights and filled with atmospheric dry ice, heightened the tension and fun. Crouching behind a pillar, Abby paused to catch her breath. So far she'd managed to evade being shot, but so had Mac. Another flash of light and in that second she saw the top of his head behind a barrier. Abby crept forward, raising her gun slowly. Her finger tightened on the trigger and she stifled a giggle.

She didn't know how it happened but the next moment she was sprawled on her back with Mac's face inches from hers.

'Trying to sneak up on me, were you?' he growled into her ear. Abby could hear the triumph in his voice. She was distracted by the heat of his body on hers, his warm breath on her neck.

His eyes bored into hers. Her heart thumped against her ribs and she knew in that moment he was going to kiss her. Her lips parted involuntarily. At the very last moment, just before his mouth came down on hers, she wriggled out from underneath him. Despite being caught off guard, he moved much more quickly than she'd anticipated. Paint splattered from their respective guns until they were both covered from head to toe in myriad colours and laughing uncontrollably.

Grinning, Mac held out his hand. 'Truce?'

Abby took his proffered hand, only to let out a yelp of

surprise when he yanked her towards him. 'I believe you still owe me a kiss. And I intend to collect it...soon.'

It wasn't long before Emma's team triumphed, and after they had all cleaned up and changed they congregated in the café.

The children chattered happily about the game, arguing over their respective tactics.

Abby smiled at Mac, sitting opposite her at the table. 'Thanks for organising today. It's wonderful to see Emma looking so happy.'

'She's a fantastic kid. You have to take some of the credit for that.'

Abby glanced over at her daughter, her heart swelling with pride. 'Don't hurt her, Mac. I'll never forgive you if you do,' she said quietly. *And don't hurt me, she wanted to add.*

Mac shook his head. 'I've no intention of doing that.'

After they had cleaned up and the other children had left stuffed full of pizza and cake, Mac turned to Emma.

'The party isn't over yet,' he said. 'I've one more treat.'

Emma grinned at him. 'Tell me,' she implored.

'You have to come out to the car.' He led the way, a bemused Abby and Emma following in his footsteps.

'Close your eyes,' Mac told Emma. 'And no peeking.'

Emma did as she was told. Mac opened the boot of his Jeep and pulled out a board and something that looked like a kite. He placed them on the ground. 'Okay, you can open your eyes now, Emma.'

Emma's eyes grew wide. 'Is that what I think it is?'

'It's your very own kite-boarding stuff. In the spring, as soon as the weather is good enough, I'm going to teach you how to do it. You picked up windsurfing so quickly I'm sure we'll have you doing tricks with the kite board by the end of the summer.'

Emma turned to Mac and flung her arms around him. He picked her up and twirled her in the air. Abby's throat tightened. She knew this was Mac's way of telling them both he planned to stick around. When he deposited her back on the ground, Emma looked at him before hooking her arms into one of his and one of Abby's. 'This is the best day of my life,' she said.

Mac looked at Abby over the top of Emma's head.

'And mine,' he said quietly.

CHAPTER FOURTEEN

As DECEMBER approached, winter began to tighten its grip. The wind was sharper and the days shorter. Emma and Mac still went mountain biking and Abby rejoiced to see her child grow ever more confident, although she still fretted until Emma had returned home in one piece. The DNA results hadn't come back yet, but Abby wasn't surprised. They had been told that it could take months.

Mac and Emma arrived back just before darkness fell. They were both spattered with mud and their cheeks were flushed from the cold.

'I'm going to beat you one of these days,' Emma teased Mac.

'I hope you're not letting her go too fast,' Abby warned Mac. 'The last thing I want is to be involved in the rescue of you two.'

'Oh, Mum, you worry too much,' Emma complained. 'Dad would never let anything happen to me.'

A chill ran up Abby's spine and as she caught Mac's eye she knew he, too, realised the import of Emma's words. She was calling him Dad. If there was any doubt in either of their minds, she knew there was none in Emma's.

'Run upstairs and shower and change out of your wet clothes,' Abby told Emma. 'I'll get supper on.'

Mac still looked in shock as Emma left the room.

'Dad!' he said. 'She called me Dad.'

'So she did. How does it feel?'

'It feels strange. Very strange. But good. Yes. Very good.'

'Would you like to stay for supper, too?' Abby asked.

Mac grinned. 'I don't even want to sit down. In case you haven't noticed, I'm filthy.'

Abby had to laugh. Mac's face was almost black with thick dust. Only his eyes, where he had been wearing his goggles, were mud free. Impulsively she leaned forward and wiped his cheek with her finger.

His hand caught hers and he looked down at her with a glint in his eye. Her breath caught in her throat.

'Careful, Abby,' he warned. 'Don't start something you can't finish.'

She pulled her hand away as if she'd been stung. They stood staring at each other.

'Tell you what,' Mac said. 'Why don't I go home, get cleaned up, and I'll organise supper for the three of us?'

'I thought you didn't cook.'

'Didn't you notice I said *organise*? I didn't say anything about cooking. There is a great Chinese a few minutes' walk away from me. That's what I had in mind.'

'Emma is going to the cinema with a friend,' Abby said, looking at her watch. 'The mother is coming to collect her in an hour.'

'In that case, why don't you come? You could feed Emma and then come over. By that time I'll have cleaned myself up. You've never seen my place.'

'I don't know, Mac. Is it wise?' They both knew what she was talking about.

Mac took a lock of her hair between his fingers. 'I promise you, you'll be safe,' he said. 'It's just two work colleagues, friends, spending time together.'

Safe? What did he mean, safe? The flash of disappointment was unexpected. Was he implying that she wasn't his type? Perhaps she had misread him? Flirting came as naturally as breathing to men like Mac. He probably wasn't even aware he was doing it. She really needed to remember that.

'Or did you have something less innocent in mind?' he said.

She flushed. Damn the man. It was as if he could read her thoughts.

'Of course not,' she said coolly. 'You and I both know that.'

'So that's sorted, then. I'll see you around eight. Don't worry, I'll let you get back in plenty of time to be here for Em.'

'Okay,' she agreed finally, knowing she was risking her heart. 'I'll be there at eight.'

Mac smiled to himself as he drove home. Abby was much more transparent than she realised. He could read every thought and emotion that flitted across her face. She just couldn't pretend. That was what he loved about her.

Good God. Where had that come from? No way was he in love with Abby. Okay, he found her attractive, well, more than attractive, sexy as hell, and she was brave and funny and good and loyal and, damn it—he was in love with her. The shock almost made him collide with a car coming in the opposite direction. He pulled over to his own side of the road and the car passed him with a blare of its horn.

No! This was crazy. It was simply that he lusted after her. She was a challenge. The first woman he had ever wanted that hadn't fallen into his arms. But he knew he was lying to himself. He was in love. For the first time. And with Abby Stevens, the woman who was the mother of his child. So to speak. This wasn't at all what he had planned. He didn't do love. He didn't do for ever.

Mac was in all kinds of trouble.

Abby knocked on the door, thinking for the umpteenth time that she should have phoned and made her excuses. Was she stark, raving mad? Every bone in her body was telling her that it was a mistake to be alone with Mac.

Just as she was thinking of turning tail, he opened the door. Her breath caught in her throat. What a difference from the mud-splattered man of earlier. He had showered and changed into a dazzlingly white short-sleeved shirt and black jeans. Her heart rate went into overdrive. He looked divine. So confident and self-assured.

'Abby!' He smiled at her as if he had been waiting just for this moment and her legs turned to jelly.

'Hello, Mac.' Damn it. She sounded breathless. She cleared her throat. 'I'm not late, am I?'

'Bang on time,' he said. 'Our food should be here shortly. Come on in.'

He stood aside to let her pass and she squeezed past him, terrified lest she brush up against him. She could almost feel the waves of magnetism emanating from him.

'Let me take your coat.'

She almost yelped as she felt his warm hands brushing the back of her neck as he helped her shrug out of her coat. Little goose-bumps sprang up all over her body.

He tossed her coat onto the sofa. 'Can I get you something to drink?'

'Some sparkling water would be nice.'

His flat was the opposite from her little house in every way possible. Where her home had cramped, if cosy rooms, his was modern and open plan, with floor-to-ceiling windows looking out over the sea. Where her home was cluttered with the everyday minutiae that living with a teenager brought, his was sparsely but expensively furnished with enormous white sofas and bleached floorboards. On one side of the room there was a small kitchen with white units and a black granite worktop. It was fitted with every conceivable appliance down to an in-built coffee maker, she noted enviously. Not that it looked used.

In front of the sofas, which were arranged to form an L-shape, was a modern gas fire that looked almost real.

As Mac was pouring her drink, she wandered over to the ceiling-height book shelves opposite the windows. She found herself intensely curious to see what he read. Apart from several well-thumbed copies of the classics, there were thrillers and medical textbooks. She found herself smiling. There were few clues here about Mac. Was that intentional?

'One sparkling water,' Mac said, holding out a glass.

As she took it from him their fingers brushed and once again she felt a zap of electricity run down her spine.

'What do you think?' Mac waved his glass at the room.

'I like it.' Taking a sip of her water, she walked to the window and took in the view. Beneath her the lights twinkled and the moon, as bright and full as she could remember seeing, lit up the sea, so that she could see the waves rolling onto the shore. The windows where she was standing were actually a set of double doors leading out onto a small balcony.

'You can hear the surf from outside on a quiet night,' Mac said, coming to stand behind her. He was close enough for her to catch a faint smell of soap. 'It's one of the reasons I bought it.'

'I've always fancied a place with a view,' Abby said. 'Who wouldn't? But at the same time just having my own place with Em is good enough for me.'

'You really love her, don't you?'

'It would kill me if anything happened to her.'

'Why have you never married, Abby?'

The question startled her. She whirled round, taken aback to find herself within inches of his broad chest. She lifted her eyes to his, trying to ignore the blood rushing in her ears. 'I never met anyone who wanted me enough to take on a child, I guess,' she said softly. Then she grinned. 'Actually, that's not the whole truth. I've never met anyone that I thought I could live with, let alone marry. And the older I get, the more used to having my independence I get. What about you?' she challenged. 'Have you never met anyone you wanted to marry?'

'Me?' Mac laughed. 'I'm not into marriage, I'm afraid. I can't see the point. Why get married only to tear each other apart? It also implies that there is only one person for each of us and I don't believe that either. Unlike swans, I don't think humans are meant to mate for life.'

'What about children?'

Mac looked thoughtful. 'Having children was something I thought I would never do. What was the point? I liked my life exactly the way it was. But now…'

'But now…?' Abby prompted.

'But now I find I like being a father.' He turned away. 'Emma's amazing. I'm proud to be her dad.' He turned back to Abby and grinned. 'I never thought I'd say that, let alone mean it. And I have you to thank.' He crossed over to where Abby was standing. 'Thank you for letting me share her.' He touched her gently on the cheek and tipped her face so that she was forced to look him in the eye. 'I've had some of the best days of my life since I got to know her…and you.'

Abby's breath caught in her throat. Her heart was hammering against her chest. Slowly he lowered his head and, tipping her chin, brought his mouth down on hers. Abby had never felt sensations like the ones that were rocketing around her body. His lips were warm and hard, demanding a response from her. His tongue flicked against her and spurts of heat ricocheted from the tips of her toes to the top of her head. Her body felt as if it were on fire.

She couldn't resist him if her life depended on it. She could do nothing except give in to the feelings that were zipping around her. Her body melted into his as if it belonged there.

He groaned and, dropping his hands to her hips, pulled her against him. She fitted there in the circle of his arms as if once they had been one, and she let her hands go around his neck as she gave in to her need.

Still kissing her, he lifted her into his arms as if she weighed nothing and carried her out of the sitting room and into his bedroom. He laid her gently on the bed and she looked at him, knowing what was going to happen yet powerless to stop it.

His eyes were dark, almost hazy, as he looked at her. Without taking his eyes from her, he slid his hands up her hips and, hooking the top of her tights with his thumbs, he began to unroll them slowly. She lifted her hips to help him. Inside she was a mass of confusion. What little part of her brain that could still think was shouting, No! Don't do this! But the far greater part was taken over by urgent need of her body. She knew she was helpless to deny him…or herself.

The only light in the room came from the lounge and the moon outside. It was dark enough to hide her shyness but light enough for her to read every nuance of his expression.

Once her tights were off he turned his attention to her blouse. He leaned over and dropped kisses in the hollow of her throat, across her collarbone, his hands all the while deftly undoing her buttons. He stopped kissing her as he drew the blouse apart. He was breathing hard as he looked down at her. Now she felt no embarrassment, no shyness, only wonder at the expression in his eyes.

Then she lifted her hips as he unbuttoned her skirt and let it drop to the floor.

'You are beautiful,' he said, his voice thick with desire.

She hated him being away from her even for a second and she pulled him back towards her. As he kissed her, she let her hands slide under his T-shirt, revelling in the feel of hard muscle under her fingertips. How could a man who was so toned be soft at the same time? she wondered as she lifted his T-shirt over his head. She pressed against him, feeling the hard warmth of his bare skin pressing against her. She wanted him so much, she didn't know if she could wait a minute longer to feel him, all of him against her, inside her.

A small moan escaped her lips as she searched for the button of his jeans, her fingers brushing the hair that travelled from his belly downwards.

This time it was him who was helping her as his jeans came off.

Then he stretched on the bed beside her. She blushed when she saw the extent of his desire for her.

He slipped a thumb inside the cup of her bra, teasing one nipple and then the other, until she didn't know how she could bear it.

Then his hand reached behind her, deftly unhooked her bra and her breasts sprang free.

He kissed her skin, running his tongue across each nipple. Her body was on fire. She couldn't wait any longer. She was going to explode.

'Please,' she whispered. 'I can't hold on...'

'Just a little longer,' he promised. 'But this time, our first time, I want to watch you.'

She shook her head from side to side. She wanted him inside her now. Moving with her. Filling this empty, aching void that she hadn't known, until now, existed.

'Shh,' he said. 'I promise you there will be time later.'

Giving in, she lay back, digging her fingers into his hair, curling her fingers tightly in an attempt to stop herself crying out as he inched his mouth downwards.

Dropping kisses on her belly, on the insides of her thighs, brushing his fingers gently between her legs. Then he removed her panties and just when she thought she couldn't bear the exquisite pain of her need any longer, he slipped his finger inside her. He raised his head and looked deeply into her eyes as she arched her

body up to him. She couldn't help the cry that ripped
from her throat as sensation after sensation rocked
through her body. He was taking her somewhere she'd
never been before, higher and higher, until at the top her
body couldn't hold on any longer and she lost all sense
of who she was.

Her head was still reeling as she clutched him to her.
She needed him inside her, and greedily she pulled him
on top of her, opening herself to him and using her hands
to guide him inside her. They rocked together, more and
more urgently, until triumphantly she heard him reach
his climax, just seconds before she followed him.

They lay, breathing deeply, their bodies hot and en-
tangled. She felt as if every cell in her body had merged
with his. She had never known sex could be like this, a
heady mix of the physical and emotional. His hands were
brushing over her hair. Lightly touching her shoulder.

'My God, you're not nearly as prim and proper as
you appear on the outside, are you?'

She blushed, but hearing the laughter in his voice she
couldn't take offence.

'I haven't had many lovers,' she murmured.

He propped his head on his elbow as he looked down
at her. 'I'm glad,' he said simply.

His hand trailed lazily over her neck and then onto
her breasts and her breath began to quicken. 'I don't
want to think of you being with anyone else,' he said
possessively. 'I want you to be mine. Just mine.'

Her heart started its hammering again. She was surprised he couldn't feel it pounding against his hand as
he continued to touch her body, searching for the spots
that drove her wild. Didn't he realise that wherever he
touched her drove her wild? Her last coherent thought
as she succumbed once more to the relentless demands

of his touch was that she loved him. Loved him, completely, irrevocably and for ever. Before she could help herself the words slipped out. 'I love you,' she whispered as he once more took possession of her, body and soul.

Mac lay listening to the gentle sound of Abby's breathing. Her hair was fanned out across his chest and he swore he could smell strawberries. It felt so right to have her curled up against him—right and peaceful.

As he began to drift off towards sleep, an image of Abby, Emma and himself came into his head. They were laughing together as they shared a meal around the table in Abby's kitchen. Abby and Emma were looking at him with such love and admiration it made him feel good. Better than he had felt in his life. But then he started. What had Abby said? She loved him. He knew women often said that in the throes of making love. They didn't necessarily mean it. He groaned quietly. But Abby wasn't any woman. She was strong and proud and honest. She wouldn't have said the words if she didn't mean them.

There was no chance of him falling asleep now. His mind was racing too fast for that. Gently he disentangled himself from Abby and eased himself out of bed. He wrapped a towel around his hips and crept out of the bedroom and into the sitting room. He opened the door to his small balcony and stepped outside into the cold air. Maybe it would knock some sense into him. He had been a crazy, selfish fool to let it get this far. He should have known better than to play with Abby. But he hadn't been able to help himself. Ever since she'd appeared back in his life, his need to take her to bed had been like an itch he'd needed to scratch. But he hadn't been thinking of her. What could he offer her? It was one thing to accept the responsibility of a child—there was nothing he could do about that, he had a duty towards Emma—but a relationship with Abby was out of the question. He hadn't changed his mind about not wanting commitment. Commitments brought trouble and pain. Commitments were not for him. Even if he loved her.

He heard the pad of feet behind him and two soft hands crept around his waist.

'What are you doing out here in the freezing cold?' Abby asked, laying her cheek against his back. Her silky hair was like a caress against his skin, and despite everything he had just been telling himself he wanted her there, always.

Suddenly she moved away from him and he felt it like a stab to his heart. He had to tell her what he felt before either of them got in any deeper.

'It can't be ten o'clock. Grief, Emma's due back at half past. I have to get home.' She had wrapped a sheet around her before coming onto the balcony and almost tripped over it in her haste to get back to her clothes in the bedroom. He smiled at her ungainly, faltering steps and had to force himself to stay where he was. If he touched her again, he'd be undone.

'My shoes—where are my shoes?' Abby's panicked voice came from the bedroom. She had slipped on her skirt and blouse and rammed her tights haphazardly into her bag.

'Hey, slow down. It'll only take you fifteen minutes to get home. Plenty of time.' He retrieved one of her high heels from under the sofa and the other from the floor halfway to the bedroom. 'Your shoes, milady,' he said.

She practically snatched them from his hands. 'It's

no laughing matter,' she said crossly. 'I've never not been there for Emma when she comes home. She'll be anxious. And anything could happen. There might be a fire. She could get trapped. Hurt herself and need me. What was I thinking, falling asleep?'

She put her shoes on and looked around feverishly. Mac picked up her coat from the arm of the sofa and held it out so she could slip her arms into it.

'C'mon, Abby. You know nothing's going to happen to her in the few minutes she'll be alone. It's just that you've been on too many rescues. That's why you're imagining the worst.'

She glared at him. 'Being a parent brings responsibility, too, Mac. And one of those responsibilities is protecting your child from any danger.'

Mac knew it was useless to argue. Besides, which would he rather? The woman who was mother to his child caring too much or caring too little? He groaned inwardly. Wasn't that the problem? Abby was the kind of woman who would always care too much. And he didn't want or deserve that.

He was aware of her lips brushing his, and then she was gone.

Happily, Emma hadn't got back by the time Abby brought her car to a screeching halt outside her little house. Everything was still in darkness. Mac was right. She had overreacted. But if anything should ever happen to Emma, she would simply die.

As she let herself in, she thought back over the evening. It had been the most exciting night of her life. A delicious thrill ran up her spine as she recalled how it had felt to be in his arms. She had never imagined that making love could be like that. Although she'd had lovers in her life before, neither of them had made her feel like that. Was it because she loved Mac? The thought frightened and excited her at the same time and she grew hot as she remembered how she hadn't been able to stop herself murmuring the truth to him.

She ran upstairs and switched on the shower. It would give her time to regain her composure before facing Emma. As she let the hot water stream over her body, she pushed aside the memory of Mac's hands. She could have sworn he wasn't immune to her. But then again, what did she really know about men?

He didn't say he loved you. The voice wouldn't go away. But that was okay. For the first time in her life she was going to throw caution to the wind and let life take her where it would. If there was one thing being with Mac had taught her, it was that life was nothing at all if you didn't take risks.

Nevertheless, she was still hurt and dismayed when over the next few days Mac was friendly but distant towards her. Although she hadn't expected protestations of undying love, neither had she expected to be treated like a one-night stand. Had she flung herself at him? Now that he had slept with her, was he no longer interested? He still spent time with Emma on a regular basis, but his invites no longer included her. It was becoming evident she had made a dreadful mistake. But one she could not regret. Making love with Mac, loving Mac, had made her feel alive. And if part of that was the dreadful pain of rejection she knew deep down that she accepted that, too. At least Emma had a father who loved and cherished her. That would have to do.

CHAPTER FIFTEEN

IT WAS another Saturday when Rebecca was on her own. Josh had gone to work, telling her that he had loads of paperwork to catch up on. Although he had promised to be back soon after lunch, it was almost three and he still hadn't returned. It was typical of Josh. In the four years they had been married she had grown to accept that his work would always take priority over her.

A few days earlier she had brought up the subject of children again. Josh had refused to even discuss it and they had argued. Since then they had been barely speaking. Josh was spending more and more time at the hospital and Rebecca had the distinct feeling that he was avoiding her.

She packed a sandwich and a flask of coffee. Josh hated hospital food. They could take their picnic and despite the cold, maybe they could find a bench and sit outside and talk. She blinked away the tears. When had they last talked properly? She couldn't remember.

As she drove towards the hospital she suddenly felt nervous. She could hardly blame Josh totally for the gulf in their marriage. She could make more of an effort, take an interest in his work, even if it did bore her senseless. She would suggest they go into London for dinner, meet up with old friends. It would be like it had been in the beginning. Her spirits lifted. Perhaps they could still find their way back to each other and then if they did, Josh might agree to have children. She would make him see that a baby would make them happy again.

She turned into the hospital car park and searched for a parking place. Then she rooted around in the back seat of her car until she found the paper bag with the picnic. Once again she checked her make-up and her hair. Was that a frown line between her eyes? She shivered. Every day she was seeing signs that she was getting older.

She hopped out of the car and took a few steps towards the door of A & E. But then, to her left, sitting on a bench under a tree, she saw them. Josh and another woman. Like Josh, the other woman was wearing scrubs, and although her hair was pulled back in a ponytail and her face was devoid of make-up, she was still startlingly beautiful in the way only certain women could be. Rebecca felt a flash of envy. She knew she was beautiful, too, but she needed the help of make-up. She didn't have the natural beauty of the woman sitting next to Josh.

She was about to call out when she froze in her tracks. Josh threw back his head and laughed at something the woman had said. His arm was draped over the back of the bench, almost touching her shoulder. There was a familiarity about the gesture that spoke volumes. Rebecca couldn't tear her eyes away. When had she last heard Josh laugh? When had she last seen him looking so relaxed, as if he didn't have a care in the world? When had she last seen him look *happy*?

The woman raised her face to Josh's and smiled into his eyes. Rebecca's throat ached and she raised her hand to brush away the tears that stung her eyes. Slowly she backed away, terrified now lest they see her. Although she couldn't bear it, she knew. Knew with a certainty that rocked her soul. Josh was in love with this woman. Rebecca could see it in every line of his body, in the way it seemed as if she were something precious he had to protect.

Tears were blinding her as she groped her way back to the car. Whatever she'd had planned, whatever hopes she'd had for her and Josh making a go of their marriage, it was too late. If Josh loved this woman, he would be with her. He was too honest to continue with a marriage when he was in love with someone else. Anger was beginning to erode some of the pain. How could she have been so stupid not to have seen what was in front of her eyes? It wasn't work that was making Josh spend all these extra hours at the hospital, it was another woman.

Rebecca gripped the steering-wheel with numb hands. He would leave her. Maybe not today, or tomorrow, but soon. He would look after her financially, she knew that, but leave her he would. And all these years she had stayed with him—giving up her dream, her longing to have a baby, giving up her happy life in London to follow him here, to a place she knew she could never be happy—had been futile.

She turned the key in the ignition. She was damned if she was going to walk away with nothing. At the very least she would have a baby to love.

The telephone was ringing as Mac stepped in to his flat after playing squash. At first he didn't recognise the voice.

'Mac? Robert here.' Mac stood still. He had almost forgotten about the doctor in charge of doing the DNA test.

'Hello, Robert. How's it going? Have you news for me?' Too impatient for small talk, he cut to the chase. He knew it was ridiculous but suddenly he was nervous.

Robert cleared his throat. 'I do. You'll get a letter confirming the results tomorrow, as will the other party, but I thought as a professional courtesy I would ring you.'

Get on with it, Mac wanted to shout down the phone, but he held himself in check. Robert could have left him to find out by letter.

'And?'

'I'm not sure if it's good news or bad, but...'

If he could have reached down the telephone line and shaken Robert he would have done so. Why didn't the man just get on with confirming that Emma was his child? As soon as he had the proof, he would ring the lawyer and start the proceedings that would allow him to be named officially as Emma's father.

'The test is negative,' Robert said flatly. 'There is no way at all she could be your child.'

The breath came out of him like an explosion. He hadn't been even aware he had stopped breathing.

'What?' he managed. He couldn't have heard right.

'Emma Stevens is not your biological daughter. As I said, I have no idea whether this is good or bad news, but that is the result. A letter is on its way to her guardian.'

Mac felt the world tip. Emma was not his daughter. He couldn't believe it. Everything in him said she was. He couldn't love her the way he did if she wasn't his flesh and blood.

He was hardly aware of thanking Robert and replacing the receiver. If it hadn't been mid-afternoon, he would have poured himself a stiff whisky.

Emma wasn't his child. Sara had either been lying or, he suspected, simply mistaken.

He was surprised at how devastated he felt at the news. What now? Would Abby stop him from seeing Emma? The thought made his stomach churn. Now he was about to lose her, he realised how much he had begun to enjoy the role of father.

And what about Emma? His heart ached for the little girl. She cared deeply about him. He knew that. How would she feel when she found out that he wasn't her father after all? He raked a hand through his hair. God, it was such a mess. Why hadn't he seen this coming? Why hadn't he reminded himself that there was always a possibility that the test would be negative?

But he knew the answer. Bit by bit he had fallen in love with the idea of being a father. He had enjoyed being around for Emma. Encouraging her to come out of her shell. All the things his father should have done for him, but hadn't. In some ways, he had been able to give Emma some of the childhood pleasures he'd never had, and it had healed something inside him.

Making up his mind, he picked up his jacket from where he'd flung it and was out of the door. He had to speak to Abby. She would know what to do.

Abby paced her small sitting room. Where was Emma? She'd promised she'd be back for lunch and it was now after one.

She picked up a magazine and attempted to read it, but there was no way she could concentrate. Emma knew Abby worried. She would have texted her had she been held up.

She had wheedled Abby into agreeing that she could go down to the beach with a friend from school. Simon was a local boy and knew the area well, so why was she worrying? They were going to go down to the beach and stop off for a burger. But Emma had promised she'd come home after that. Abby checked her watch for the hundredth time. Only five more minutes had passed, although it felt like a lot longer.

She almost jumped out of her skin when her mobile rang. She leaped on top of it. It was bound to be Emma, probably apologising for not being home, for forgetting the time.

And it was Emma. At least, she thought it was. The signal kept fading and all she could hear were muffled snatches of words.

'Em? Is that you? I can't hear you. Can you go somewhere where you can get a better signal?'

'No...stuck...help...'

Abby's blood ran cold. She could hardly make out the words but there was no mistaking the fear in Emma's voice.

'Em? Where are you?'

More static. Then three words that made her physically ill. 'Trapped...cave...tide...' Then all of a sudden Emma's voice came over clearly. 'Help us, Mum.'

Her daughter, her beloved Emma, was in trouble. Abby forced back the waves of terror that threatened to overwhelm her.

'Stay calm, Emma, and tell me where you are.'

'Cave...beach...hurt...'

'Are you hurt? God, Emma!'

But there was only more static on the end of the phone. 'Look, Emma, I don't know if you can hear me, but leave your phone on. I'll find you. I promise. Keep calm, I'm coming.'

'No time... Hurry—' And then the phone cut out.

Abby was almost sobbing with terror. She had to find Emma. But where to start?

For a second she couldn't think what to do, and then suddenly the door opened and he was there. Mac! Relief made her knees go weak.

'I knocked,' Mac started to apologise, but the expression on her face must have told him something terrible had happened. He was by her side in seconds, pulling her close. 'Breathe, Abby. That's it. Slow, deep breaths, and tell me what's happened.'

This was wasting time! She pushed him away.

'It's Em. She phoned. Just now. I couldn't hear properly. Just enough… Oh, my God. I have to go to her.'

Mac reached out for her and pulled her round to face him. His face had lost all colour and his eyes were as dark as ink.

'Tell me,' he said.

'She's trapped. And hurt. She needs us, Mac,' Abby moaned. 'Help me, find my baby. Our child. Please, Mac. You have to help me.'

'Listen to me.' He grabbed her by the shoulders. 'Look at me, Abby.'

She looked into his eyes. She saw fear and something else. Conviction.

'We're going to find our girl. Do you hear me? And she's going to be all right. But I need you to tell me everything.'

'She went to the beach with a boy from her class. Simon. That was almost three hours ago. She said she'd be back by one. She promised.' She took a gulp of air. Mac was right. Panicking now wouldn't help Emma. 'She phoned. The signal was bad. I could hardly hear her. All I could make out was that she was trapped. In a cave. And hurt.' She took a shuddering breath as terror returned. Her baby. Out there somewhere. Alone and scared.

Mac was already on his phone. 'I'm going to alert the rescue services. We need to get the coastguard and the other services out looking.' Abby paced as he spoke into the phone for a few minutes. All she could hear was Mac's side of the conversation, repeating what she had told him. When he finished the call, he looked grimmer than ever.

'What is it?' Abby asked. 'What did they say?'

'They said they'd mobilise a sea and air rescue,' Mac said. But Abby could tell there was something more. Something he wasn't telling her.

'Tell me everything they said.' She kept her voice level. 'I have a right to know.'

He hesitated.

'Please, Mac, tell me.'

'The tide is coming in,' he said. 'And it's higher than usual today. If they are trapped somewhere, it's only going to get worse.'

Abby cried out and sank to her knees. In a flash Mac was by her side. He lifted her into his arms and held her tight before placing her on the sofa.

'You stay here, Abby. In case Emma phones. Keep trying her mobile. I've got to go.'

Abby struggled to her feet. 'I'm coming, too.'

'It'll be best if you don't.'

'Don't even think of trying to stop me,' she said. She took a deep shuddering breath. 'I'll be okay. I promise. I won't panic and I won't get in the way. But I'm coming.'

Five minutes later they were prowling the cliffs above the beach front. Mac had managed to get hold of Simon's parents. They were also panic-stricken but had told them of a cave that Simon liked to explore. They told Mac that they had forbidden their son from going into the cave, but suspected that he, trying to impress his new friend, might have ignored their warnings. The cave was easily accessible when the tide was out but, depending on the size of the tide, could become filled with water, preventing escape. Instinctively Abby knew that this was where Emma was. At the very least they had nowhere else to try. When it arrived, the Royal Navy helicopter would keep searching from the air and the coastguard would search the shoreline.

As soon as Abby and Mac got the information about the cave, they ran towards the part of the beach where it was. Although Abby knew the tide was rising, she couldn't help a small cry when she saw that the beach had completely disappeared under the sea.

How would they get to the stranded children, and even if they did find them, how would they get them out?

'We need divers,' Mac was speaking into his mobile. 'The navy will have them. Get them down here immediately.'

Divers! If they needed divers to get to the children, they were in deep trouble. It would take time to get them here. And time was what they didn't have. With every minute, the tide was rising higher.

Mac ran into a shop selling gear for watersports. He returned a few minutes later with flippers. The kind divers used. 'I can move much faster with these. Try and get Emma again,' Mac said. 'Even if you can't hear her, she might be able to hear you. Tell her help is on the way. Try texting her, too. Sometimes a text will get through even if a call won't.' Uncaring of who might be watching, Mac stripped off his clothes until he was down to his boxers and T-shirt. Tossing his clothes to one side, he pulled on the flippers.

While he was doing that, Abby tried Emma's mobile again, despairing. She had tried every minute or two since she had got Emma's call, but it was hopeless. Her fingers fumbling with the tiny buttons, she sent a text.

Coming for you. Dad is here. Hold on. We love you.

As she pressed 'Send', Mac declared he was ready.

'We don't have time to wait for the rescue services. I'm going to go down there now. As soon as the Sea King gets here, make sure they know exactly which cave I'm searching. The coastguard, too. They'll have a pretty good idea of where the cave mouth is. The air ambulance is on its way with Lucy and Mike.'

He looked down at her and gently raised her chin, forcing her to look at him. 'I'm going to get her, Abby. I promise you. She'll be home safe with you soon.'

'Isn't it better to leave it to the Navy divers?' she had to ask.

Mac shook his head. 'She might be hurt. Or him. Or both. They may need medical attention. It has to be me.'

Abby nodded. Despite her terror, she knew Mac would do everything in his power to save their child, even if it meant sacrificing his own life. The thought of losing him, too, rocked her soul.

Just as he had done those weeks before, Mac disappeared over the side of the cliff. But this time the stakes were higher.

The water was freezing and murky. Mac forced himself to wait a minute or two to let the water settle. He had to be methodical and not let his impatience to get to Emma and her friend cloud his judgement. As he had hoped, after a few agonising seconds the water cleared and he was able to see the entrance to the cave. There was still a gap between the mouth of the cave and the sea, but Mac knew it wouldn't be long before that small opening disappeared.

He used his fins to propel himself towards the cave. The tide was so high. Would he be rescuing two corpses? No! Thinking like that did no one any good. He had to believe that Emma and her friend had found a high ledge to wait on.

He swam underwater towards the cave opening. After a few metres he stopped and raised his head to get his bearings. He was in a cave that stretched a metre above his head. It was almost completely dark inside and Mac had to strain to see anything. Damn it!

'Emma!' he shouted, his voice echoing in the semi-darkness. His heart plummeted when there was no reply. Had they got it completely wrong and were searching in the wrong spot? Or, even worse, was it too late?

He heard a noise coming from his right. He whirled round, trying frantically to make out in the gloom where the noise had come from. Then he saw them. Two small figures huddled together on a ledge. Relief coursed through him, to be replaced almost instantly by anxiety. They were still in desperate danger. The rising tide was lapping at their feet.

'I'm coming,' he yelled, frantically searching for another ledge. A higher one, where the tide couldn't reach. But there wasn't one. He had to get the children out. But how?

Quickly he swam towards the children.

'Hey, there,' he said softly. 'How're you doing?' He knew the children would be very frightened.

'Dad!' It was Emma's voice, Mac noted. Whatever injuries she might have, at least she was conscious. 'You found us. See, Simon? I told you my dad would find us. He rescues people all the time.'

The irony wasn't lost on Mac. The first time she really needed him was the day he'd found out that he wasn't her father. But that didn't change the way he felt. Not one iota. He couldn't love Emma any more if she were his biological child.

'Dad. Simon's hurt his leg. We think it's broken. That's why we couldn't get out. When the tide started coming in we managed to get up here, but we couldn't go any further.'

And you didn't think of leaving your friend and saving yourself? My brave, darling child. She was so much his and Abby's child, whatever the DNA test said.

Mac heaved himself out of the water and onto the ledge beside the children. There wasn't much space. A quick examination of Simon's leg told him Emma was right. It was broken. And not just broken—the boy had a compound fracture and was bleeding badly. The loss of blood, combined with the cold and fright, was having a bad effect on the young lad. He was shivering uncontrollably. They had to get him to hospital, and soon.

'I'm going to strap your leg as best I can,' he told the boy, 'and then I'm going to get you out of here, okay?' As he spoke he struggled out of his soaking wet T-shirt. It wasn't a great bandage, but it was all he had.

'I'm sorry, but this will hurt a little,' he told Simon. He straightened the leg as best he could before strapping it with his T-shirt.

'Emma, I'm going to have to take you out of here one at a time, do you understand? And I'm going to have to take Simon first. He's the one in need of help most urgently.'

It broke his heart to see the fear then resolve on Emma's face. She lifted her chin. 'That's okay,' she said. 'I can wait.'

He was so proud of her. Any other child would be crying, but not his Emma.

'Abby is waiting for you outside.'

He explained to Simon what he wanted him to do. 'Lie on your back and don't, whatever you do, try and fight me. I'm going to put my hands on either side of your head, and pull you out. As long as you don't panic, you'll be fine.' There was just a big enough gap between the top of the entrance to the cave and the water for him to make it out with the boy. But would there still be a gap by the time he returned?

Mac was facing the worst dilemma of his life. How could he leave Emma? What if he didn't make it back in time? How would he live without Emma? How would Abby live without the child she loved?

But if he had any chance of saving Emma, he had to act now.

'I'll be back as quick as I can,' he said. 'Hold on.'

He grasped Simon around the head and pulled him out of the cave, taking care not to let water splash in the boy's mouth. If the boy panicked now, it could be fatal for both of them. As he swam, his heart and soul was back in the cave.

He found the rock where Abby was still waiting. She had been joined by the crew of the air ambulance. Lucy and Mike were standing by, waiting to help him. From the corner of his eye he could see the lifeboat circling nearby. He knew they couldn't risk getting any closer. There was no sign of the Sea King. It must still be waiting for the divers.

'Where's Em?' Abby's face was white.

'She's still in the cave. I'm going back for her. I couldn't take her as well as Simon.'

Mac was helping Lucy and Mike carefully lift Simon out of the water and onto a stretcher. Before he could stop her, Abby jumped into the water and was swimming towards the entrance of the cave.

'No, Abby, wait!' he shouted, but either she couldn't hear him or she was ignoring him. She carried on swimming towards the cave.

Muttering a curse, Mac gave one final heave and his arms lightened as the injured boy was taken out of his arms. He plunged back into the water after Abby. Didn't she know that she, too, could drown? He could lose both the people he loved most in the world. The realisation cut through his fear. He loved Abby. He loved her more than his life itself. He had been running away from it but now, when he could lose her, he knew a life without her and Emma was no life at all.

The realisation added strength and soon he was back in the cave. By now there was no longer a gap between the top of the cave entrance and the cave and Mac had to take a deep gulp of air and swim underwater. His lungs were bursting as he once more emerged into the cave. To his horror he saw that the water was now up to Emma's waist, even though she was standing on the ledge. Abby was treading water nearby.

'Emma, we have to go now. You, too, Abby,' Mac said, trying to keep his voice even.

Emma was staring, her eyes wide with fear. 'I can't,' she said. 'I've hurt my arm.'

'Yes, you can, my love. Mac and I will each take one side of you. And we'll help you through. We won't let anything happen to you, I promise,' Abby said.

Mac marvelled at Abby. The fear was gone from her voice. It was steady and calm, as if she was suggesting a walk in the park.

'We'll be underwater for thirty seconds. But your mum and I will be on either side of you. All you have to do is keep as still as you can and let us pull you along. Can you do that?' he said.

'Yes,' Emma replied.

'Good girl. But we have to go now.' Mac slid back into the water. Abby held onto Emma's good arm as she slipped into the water and then she jumped in beside them. Mac's heart lurched. Getting through the channel, swimming against the incoming current, would be a challenge. But what choice did they have?

'Okay. On my count of three, we're all going to take a deep breath and then go under. Okay?'

Abby and Emma nodded.

'One, two, three,' Mac said, and then between them he and Abby had Emma. He gripped Emma around the waist, careful to avoid her injured arm. To his relief, the rising tide meant that the current wasn't as strong as it had been. But still he felt every second of the time they spent underwater. True to her word, Emma relaxed, letting them pull her along.

At last, when he thought Emma wouldn't be able to hold her breath any longer, they broke through into the fresh air. The three of them trod water, breathing in deep lungfuls of fresh, clean air, and then the lifeboat was beside them and men were dropping into the water, helping them lift Emma gently onto the boat.

As soon as they were all safely on board, the boat

sped off towards the shore. Over the top of Emma's head Mac and Abby shared a look. In Abby's eyes there was relief and gratitude and something else—love. Soon, when all this was over, he would tell her about the DNA test, but all that mattered right now was that he had his small precious family safe and well beside him.

CHAPTER SIXTEEN

'I WAS scared,' Emma said, 'but I remembered what Dad told me once and that helped me stay calm.' She was sitting on the hospital trolley. Her arm had been X-rayed and, as they'd expected, found to be broken. It had been put in a cast but the staff wanted to keep in her in overnight for observation. The bruise that was blossoming on her forehead suggested she had knocked her head, too.

'And what was that, darling?' Abby asked.

'He told me that panic kills more people than anything else. He said if you use your head, there is always a way out of most problems. So that's what I did.'

Abby slid a glance at Mac. Emma was more her father's daughter than she had realised. 'When Simon fell, I knew he had hurt his leg quite badly and I knew we couldn't walk out of the cave together. Not through the tide. So I climbed down to stay with him. But I had to get help. My mobile wasn't working. I could hear you, Mum. Some of the words, at least, but not everything. I didn't know for sure if you could hear me.

'I waded out, the tide wasn't so high then, and I waved my arms until I got someone's attention. Then I went back to stay with Simon.' Her voice trembled slightly. 'But on the way I fell over a rock that I couldn't see in the water and bumped my head. I think that's when I hurt my arm.'

'You were very brave. It must have been difficult to climb back up to Simon with only one arm.'

Why didn't you stay out of the cave once you got out? Abby wanted to ask. But she knew the answer. Her heart swelled with pride. Abby hadn't wanted to leave her friend alone and hurt by himself. As Mac had pointed out, she couldn't change her daughter's nature. And despite everything she had been through in the last hour or two, she wouldn't change her daughter for the world.

Eventually, Emma closed her eyes, the exhaustion and the excitement of the last few hours catching up with her.

Abby reached for Mac's hand as they watched her breathing deeply. To her surprise he didn't pull away. Instead, he brought her hand to his mouth and kissed each finger tenderly.

'My God, Abby. For a moment I thought I was going to lose you and Emma. Don't ever do anything like that to me again.' His voice was ragged.

'Don't want to have to train a new teammate?' she said lightly.

'I don't want to lose the woman I love,' Mac replied quietly.

Abby's heart kicked against her ribs. He'd said he loved her. Did he mean as a friend or a lover? She had to know. Silently she waited for him to go on.

'Two months ago I thought I was happy. I had a job I loved, a decent place to live where I could do the sports I enjoy whenever I wanted. It was a good life, a perfect life, until you walked into it.'

Abby couldn't stop her smile. He sounded almost

annoyed. But she knew his life had been empty of all that was important, even if he didn't.

'And then I found out I had a child. This child.' He bent over and kissed Emma gently on the cheek. 'At first I could hardly take it in. I didn't want it to be true. Emma would be nothing except a duty and while I knew I couldn't ignore my responsibilities, I never thought that she would become such an important part of my life. And as for you...' He sighed. 'You drove me insane almost from the moment I set eyes on you. Not just those cat eyes, or that mouth that just cries out to be kissed, or your body, which would make most women weep— those are the things that counted in my other life, but as I got to know you, I realised I was falling hard for you. And it frightened me.' He half smiled. 'That was a new one for me. I didn't think I was scared of anything but I was. I was scared of being in love.'

A warm glow was spreading upwards from her toes and surrounding her heart like a blanket. But she still couldn't be certain he was saying what she so desperately wanted to hear.

'I thought if I took you to bed, that would break the spell. But I was wrong. If anything, I wanted more. I wanted nights and nights with you. I couldn't imagine a time when I would no longer want you. Then you told me you loved me and that frightened me even more. What if I couldn't live up to your expectations of me? What if I let you—and Emma—down? What if I turned out to be like my father? I'd be dragging you and Em down with me. I couldn't do that. I tried to stay away from you, Abby. I wanted you to find someone else, even if the thought ripped me apart. And if it meant losing Emma, too, I knew the man you chose would be a good man. Someone who would love Emma the way she deserved.'

'Do you still believe that?' Abby clasped her hands together to stop herself from reaching out and pushing a wayward lock of hair out of his eyes. Didn't he know that she would never love another man as long as she lived?

'No. I don't. I came close to losing you and Emma today. I knew then that I couldn't let you go. I'm not strong enough to do that.'

Abby came and crouched by his side. Taking his hands in hers, she looked up into his eyes. 'You are the strongest man I know, Mac. In the truest sense of the word. You are not your father. And even if you were I would still take my chances with you. I would rather have a tempestuous life with you than one without you.'

He stood up abruptly, forcing her to drop her hands. 'But that's not all. The lab that took our DNA for testing called today. That's why I was on my way to see you.'

A tendril of fear curled around her heart. The look in Mac's eyes told her something was far from right.

He lowered his voice. 'Abby, Emma is not my child.'

'What?'

'Whatever Sara told you, Abby is not mine.'

Abby's head was reeling. 'But why did she say you were?' As soon as she said the words she guessed the truth. Sara probably hadn't been sure who the father was and that was why she hadn't wanted to give Abby a name at first. But when she'd known she was going to die, she'd given Abby the name of the man she would have liked most to be the father of her child, Mac. Perhaps in her heart she had harboured a dream that once her child was born, she would go to Mac and persuade him Emma was his. They would never know.

'Whoever the biological father of Emma is, it isn't me.'

The pain and disappointment in his eyes shook her.

What now? What would he do? There was no reason for him to continue with the relationship. He would walk out of Emma's life and what would that do to Emma?

'Emma's going to be devastated. She adores you. She's so proud to call you her father.'

Mac's jaw tightened. 'No prouder than I was to think she was my daughter. And I love her.' A small smile curled his lips. 'I never thought the day would come when I'd say that.' The smile faded from his eyes. 'I don't care what the test says. I don't care who the biological father is. Damn it, Abby, Emma is my daughter. I don't want to lose her.' He looked away. Emma was still sleeping peacefully.

He reached out and took Abby's hand and pulled her to her feet.

'Come with me. There's something I want to show you.'

'But, Emma... I don't want to leave her.'

'She'll be out for the count for an hour or two. We won't be that long. I'll ask them to bleep me the minute she wakes up.'

Abby hesitated.

'Please, Abby.'

She couldn't resist the appeal in his blue eyes. He was hurting.

She followed him out to the car park. He opened the door to his Jeep and helped her in.

'I don't suppose you're going to tell me where you're taking me?' she said.

He smiled at her and her heart cracked. She loved him so much it hurt. She would have given anything for Emma to be his child.

They drove in silence, turning onto the track where Mac had taken her a few weeks earlier. Abby was baffled. As they drove they passed diggers and lorries. There was obviously work going on.

Mac helped Abby out of the car.

'You and Emma are everything I wanted. I just didn't know it. I love you both.' He turned to Abby, pinning her with the intensity in his blue eyes. 'I'm in love with you, Abby. I'm not good at finding the words, but I know I couldn't bear to live without you. I want to wake up every morning with you beside me and I want yours to be the last face I see when I go to sleep. I want to live my life with you and Emma by my side. I want to have breakfast and dinner with you and Em, take you to Tiree to show you the place I grew up. The works.'

Abby's heart started to pound.

'I thought I could run from you. But I couldn't. I wouldn't let myself accept that I was falling for you.' He smiled sadly. 'Thinking I was a father was shock enough and even though it turned out to be the best thing that ever happened to me, I didn't know if I could commit myself to a wife. All I knew was that I didn't want to let you go.'

He gestured to the building site. 'When you refused to let me build this house for you, I thought I would build it anyway. I began to realise that I was putting down roots. Then, when I was discussing the plans with the architect, I saw the little sitting room with you in it, looking out to sea, a book in your hand. The garden where you would grow your roses. The kitchen where we would eat, the bedroom where I would fall asleep with you in my arms and the starlight shining in the window. Everywhere I looked, there you were. You and Emma. My family. My heart. My reason for living.'

He reached out and tipped her chin so she was looking into his eyes. 'Abby, I love you. I want you to marry me. I want you and Emma to be my family. I know she's not my biological child and that one day she might want to find her real father, but until then, could you love me enough to spend the rest of your life with me?'

A frisson of joy was spreading through Abby's body. Happiness swelled inside her. He loved her. But she had to be sure that this wasn't his way of hanging onto Emma.

'I'll never stop you seeing Em, whatever the results of the test say, and as long as she wants you in her life, which, knowing Em, is going to be for ever. You do know that, Mac?'

He glared at her. 'You don't think I'm saying all this simply because of Em, do you?' He smiled grimly. 'I love you. Heart and soul. For ever. I want babies with you, to grow old with you. To laugh with you. Argue, too, if it comes to that.' He pulled her into his arms. 'I love you, Abby Stevens. Will you get that into your stubborn head?'

The blood was singing through her veins. The way he was looking at her left no doubt in her mind. She brought her face up to his. 'For heaven's sake, how long do I have to wait for my fiancé to kiss me, then?'

And then he was kissing her as if he would never let her go, and she knew at last they had both found the place they were meant to be.

* * *

Emma was just waking up when they tiptoed back into her cubicle. One look at their faces must have told her something was up.

'Hey, what's going on with you two?' she asked.

Mac and Abby sat on the bed on either side of Emma, careful not to bump her injured arm.

'We have two things to tell you. Both are surprises. The first you're going to have to prepare yourself for, the second we think you'll like.'

Emma eyed them warily. Then she broke into a wide smile. 'I know what one of the surprises is,' she said. 'You two are getting married. Am I right?'

'You are. But how did you guess?' Abby said.

'Grown-ups can be so silly,' Emma said scornfully. 'I knew you were in love ages ago. Anybody, even a kid like me…' she slid Abby a mocking glance '…could see it a mile away. Even if you are old.'

Abby and Mac laughed. 'Hey, we're not that old,' Mac protested. 'There's still a few years before we get really ancient.'

'So you're okay with us getting married?' Abby asked.

There was no need for a reply. The smile that lit up Emma's face was all the answer Abby needed. 'I wished you would get married. Does that mean we'll all live together? For ever? Like a real family? I'll have my mum and my dad just like all the other children?'

Despite her happiness, Abby felt a chill. It was going to be a blow to Emma finding out Mac wasn't her biological father.

'Emma,' Mac said, taking her hand. 'I have something to tell you. But first I want you to know that I couldn't love you more than I do now.'

The smile left Emma's face. 'What's going on?' she whispered. She clutched Abby's hand again.

'Remember that test we had? To prove I was your dad?'

'When you and me went to the hospital?'

'Yes, that one.' He took a deep breath and Abby knew he was having difficulty finding the right words. 'It turns out that I'm not your father. At least, I never made you.'

'You mean it wasn't your sperm with my real mummy's eggs?'

Mac looked so shocked that Abby had to laugh. 'I've always told Emma the truth. And it seemed silly to wait until some other child gave her the wrong information. Emma knows how babies are made. At least,' she rushed on, in case Mac misunderstood, 'the biological basis.'

Emma frowned. 'I thought you said people made babies when they loved each other. But my real mum didn't even know who my father was.'

Oh, dear. Abby thought. This was going to take some explaining...

Luckily Mac stepped in. 'Your mum, Sara, was a kind, lovely person. But she was a little lonely. Sometimes people make babies because they want someone to love and look after. I think that's why Sara made you. Whoever your real father is, your mother made you out of love.'

'And you always have to remember that,' Abby said softly. 'She loved you more than anything in the world. So much she didn't want to share you.'

'But if Mac's not my real dad...' Emma's lip trembled and tears spilled down her cheek '...then we're not really a family.'

'Emma, look at me,' Mac said firmly. He waited until

Emma turned her blue eyes to his. Abby's throat tightened when she saw the trust there. 'You and Abby are my family. I love you both more than anything in the world. I want to be your dad for as long as you'll let me. I want to be the one who chases the boyfriends away, who picks you up from parties.' His voice softened. 'Who walks you up the aisle. We can carry on looking for your real dad, but if you let me, us...' he turned to Abby '...we want to adopt you, so you really belong to us. What do you say?'

Emma cuddled into Mac, snuggling deep into his arms. He stroked her hair, comforting her.

'I say yes,' Emma said. Then she pulled away and took hold of Abby's hand, too. 'So does that mean I can go to night-time parties now?'

EPILOGUE

ABBY stood by the window of her new home. In the sitting room, her mother and Mac's were chatting ninety to the dozen, each trying to outdo the other. Mac's mother had come down for the wedding and although she had grumbled about being away from Tiree almost constantly since she had got to Cornwall, Abby suspected she was pleased and touched that Mac had asked her to come to their wedding. Two more days then she'd be walking down the aisle with Mac, and she still couldn't believe it.

She felt his arm slip around her waist and she leaned against him, savouring the warmth and security of his embrace.

'Happy?' he whispered into her ear.

She nodded. Two more days and he'd be coming to live with her and Emma. He had refused to move in before, saying he wanted to wait until after they married. The house was everything he had told her it would be. Although enormous windows captured the view from every side, it was still cosy.

'You must come to Tiree to visit me,' Mac's mother was saying. 'I don't live in a grand house like this,' she sniffed, but Abby was beginning to realise that she didn't mean half of what she said, 'or in London, where all the fancy people live, but my house is good enough for me.'

'Your house is so sweet, Gran MacNeil,' Emma protested. 'I love it. Especially the chickens. And so is yours, Grandma Stevens,' she added hastily.

Abby smiled. Emma was ever the diplomat. Whatever differences the two older women had with their own children, there was no doubt they doted on their grand-child. Indeed, they spent all their time trying to compete for her affection.

Behind her, she heard Mac stifle a laugh. He had learned to be tolerant of both parents. 'At the very least,' he had told Abby, 'we both know how not to do it.'

Emma left the two old women to their bickering and came to stand next to Abby. She was to be bridesmaid at their wedding and was barely able to control her excite-ment about having a brother or sister to boss around in a few months' time. Mac reached across to pull her into the circle of his embrace.

'My two best girls,' he said. 'My daughter and my wife-to-be.' Mac and Abby had formally adopted Emma. His voice turned serious. 'Have I told you both that I consider myself to be the luckiest man alive?'

Emma giggled. 'Only all the time. You're so sad, Dad.'

He placed a proprietorial hand on Abby's stomach, where her body was just beginning to swell with her pregnancy.

'No, not that. Not any more.'

Abby raised her face to his. She never got over seeing her love reflected in his eyes.

'I have the best life,' Emma sighed happily.

'The best life. That's what we have. No one could be luckier.'

Together they watched as the sun melted into the sea.

ST PIRAN'S:
THE BROODING
HEART SURGEON

ALISON ROBERTS

CHAPTER ONE

IF LOOKS could kill, Luke Davenport would be a dead man.

Dr Anna Bartlett had finally deigned to join him in Theatre for her assigned job of assisting him in a potentially complicated procedure, and she was clearly less than impressed that he had decided to go ahead without her.

Sure, he'd received a message while reviewing his patient's notes that she was caught up in the emergency department of St Piran's hospital with a chest trauma case requiring a thoracotomy and would therefore be late, but what had she expected? That he would delay the case until she arrived? This patient had already had to wait longer than he should have for his surgery. In any case, if the patient in Emergency survived the aggressive procedure to try and stabilise him, Dr Bartlett would be the only person available to take them to another theatre and that left Luke in precisely the same place—having to find someone else to assist him in surgery. Thankfully, this wasn't that difficult given the talented staff this hospital could boast, and paediatric cardiac surgeon James Alexander had been available and only too willing to assist the returning head of department.

James had joined the staff in the eighteen months Luke had been away. He was not only settled in the area but married to Charlotte, a senior registrar in the cardiology department. Just one of a countless number of changes. So many it was hard for Luke to imagine he'd once been a part of all this. It was frightening how one's world could change in a heartbeat.

Like Luke's had done when the news of his younger brother's death had rocked the seemingly solid foundations of his life and prompted the radical decision to join a military medical unit. Nothing would ever be the same and yet here he was, trying to pick up the pieces of his old life.

If it felt wrong to him, it was no wonder he was an unwelcome disturbance in Anna Bartlett's world. She'd had enough time to become part of this medical community. To stake a claim and make this department her own. Maybe that was the real reason for the resentment he could detect. That he was in charge again.

It would be a bit of a blow to anyone's ego, wouldn't it, being bumped from a position as top dog? Everybody had known that his replacement was temporary but nobody had expected him to return so abruptly. Maybe Anna had secretly thought he might never return from Iraq. To add insult to injury, it wasn't the first time Luke had taken the position from her. He'd been the winner three years ago when he'd been chosen over her for the prestigious role of head of St Piran's specialist heart surgery unit.

Yes. That could well explain the death glare he'd

caught from over the top of the mask as Anna had finally entered the theatre. She stood outside the cluster of staff around the operating table now, gowned and masked, her gloved hands held carefully away from her body. Taller than average, he noted in that split second of noticing her arrival, and her eyes were green. Very cool right now because she was displeased and that made them seem hard—like uncut emeralds. Unusual enough to make a lasting impression. As did her body language. The way she was standing so absolutely still. It advertised the kind of attention to detail, like not contaminating anything, that came from being not only well trained but highly disciplined.

He'd heard that about her from James as they'd scrubbed in together. That his missing assistant was skilled and meticulous. Uncompromising. Single because she chose to be. Or maybe no man could compete with a job that someone lived and breathed to the exclusion of anything else.

'She's good,' James had added. 'Very good. You'll be pleased she's taken on the job of Assistant Head of Surgery. With the reputation she's built here, she could have gone anywhere she chose.'

James obviously respected Dr Bartlett but he'd also said he didn't really know her. Not on a personal level. The way his sentence had trailed off in a puzzled tone had suggested that maybe she didn't have a personal level.

It was James who acknowledged her presence now, however.

'Anna! That was quick.' He gave his colleague a closer glance and frowned. 'No go, huh?'

'No.' The word was crisp. The attempt to save someone in the emergency department had failed. That was that. An unsuccessful case. Time to move on to the next. 'Want me to take over?'

'If that's all right with Luke. I am rather late to start my ward round now and I've got my own theatre slot this afternoon.' James sealed another small blood vessel with the diathermy rod and then looked up at the surgeon across the table. 'Luke? Have you met Anna already?'

'No.' His response was as curt as Anna's verdict on her emergency case had been.

He carried on with the long, vertical incision he was making in his patient's chest, not looking up until James moved in to control the bleeding.

She was standing closer to the table now. A mask covered the lower half of her face and a disposable hat hid her hair and ears. All he could see were those green eyes and for a split second the accusation in them hit home.

Yesterday he had been supposed to meet the woman who'd looked after his job for eighteen months, but there'd been that hassle at his house with a burst pipe and there had been no water supply. There'd been a problem getting power reconnected as well, after such a long period of being empty, so he'd had no way of recharging the battery for his mobile phone when it had died. The hassles had underscored the fact that he wasn't exactly thrilled to be back here anyway and...and she hadn't waited for him, had she? He'd been less than an hour late but she had gone home and hadn't left any message other than the theatre list for this morning.

And now she was glaring at him as if accepting her

belated assistance for this surgery was only the first challenge he had coming his way. Well, she could take her attitude and deal with it on her own time.

'If you plan to assist,' he said curtly, 'now's the time to start. I don't like my surgeries being disrupted and I'd prefer to start the way I mean to go on.'

A tense silence fell around them as James stepped back and Anna smoothly took his place. The familiar ache in Luke's leg kicked up a notch but that only served to increase his focus. He turned his head to the scrub nurse hovering over the trolley beside him.

'Sternal saw, thanks.'

The nurse jumped at his tone and handed him the requested item with commendable speed. Then the whine of the saw cut into the silence he could still feel around him. Luke concentrated on splitting the bone beneath his hands. For a short time at least, he had no need—or inclination—to look at the woman now opposite him.

So this was Luke Davenport.

The war hero she'd been hearing so much about in the last few days. Too much. As if it hadn't been bad enough to have her position as head of department cut short, no one hesitated in rubbing salt in the wound by telling her how marvellous Luke was. What a great surgeon. And soldier. How he'd single-handedly saved everybody he had been with when they had come under attack, dragging them from a burning vehicle despite his own badly broken leg and then providing emergency care that had kept them alive until help arrived.

She could believe it. One glance from a pair of the

most piercing blue eyes Anna had ever seen and she knew she was meeting someone just as ambitious and determined as she was herself. Two horizontal frown lines at the top of his nose, between dark eyebrows, added to the intensity of the glance and made her catch her breath. To have him treating her like a junior fresh out of medical school might be unacceptable but it wasn't totally surprising. This man had seen and dealt with things she couldn't begin to imagine experiencing.

'An honourable discharge from the army,' someone had said. 'He's up for a medal.'

St Piran's was so lucky he had come back. The hospital, the patients, the whole damn community was feeling lucky. Anna had had to hide disappointment strong enough to morph very easily into burning resentment. Had to try and smile and pretend she felt lucky that she was being given the opportunity to be the hero's assistant from now on.

No wonder the guy was so full of himself he hadn't even bothered to come and introduce himself yesterday. She'd given him the courtesy of sending an apology for being late for this theatre case and look at his response! He didn't like his surgeries being disrupted. The voice had been deep and the words clipped. This was a man who was not only used to giving orders, he expected them to be obeyed.

Anna's spirits—already well dampened by the unsuccessful struggle to save a life in Emergency—slipped a little further. The only way through this, as she'd discovered with any previous difficult episode in life, was to focus on her work to the exclusion of anything else.

It wasn't hard. 'Good grief,' she couldn't help but comment when the rib spreaders were locked into position and the target of this surgery was exposed. 'Look at that.'

The sac of membrane enclosing the heart had calcified and become a thick, white casing—a kind of scar from the inflammation a virus had caused and so solid it was preventing the heart from beating effectively. Luke was about to perform a pericardectomy and peel this hard layer away from the heart tissue. A tricky, fiddly procedure that Anna had studied but never performed herself.

She would have been happy enough to do the surgery if a better option hadn't been available, but she would definitely have preferred to have the patient on bypass and a still heart to work with. Luke was sparing this man the additional risk of being on a heart-lung machine. He was going to do the procedure with the heart moving beneath his scalpel.

'Your investigations showed the extent of the calcification.' Luke sounded mildly surprised by her exclamation of astonishment. 'Right-sided filling was poor and the stroke volume was abysmal. It's a wonder he's been able to function at all.'

'The first sign that it was anything serious only came when he collapsed at work three weeks ago.'

Anna watched as Luke used a scalpel to cut through the hard, white tissue, his hand large enough to make the small instrument almost invisible. She could see how much pressure he was needing to apply but how careful and controlled that pressure was. He needed to open the scarred tissue but not penetrate the heart beneath.

His response of a grunt to her statement could have actually been satisfaction at the gleam of healthy, pink tissue revealed, but Anna caught something that seemed more like a reprimand that it had taken that long to diagnose the condition correctly and arrange livesaving treatment.

The criticism was unfair. This patient, Colin Herbert, had avoided even going to his GP for years, putting his shortness of breath down to being unfit and his tiredness to the broken nights of helping to parent two young children. Even initial investigations hadn't pointed to a cardiac cause for these symptoms in the thirty-seven-year-old. It had taken a CT scan and then cardiac catheterisation to reveal the rare condition, and that had left Anna having to decide whether to attempt an unfamiliar surgery herself or refer Colin to someone more experienced.

The news of Luke Davenport's return had made it worthwhile delaying the surgery for just a little longer. If Colin could stay in St Piran's, close to his family and friends, it would probably speed his recovery. It would certainly make this period far less stressful for his wife and children.

Luke had now begun peeling the pericardium away from the heart muscle. The anaesthetist, amongst others, was peering into the wound with fascination.

'Looks like plastic,' one of them commented.

Another grunt came from the surgeon and then silence fell in the theatre again. His requests for instruments or responses to updates on monitoring were curt. He barely acknowledged Anna's assistance. Surgery with this man was never going to be a relaxed affair, then. Not that he shouldn't be concentrating fiercely on the task at hand, but that had never stopped Anna from involving her colleagues. Testing their knowledge and sharing her own. Discussing problems and allowing contributions to any trouble-shooting needed. The way mentors had done with her in the past.

Being Mr Davenport's assistant might be like treading water as far as her career was concerned. Demoted to second best but only allowed to learn anything new by observation. Anna could feel the frustration creeping in already. She might well have to bite the bullet and start fighting for the chance to prove herself elsewhere. Having to apply for sought-after positions where most of the applicants, as well as those making the final choice, were male. Skilled, powerful, alpha men like the one working opposite her right now. Men who needed a lot of convincing that a woman was capable of being their equal.

But even as Anna felt the tightening knot of a tension she'd been aware of for her entire career in medicine, something else was pushing into her awareness. The skill Luke was demonstrating here told her that, merely through observation, she could learn from him. His timing was exquisite as he allowed the heart to beat and squeeze out blood, then advancing his scalpel to free the casing a little further in each fraction of time when the heart was filling again and, therefore, still enough to be safe.

The equipment and the technician needed to put the patient on bypass were standing by. Peeling the pericardium from the back of the heart would be the most difficult part of this procedure and Luke was keeping the option of using cardiac bypass available.

He would prefer not to, however, and so far things were going smoothly. The staff were more than competent and he had no complaints about Dr Bartlett's assistance. She was good. Somehow she had instantly tuned in with how he worked, and it was like having an extra pair of his own hands in action. Smaller hands, of course. More nimble ones. It was quite possible that Anna would be better suited to continue this when he got to the tight patches around the back.

The thought was embryonic. Barely registered, in fact, because Luke was so focused on what he was doing. Anna had the edge of the hardened pericardium caught in a pair of forceps, holding it up and helping to peel it away as he cut carefully beneath it.

He was using the scalpel with absolute precision. Tiny cuts as close to the hard casing as possible. There was less than a millimetre of space to work in. Luke was vaguely aware that the atmosphere around him was tense and that he could change it by relaxing a little and talking more, but he had no desire to do that.

He was being watched in this, his first surgery on returning to his role as head of department for cardiac surgery. Being watched and judged. They were wondering if his experience in the army had changed him—as a surgeon or as a person.

Of course it had. He had honed skills and one of them was the ability to focus no matter what kind of distractions were around. What anyone else, including

Anna—no, especially Anna—might be thinking of him was irrelevant. What mattered here was a good outcome for his patient. His focus was on that scalpel. Right on its tip, which was the only part of the blade he was using.

The blood seemed to come from nowhere. There'd been small bleeders up to now that Anna had dealt with but this was a sudden gush that drowned his scalpel, washed over the fingertips of his gloves and began to form a pool. The beat of the heart made it appear briefly and then the blood washed over it again, totally obscuring his vision.

Red.

So red.

And warm. He could feel it on his fingers. Sticky life blood, ebbing rapidly from where it was supposed to be.

Someone was dying.

He could hear their screams. He could hear the sound of gunfire, too, and smell something burning.

He had to do something.

But he couldn't move.

Anna saw the moment the small artery got nicked by the tip of the scalpel. It needed more than diathermy. Clamping and tying it off shouldn't present more than a momentary delay. She picked up a clamp, ready to hand it to Luke, already eyeing up the suture material he would need.

But he didn't request the clamp. The hand that was holding the scalpel was as still as stone. Frozen.

And then the surgeon looked up, straight at her,

and Anna's own heart missed a beat. He was looking at her but he was seeing something very different. Something that had absolutely nothing to do with this room or this patient or the surgery he was in the middle of performing.

He was seeing something...terrifying?

Her heart missed only a single beat. With the next one she was moving smoothly. Using the clamp in her hand and then a suture. To those around them, it would look as though Luke had silently requested her control of the nuisance bleeding. Given his virtually silent technique up until now, it wouldn't have surprised anyone. But Anna had been the only one to see the look in his eyes. Had felt the way he had frozen, and it had quite possibly been the most disturbing moment she had ever encountered in Theatre.

It took only moments to deal with the artery and a nurse used suction to clear the operating field again. Anna heard Luke's indrawn breath and looked up to see the way he blinked with such deliberation it gave the impression of a switch being flicked off. And then normal service was resumed. The surgery carried on as though nothing awkward had happened.

But something had changed. Maybe it was an acknowledgment of the way Anna had rescued the situation. Or maybe it was the beginning of the kind of bond that could weld a tight team together.

'If I tilt the heart,' Luke said quietly a short time later, 'you're in a much better position to deal with that patch at the back. Are you happy with what you've seen of the technique?'

'Yes.' The increase in her own heart rate wasn't trepidation. It was far more like excitement. The challenge of trying something new. The idea that she might be on a new journey to learn skills that nobody else could teach so well. There was something like relief mixed in there as well because her future here at St Piran's looked a little less bleak. There was even a letting go of a little of that resentment towards the man who had reclaimed his job. The job she had desperately wanted to keep.

Thank goodness her hand was steady as she took hold of the scalpel. Even better was Luke's quiet praise as he watched what she was doing.

'That's excellent. Keep going. The more of this we can remove, the better the outlook for this patient will be.'

By the time the surgery was complete, the outlook was good and Luke finally stood back from the table and stripped off his gloves, thanking everyone for their contribution to the successful procedure. As he turned to leave, he tugged at his mask, breaking the strings that held it in place, and for the first time Anna saw more than those intensely blue eyes.

She saw a rugged, unsmiling face, with deep furrows from his nose to the corners of a mouth wide enough to balance the size of his nose. He wasn't what you'd call classically good-looking but it was hard to look away. The raw, unpolished masculinity was compelling. Those frown lines were still there at the top of his nose so maybe they were a permanent feature. When Luke started tugging off his bloodstained gown as he neared the swing doors of the theatre, Anna saw the lean muscles of deeply tanned arms. She could have sworn that those doors opened of their own accord, which was impossible but there was something about the commanding height and the way this man moved that made the notion perfectly feasible.

Luke Davenport was a soldier as much as—or possibly more than—he was a surgeon.

Every female in the room was watching as he made his exit, no doubt equally impressed, but Anna knew she would be the only one who found the image conflicting. Downright confusing, really.

Yes, Luke had lived up to his reputation as a gifted surgeon and he was apparently prepared to let her close enough to absorb valuable new skills but...what the heck had happened back when that bleeding had occurred?

Was Luke even aware of the way he had zoned out like that? He certainly hadn't acknowledged her contribution to the situation. He'd been injured during his time on the front line. An injury that was serious enough to prevent his return to his army position. Maybe he'd received wounds to more than his leg? A head injury perhaps that had left him with a form of epilepsy? Absence seizures where the sufferer was unaware of their surroundings and could freeze for up to a minute or so would explain it, but if that was the case, there was no way he should be still holding a scalpel.

That explanation didn't seem plausible, however. A seizure would have someone looking blank and Luke hadn't looked blank at all. He'd looked... *Haunted* was the word that sprang to mind. As though he'd been sucked into a flashback that he hadn't been able to escape from. This seemed far more likely but no less excusable.

What if he'd been close to the pulmonary artery? Or, worse, the aorta? Even a few seconds of delayed response in trying to control the kind of bleeding those vessels were capable of producing could have been disastrous. What really bothered Anna was knowing that she was probably the only person who had noticed the incident, which meant that saying anything might be seen as a form of professional sour grapes. Revenge, even, for the reprimand she'd received because of her late arrival for the case. Everyone knew that she'd missed out on the job as departmental head when she'd first applied. Now they'd be watching to see how she was handling her new role. To make an accusation that could have major repercussions on Luke's career within the first few hours of them working together was unthinkable.

There was only one person who might accept and understand her concerns. The same person who could provide an explanation that could possibly negate the need to take it any further. If nothing else, Luke deserved the courtesy of direct communication but it was also a conversation that needed to happen in private.

Right now her focus had to remain with their patient as he went into Recovery and was then settled into the intensive care unit for monitoring and post-surgical care. She had surgery she was due to perform with a registrar to remove sternal wires from a patient who'd had heart surgery a long time ago but was continuing to suffer pain that was probably a reaction to the foreign material in her body. The procedure wouldn't take too long and she'd planned to use her lunch break after that to talk to Luke and suggest a detailed ward round to bring him up to speed with all the cardiac inpatients.

Maybe she'd better use that time for something rather more personal. To make a judgment call on the integrity of the man she had to be able to trust if she was going to work with him at all. For some reason, the prospect of getting that close to Luke Davenport was more intimidating than anything Anna could remember facing.

She needed to think of it as nothing more than a new professional challenge. Backing away or trying to make it easier was not an acceptable option. She'd take it face on. Anna gave a decisive nod as she followed Colin's bed out of Theatre. She actually found herself almost smiling, having made the decision to confront Luke. If the situation had been reversed she had no doubts at all that Luke would be addressing the issue. He would probably have done so on the spot, with no thought of sparing her the humiliation of an audience.

Maybe this was a subtle opportunity to demonstrate not only her ability to do the job he had reclaimed but that her way of doing it might be better.

The prospect of the private interview with Mr Davenport was no longer simply intimidating.

It was…exhilarating.

CHAPTER TWO

THE need to escape was overwhelming.

And impossible.

Having ripped off the theatre scrubs, Luke had gone straight to the showers in the changing room but he couldn't wash away the aftermath of those few seconds in the middle of Colin Herbert's surgery. Turning the water to lukewarm hadn't brought its recent comfort of familiarity. Even the icy cold blast he finished with couldn't shock it out of his head the way it could chase nightmares away.

His clothes felt wrong, too. His trousers and an open-necked shirt felt too smooth against skin used to the thick fabric of camouflage overalls. At least he didn't have to knot a tie around his neck, like tying a bow on a pretty parcel. How ridiculous would that seem when he would far rather be fastening the Velcro straps of a Kevlar bulletproof vest over his shoulders. Feeling the weight of the armour plating and the bulkiness of pockets stuffed with whatever he might need at a moment's notice.

He felt too light as he strode out of the theatre suite

without a backward glance. Almost as though he was floating.

Lost.

The corridors were full of people going about their business, but it was all so slow. There was no sense of urgency as beds and wheelchairs were propelled to new destinations or staff moved from one task to another. They had time to stop and chat to each other. He saw people smiling and even heard laughter at one point. Someone said hello to him and Luke managed to smile back, but the facial contortion felt grim.

He didn't belong here any more. This was a joke that wasn't the least bit funny. Like the whole of civilian life. It was a game. A pretence. Meaningless.

Going outside was better. A brisk walk around the sprawling, modern structure that was busy St Piran's hospital. A helicopter was coming in to land, no doubt bringing a trauma patient to the emergency department. Luke's eyes narrowed as he watched it intently and soaked in the sound of its rotors. If anything was likely to give him a flashback, surely that was?

It wasn't going to happen. He knew that because he was aware of the potential and he was focused. In control. The way he should have been for every second of that surgery. He kept watching anyway. Testing himself, until the helicopter took off again and disappeared into the distance.

A tempting distance. He could start walking again and just keep going. Stride down the cobbled streets of this picturesque market town until he got to the harbour. Or, better yet, a stretch of beach where he could push himself with the added difficulty of walking in sand. Or hurl himself into the surf with its magic, albeit temporary, ability to numb his body and brain and wash everything away. An effect a thousand times better than a cold shower.

But this was early December. It was freezing and his wetsuit was hanging to dry on his back porch after his early swim that morning. His leg hurt, too, thanks to standing so still for so long in Theatre. And he was here because he had a job to do. A job he had been lucky to be able to come back to. An anchor. Something to build on and the only thing he had, really. Given time, this might start making sense again, giving him the bonus of feeling like he was doing something worthwhile even, though after this morning that goal seemed further away than ever.

At least the patient who had been unfortunate enough to be his first case back here was doing well.

It was nearly an hour later that Luke arrived in the intensive care unit and Colin was awake, though very drowsy. A nurse was by his side and she smiled warmly at the surgeon.

'I've been hearing all about the surgery,' she said to him. 'I wish I could have seen it. I hear you did an amazing job.'

Luke made a noncommittal sound without looking away from the monitor screen giving detailed recordings of what was happening inside Colin's heart thanks to the catheter that had been positioned at the very end of the surgery.

Surgery that could have been a total disaster.

An amazing job? He didn't think so.

The nurse was still hovering. He heard the intake of her breath. She was about to say something else. Possibly another admiring comment. Luke shifted his gaze to give her what he hoped would be a quelling glance. Sure enough, her mouth snapped shut, a flush of colour stained her cheeks and she turned to fiddle with an IV port on her patient's arm.

Colin's eyes flickered open. He saw the surgeon standing beside his bed and smiled weakly.

'I'm still here,' he said, his voice slightly raspy. 'Thanks, Doc.'

Luke returned the smile. 'You're doing fine. We'll keep an eye on you in here for a bit and there's a few tests we need to run later today, but we'll get you onto the ward as soon as possible. Do you have anything you want to ask me about?'

Colin's head moved in a slow shake. 'I think my wife's asked everything already. Dr Bartlett seems to know what she's talking about. I'm still a bit groggy to take it in but I'm alive and that's what matters.' He smiled again, his relief obvious.

'I'll be back later. I can talk to you and your wife then.'

'Dr Bartlett said how well things had gone. What a great job you did.'

'Oh?' That surprised him. Or did Anna not worry about embellishing the truth when it came to reassuring her post-operative patients?

'The wife's just gone to find my mum downstairs

and look after the kids so Mum can come in for a visit. Hey, did I say thanks?'

'You did.'

Luke knew he sounded brusque. He didn't need the nurse to give a look vaguely reminiscent of the glare he'd seen more than once in Theatre from Anna. Did she know? Had word spread that his new colleague had had to leap in and prevent the error he'd made during surgery becoming a potential catastrophe?

'Where is Dr Bartlett?' he asked the nurse as he signed off a new addition to the drug chart and prepared to leave the intensive care unit. 'I need to have a word with her.'

'Back in Theatre, I expect.'

Of course she was. He'd seen the case listed on the whiteboard in the theatre suite. A sternal wire removal. In the same theatre Colin had been in. With the same theatre staff, presumably. Would Anna be checking whether anyone else had noticed the incident and could back up her report on the concerns she now had about the abilities of the returning head of department?

She hadn't said anything at the time. Hadn't even sent a significant glance in his direction, but that said something in itself, didn't it? She hadn't bothered to hide what she thought of him returning to take her job in those early glares. It suggested that she was weighing the implications. Making sure she used the ammunition he had handed her to best effect by choosing the best time and place.

Dammit! How the hell had it happened? He was well used to the nightmares, but to have a flashback like that happen during the day? In the middle of surgery? It was appalling. He wasn't quite sure of how long he had lost his focus but he had no doubts about what could have happened if there hadn't been someone as quick as Anna on the other side of that table.

It wouldn't happen again. He'd lost focus because that had been his first slot back in a civilian theatre. His concentration had been too much on a procedure that couldn't have been more different to the kind of work in an Iraqi field hospital or, more particularly, as a member of the medical emergency response team on a mission on the front line. It had been slow and fiddly compared to the aggressive, lifesaving measures of treating major trauma under circumstances as tough as they got. It had been a mental ambush, triggered by the unexpected amount of blood he'd seen, or the way it had pooled, maybe.

Whatever. It wouldn't happen again because he'd be ready for it and wasn't going to allow a loss of control. Luke was perfectly confident of his ability to do just that.

But would Anna believe it?

A pair of green eyes came to mind. Framed by dark lashes that were unadorned by any mascara. Angry eyes. Accusing and assessing at the same time. What would they be like, softened by trust?

Even more compelling, no doubt, but Luke had to wonder if he would ever witness such a change.

Winning Anna's trust was not even the priority it probably should be because this underlying tension… this waiting for something potentially unpleasant to

happen, was oddly welcome. It made him feel a little
more alive than he had ever felt since he'd been shipped
home.

He was there, in the hospital canteen. Sitting alone near
a window.

Brooding was the word that sprang to Anna's mind.
Hunched over a plate of food he appeared to be toying
with rather than eating. The big room was well popu-
lated and noisy. Was that why the table with its single
occupant seemed to stand out like a beacon? Or was
her glance drawn there like a magnet because so many
other people were eyeing the newcomer and probably
talking about him?

She could understand not wanting to be in there and
either listening to or being the object of the kind of spec-
ulation and gossip rife in any group of people as large
as the St Piran's staff was, but why on earth hadn't he
done what she almost always did—buy a sandwich and
some fruit to take back to the privacy of an office?

Was he hoping for company? There must be so many
people there who knew him but there was a hierarchy involved and maybe there weren't any of his peers around.
Anna found herself hoping that by the time she got to
the end of this long queue someone would have joined
Luke. That way, she wouldn't need to feel guilty about
not doing so.

Not that she didn't want the chance to talk to him, but
this was hardly the place to have the kind of conversation she had in mind, and the idea of making small talk
with this man was not appealing. It would be dishonest,

in a way, when they both knew what needed to be discussed—the kind of game-playing Anna had never had the slightest inclination to indulge in. Besides, Luke was making himself look so very unapproachable. Self-contained and cool. If he knew and agreed with all the praise going on behind his back, his self-image would have to be more than a little inflated. Maybe his own company was enough?

Like Anna, Luke had changed out of his scrubs and was dressed neatly. Professionally. Anna slid her tray along the metal bars in front of the food cabinets and found herself running her hand down the side of her close-fitting skirt to make sure it wasn't creased. And then touching her hair to ensure that no tendrils had escaped the sleek knot at the back of her neck. She could do professional, too. Better than anybody, which was no surprise given the amount of practice she'd had.

'Anna… Hi!'

A new burst of hungry staff members was milling behind her, settling into the queue. The greeting had come from Charlotte Alexander, one of St Piran's cardiology staff members, who was behind a couple of nurses who'd stopped to stare into a chilled cabinet containing rolls of sushi.

If Anna made personal friendships among her colleagues, which she didn't, Charlotte would have been at the top of her list. While their relationship was friendly, it was still as professional as Anna could keep it. Even now, when the loose top Charlotte was wearing reminded her that she'd noticed the obvious increase in weight a week or two ago and it had occurred to her that Charlotte could well be pregnant, she wasn't about to ask such a personal question.

Girl stuff, like heart-to-hearts or sharing secrets and especially wedding or baby talk, was never going to happen. They were in the same category as frilly clothes or loose hair or make-up. Badges of femininity. Barriers to acceptance as an equal in a male-dominated profession. How did women like Charlotte manage it? Looking and dressing in a way that accentuated their best features but still having the respect of both colleagues and patients?

It made Anna feel like she had some kind of split personality, but it was so engrained now it was getting hard to know whether it was the Anna at home or the Dr Anna Bartlett at work that was the real her. The only thing she could be sure of was that never the twain could meet.

But sometimes…like right now…it struck Anna that her work persona was simply armour. Concealing anything feminine and vulnerable. Giving her focus and strength. Her gaze strayed of its own accord back to the solitary figure of Luke Davenport. What was it about him that made her even more aware that she didn't look as feminine or, God help her, attractive as she could? Just as well her work persona was so firmly engrained. If armour was what it was, she might need its protection more than ever.

Charlotte had been held up too long. She moved around the nurses who couldn't decide between the teriyaki chicken or smoked salmon.

'Hi.' She smiled at Anna. 'How's it going?'

'Very good. Theatre's over for today and both patients are doing well. I just took the sternal wires out of your Violet Perry. I'm sure the irritation will be gone and she'll be pain-free in no time.'

'That's great.' Charlotte was peering into the sandwich cabinet. 'Hmm. Chicken and Camembert sounds nice. Or turkey and cranberry. No...we'll be sick of that soon. Have you seen how many Christmas decorations are up already?'

'Mmm. Way too soon, in my opinion.' Anna found the seasonal celebrations at work disquieting. Too much of a bridge to personal lives.

'Ham salad,' Charlotte decided, reaching for one of the triangular plastic boxes. 'Oh...weren't you in Theatre with Davenport this morning? Doing Colin Herbert's pericardectomy?'

'Yes.' Again, Anna's gaze strayed towards Luke.

'How did it go?'

For a split second Anna considered confiding in Charlotte. Telling her all about how Luke had frozen and she'd had to take over the surgery. If she did, she'd be taking a step she could never undo. Charlotte would tell her husband, James, and the snowball effect might sweep them all into places they would rather not go. This man was going to be her professional partner from now on. They would be working closely together. Closer than she was with Charlotte or James or any of the other cardiology or cardiac surgery staff. She and Luke would share duties in Theatre, on ward rounds, during outpatient clinics.

As though he sensed her stare, Luke raised his head

to look up. Straight at Anna. Just for a heartbeat she held his gaze and tried to analyse what she could feel in that connection.

Maybe he wasn't bad tempered and brooding, she decided as she looked swiftly away. Strangely, for that moment in time, it had looked more like something deeper. Possibly even unhappiness? What reason could he have?

He had been forced to leave the army early due to his injury, hadn't he? Perhaps Luke didn't want to be here just as much as Anna didn't want him to be.

She looked away but not before she felt an odd squeeze beneath her ribs. She knew what it was like to feel unhappy.

Lonely.

Did she really have to kick someone who might already be down? Maybe she was overreacting. She had stepped in so fast, after all. If he'd been about to move at the same time it wouldn't have been such a big deal at all. Not that she'd had the impression he would have moved that fast, but it wouldn't hurt to think about things a little longer.

'It was amazing,' she heard herself telling Charlotte, absently picking up a pack of chicken sandwiches. 'I've never seen a technique quite that precise. I got to do a patch behind the left ventricle and it wasn't easy.'

'Wish I could have seen it,' Charlotte sighed. 'Did you know he'd ordered the observation deck closed?'

Her disappointment was clear. It was an opportunity to express caution about the man's personality or even say something negative. Curiously, Anna felt the need to defend Luke.

'I guess you wouldn't want too many people watching when you're doing your first case after a long time away.'

'I guess. How's Colin doing now?'

'Really good. We might be able to move him to the ward later today. Tomorrow, anyway, if he stays this stable. We should be well past the danger period for complications from acute dilation of cardiac chambers but his heart's still got to get used to dealing with much more of a blood flow.'

'I'll get up to see him this afternoon. Here's hoping the surgery report won't be far away. I'll be very interested to read it.'

So would Anna, but her agreement was silent. If she'd voiced it, her tone might have suggested that there would be more to read about than Charlotte might expect. They were getting near the cashiers' part of the counter now and she turned her attention to the baskets of fruit. An apple, she decided. The nice-looking green one on the top of the second basket.

The crash that came from somewhere in the kitchens behind the food counters was astonishingly loud. Metallic. Jarring enough for every head in the cafeteria to swivel sharply in that direction and for conversation to cease abruptly.

And in that second or two of startled silence a scream rang out. And then a cry for help.

Jaws dropped as staff members looked at each other

as though trying to confirm the reality of what was happening. Anna heard Charlotte's gasp behind her but she was watching something else. Weirdly, her instinct had been to look away from the source of the sound so she had seen the first movement in the crowd. A reaction time so fast it was hard to process.

Luke Davenport was on his feet. His chair tipped backwards and he pushed at the table in front of him rather than stepping around it. The table also tipped, the tray sliding off to send china and cutlery crashing to the floor but Luke didn't even spare it a glance. He was heading straight for the kitchen.

Access was blocked by the tall, glass-fronted cabinets apart from the space where Anna was, beside the tills and the fruit baskets. There was a flap in the counter beside the last till where kitchen staff could go in and out with the trolleys of used dishes but Luke didn't bother to stop and lift it. Or maybe he didn't see it. He swept the baskets clear to send apples and oranges bouncing around the feet of those still standing motionless and then he vaulted the space, making the action seem effortless.

Kitchen staff were backing away hurriedly, but not quickly enough for Luke.

'Move!' he barked. 'Clear the way. What's happened?'

'Over here,' someone shouted. 'Oh, my God... I think he's dead.'

Luke took several steps forward. Between the tills, Anna could see the blue uniforms of kitchen staff moving. Clearing a space near the stoves in front of which a large man in a white jacket lay very still.

Luke took in the scene. He turned his head with a single, rapid motion.

'Anna!' he shouted. 'Get in here. I need you.'

Someone had raised the flap now but, if they hadn't, it occurred to Anna that she might have tried to leap over it, too. Luke needed her?

The man was obviously one of the chefs. His white hat had come off when he'd collapsed and was lying amongst the pots and pans of an overturned rack.

Luke kicked one of them aside as Anna raced into the kitchen. 'Get rid of those,' he ordered. 'Someone help me turn him. Did anyone see what happened?'

'He just fell,' a frightened woman offered. 'One minute he was cleaning down the cooker and then he toppled sideways.'

'What's his name?'

'Roger.'

The man had been rolled onto his back now. Luke gripped his shoulder and shook it firmly, hunched down so that he could lean close and shout.

'Roger? Can you hear me? Open your eyes!'

He barely waited for the response that didn't come. His hands on Roger's chin and forehead, he tilted the head back to open his airway.

'Does anyone know him?' he demanded. 'Medical history?'

'He takes pills,' someone said. 'For his blood pressure, I think.'

'No, it's his heart,' another voice added.

The few seconds that Luke had kept his fingertips on the side of Roger's neck and his cheek close to his face had been enough to let him know that there was no pulse or respiration to be felt or seen. Anna crouched on the other side of the collapsed man as Luke raised his fist and brought it down squarely in the centre of the man's chest. A precordial thump that was unlikely to be successful but was worth a try.

Ready to start CPR, Anna was thinking fast, compiling a mental list of what they would need. Luke was way ahead of her.

'Get a crash trolley in here. Find a cardiac arrest button. Send for someone in ED or wherever's closest. Anna, start compressions.' He looked up at the silent, horrified onlookers. 'Move!'

They backed away. Anna heard someone yelling into the canteen for the cardiac arrest button to be pushed. If there wasn't one in there, it wouldn't be too far away. She positioned her hands, locked her elbows and started pushing on Roger's chest. He was a big man and it was hard work to compress the sternum enough to be effective.

Ten...twenty...thirty compressions. At least someone would arrive with a bag-mask unit very soon so she didn't have to worry about the implications of unprotected mouth-to-mouth respirations on a stranger.

The faint possibility of contracting something like hepatitis didn't seem to occur to Luke. Or it didn't bother him.

'Hold it,' he ordered Anna, pinching Roger's nose and tilting his head back as he spoke. Then he sealed the man's mouth with his own. One slow breath…and then another.

Anna started compressions again, the image of Luke's lips pressed to someone's face emblazoned in her mind. The kiss of life… She'd seen it before, though it was a rarity in a medical setting. Was that why it was so disturbing this time? Shocking, in fact. She had to concentrate on her silent counting until it was time to warn Luke.

'Twenty-seven, twenty-eight, twenty-nine, thirty…'

By the time they had completed another set of compressions and breaths, there were new voices nearby and the rattle of a trolley.

'Crash team,' someone announced. 'We'll take over now.'

'I've got it, thanks,' Luke growled.

'But it's what we—'

'We just need the gear,' the surgeon interrupted. 'And some assistance.'

Anna could feel the resentment at not being allowed to do what they thought they had been summoned for, but a life pack was lifted from the trolley and put on the floor along with an IV roll, a bag mask and a portable oxygen tank.

She carried on with the chest compressions, pausing only to let Luke rip the chef's jacket and the singlet underneath open to expose the chest and stick the pads in place. On direction, one of the doctors in the crash team secured his airway and attached oxygen to the bag mask, holding it in place until Anna paused again.

Could she ask to hand over compressions to someone else? This was enough of a physical effort to make her aware of perspiration dampening her shirt. No, she wouldn't ask. She was with Luke on this.

He had been the one to respond and identify the crisis, which made this man his patient until he chose to hand him over. And he'd asked for Anna's help. Roger was their patient and they could do this as well, probably better, than the junior doctors assigned to crash-team duties for the day.

'Stop compressions.' Luke was watching the screen of the life pack, waiting for a readable trace to appear. 'V fib,' he announced moments later. 'Charging to three hundred joules. Everyone stand clear.'

The junior doctors inched back, exchanging glances.

'Who is this guy?' Anna heard one of them ask another.

'Luke Davenport,' came the response. 'You know, the surgeon who's just got back from Iraq?'

'Oh...'

In the short space of time it had taken for three stacked shocks to be delivered, the atmosphere in this inner circle around the victim changed. The crash team, who had been busy resenting not being allowed to showcase their skills in managing an arrest, suddenly couldn't do enough to help their leader.

'Do you want an intubation kit, Mr Davenport?'

'Shall I draw up some adrenaline? Atropine?'

'Here's a sixteen-gauge cannula. And a flush.'

'Dr Bartlett? Do you need a break?'

Anna sat back on her heels, nodding. There was plenty of scientific evidence that compressions became less effective after two minutes unless someone else took a turn. She didn't move far away, however. She watched, totally amazed by the speed at which Luke worked. And she noticed things she hadn't noticed before.

Like the streaks of grey in his short brown hair. They had to be premature because she knew he was only a few years older than her and couldn't have hit forty quite yet. He had such neat fingernails too and his hands looked so different without gloves. Far more masculine, which made their speed and cleverness more impressive as he gained intravenous access and secured the line.

His brain was working just as fast. He seemed to be able to think of everything at once and keep tabs on what everybody was doing, but most of all, Anna was caught by the way he'd taken a trolley of equipment and a group of young medics who hadn't been thrilled not to be allowed to take over and forged them into a team that was now working under difficult conditions as well as they could have in a resuscitation bay in Emergency.

It was a team that had achieved success even before Luke had made a move to secure Roger's airway with an endotracheal tube. When the static cleared from the next, single shock delivered, the flat line suddenly gave a blip. And then another…

'Sinus rhythm,' one of the crash team said triumphantly. 'Yes.'

'Have we got a stretcher?' Luke still hadn't relaxed. 'Let's get this man into the ED. Or CCU.'

Charlotte had edged her way to the back of the

kitchen. 'Great job, Mr Davenport. Would you like to hand over now?'

'Call me Luke,' he said, still watching the monitor. The rhythm was picking up steadily and Roger was taking his own breaths now. The chef's eyes flickered and he groaned loudly.

And, finally, Anna saw the grim lines of Luke's face soften a little. He leaned down and gripped Roger's shoulder again with his hand—the way he had when he'd first begun this resuscitation effort. He didn't shake it this time. This was a reassuring touch.

'Just relax,' he told Roger. 'We're looking after you. Everything's all right.'

He looked up at Charlotte and gave a nod to indicate transfer of responsibility. Charlotte moved closer to talk to him, but as she moved, Luke shifted his gaze to Anna.

And something inside her tightened and then melted.

From the moment this incident had started—from when she'd heard the scream and seen Luke's instantaneous response, she'd been aware of his total command of the situation. Of his faultless performance and ability to absorb additional resources and personnel and then… right at the end…an indication that he really cared about this patient.

An impressive mix. If his glance had been in any way smug, it could have driven Anna into a defensive corner she might never have emerged from, but there was no hint of smugness. No self-satisfaction even. The fraction of time he held her gaze sent a message that was more like, We did it. This time, at least.

The triumph that was there was on the patient's behalf. Behind that was the acknowledgment of defeat in other cases and the sadness that they couldn't always win. Shining over both impressions was a kind of promise. A determination to always fight the odds and do the best possible job.

It sucked her right in.

She could work with this man. Could respect him. Like him.

More than that, in fact, judging by the odd ripple of sensation that caressed her spine and sent tingles through the rest of her body.

Dear Lord, she was attracted to him? No wonder she'd been so aware of her own appearance when she'd been standing in line with Charlotte. It explained a lot but it was a reaction that had to be crushed instantly. Allowing something that personal to threaten a professional relationship would be the ultimate play on femininity.

The reason women couldn't be seen as equals in this arena was largely because of the perception that they allowed emotion to cloud their judgment. Or, worse, they put a priority on relationships and undermined their careers by taking time off to have babies.

Not Anna Bartlett. It wasn't on any agenda she'd ever had.

Luke's return and—worse—his attractiveness were roadblocks. Ones she could detour around, which would see her working somewhere else, or deal with if the pull to stay put was strong enough. Either way, getting even remotely close to Luke Davenport would be a mistake.

It was Anna who broke the eye contact.

And turned away.

CHAPTER THREE

THE crisis over, Luke found he couldn't drag his eyes away from Anna.

Not that he hadn't spotted her the moment she'd walked into the canteen. He'd taken a good look then because he hadn't been sure it was her. Something about the height and body shape of the woman had seemed familiar but he'd only seen her eyes before this so it could have been anybody.

Just an attractive female member of staff. A senior member, obviously, because of the way she held herself. The way she moved with the confidence of someone who knew she was very good at what she did. And maybe he recognised something in the way this woman was dressed. Power dressing, really, with that pencil skirt and neat shirt. She probably had a matching jacket that would make the outfit the female equivalent of a man's suit. And what was that horrible thing she'd done to her hair? It was all scraped back into a round thing that made her look like a cartoon version of a librarian or frumpy secretary. All she needed was some thick-rimmed spectacles to complete the picture.

When her head had turned to scan the room, he hadn't

needed to be close enough to see the colour of her eyes to recognise that this was, indeed, Anna Bartlett. While she wasn't radiating resentment right now, there was an air of containment about her that suggested she didn't change her mind easily. A reserve that could well morph into an arctic-type chill when she saw him. A woman that knew her own mind and woe betide anyone that got in her way. Like him.

Luke almost sighed as he dropped his gaze back to a meal he wasn't particularly interested in. He wasn't enjoying this lunchtime experience much at all, in fact. He knew that many of the people around had to be talking about him. Gossiping. The happy chatter and laughter going on around him, even the smell of abundant, hot food all seemed irrelevant. Superficial.

The crash and then the scream had been real, though. He'd reacted on autopilot. He wasn't sure what had made him demand Anna as an assistant. Possibly because she had been the only staff member nearby that he could call by name. Or maybe it was the memory of how well they had worked together in Theatre only a short time ago.

It had been a good choice. The crisis had been dealt with and a life had been saved and it had only been then, when it was virtually done and dusted and he was handing his patient into the care of a new team, that Luke had allowed anything else to enter his head. It was then that he'd had his first close-up look at Dr Bartlett and he'd had the curious impression that he'd been looking at something he wasn't supposed to be seeing.

No wonder! The cool professional he'd seen queuing

for her lunch was absent. This woman, standing in the canteen kitchen with a creased skirt and a shirt that had come untucked on one side, was…wrong, somehow. Even more disconcerting was that a thick lock of dark blonde hair had escaped the bun thing and lay against a long, pale neck.

Her cheeks were flushed. From the exertion and stress of doing CPR or was she embarrassed at being dishevelled? Even her eyes looked different. Enlarged pupils made them seem softer. Warmer.

Good grief…she was rather lovely.

Any impression of warmth vanished, however, as Luke stared at her, unable to drag his gaze away.

And then she dismissed him! Simply turned on her heel and walked away.

How rude. No genuine warmth there, then. Anna Bartlett was clearly a career woman through and through, and she probably saw him as nothing less than an obstacle in her scramble to the top of that ladder. Any hope that she might discuss this morning's incident with him before reporting it to a higher authority faded and disappeared.

Charlotte, the cardiologist, was saying something to him, he realised. Something about whether he'd like to come with them to the emergency department to see what the investigations Roger needed would reveal.

'Yes,' he said. 'Please.'

'You'll remember Ben Carter?'

'Of course.'

'And have you met Josh O'Hara? No, you wouldn't

have. He joined the A and E staff while you were away.'

Luke kept up with the pace set by the people pushing the stretcher, heading away from the canteen and any areas that his assistant was likely to be heading for.

He'd see Anna again soon enough. Doing a ward round later today or perhaps in the departmental meeting scheduled for early tomorrow morning. Given how he felt about her in the wake of that dismissal, it might even be too soon.

The aura of the war hero already surrounding the return of Luke Davenport to St Piran's had evolved into something far more tangible by the time Anna was halfway through her ward round later that afternoon.

He had become a living legend.

Thanks to the crowd in the canteen at the time, accounts of the incident would have spread like wildfire and reached every corner of this institution in no time flat. Spilling into ears eager for the smallest details.

The junior nursing staff on the cardiology ward were discussing it when Anna paused outside the central station to collect some patient notes she needed.

'It was like something in the movies,' someone was saying in awed tones. 'He just pushed everything off the counter and jumped over it.'

'I heard he did mouth-to-mouth without even using a face shield.'

'Yeah...'

'Is the guy still alive?'

'Apparently he's in the cath lab right now. He'll

probably get admitted in here or CCU when they're finished.'

'Do you think Mr Davenport will come down with him?'

'Ooh…I hope so.'

The giggling from the young nurses was irritating. Anna decided it was because her own participation in the incident had been totally eclipsed by the actions of St Piran's new superhero. Except that she couldn't convince herself to be that petty. The irritation was really there because part of her was as star-struck as everyone else seemed to be. The man was intriguing. Compelling. Apparently trustworthy. And that was disturbing because Anna felt that she knew something about him that no one else knew. Or would believe.

If she wanted to discuss her concerns with someone, the obvious choice would be Albert White, the CEO of St Piran's. He would listen to any concerns she might have about Luke's abilities. He might even believe her and, if he did, he might set some kind of probationary programme in place. Things like that did not remain confidential. Eventually, it would leak. Given his performance in the canteen and new status amongst the staff, nobody else would believe Anna.

She might find herself more alone than she'd ever been in her struggle to break through the glass ceiling of her gender. It could affect how well she was able to do her own job. She stood to lose the trust and possibly even the co-operation of the people she worked with and teamwork was vital in this line of work.

Tread carefully, she reminded herself, even when her

demotion from being team leader had been rubbed in when a flurry of activity had heralded the new arrival in the coronary care unit adjacent to the ward and more than the necessary staff numbers flocked to greet both the patient and the new head of department.

Roger the chef was made comfortable and wired up so that every beat of his heart could be monitored, the trace and its extra information like blood pressure and the level of oxygen in his blood appearing on one of the screens flanking the central nurses' station. It was there that Luke caught up with Anna.

'He needs urgent revascularisation,' he informed her. 'I'm hoping you can fit him in on your list for tomorrow.'

Anna closed her eyes for a split second as she groaned inwardly. She opened them to find herself under intense scrutiny.

'Is that a problem?' Luke asked. 'You don't have any elective patients on the list?'

'I do, but I've just been talking to a Mrs Melton and reassuring her. She's stable but has severe triple vessel disease. This is her third admission for surgery because she's been bumped off the list for urgent cases on the last two occasions.'

'Has she had a major infarct? An arrest?'

'No.'

'Come and look at Roger's films and then we can discuss it. Have you got viewing facilities in your office?'

She did, but Anna was aware of a strong reluctance to take Luke there. She had chosen not to take over his office in his absence and her space was relatively small. It was also the most personal space she had here at work.

She was already a little too aware of this man. His size and reputation and…and whatever it was that was exerting a tugging sensation on something emotional. Not to mention the danger that frisson of potential attraction had represented. She didn't want him invading a personal space. Not yet. Not until she felt a lot more confident in her interactions with him and that wasn't going to be until she'd resolved the dilemma she was in.

'The seminar room's closer. Where we hold the departmental meetings.'

'Of course. Have you got the time now?'

'Yes. I've finished the ward round.'

The round Luke had been supposed to join her for, but if he noticed any reprimand in her dry tone he gave no indication of it. He led the way down the corridor, his pace fast enough to keep Anna a half step behind. The hint of asymmetry in the way he moved had become a noticeable limp by the time they reached the lifts but Luke didn't pause. He pushed open the fire-stop doors and headed up the stairs.

Commenting on something as personal, not to mention physical, as the aftermath of his injury seemed inappropriate. In the same ball park as asking Charlotte if she was pregnant, and this wasn't remotely like the far more social setting of the hospital canteen with its 'time out' from work atmosphere. This was work and Luke's focus was entirely professional. He had no difficulty using the computerised system to bring the images from the catheter laboratory onto the large screen in the meeting room.

'As you can see, there's a seventy to eighty per cent stenosis on the left anterior descending and diffuse disease over a significant segment of the vessel. And that's not all. There's a critical stenosis in the circumflex. Here...see?'

'Yes.' Anna watched and listened. It was quite obvious that Roger was in more urgent need of surgery than her Mrs Melton. As the head of department, Luke would have been within his rights to simply order her to juggle lists but instead he was taking the time to put all the information in front of her, presumably with the intention of giving her the opportunity to make the call.

Exactly the way they should be interacting as colleagues. There was every reason to take a moment to admire the way he was dealing with the situation but there really shouldn't have been any space in Anna's head to be so aware of the way Luke moved his hands as he spoke. Of how elegant those movements were for those large hands with their clever, tapered fingers.

It was quite reasonable to appreciate the way he spoke so clearly too and the transparent speed with which his mind worked, but that didn't excuse the enjoyment Anna found she was getting from the timbre of that deep voice. She brushed off the visceral reactions. So he was intelligent and articulate. She should have expected nothing else in someone who had beaten her in a job application.

But perhaps that underlying awareness of him as a

person and not simply a surgeon made her more aware of his physical issues. When they had finished coming to a mutually agreeable compromise on theatre lists, which would see Mrs Melton staying on as an inpatient until her surgery could be scheduled, Luke stood up. His face was grim and he blinked with slow deliberation, as though he was in pain but determined to ignore it. Or switch it off. The action took Anna straight back to their time in Theatre that morning and she knew she couldn't avoid broaching the subject.

'How's your leg?' she found herself asking. 'I understand you suffered a fairly serious injury?'

'I survived.' Luke's tone told her it wasn't a welcome subject for discussion. 'It's improving all the time.' His stare was expressionless. 'Why do you ask?'

Anna had to fight back the urge to apologise for asking a personal question. His eyes were so blue. So intense. No way could she simply dismiss that sharp squeezing sensation occurring deep in her belly. It might have been a very long time since she'd experienced a shaft of desire but it was all too easy to recognise. She looked away.

'I've taken on a position as your assistant. If you have problems that I could help with, please don't hesitate to tell me.'

Luke made an incredulous sound, as though Anna would be incapable of giving him any assistance. That she had no idea what she was talking about. The sound rankled. She looked up to meet his gaze again.

'If, for example, you find it hard to stay on your feet for a long theatre session.'

A corner of his mouth lifted. Just a fraction. A sardonic twist but enough of a curl for Anna to realise she had yet to see Luke smile. He certainly wasn't about to now. His expression was anything but friendly or relaxed. Her heart skipped a beat and then sped up but it was too late to swallow any words that had been spoken and try to get back onto safe ground.

She had seen his pain when Luke knew how good he was at hiding it, and it seemed like he was exposing a physical flaw. Almost as bad as that loss of focus in Theatre that morning had been. Anna had been the only person to pick up on that, as well.

He'd barely met the woman and yet it felt like she was inside a very personal space. As for offering to help with his problems. Ha! She didn't know anything.

No one here did.

And yet the idea was appealing. To have someone in his corner who was prepared to listen even if they couldn't begin to understand.

To have someone to hold at night…

Whoa! Where the hell had that come from?

Luke could manage being alone. He had to. Just as well he'd learned to bury the kind of emotional involvement that could make reality too hard to deal with. He might be back in a very different reality now but the ability to remain detached at some level was just as important. More important, maybe, given that he felt the despair of a meaningless existence pressing in on him from all sides.

He was looking into a future that had only one bright

spot. His work. And Anna was trying to undermine it. Something like fear made him straighten and defend himself by attacking.

'Are you suggesting I'm physically incapable of doing my job?' He had her pinned with his gaze. 'Hoping that it might prove too much and I'll quietly go away and let you take over again?'

He saw her eyes widen and felt a flash of remorse at being so harsh. He also heard the swift intake of her breath but he didn't give her time to speak. He couldn't afford to back down. Admitting defeat wasn't something Luke Davenport did willingly.

'This is my home,' he continued. 'Where I live and where I work. Where my future is. I'm back and I have no desire to go anywhere else.'

Which one of them was he trying to convince here?

'I wasn't suggesting anything.' Anna's tone was clipped and very cool. 'Maybe I was hoping there might be a satisfactory explanation for what happened in Theatre this morning. For your slow response to a significant bleed.'

A moment's silence hung heavily between them. Not that Luke had any intention of denying the accusation or trying to excuse himself.

'I lost focus,' he admitted simply. 'It won't happen again.'

He saw the way her features softened at his honesty. She wanted to believe him. But he could also see confusion in the depths of those astonishing green eyes. What had he been thinking, attacking her for asking what had been a perfectly reasonable question? No wonder she felt torn.

'Are you intending to report the incident?'

She held his gaze. She had courage, this woman.

'Would you?'

'Yes,' Luke responded without hesitation. 'Sloppy performance is never acceptable.'

Anna tilted her head in agreement but said nothing. They left the meeting room in silence. There seemed to be nothing more to be said.

So that was that. The subject was out in the open and he'd all but told her he expected it to be reported. All he had to do now was wait until someone, presumably Albert White or one of the other hospital administrators, came to have a little chat with him.

It didn't happen the next day.

If anything, Luke got the impression that Anna hadn't said anything at all about him that wasn't complimentary, judging by comments made in the departmental meeting the next morning.

More than one member of the cardiology and cardiothoracic surgical staff said admiring things about Colin Herbert's surgery. The congratulatory buzz when Roger's case came up during the discussion on revised theatre lists was actually embarrassing.

Luke cut it short. 'I had some very able assistance from Dr Bartlett,' he told the group briskly. 'And she's the one with the real work to do with his CABG today.'

That coronary artery bypass grafting was well under

way by the time Luke left his administrative tasks and headed for the theatre suite. He didn't don a gown or mask and enter the theatre. Instead, he slipped quietly into the observation deck and sat, probably unnoticed, in the far corner. You could see what was going on and hear what was being said and, if you wanted, you could focus on one person and make judgments about their ability. Their personality even. That was why he had requested that the space be closed during his surgery yesterday. An unusual case would have attracted as many people as could have squeezed in here and, on some level, he would have been aware of it.

Anna wasn't aware of him. He could watch every movement and hear every comment. He could feel the time and care she took with every meticulous stitch as she took the veins harvested from Roger's legs and used them to make new conduits to take blood to where it was needed in the heart muscle. Her voice was as calm as her movements. She was polite in her requests and prepared to discuss anything with the anaesthetist or bypass machine technicians. She spoke frequently to her registrar as well, asking questions and explaining her own decisions. A natural teacher, then.

With a voice that he couldn't imagine getting tired of listening to. Not when it was coupled with a brain that was clearly as focused but as flexible as her hands were. An impressive mix.

He stayed where he was only until the blood flow in the new coronary arteries was deemed acceptable and Roger was successfully taken off bypass. He would see Anna again today and maybe she would let him know who she had decided to speak to. He couldn't pre-empt her by speaking to someone himself because that would make it a bigger issue than it actually was. It wasn't going to happen again because he was in control now. Of every waking moment, at least.

But nothing more was said about it despite their paths crossing frequently when they shared a busy outpatient clinic and more than once during ward rounds and departmental meetings. By Friday, both Colin and Roger were on the ward and recuperating well and finally, late that afternoon, Luke got a call to the office of St Piran's chief executive officer.

'Luke.' Albert White shook one hand and gripped Luke's other shoulder at the same time. 'I'm so sorry this has taken so long. It's been a hectic week that included a day or two in London. Welcome back. It's good to see you.'

'It's good to see you too.' And it was, except that he could feel the distance between them. He'd been on another planet since he had last worked here. But Albert was a familiar face. Part of the anchor that Luke hoped to use to stabilise his life.

'How's the family?'

'All well when I last heard any news.'

'I was astonished to hear that your parents had taken off to New Zealand, of all places. I hear they're living on a military base in North Island?'

'They are indeed. Dad's taken an administrative position. He calls it a semi-retirement but I can't see him ever not being full-time army.'

'No. And your older brother?'

'Currently in Australia. Helping train their SAS.'

Albert shook his head. 'Army family through and through. At least we've got one of the Davenport boys back again.'

'Yes.' The word was clipped. Luke didn't want to discuss the 'Davenport boy' who would never make it back.

There was a moment's silence, which seemed appropriate, and when Albert spoke again his tone was more serious, acknowledging so many things that were not going to be said.

'How's the leg?'

'Oh, you know. Still attached. Still works. I'm not complaining.'

Albert chuckled. 'Works pretty well from what I've been hearing. What's with the commando techniques in the canteen? Leaping tall buildings on the agenda, too?'

Luke summoned a smile. 'I don't think so.'

'Well done, anyway. I hear the chap's doing really well.'

'He is. Dr Bartlett did a quadruple bypass on him. She's an excellent surgeon.'

'She is indeed.' The glance Luke received held a hint of relief. Any awkward subjects were being left well behind. 'So things are working out, then? You two going to be able to work as a team?'

Luke couldn't detect even a hint that the CEO might be fishing for any confessions regarding a bumpy start. Maybe he should say something about it himself but if Anna had chosen not to, perhaps he should respect her decision. Albert didn't seem to notice that his silence was covering a moment of confusion.

'Not that I expected any problems, but it was good to hear Anna singing your praises the other day. A pericardectomy, I hear?'

'Um…yes. First case. What did she say?'

'That you did the entire procedure off bypass. That she was delighted to have the opportunity to learn something new.'

About the procedure? Or about him?

This meeting was nothing more than touching base. A welcome home.

'Come and have dinner some time soon. Joan would love to catch up.'

'Sure. Maybe when I've had time to find my feet properly.' Luke hoped his vague acceptance would not seem rude but he wasn't ready to get drawn into a segment of the St Piran's community that knew his family so well. He wasn't here because of the family connection. He was here because he'd had nowhere else to go.

Besides, he was getting into a routine now. An icy swim in the ocean at daybreak to chase away the night's demons. As many hours as possible focused entirely on his job and then exercise and work-related reading until he was hopefully exhausted enough to sleep for more than a few hours. He didn't want to tamper with what seemed to be working. Or remind himself of the past, which would only emphasise too clearly how different life was now. Control was paramount.

Control could be undermined by confusion, however.

Anna had had a whole week to decide how to present her concerns about his skills but she hadn't done so.

Why not?

Not that Luke wasn't grateful but he was definitely puzzled. She'd agreed that the matter should be reported. That sloppy performance wasn't acceptable. And yet she had apparently accepted his.

Why?

He would have spoken to her about it before leaving work that day but it was late and she had already gone. It wasn't hard to use his influence to find her contact details but Luke discovered that she was living well along the windy coast road that led to Penhally.

A phone call to thank her for making his first week back smoother than it might have otherwise been seemed too impersonal. What he said might even be taken the wrong way—tacit approval for not reporting the incident perhaps. Taking a fifteen- or twenty-minute drive to what was quite possibly only a small collection of dwellings and knocking on her door after dark was a long way too far towards the other end of the spectrum, however. Far too personal. Why was he even considering it?

It didn't seem nearly as inappropriate on Saturday morning. Especially as the world in general seemed a brighter place. Days and days of grey skies and intermittent rain had been blown inland by a stiff sea breeze and the sun was making a determined effort to raise the temperature by at least a degree or two. The surf had been high enough that morning to make his swim an

adrenaline rush, and his leg hadn't collapsed under him
when he'd attempted a slow jog on the softer sand.

Yes. For the first time since arriving back, Luke felt
that things were a little less bleak. Some time out on
a day like this to drive up to Penhally and revisit old
haunts was an attractive idea. He might have intended
to wait until Monday to give Anna the excellent article
on restrictive cardiomyopathy he'd come across in one
of the journals he'd been reading until the early hours
of that morning but if it was in the car, he'd have the
perfect excuse to drop in at her house on his way past
if he chose to.

He did choose to.

Maybe because the signpost to the lane she lived
on was so easy to spot. Or perhaps because the house
he found at her address was so unlike what he might
have expected. Not even a house. More like a cottage
with its latticed windows and some kind of evergreen
creeper scrambling along the faded shingles of its roof.
The small garden was overgrown and…it had a picket
fence, for heaven's sake!

If someone had asked him where he thought Dr
Bartlett would be living, he would have imagined a
modern apartment. Streamlined and minimalist. Devoid
of personality—hers or its own. This cottage probably
had tourists stopping to take its picture and a name
somewhere under the tangled, prickly branches obscuring half the fence. Bay View Cottage perhaps, given the
glorious sweep of Penhally Bay on display. It was only
a short walk down the hill to get to a beach and, given

the rocky coves he had noticed just before turning off the main road, the coastline was due to provide one of those gems that surfers searched for.

Sure enough, when he left the car and went a little further uphill towards the front door of the cottage, he could see a stretch of white sand beyond the boulders. This cottage might be rundown but it was sitting on valuable land. Any closer to Penhally or St Piran and it would be worth an absolute fortune. Was that why Anna had chosen it? As an investment?

That made far more sense than a desire to inhabit what had to feel like an alien space. Having come to terms with the apparent contradiction, Luke was now hesitant in knocking on her door. Had he passed a letter-box? He could leave the article in there and then explain it on Monday.

He might have done exactly that if it hadn't been for the sudden loud noise from inside the cottage. A crashing sound not dissimilar to the one he'd heard in the canteen earlier in the week.

No scream followed the sound but he could hear the dismay in Anna's voice.

'Oh…no!'

CHAPTER FOUR

'ANNA?' Luke didn't bother knocking. He tried the doorhandle and found it turned, so he shoved the door open. 'Are you all right?'

There was no response. Cautiously, Luke advanced along the narrow hallway. He could hear Anna's voice again. It was much quieter now. Soft and soothing.

'It's all right,' she was saying. 'Poor baby, you gave yourself a big fright that time, didn't you?'

Maybe he was in the wrong house.

'Anna?'

'Who's there?'

'Me,' Luke said as he stepped into a doorway on his right.

'Luke? Good grief! What on earth are you doing here?'

She sounded surprised. No, more like appalled. Luke opened his mouth but no words emerged. This was Anna?

She was sprawled on the floor, her arms around a large dog that was virtually in her lap and making enthusiastic attempts to lick her face. There were newspapers spread around them both, a collection of paintpots and an aluminium stepladder lying on its side.

'I was just on my way to Penhally. I heard the crash.'

'From the road?'

'No…I…er…had an article I wanted to give you.' It was weirdly hard to string a coherent sentence together so Luke gave up. He stared at Anna instead, trying to take in the faded, ripped denim jeans she was wearing. The paint-stained jumper. The soft waves of her loose hair that reached her shoulders. Those amazing green eyes that were staring at him in utter bewilderment right now.

Luke dropped his gaze. The dog was staring at him too. Warily. Pressing itself further into Anna's arms and visibly shaking.

'What's wrong with the dog?'

'He's scared.'

'Of what?'

'You.'

She should probably be scared herself, Anna thought. A large man she hardly knew had just come into her house uninvited. Into her bedroom. Well, it would be her bedroom again when she'd finished renovating it. Right now it was just a mess.

Like her head.

Luke was wearing some jeans that were probably as old as her own. He had a black woollen jumper on with the sleeves pushed up to reveal bare forearms. His hair looked windswept and there was a tension about him that suggested he could leap into action at any moment. To save a life or rescue a damsel in distress.

He'd thought she was in distress.

He'd come into her house to rescue her.

And here he was, looking rugged and grim and... and...gorgeous.

Thank goodness she had her arms full of warm, shivery puppy. She hugged him more closely.

'He's a rescue puppy,' she told Luke. 'I've only had him a couple of weeks. My neighbours, Doug and June Gallagher, own a farm and they found him in the creek. In a sack. They would have kept him but they've already got a lot of dogs and he was terrified of Doug. June reckons he's been badly treated by a man.'

'So you took him? You're going to keep him?'

He sounded as though she'd just informed him that she intended to fly to the moon. Anna almost laughed but she felt absurdly close to tears. This wasn't supposed to happen and the earth had just tilted beneath her feet.

Dr Bartlett didn't do feminine or personal. She didn't do attraction to her colleagues.

Mr Davenport wasn't supposed to meet Anna. And there were no rules about Anna feeling attracted to a man. There hadn't needed to be for too long to remember.

This was threatening to do her head in completely so she dragged her gaze away from the towering figure by the doorway and buried her face in the expanse of woolly hair in her arms.

'You're all right,' she soothed. 'He's not going to hurt

you.' The reassurance seemed to bounce back at her and it sounded good. The warmth and smell of her dog was good too. Comforting. Anna raised her head to find that Luke was closer. He had dropped to a crouch and he was looking at the puppy.

'What is he, exactly?'

'We're not sure. The vet thinks he's about four months old. She reckons he's part poodle because of the wispy hair. Or maybe there's some wolfhound in there. A designer dog gone wrong, we decided, and that's why nobody wanted him.'

'A poodle and a wolfhound?' Luke seemed to be making a valiant attempt to imagine such an unlikely combination.

He looked intrigued and, with his focus so completely on the puppy, Anna got the chance to look at him.

He looked so different. Was it the casual clothing or the fact that he was here, in her home? No. It was more than that. The grimness she was getting accustomed to in his face had lightened. The puppy had distracted him and caught his interest. Was it possible it might even amuse him? Make him smile?

Anna really wanted to see Luke smile.

'It could be possible,' she said, her tone deadpan. 'As long as they'd had a staircase handy.'

Luke's gaze flicked up. He gave a huff of sound that could have passed for laughter but there was no matching curl to his lips. Instead, there was an incredulous expression in those amazingly blue eyes. As though he was seeing someone he didn't recognise at all.

Because she'd cracked a fairly pathetic joke?

Or because of the reference to parentage? Canine sex.

Sex...

Oh, Lord! Anna closed her eyes. She couldn't hold the puppy any more tightly because she could feel his ribs too well already. Poor thing, he'd had a hard time in his short life so far. At least he'd stopped shaking, though.

'What's his name?'

'I can't decide. Every time I come up with one, I try using it but it doesn't feel right. Herbert was my last effort.' To her dismay, Anna realised that Luke would make the connection. That the surname of his first surgical case had seemed like a good name for her pet. How unprofessional would that seem?

Probably not as bad as talking about dogs mating on the stairs.

And did it really matter? This wasn't work. It was home. Different.

Confusing.

'He's got big feet.'

'Mmm. He's growing fast, too. I think that's why he's so clumsy. He got underneath my ladder and tried to turn around and that's how it tipped over.'

Luke was silent for a moment but then he looked at Anna and she saw that the grim lines were still missing from his face. There was a hint of amusement there but it was lapped by a sadness she could feel all the way to her bones.

'I knew someone once,' he said quietly. 'He grew

too fast and looked a bit goofy, with his hands and feet always looking a bit too big for him, and he was such a clumsy kid we all called him "Crash". He grew up, though. Into the strongest, bravest guy I knew.'

He was talking about someone important. A fellow soldier, maybe? Someone he had loved who had died? Why was he telling her something so personal?

'I heard a crash,' Luke added. 'That's why I came inside.'

Anna swallowed. Luke's lips were moving. Slowly but surely they were curling into a smile. A real smile. One that changed his whole face, deepening those furrows to his nose but adding a sparkle to his eyes that made him seem so much more…alive.

It faded all too quickly and instinct told Anna that she had been given a glimpse of something normally well hidden. The real Luke? A letting down of some guard that not many people got to see, anyway. A real smile and he had chosen to bestow it on her.

Something deep inside her was captured. Something huge and warm and wonderful. Anna knew she would remember this moment for ever.

'It's a great name,' she said softly. 'Crash?'

The big pup wriggled in her arms and looked up at her. He tried to prick up his ears but they were too heavy and stuck out sideways. Liquid brown eyes were full of trust and a long tail gave a thump of approval.

'Crash it is,' Anna announced. She smiled up at Luke. 'Hey, thanks.'

'No problem.' But the smile had well and truly vanished from Luke's face and he stood up.

He was leaving. Something oddly like panic made Anna's heart skip a beat.

'Would…um…would you like a coffee or something?'

'No. You're busy and I'm on my way to Penhally. I'll leave the journal.' He dropped it onto a chest of drawers by the door. 'There's a good review of restrictive pericarditis in there. I thought you'd be interested.'

The reminder of work was timely. She had to work with Luke. Work and home couldn't mix. Professional and personal couldn't mix. What had she been thinking, blathering on about her rescue puppy? She scrambled to her feet.

'Thank you.' There wasn't a thing Anna could do about what she was wearing or what her home looked like, but she could summon as much as she could of Dr Bartlett. Lifting her chin, she could feel the shell of professionalism beginning to enclose her. Protect her.

'That was thoughtful of you. I did do as much research as possible when Colin was admitted but it might well be something I didn't come across.' She looked pointedly at the door. 'I'll see you out, shall I?'

'No need.' Luke turned to leave but then paused. 'Actually, there was something else.'

'What?'

The hesitation was almost imperceptible. 'You don't seem to have reported that incident from Colin Herbert's surgery. Or not that I've heard about.'

'No. I decided not to.'

'Why not?'

'Because you said it wouldn't happen again.' *And I*

believe you, Anna added silently, looking away so that he wouldn't see any crack in her newly formed shell. *I trust you.*

Luke didn't say anything. After a long moment he broke the eye contact and gave a single nod.

'Thank you,' he said, the words somewhat curt.

And with that he was gone.

Anna stood very still. She listened to the sound of her front door closing. And then the sound of a car engine starting up and a vehicle moving away.

Even then she didn't move. Standing like this, she could feel that shell cracking and falling away, exposing something tender. She could almost feel Luke's presence still in the room. She could still see that amazing smile.

And, heaven help her, but she wanted to hang onto it for just a little longer.

The sound pierced his eardrums, his body rocking from the force of the impact. Through the painful buzzing that came in the wake of the explosion he could hear the cursing of his companions. The screaming.

'Get out!'

'Get down!'

The ping of bullets ricocheting off the metal of their armoured vehicle came faster. An unearthly shriek from someone who had been struck ripped through the sounds of chaos.

Of panic.

He could feel the heat now. Not just the normal strength-sapping attack of the desert sun but the kind of heat that could sear flesh. A lick of flames that could bring death with far more suffering than a bullet.

The dust was thick. Getting thicker. The chop-chop-chop of a nearby helicopter was stirring the ground. Bringing assistance, but it was going to be too late. It was getting hard to breathe. He could smell the dust. Taste it. Dust mixed with blood to become a suffocating soup.

His companions needed help. The driver was slumped over the wheel, others bleeding. The young paramedic was crying. Facing death and terrified.

He could feel that terror reach out and invade his own mind. He was frozen. Becoming aware of the pain in his own leg. Terrible, unimaginable pain. He couldn't breathe. Couldn't move...

They were his brothers, these men. All of them. And he was going to watch them die.

He was about to die himself. He could see the enemy emerging from the clouds of dust, their bodies shrouded with the clothing of the desert, their faces disguised by heavy, dark beards. He could see the cruel muzzles of the weapons they were pointing at him but he couldn't move.

Couldn't even breathe...

The sound of his own scream was as choked as the air around him.

Arghhh!

The desperate, strangled sound that finally escaped his throat was, mercifully, enough to wake him. Even as his eyes snapped open, Luke was throwing back the covers on his bed, swinging his legs over the edge so that it was a continuous, flowing movement that had him sitting, hunched on the side of his bed, his head in his hands as he struggled to drag in a breath.

The feeling of suffocation—of imminent death—was still there.

He couldn't afford to stay still. He knew what he had to do.

The warm, fleecy trackpants were draped over the end of his bed. His shoes were right there to shove his feet into. Running shoes.

It wasn't real, he reminded himself as he pulled the laces tight. It hadn't even happened that way. He had never seen the enemy. He had been able to move. To drag his companions to shelter behind the vehicle as the helicopter hovered overhead. He had staunched the flow of blood and kept airways patent. None of them had died.

But the nightmare was always the same.

He was watching his own brother die. Feeling the fear. Unable to help.

Matthew. Mattie. The clumsy kid with the happy grin who'd had to tag along with his older brothers and do everything they did. Crash.

Oh...God! What on earth had possessed him to suggest that Anna Bartlett use that precious nickname for that skinny, ridiculous-looking dog?

What was she doing with a dog in the first place? How could she keep a pet that needed so much time and love with the kind of hours he already knew she put into her career? She did love it. He had seen that in the way she held it and soothed it. The way her face had brightened with joy at finding a name she really liked.

He had now pulled on the coat hanging by the door. Within seconds he was lurching down the rough track that led to the beach. It didn't matter that it was the middle of the night. His night vision was better than most people's and he was getting very familiar with this route.

Maybe it didn't matter that he'd given his brother's name away to a dog. It wasn't as though he was planning to visit that unlikely little cottage again and they were hardly likely to be chatting about it at work because they never talked about anything remotely personal.

In fact, he was having enormous difficulty reconciling the woman who was his assistant head of department with the person he'd found on the floor of that room cuddling...Crash.

Sea air so fresh that it bit into his lungs and numbed his face barely penetrated his awareness. He could feel the shifting of sand beneath his feet and hear the sound of the surf crashing in right beside him but his mind had fastened onto that picture of Anna on the floor.

With her hair in a soft tumble of curls. Her arms holding a vulnerable creature. Comforting it. Protecting it. He had felt the love. That was what had hit him in such a poignant place. What had reminded him of the kid brother who had never come home.

He'd reached the end of the beach now. Turned to go home again. He might even manage another couple of hours' sleep before daylight came. Usually, by the time he had done this punishing circuit, the nightmare had faded.

And it was only then that Luke realised he hadn't had to fight the remnants of that terrible dream the way he always did. From even before he'd left his house, all he'd been thinking about was Anna.

Or rather the two Annas.

Now that he'd seen her at home, he'd be able to recognise what he'd missed at work so far, surely? Some signs that hidden beneath that power-dressing, uber-professional, calm, cool and collected surgeon was... the most compelling woman he'd ever met in his life.

He was watching her. And he was puzzled.

Anna could feel the unasked questions hanging in the air between them.

Had it been real? Had he really found her wearing scruffy clothes, with her hair in an untidy mop, living in a shambolic house with a rather large and definitely unhygienic animal? Did she really have a sense of humour?

It was easy to emanate denial because that wasn't who she was at work. She'd also had years of practice in deflecting any line of communication that threatened to become personal. Patients could be so useful.

Like first thing on Monday morning when the anticipation of seeing Luke for the first time since he'd been in her house was making Anna feel more nervous than she had since her junior years as a doctor when she'd had to perform in front of some eminent consultant.

Luke hadn't looked any different.

'Good morning, Anna. How are you?'

'Very good.' She wasn't going to return the query. Luke wasn't one of her patients.

'How's—?'

Crash? She knew that was coming next and she had to stamp on that topic of conversation before it could start. The temptation to talk about her puppy was too strong. She wanted to tell Luke that Crash had learned to sit. That he had stepped on an overturned lid of a paint tin and made a giant pawprint on her wooden floor and it had been such a perfect signature she'd been reluctant to clean it off. Would that make him smile again? She couldn't afford to find out.

'Mrs Melton?' She interrupted smoothly. 'Finally getting to Theatre, thank goodness. I know it's your slot this morning but I'm more than happy to do the surgery. Or assist.'

'It's a long time since I did a CABG.' He knew exactly what she'd done in changing the subject. She could see him taking it on board that her private life was not up for discussion. Could see the focus as he let it go. 'Might be a good idea if you assisted.'

Was this a challenge? To see if she did trust him to operate safely on his own? A sideways glance as Luke fell into step beside her made her notice that his hair was damp. Just out of the shower? That image was disturbing. Anna dragged in a breath, only to catch a whiff of something fresh and clean. Like a sea breeze. Good heavens, she could almost imagine Luke had just been for a dip in the ocean. In the middle of winter? Who would be that crazy?

Her senses were threatening to override her train of thought. What had he asked? Oh, yes… Was he offering her the opportunity to observe and judge his capabilities in Theatre or might he want her company for an entirely different reason?

'I can't imagine that you'll have any problems,' she said calmly. 'But I am a little concerned about the quality of her saphenous veins. I'm wondering about harvesting the lesser saphenous or possibly upper extremity veins, in which case I could probably be more helpful than a registrar.'

Your choice, she threw at him silently. I'm available.

He simply nodded. 'Excellent. Have we got time to review her films? I'd like to have a word with her as well and introduce myself.'

'Sure. I'm heading to the ward right now.'

Mrs Melton was thrilled to hear that the head of department would be doing her surgery. She beamed at Luke.

And he smiled back. Anna was watching and she could see that it was a purely professional sort of smile. It still softened his face and reminded her of when he'd smiled at her but it wasn't anything like the same. It didn't make his face come alive. It didn't come anywhere near his eyes.

She found herself watching him just as intently as she suspected he was watching her. She saw him smile in greeting colleagues. She saw him smile in satisfaction when he was informed of how well a patient was doing. He even smiled directly at her on one occasion. All mechanical gestures. Done because it was expected and it would be impolite not to.

Anna wanted to know what those shadows in his eyes were from and why they were dense enough to smother real smiles. She wanted to know who the real 'Crash' had been and why talking about him had cracked open the armour Luke wore.

For that was what it was. Anna could recognise it because she had her own. By the end of their second week of working together, she had the weirdest sensation that they were like actors. Playing their part on stage but with each of them knowing perfectly well that the role the other was playing was not the real person.

Even more disturbing, Anna was becoming obsessed with wondering about the real Luke. The man that had really smiled at her. Why did he come to work each day with his hair damp and smelling of the sea? The temptation to ask was becoming unbearable. Or maybe it was the desire to touch his hair...to press her face against it and see if that was where the impression of the outdoors and punishing exercise came from.

She wanted to know why he refused to admit that his leg hurt even when it was obvious it did. When there were lines of pain in his face at the end of a long day that she could feel herself. She could smooth those lines away. With her fingers. Or her lips. If he let her.

If she let herself...

The intrigue refused to go away. The pull became stronger but Anna was fighting it. Anyone seeing Mr Davenport and Dr Bartlett together would see nothing more than a purely professional association. Reserved but respectful. Discussions might be animated but they were only about their patients. Their work. Current research. New technologies. Endless topics to talk about.

A seemingly endlessly fascinating man to talk to.

If it wasn't for the puzzle that Anna represented, Luke might have been tempted to admit defeat.

Every day was the same. Enclosed within the walls of an institution that sometimes felt like it was filled with people who had created their own illnesses. Heavy smokers who seemed surprised that they'd had heart attacks because of their damaged blood vessels. Morbidly obese people who still expected lifesaving surgery.

What for? So they could carry on with their meaningless lives? Lie in bed and keep eating junk food?

'I'm not going to operate on Walter Robson,' he informed Anna after a ward round late that week. 'I refuse to spend my time patching someone up just to give them longer to indulge in slow suicide by their appalling lifestyle choices.'

If he'd hoped to get under her skin with such a terse and controversial statement, he was disappointed.

'I agree he's a poor candidate for surgery,' she said calmly. 'Maybe that will be enough of an incentive for him to stop smoking and lose some weight. If we can reduce his level of heart failure and get his type-two diabetes and cellulitis under control, it will reduce the surgical risk.'

Luke almost exploded. Thumped the wall beside

them or walked away from his colleague. Told Anna what he was really thinking.

That she knew nothing about risk. Real risk—the kind that young, healthy people took for the benefit of their brothers-in-arms, if not for the much bigger human-rights issues. That patching them up was the kind of lifesaving surgery that had some meaning.

But that would open floodgates that had to remain shut. It would take Anna into a life that didn't exist for him any more except in his nightmares, and winning freedom from those nightmares was the hurdle he had to get through to survive.

He had discovered a new way of dealing with both the terrors of the night and the feeling of suffocation he could get ambushed by at work. He could distract himself by thinking about Anna. Just for a few seconds. Like a shot of some calm-inducing drug.

Her voice became a background hum as she talked about dealing with Walter Robson's anaemia and whether his chronic lung problems would improve if he carried through his vow to quit smoking.

Luke let his gaze stroke the sleek hair on top of Anna's head and then rest on the tight knot nestled at the nape of her neck. That clip thing would be easy enough to remove. The hair might still be twisted and squashed but he could bury his fingers in it and fluff it out until it bounced onto her shoulders.

His breath came out in a sigh. It was enough…the feeling of desperation was fading again.

'Luke?' Anna had caught the sigh. Fortunately, she

misinterpreted it. 'The decision has to be on medical grounds, not moral ones.'

'Of course.'

This wasn't the place to discuss the ethics of what represented a significant part of their careers. Much of the workload was genuine and worthwhile. He knew that. He used to get more than enough satisfaction from it.

Why did everything have to be so different now? So difficult?

And why couldn't he see what he knew was there—hiding behind the person Anna was within these walls?

She wouldn't let him. That was why. The boundaries had been marked and were being reinforced every time she changed the subject if he tried to talk about something personal, like the puppy he had named for her. Or had she even kept the name?

No wonder James had sounded puzzled back on his first day when they had been scrubbing in together. As though he had no idea of what Anna was like out of work hours.

Maybe Luke was the only person here who'd had a glimpse of that side of Anna.

He liked that notion.

He liked it a lot.

CHAPTER FIVE

'I'M HAPPY to cover Christmas Day.'

'So am I.' Luke's nod was matter-of-fact. 'Thanks, Anna. That's the holiday roster issues sorted, then. Let's get on with the rest of the agenda.'

Anna couldn't help but notice the look that passed between James and Charlotte Alexander, who were sitting together in this departmental meeting. No mistaking the look of relief. Joy even at the prospect of spending a special day together with no danger of being called in to work.

The movement of Charlotte's hand was probably unconscious. She seemed to be listening carefully to Luke as he introduced a new grading system for cardiac patients.

'It's hoped that this will be brought in nationwide to try and standardise criteria and address the increasing numbers of people that are dying while on waiting lists for surgery. We've been asked to implement this at St Piran's as of the first of January as part of a multi-centre trial, so your feedback is going to be important.'

Anna was listening, too, but she'd already read the proposal and she and Luke had discussed it at length.

It was hardly surprising that she caught that movement from Charlotte in her peripheral vision. A hand that gently smoothed the loose fabric of her top, gathering it up as it came to rest cupping her lower belly. There really was no doubt now that she was pregnant. It would be a special Christmas for them, wouldn't it, with the extra joy and dreams that came with knowing they were about to become a family?

'As far as degree of valvar dysfunction goes, we're staying with the New York Heart Association functional classes. As you can see, mild is class one and scores two. Severe is class three and scores fourteen. If there is coronary artery disease present as well, it puts it into class four and we can add ten to the overall score.'

Luke had the score sheets projected onto the wall. He was going to cover all the non-coronary revascularisation type of patients like valve replacements and then he'd run through the more complex scoring system for patients who had arterial disease. He was being clear and methodical and making sure everyone understood. People were nodding approvingly. A system like this could make prioritising people on the waiting lists much more straightforward.

Charlotte was one of those nodding. As though she would be only too happy to be filling in the score sheets on her patients and adding her comments to the feedback that would be required. But how long would she be around to be doing that?

It was all very well having secrets but it was also annoying. When were they planning to share the information and allow arrangements to be made for Charlotte's absence for maternity leave? For James to be covered at the time of the baby's arrival? For a new member of staff to be advertised for, if necessary?

No wonder there was such prejudice against women in top positions. Imagine if she was pregnant herself? Even if she worked up to the last possible moment and then took minimal maternity leave, the disruption to the department would still be huge.

Unthinkable. It always had been.

So why was she watching Charlotte surreptitiously right now instead of focusing on the information Luke was presenting? Wondering what her colleague was thinking and how she'd come to the conclusion that having a baby was more important than her career. What it might be like to feel a new life growing and moving within your own body. To face the enormous responsibility of caring for that baby when it was born.

The disturbing niggle was annoyance, not envy. Luke needed to know. He had quite enough on his plate settling back into running such a busy department and working the kind of hours he did with the extra stress of recovering from a major physical injury. Maybe it wasn't her place but Anna wanted to warn Luke. She could help him put arrangements into place to make sure they could cope with the inevitable disruptions.

Her gaze was on the head of department now. He was talking about the Canadian Cardiovascular Society's criteria for grading angina.

'The class is assigned after appropriate treatment, not at the time of admission or diagnosis.'

Luke stood tall but relaxed and his voice was clear

and authoritative. What was the X factor in the way he presented himself that got people on side so easily? Anna found herself biting back a smile. It certainly wasn't his warm and friendly countenance. He was always so serious, often looking grim, and he could be downright impatient with staff who couldn't get up to speed quickly enough. He was utterly closed off on a personal level and yet he drew everyone in.

Already this department felt more cohesive than it had under her own leadership. There was enthusiasm for all sorts of projects that might otherwise have been seen simply as more paperwork and stress. In the space of just a few short weeks they had a new rostering system in place, had been chosen for this pilot centre for an important national initiative and several new research projects had been kicked off.

Maybe that X factor was because of the sense that Luke was driven, despite—or perhaps because of—the physical challenges it now incorporated. Anyone could see how hard it was for him to be on his feet all day and keep up with such a demanding schedule. This job was his life and he was going to do it so well that anyone who chose to get on board would have an unexpectedly satisfying ride.

And she was one of them. Funny how the resentment she'd felt at Luke returning to take his leading role in the department had faded so quickly. Perhaps it had been pushed away completely because she'd been watching him so carefully and the more she saw, the more compelling this man was becoming. Had she really thought she wouldn't learn from him? It wasn't just his technical excellence in Theatre. Apart from that momentary wobble on his first day back, Anna hadn't seen anything that would have undermined her opinion that he was one of the best in his field. It was rare for someone so good on the practical side to be so competent at administration, but Luke really seemed to enjoy the challenge of running a large department effectively.

Yes. The closer she could stay and work with Luke the more she could benefit. She wanted them to be a close team.

How close?

The odd question came from a part of her brain that was normally closed off at work. The kind of disruptive thought that had never been a problem in the past but, curiously, had started to plague her out-of-work hours lately. She couldn't distract herself easily right now either. She was trapped, motionless, and she had already been distracted by the people around her.

'Scores for the ability to work or give care are a little more subjective,' Luke was saying. 'Especially the middle category when it's threatened but not immediately.'

Anna's concentration was certainly threatened. She didn't need a sideways glance at the Alexanders to remind her of married couples amongst her colleagues. It happened all the time. Didn't they say that you were most likely to meet the person you were going to marry amongst the people you worked with?

It wasn't going to happen to her. The desire for a husband and family—if it had ever been there—had been dismissed long ago. About the time she'd discovered the passion she had for surgery and it had become obvious that if she was going to have any chance of getting to where she wanted to be, it had to be the only thing that mattered in her life.

Adopting a puppy had been extraordinary enough. A substitute baby? No. You couldn't leave a baby in the house for a helpful neighbour to collect and care for while you were at work. Or leave a pile of newspaper on the floor so you didn't have to get up in the middle of the night to deal with toileting issues. She still had to factor in collecting Crash every day from the yard he shared with June and Doug's dogs. To take him for a walk on the beach and spend time training and playing with him. To listen to the snuffles and odd whimpers in the night from his bed in the corner of his room. All in all, it was a major upheaval in her life. Not that she wasn't getting a lot of pleasure from it. And if it was a substitute child it was as close as she ever wanted to get, that was for sure.

No family, then. And what was the point of a husband if you weren't planning on having a family?

A partner was something different, however.

A lover.

At this point in the meeting Anna very uncharacteristically stopped listening to anything being said around her. She was watching Luke's hands as he shaped the size of whatever it was he was talking about. Strong, tanned, capable hands.

She couldn't stop herself imagining them running down the length of her spine. It would be no effort to fit the curve of her bottom into their grip and he would be able to pull her against his own body with no more than the slightest pressure. It would feel lean and hard, like his face.

And he would have turned that blinding focus onto her. Those incredible blue eyes would be on her face. On her lips as he dipped his head…slowly…to kiss her.

Oh…dear Lord… With a huge effort, Anna managed to tune back into her surroundings just as the meeting was wrapping up. People were closing diaries and starting to chat. Charlotte pushed back her chair and stood up.

'Just before you all go…'

The buzz of conversation died. Here we go, thought Anna, but the announcement wasn't what she expected.

'I've been involved in organising the staff Christmas function,' Charlotte said with a smile. 'It's in the canteen on the twenty-second, seven p.m., in case you haven't seen the flyers. There's going to be lots of nice food and plenty of non-alcoholic drinks if you're unlucky enough to be on duty. It's a chance for everybody to get together in the spirit of the season, so I hope you can all make it. Partners and families are welcome. There's going to be a Secret Santa. Bring a small gift and put it under the tree and then you'll get one yourself at the end of the night. Or just bring one for any children that might be there and if they're not needed they can go to the children's ward.'

Anna looked away from Charlotte. Towards Luke. Their senior cardiology registrar should be talking about her upcoming maternity leave, not a Christmas party. Luke had an odd expression on his face. As if he couldn't believe that something so trivial was being announced in a departmental meeting.

As though a party or celebrating Christmas was absolutely the last possible thing he would have any desire to do.

Did he ever relax? Let his guard down and enjoy something social?

Something intimate?

She gathered up her folder of papers and stepped around the table. Towards Luke. She couldn't stop herself. The wanderings of her mind during the meeting might be under control now, thank goodness, but they'd left an odd kind of physical yearning and it was like a magnet, pulling her towards Luke. She did her best to disguise it. Her professional mask was quite intact, on the outside at least.

'Good presentation,' she offered. 'I think we'll have full co-operation in the trial period.'

'Yes.' Luke was shutting down the program in his laptop. 'I'm hoping so.'

Anna's thoughts were tripping over each other. She had a strong urge to engineer a way to spend some time with Luke and it would be easy enough if she asked to discuss something professional, like the planned research project she was taking on to analyse post-operative infection rates in cardiac patients.

But something new and rather disturbing was happening. She could actually feel the war going on between her head and her heart. She didn't want a professional kind of interaction. She wanted…

Oh, help… Was she actually thinking of asking him for some kind of a date?

No, of course not. She didn't do work relationships. Of any kind. This was Anna getting rebellious, trying to claw her way through Dr Bartlett's armour. It simply wouldn't do.

Her thoughts might be running with the speed of light but she had been standing there for a shade too long judging by the quizzical set of Luke's eyebrows when he glanced up at her.

Anna was aware of the final staff members exiting the meeting room, including Charlotte. She hoped her smile was offhand.

'You planning to go to the Christmas party?'

'No. Are you?'

Anna couldn't look away. Her mouth wasn't going to wait for her brain to mull over what seemed to be a perfect compromise between professional and personal. It just widened its smile and opened to say something extraordinary.

'I will if you will.'

Something flickered in Luke's eyes. Astonishment? Interest?

'I don't like parties,' he said.

'Neither do I,' Anna agreed. She could have left it there. What was wrong with her today? 'But this is a staff function. It's polite to put in an appearance. Especially for HODs.'

Luke was frowning now. 'You think I should go?'

'I think there must be a lot of people in St Piran's who would enjoy the chance to welcome you back.

Good relations both within and between departments are useful.'

Luke grunted. He looked up as the meeting door swung shut behind the last person. 'Did you know Charlotte Alexander's pregnant?'

Was he trying to change the subject? 'I guessed. How did you know?'

'She told me. We need to look at possible replacements amongst the registrars we have available. Or get in a locum.'

'Yes. How much time have we got?'

'We should look at getting it sorted next month.'

'It's going to be a busy start for the New Year. Which reminds me...' The rebellious part of Anna had finally been quelled. Maybe it was just as well Luke was so good at sticking to professional. 'I wanted to have a chat to you about the parameters for this infection study. How retrospective do you think we should make it? I've got my registrar primed to start digging through records.'

'Let's have a look at our diaries. We should be able to squeeze in a meeting. You can bring anyone else you want involved along as well.'

'I will.'

Not that it was likely to help, Anna thought, her heart sinking. If she was capable of having totally inappropriate thoughts about her boss when there were a dozen or more members of the department around her, what hope did she have by flanking herself with a couple of junior doctors?

She needed to escape. To get home and get a grip. Heading purposefully away from work, Anna barely registered the huge Christmas tree in the hospital foyer with its twinkling, coloured lights but she thought of it again as she turned her car towards her cottage.

This was the silly season, she reminded herself. Everything would settle down, including whatever it was that making her feel so…unsettled.

The Christmas party was well under way by the time Anna managed to get there.

The canteen was noisy and crowded, warm with the inviting aroma of hot, savoury food and people determined to enjoy themselves. There were bright balloons and streamers and huge, shiny silver stars hanging from light fittings. There were flashes of even brighter colours as well. Where on earth had people found their accessories?

A trio of nurses wore headbands with big yellow plastic stars that flashed on and off. Steffie, the staff nurse from the cardiology ward, had earrings and a matching necklace that had red and green twinkling lights. Anna spotted a set of glowing reindeer horns and Santa hats made of shiny red sequins. She passed a registrar who wore a large badge. Rudolph's nose was flashing and a tinny version of a Christmas song could be heard competing with the background carol music in the room. More than one person rolled their eyes as the owner of the badge reached to push the nose as the song finished.

'Not again, Peter. Please.'

A very young-looking nurse was dressed in a naughty Santa costume, the rim of white fluff on the bottom of her dress barely reaching her thighs. Anna groaned inwardly. This really wasn't her scene at all. She knew she must look as out of place as she felt. Prim, in her skirt and jacket. It was getting harder to respond to the smiles and greetings of people when she was completely sober and they were clearly making the most of the party drinks available to those not on duty.

She felt like an island. A rather barren, rocky one, moving through a sea of festivity. She had to be the only person there who didn't have at least a string of tinsel tied on to signal that they belonged.

And then she spotted Luke.

Another island. Even rockier, given the tight body language and an almost desperate look on his face as Anna edged through the partygoers to join the group of familiar faces.

'Anna. Merry Christmas!'

'Thanks, Ben. Hi, Lucy.' Anna smiled at Ben's wife, her gaze dropping to the bundle snuggled against the front of her body with a sling. 'I heard you'd had another baby. Congratulations.'

'Thanks. Yes, this is Kitty. She's ten weeks old now.'

A small girl was peeping out from behind Lucy's legs.

'This must be Annabel.' Anna searched her memory. 'It's her birthday soon, isn't it?'

'Christmas Eve.'

'Just as well she's a party animal.' Ben grinned. 'She's loving it.' He was holding Annabel's little brother, Josh, but he reached down to touch his daughter. 'Tell

Dr Anna how old you're going to be on your birthday, darling.'

'Free,' Annabel said shyly. Ben tickled her head and made her giggle.

Who could help smiling at the joyous sound? Glancing up, Anna saw Luke's lips curve and it was, almost, the kind of smile he'd given her that day. Poignant. Real.

But not happy. The sound of laughter around them was virtually constant and Anna wanted to hear Luke laugh. To see and hear him forget himself in a moment of happiness. The feeling that he might never do that was heartbreaking. She tore her gaze away swiftly. Towards another smiling face.

But Josh O'Hara's smile looked forced and the petite, blonde woman standing beside him wasn't smiling at all. She was draining a glass of wine.

The A and E consultant noticed the direction of her gaze. 'Anna? You won't have met my wife. This is Rebecca.'

Charlotte and James Alexander joined the group, along with another man whom Anna recognised as Nick Tremayne, head of the Penhally medical centre.

'Has anyone seen Kate? I told her to pop in while I was upstairs visiting my patient but I can't find her anywhere in this crowd.'

'Nick!' Ben stepped closer to the newcomers. 'So you got in to see Mrs Jennings?'

'Yes. The surgery went well. She should be up and about with her new hip in no time. Home for the new year.'

'How's Jem?' Anna asked. 'He was the talk of the hospital there for quite a while.'

'He's great. Started senior school in September and seems to be loving it. Still gets a bit tired but it's been a big year for all of us.'

'Sure has.' Charlotte smiled. 'It's going to be a special Christmas this year. Your first together as a new family.'

'It's going to be wonderful. If I can find my wife, that is. Excuse me. Carry on enjoying yourselves. Oops!' Nick almost collided with a waiter bearing a tray of brimming champagne glasses.

Anna caught Luke's gaze and there was a moment of connection there. Neither of them was enjoying themselves in this setting.

It might be better somewhere else, Anna's response of a smile suggested. Somewhere without any of this crowd and noise. Somewhere they could be alone. Together. It had to be her imagination but Luke seemed to be silently in agreement. If nothing else, he certainly recognised the connection.

'Drink, Anna?' someone asked.

'No, thanks. I've still got patients I want to check on before I head home.'

'Definitely not for me,' Charlotte said happily.

'Or me,' James chimed in valiantly. 'I've climbed on the wagon with my wife.'

'Oh?' Ben's smile broadened. 'For how long, might I ask? Seven or eight months, perhaps?'

'Um…actually, there's something we probably should have told everyone quite a while ago now.'

The tray was still within reach and Josh's wife swapped her empty glass for a full one. Anna caught the expression on Josh's face. He's embarrassed, she thought in surprise. He doesn't want her drinking any more. No. The tension was deeper than that. It was hard not to get the impression that he wasn't comfortable having his wife there at all.

She took another glance at the woman she'd never met before. Rebecca had the kind of grooming that came, in her experience, with women who had plenty of money and too much time to spend on how they looked. Flawless make-up. Shoulder-length hair that was beautifully cut and exquisitely highlighted. Her nails sported a perfect French polish and her figure might be curvy but it looked well toned.

Rebecca had also caught the look from her husband. 'What?' she snapped. 'You think I've had enough?' A tiny snort suggested that an unhappy exchange was nothing new to this couple.

It was Anna's turn to feel embarrassed. She looked away to where Lucy was giving Charlotte a one-armed hug that wouldn't disturb the sleeping baby in the sling. Ben and Luke were both offering their congratulations to James and they all seemed unaware of the sudden atmosphere Anna was separating them from.

'Maybe I have had enough,' Rebecca said, too loudly. 'Of everything.'

'I'll order a taxi for you,' Josh said. 'I've still got some work I need to do tonight.'

'Of course you do.' Rebecca's laugh was brittle.

'Let's go.'

'When I've finished my drink. It's not as if I have any reason not to, is it?'

Josh's voice was too low for anyone but Anna to hear. 'I think we should go now. This isn't the place.'

'But it never is, is it, Josh?' Rebecca raised her glass but, to her dismay, Anna saw that the woman's lips were trembling too much for her to take a sip and tears were filling her eyes. Debating whether she should say something when it was obviously none of her business, Anna was relieved to see Rebecca blinking hard. Making a determined effort to control herself.

But then she shifted her gaze to where Lucy was standing with her tiny baby and Charlotte had pulled her top tight to show off her rounded belly, and Rebecca's face just crumpled. She pushed her glass at Josh and turned, tears streaming down her face as she fled. The others all turned in surprise.

'Oh…God,' Josh groaned. 'Sorry about that. I need to… Would you…?'

'Give it to me.' Anna took the champagne glass and Josh elbowed his way through the throng in pursuit of his wife.

'What was that all about?' Lucy looked worried.

'What happened?' Charlotte looked bemused.

'Josh and his wife. They didn't look very happy.'

Oh, no. Was this social occasion about to become the kind of gossip session Anna refused to engage in?

'Not everyone appreciates Christmas,' Luke said levelly.

'That's true.' Ben nodded and went along with making

the subject about generalities. 'Look at the increase we see in A and E for things like self-harm.'

'The hype doesn't help.' Anna was more than happy to direct conversation away from colleagues and their probable marriage woes. She gave Luke a grateful glance and then waved her hand to encompass the party and all the decorations. 'There's this huge expectation put out that it's going to be the happiest day of the year. Brimming with fun, family times and the best of everything. No wonder it just serves to underline what some people aren't lucky enough to have.'

There was a moment's silence and Anna could have kicked herself. Had she been responsible for the atmosphere in this group going from joy at James and Charlotte's news to entirely unnecessary gloom? She bit her lip.

'I'm just hungry,' she said apologetically. 'Take no notice. I might go and find a sausage roll or something.'

'And I'd better take these guys home,' Lucy said. 'We need to pace ourselves to get through all the parties lined up for the rest of this week.'

'And I...' Luke was obviously trying to think of a reason to excuse himself as well.

No surprises there. The noise level around them was increasing. Music had been turned up to compete with the laughter and happily raised voices, and there was a new sound mixed in with the general hubbub. A sharp cracking. People cheered and then there were more muted bangs. Someone was handing out Christmas crackers and people were pulling them with gusto.

The sound was not unlike distant gunfire. Anna's gaze flicked back to Luke. He didn't like parties anyway. How much worse would this be when it couldn't fail to remind him of being in a war zone? She could see his tension escalating. Instinctively, she found herself moving closer. Wanting to protect him. He looked straight at her and she had never seen him look so grim.

James was handed a cracker. 'Here we go.' He laughed, holding it out to Charlotte.

This bang was much louder. Charlotte squeaked in surprise, Annabel buried her face in her father's shoulder and little Josh burst into tears.

But Anna was still watching Luke. She saw the exact moment he stopped seeing her. When his face took on the same expression it had had in Theatre that first day. One of horror.

'Luke.' Anna put her hand on his arm and she could feel muscles as unyielding as steel beneath her fingers.

'Luke.' Her tone was more urgent now. She had to get through to him. Snap him out of this flashback before anyone else noticed.

But he didn't seem to feel her touch. Or hear her. He started moving away and seemed unaware of the people in his path. Someone got jostled and spilled their drink.

'Hey! Watch where you're going.'

Ben and James were watching where Luke was going. Anna caught the glance the two men exchanged. Frowning, Ben opened his mouth to say something but Anna shook her head.

'I'll go,' was all she said.

It was quite easy to follow Luke. People were stepping aside like a wave as they saw him coming. Smiles faded from faces to be replaced with dropping jaws. Anna didn't catch up with him until he was well past the doors of the canteen. She barely noticed Josh coming in the opposite direction. Good grief, this party wasn't proving very enjoyable for more than one person.

Finally, she got close enough to catch hold of Luke's hand but he didn't stop. He towed her along until he reached the end of the corridor. The noise from the canteen was muted now, like the lighting in this junction that contained the lifts. Two big pot plants on either side of a bench seat had some tinsel draped over their leaves.

Luke stopped and his head turned swiftly from one side to the other. At some level he was making a decision on what direction to take next. He still felt just as tense. Just as distant.

Anna had to distract him. Bring him back to the present. She stepped in front of him and reached up to hold his face with both hands.

'Luke...' She tilted his face, forcing him to look down at her. 'It's me. Anna.'

He was still caught somewhere else. A long way away in time and place. Somewhere dark.

Anna had to do something. Without thinking, she stood on tiptoe, still holding Luke's face.

And then she kissed him.

CHAPTER SIX

LUKE knew that Anna was kissing him.

Just as he'd known that she had followed him from the canteen and had caught his hand. He'd heard the urgency in her voice.

But it had all been on another level of his consciousness. Maybe that was what it was like for people in a coma. Or coming out of one, anyway. They could hear the voices and feel the touch but there was a transition period before they were able to enter the same reality.

Something had snapped inside him with the sound of that cracker and he'd known he was getting sucked into a flashback. He'd tried to fight it off as he'd stormed out of the canteen. Tried to shut down the even louder cracks of the real gunfire he could hear. The explosions of landmines. The screams of dying men. But the pull had been huge. Even the smell of savoury food became acrid. Like smoke. Rusty. Like blood.

By the time he was in the corridor all Luke had been aware of had been the need to escape. To find somewhere he could be alone and bury his head in his hands until, somehow, he could wrestle the monster into submission and regain control. And then he'd felt Anna's grip on his hand and heard her voice calling his name.

He tried to clear his head. Tried so hard. He wanted to get back to her. He was caught in the horror of a battlefield and she was there but not there. If he could just reach her, everything would be all right. Couldn't she hear him shouting? That he was trying, dammit. Doing his utmost to get to her.

Maybe she had heard. Maybe that was why she was holding his head and pulling it down. Pressing her lips against his with such intensity.

God...he recognised this form of escape. Distraction. Release. An affirmation of life. Passionate sex that carried no strings because if you got involved you only risked more of exactly what you were using it to escape from.

How did Anna know?

It didn't matter.

Luke could feel the force that had taken over his mind receding. He was in control again but instead of pulling away his lips moved over hers and his arms went around her body. He drew them both into the shadowy area between the bench and the giant pot plant.

He let his hands shape her body. Feeling the trim curve of her waist and the neat rounds of her buttocks and then up, beneath the layer of the tailored jacket. Up to the solid anchor of her shoulder blades and then around to the softness of her breasts. He cupped them and brushed his thumbs across the nipples that he could feel like tiny pebbles beneath the silky fabric of her blouse.

And all the time his lips moved over hers. Encouraged when they parted beneath his. Excited when his tongue made contact with hers. Aroused beyond belief when she responded, her tongue dancing with his and her hands touching his body.

This was Anna, for heaven's sake! At work. The place where she had no personality or, at least, no personal life anyone was allowed to encroach on. Had she been drinking? No. She'd refused alcohol at the party because she had work she still needed to do. They were both sober. Sober enough to realise that this was totally inappropriate.

How long had they been standing here, locked in each other's arms, lost in a flash of physical release that had exploded like a cork from a champagne bottle?

Too long. Not nearly long enough.

Had anyone seen them?

He had to stop but it was too hard not to taste her for just a moment longer. To hold her against the length of his body and imprint the feel of her into his brain. He would need that memory and it was too important not to make sure that it stuck.

He was kissing her back.

Anna had only intended to distract him. A brief, hard kiss that was supposed to have the same kind of shock effect that a slap on the face might provide to someone in the grip of hysteria.

But after that first stunned beat of time he had kissed her back. His lips had softened and moved beneath hers and his hands had touched her body and something inside Anna had simply melted.

He hadn't seemed to hear her voice or know she was there as she'd followed him. Maybe he didn't actually know who he was kissing. She could be anybody so she didn't have to be Dr Bartlett, did she?

She could just be Anna.

An old version of herself, even. One that had been lost too many years ago to count. The young girl who had dreamed of finding true love. A prince who was going to think she was the most wonderful person on earth. Who would love her for being exactly who she was. For ever.

And layered on top of that dreaming girl were flashes of everything she'd discovered about herself later. The yearning for a soul mate. The ability to give love and the need to receive it. Wild things like a need for physical release. All the things that had had to be buried so that they couldn't become a torment.

For just a few seconds Anna let herself sink into this astonishing kiss because she knew she would never experience anything like this ever again and she wanted to remember it, but the insanity began to fade and maybe she transmitted a tension that had nothing to do with desire. Something changed, anyway. She couldn't have said who actually broke the kiss and pulled away.

Maybe they both did.

For a long, long moment they stood there, still close enough to touch but not doing so. Staring at each other. Anna could see it was Luke looking down at her, not a tormented soul who was caught in a different reality. He knew who he was. Where he was.

And who he had been kissing.

Oh…Lord…

Anna swallowed hard. How on earth was she supposed to handle this? And not just the kiss. She'd witnessed another flashback incident. He'd said it wasn't going to happen again but it had. OK, so he wasn't in the middle of surgery and it hadn't endangered anyone, but there was no way her conscience would allow her to make excuses or ignore the implications of this.

She had a professional responsibility here and she had just complicated it to the nth degree by not thinking and by doing something as outrageous as kissing her new boss.

Then again…maybe that gave her a way in. An opening to talk about what had happened and what they were going to do about it.

She took a deep breath.

'Feeling better?'

She knew.

Too much.

Luke could feel himself closing off. Slamming mental doors in an effort to protect himself. To protect her?

'Maybe I should ask you the same thing,' he said coolly.

'Sorry?'

'You kissed me.' He managed to sound offhand, as though it hadn't blown him away. Like it hadn't meant anything at all.

He could see the way her eyes widened in shock as though he'd physically slapped her. The way she collected herself and looked away.

'You needed distraction.'

She couldn't know. Not everything. Not that she was already a distraction that he held onto every single night. That she represented a kind of rope that he could use to haul himself back to where he needed to be. A link that he had now tied firmly into the horrors of the past but one that led back to the present. To the future. A rope that he just needed to run his hand along to save his sanity. He would get where he intended to go eventually, as long as he could feel it running beside him.

The rope had been formed largely due to the intrigue that the contrast between what this woman was like at home and at work had sparked. Appreciating the fact that she was an attractive woman had woven another strand into it. But this…this blinding demonstration of what physical passion she was capable of did more than thicken the rope. It had come alive. It was warm and soft and he could stay glued to it with no effort at all. He didn't even need to touch it because a part of his mind could see it. Glowing.

'It was the Christmas crackers, wasn't it?' Anna asked. 'That sound like gunfire. You had some kind of flashback, like you did that day in surgery.'

'Nonsense.' It was. It had to be because if it wasn't, it would mean he would lose his job and that was all he had to fill his future.

And if he lost his job, he would lose Anna.

'I didn't like the noise,' he admitted stiffly. 'I told

you I didn't like parties. I left because I'd had enough.
The noise of the crackers was just the last straw.'

'Do you actually remember leaving the canteen?'

'Of course I do.' And he did, in a vague, dream-like
way. A background that had faded rapidly as he'd got
sucked into the flashback. He remembered that Anna
had been following him and… 'I…bumped someone,'
he said aloud. 'They spilled their drink.'

That surprised her. 'You didn't look like you were
aware of what you were doing.'

'I was…angry.'

'Why?'

'The party. The noise. All that food and drink and
the silly costumes. It's all such a waste of time and
money.'

She wasn't convinced. 'You didn't stop, Luke. You
didn't hear me calling you. I kissed you because I
couldn't think of anything else that might shock you
enough to get you off whatever planet you were on.'

'And I hope you plan to include that little gem in
whatever report you're obviously intending to make.'

A spark flashed in Anna's eyes. 'For God's sake,
Luke. This isn't about reports or jobs or whether someone gets embarrassed. This is about the fact that if
there's any chance of you "losing focus" or having a
flashback or whatever the hell that was really all about
that you're obviously not prepared to talk about, then
you can't operate on people.'

Luke watched the play of expression on Anna's face.
Her distress was all too easy to see in the frown lines
framing her eyes. In the way her lips trembled.

'I'm not out to get you,' she said fiercely. 'I want to help you.'

It was more than that, Anna realised as the words left her mouth. Had it been growing within her all the time she'd been watching Luke so carefully? Hoping to see him smile? Thinking so often about that short space of time when they'd been alone in her house and tumbling ever further into the confusion of her response to him. She could see the shadows that clouded his life and his eyes. There were things that haunted him and closed him off but she'd had a glimpse of the man he'd once been. Or could be.

She wanted, more than anything, to dispel those shadows. To get close enough to be allowed to help him.

She cared about him, Anna realised with something like dismay. She couldn't pinpoint when it had happened. Maybe the evidence had been there for days and days. A sum of everything she had seen or imagined. Elements that had floated in an uncoordinated fashion until the fear she had felt in seeing Luke virtually run from the canteen.

Something else had been added in when she had felt him respond to her kiss. A confused medley of caring and attraction. Not something she wanted to try and analyse and she certainly couldn't possibly tell him about any of it. Not when it was beyond the realms of possibility that he could feel anything like the same connection. Or that someone like him would want help from someone like her. He was more qualified than she was in so many ways. He was older. More skilled. He had seen and done things she would never want to do.

No wonder he was looking at her in a stony silence that took a little too long to be broken.

'Help me?' The words were bitten out scathingly. 'How do you propose doing that, exactly, Anna? By spreading a rumour that I might be unfit to do my job?'

'No.' Anna tried to catch his gaze but Luke was looking at the blasted potted tree they were standing beside. 'I think if you have the time, you'll get on top of whatever it is or find the help you need from someone a lot more qualified than I am.'

The snort of sound was incredulous. 'A shrink, you mean? Cheers, Anna.'

She ignored the rejection. She'd be angry, too, if someone suggested she couldn't handle her own issues. 'What I was going to suggest is that you don't operate unless I'm assisting you. For the protection of everybody involved.'

'You think I need supervising? By you?'

Anna flinched, biting back the observation that he had needed her during Colin Herbert's surgery. Something told her that Luke was trying to turn this into a confrontation he could feel justified in dismissing. She had to find a way to rescue this discussion or she would lose him. For ever.

The lift suddenly pinged into life close by. The doors slid open.

'Oops, wrong floor,' a masculine voice said. 'Hey... sounds like there's a party going on.'

'Yeah. Staff do, mate. Doctors and nurses. Security wasn't invited.'

'Shame. Wanna crash it?'

'Nah. More than our jobs are worth. Come on. Push the damn button.'

The doors slid shut again but a single word of the exchange lingered in Anna's ears.

Crash.

The kiss seemed a very long time ago. Hard to believe it had happened, even. But it had and for a brief time Anna had felt the same kind of connection she had that day he'd told her about his friend 'Crash'. It was possible to find a chink in the armour he wore.

'Actually,' she told Luke quietly, 'I was thinking of it more in terms of it being beneficial to both of us.'

'So I get a supervisor. What do you get?'

'A mentor,' Anna said. 'The chance to learn from someone whose work I already respect.' She managed a smile as Luke finally made eye contact again. Had she also managed to placate him? 'Think about it. I'm going to go back to that party for a bit. I need some food.'

Going back into the canteen was the last thing Luke wanted to do but he found himself following Anna after a brief hesitation. He needed to prove he could. To Anna and to anyone else who might have raised their eyebrows at the manner in which he'd left. Most of all, he needed to prove it to himself.

He could see Anna walking well ahead of him.

He didn't need a babysitter. Or help.

He didn't need somebody kissing him because they thought he was on 'another planet' either. Because they felt sorry for him?

No. Anna had said she could learn from him. That she respected his work. That didn't suggest she felt sorry for him. That kiss hadn't held any hint of unwillingness. Quite the opposite.

She'd kissed him because she'd wanted to kiss him. And what's more she'd wanted to keep on kissing him. It wouldn't have been difficult to pull away as soon as he'd responded. What she was saying was at odds with her behaviour. As much of a contradiction as her smart suits and paint-splattered old clothes. It was a puzzle and Luke liked that. He liked having Anna to think about. To ponder over. He was like a boat being tossed on a stormy ocean and Anna was his anchor. Maybe he could get to his future without her but it would be hard.

Lonely.

Luke was walking slowly. He could see the brightly lit interior of the canteen now, beyond the doors that were propped open by chairs. Anna had vanished into the crowd.

A couple stood on the shadowy side of the doors, partly screened because one of the chairs had shifted. A man and a woman. He wouldn't have taken any particular notice of them except that he could feel the atmosphere as he got closer.

A palpable tension. Maybe he recognised it because the air had the same charged feeling as it had had in those stunned moments after kissing Anna.

Sexual tension.

The man raised a hand to shove his fingers through his hair and then rub his forehead with the palm of his hand.

It was Josh O'Hara, Luke realised with astonishment. The A and E consultant he'd met the day he'd accompanied Roger into the emergency department after his cardiac arrest. The man last seen going after his distressed wife when she'd fled the Christmas party.

This woman was definitely not his wife.

She was quite tall and very beautiful, with long dark brown hair tied loosely into a ponytail.

'I saw her leave,' the woman was saying. 'She looked dreadful, Josh. You should go home. Talk to her.'

'I know. I will. But she had gone by the time I got outside and I just had to... Oh, God, Megan...'

It was only a snatch of conversation that he overheard and Luke wished he hadn't. There was something going on and he didn't need to know about it. It was none of his business how difficult or miserable other people were making their lives.

He had more than enough to deal with in his own.

Something made him turn his head again, however, as he pushed himself back into the party.

He saw Josh move his head. Tilting it further into the space behind the door that no one in here could see. Luke could sense the intent. Josh was planning to kiss this Megan. But almost at the same moment his head jerked backwards and he saw the shadowy figure ducking from reach as she emerged. She was shaking her head and she walked away without a backward glance.

Almost ran away, in fact.

That's what he should have done when Anna had gone to kiss him. Ducked the gesture and gone.

So why did he feel relieved that he hadn't even thought of doing so at the time?

Sleep proved elusive for Anna that night.

She couldn't close her eyes without thinking about that kiss and thinking about it brought it unerringly back to life.

She could still feel it.

The way his lips had moved over hers. Exploring them. Claiming them.

The strength in his hands. Their sure grip when he had pulled her close.

That incredibly gentle touch of his thumbs on her breasts.

And every time she relived that particular moment, her nipples tingled and a shaft of desire pierced her belly. And every time it got stronger. Feeding on itself. Taking on a life of its own. Becoming so intense it was physically painful.

With a groan, Anna shifted her body, turning over in her bed yet again. She had to stop thinking about it before day broke and she found herself on duty having had no rest.

Becoming aware of an odd thumping sound a moment later, she dragged her eyes open to find another set of eyes disturbingly close to her own. A long, wet tongue emerged to lick her face and the thumping accelerated when Anna laughed and wiped her face on her pillow to dry it.

'You're supposed to be asleep, Crash. On your bed.'

The puppy wriggled with delight at hearing her voice.

He obviously had no objection to being awake in the middle of the night.

'It's all right for you.' Anna pulled her hand out from under her pillow and reached to stroke the dog. 'You can sleep whenever you want to in the daytime. I need to sleep now and I can't.'

Crash leaned against the side of the bed, his chin tilting up against the mattress.

'He made out it was all my idea,' Anna informed Crash indignantly. 'And maybe it was, to start with, but you know what?'

Big ears twitched into their endearing sideways position and Anna smiled as she stroked them.

'He liked it as much as I did, that's what. He could have backed off and he didn't. He kissed me back.'

And how!

Anna let her breath out in a long sigh. A release that was partly pure pleasure at the memory but it also held a good whisper of frustration and more than a hint of anxiety about the implications of it all.

Silence gathered around them both as Anna's thoughts drifted on the breeze of that sigh. Her hand stilled and finally Crash heaved a sigh of his own, folding himself into a lumpy shape on the floor. He didn't go back to his own bed. He was still there, right beside her, prepared to share any vigil.

But Anna's eyes had drifted shut. One thing was certain. That kiss couldn't be undone and it put her and Luke on new ground. Unexplored, potentially dangerous but undeniably exciting territory.

Was Luke awake right now?

Would he remember that kiss?

Oh, yes. Anna was as certain of that as she was about the fact that the kiss couldn't be undone. Curiously, the knowledge was comforting and sleep finally came, but it didn't quite erase the tiny smile curling her lips.

CHAPTER SEVEN

IF LOOKS could kill...

Anna had to bite back an ironic smile as she pressed her foot on the control to start the water flowing and reached for the small, soap-impregnated scrubbing brush.

She'd probably been glaring at Luke in a very similar fashion that first day they'd been in Theatre together. Resenting his presence. Resenting him. Knowing that she was perfectly capable of doing the job without him being there. Feeling demoted in some way.

Now it was his turn. This was his first theatre slot following that little talk they'd had after she'd chased after him out of the staff Christmas party. The issue had been ignored for the day or two since then. In fact, Anna had had the impression that Luke had been avoiding her and that had been fine because any embarrassment lingering from the kiss had been somehow watered down until it didn't exist any more. Maybe he was hoping she would also forget her intention of scrubbing in with him for the safety of everyone involved but she hadn't forgotten. She hadn't waited for an invitation either, she had simply arrived.

Luke was apparently focused on scrubbing his hands and forearms with commendable thoroughness. Under his nails and between his fingers. Carefully angling the water flow so that it chased soap from the wrists up to his elbows and then dropping his hands to rinse from the wrists to his fingertips.

He muttered something under his breath as he reached for a sterile towel to dry his hands. It sounded like, 'Blackmail'.

'Sorry?'

'Nothing,' Luke growled. He stepped towards a theatre nurse waiting to help him don his gown and tie it. He cleared his throat and raised his voice. 'Good that you had the time to join us this morning, Anna.'

'Wouldn't have wanted to miss it,' she responded calmly. 'Pretty complicated case. I'm sure I'm going to learn a lot.'

The nurse made an approving sound. 'We all are,' she said admiringly. 'The gallery's a very popular place today. Full house.'

Anna looked up and smiled at Luke.

See? the smile said. Nobody's going to blink an eye at me being in Theatre with you. We are the only two people who know the real reason I have to be here and we both know why it has to be this way. Her smile faded but she held his gaze. Get used to it, she advised silently. You don't have to like it but you do have to deal with it.

Not that she expected him to deal with it in quite the way he did. By making her the lead surgeon. Talking her through the more complex aspects but only taking over for a few minutes at a time. It was a long and complicated surgery. The middle-aged female patient had a tumour in one lung that had spread to send tentacles around the major vessels that returned blood to the heart. The diagnosis had not been made until the reduction in blood flow due to the compression had given her heart failure. Swollen ankles and shortness of breath had finally made her seek medical help.

Fortunately, they found no cardiac involvement, but the dissection needed to remove as much of the tumour as possible was tricky. The patient was on bypass for nearly five hours as Anna and Luke worked to free the blood vessels and remove a lobe of her lung. By the end of the procedure Anna was exhausted. It wasn't until their patient was off bypass and her heart was beating again effectively that she could relax at all and it was then that she realised how Luke had 'dealt' with what he'd taken to be her supervision. He'd made her do the work and put so much pressure on her that she hadn't had time to even think about how focused he had been.

If that was how he wanted to play this, it was fine by her. Brilliant, in fact. In order to watch her and challenge her to improve her own skills, he was having to focus just as intently as he would if he was doing the procedure alone. More so, in some ways, because he had to think ahead in several directions so that he could troubleshoot if she wasn't on exactly the same wavelength.

Not that any major discrepancies in thinking had occurred. They had been amazingly in tune. So much so that Anna would have noticed instantly if Luke had lost focus. He hadn't. She had been challenged. She'd learnt a lot. To outward appearances they had worked as a close, harmonious team. The initiative had been a huge success as far as Anna was concerned and not only from a personal perspective. The patient's quality of life had been improved immensely and, if she was lucky, the length of it might be well beyond current expectations.

While Luke might not be prepared to recognise it yet, there had also been an additional, albeit secret bonus. He had done more than save face. Nobody watching—and there had been plenty of them—would have thought there were any undercurrents. They would have seen a head of department using exceptional skills in both surgery and teaching. His kudos had probably been raised by several degrees.

She might be exhausted now but she was also delighted. This could work.

And maybe it was a good thing that Luke was grumpy about it. Anna found she was frequently the recipient of glares over the next few days. Surprisingly often, and not just when she might have expected to cross paths with her senior colleague on ward rounds or in meetings.

It was getting so that she could sense that brooding, intense look from a considerable distance. From the end of a corridor, for instance, when she got out of a lift. Or from across the canteen when she joined a lunchtime queue. He seemed to be everywhere. All the time. It didn't matter how late she stayed at work to catch up on paperwork or how early she arrived to get ahead with whatever her day held. He was always there. Or was it just that she was so much more aware of it?

Too aware.

So, yes, it was good that he was grumpy. It meant that he wasn't thinking about that ill-advised distraction of kissing him. Or, if he did think about it, it didn't make him happy. Either way, he wasn't going to want a repetition of anything like that and that was exactly what Anna needed to push herself forward. To get over it and get on with her career and her life.

It was good.

It was. And if she reminded herself of that often enough, it would be true.

It should have been a relief to get Christmas and the start of the new year over with.

To get back to business as usual and away from all the forced cheerfulness of so many people trying to spread the joy of the season. Even patients were wishing him a happy new year, and there'd been far too many invitations to social events to find plausible excuses to avoid. So many smiles to produce.

Theatre had been the best place to be, of course. No tinsel allowed in there and nurses had to remove any silly seasonal earrings. He didn't tolerate small talk either so he didn't have to hear people talking about how excited their children had been as they had counted down the sleeps or what people were planning to do to see in the new year.

The only downside of being in Theatre had been that Anna had followed through her threat of supervising him. His response had been a form of attack in a way. If she wanted it to be like this and pretend she was there to improve her knowledge and skills then she could jolly well put the hard yards in instead of watching.

To his surprise, Anna had embraced the perspective and anyone in the gallery would have been convinced that that was the only reason she was in Theatre with him. Even more surprising was how much he enjoyed teaching her. At some point during that first operation on the woman with that nasty tumour threatening her cardiac function, Luke had stopped watching like a hawk to catalogue things he could be doing better than Anna and, instead, began channelling his knowledge and watching how quickly she understood what he was saying and how deftly the information was put into use.

He not only enjoyed the session, if he was really honest with himself, it had also been a relief to have her there.

Just in case.

Having watched Anna so closely during that surgery, Luke found himself continuing to watch her. He justified the scrutiny by telling himself he was watching her to see whether she was watching him. He watched her on ward rounds and in meetings. Even in the canteen. It was easy to create any number of opportunities to watch his assistant. He could find patients in the intensive care unit whose condition needed review. Departmental issues to discuss. Research projects to plan and monitor.

He discovered that Anna spent almost as much time in the hospital as he did. Way too many hours to have any kind of life away from a career. How did she find time to work on renovating that small cottage she lived in or to give her pet the attention it needed? Not that it was any of his business.

Or was it? At one point, he had to wonder if Anna's willingness to put in so much extra time was purely due to her dedication to her career or whether it had something to do with him still being in some kind of probationary period. Was he just aware of it because he was trying to keep one step ahead of her?

Or…was he watching for a signal of some kind that she remembered that kiss?

That she might find herself thinking about it as often as he did? Sometimes he would catch her gaze and he'd feel an odd buzz. A hint that she might remember.

That she might be wondering if it would be as extraordinary if it happened again.

Wanting it to happen again…

On one of the first days of the new year, Anna was with Luke and one of her registrars in his office. They were discussing one of the new research projects due to get under way.

'The main causes of prolonged hospital stay, morbidity and mortality following cardiac surgery are haemorrhage and infection,' Luke was reminding the young doctor present. 'And, quite often, infection is one of the sequelae of haemorrhage.'

Anna was listening quietly. This was an occasion when she was in Luke's company but his attention was on someone else. Even when he involved her in the discussion, he would forget to glare at her and the simmering undercurrent that she was waiting on for further evidence that Luke was unfit for the position of responsibility he held vanished. She could interact with—and enjoy—the company of an intelligent and stimulating colleague.

Bask in it even.

The registrar was nodding. 'Is that because they're more susceptible to infection due to a low cardiac output?'

'That's one of the parameters we need to keep in mind. There's also the issue of how long the chest has been open, whether they've been on bypass or whether hypothermia has been employed. There's a lot of stuff that's been written on aspects of this in other studies. What we're aiming to do is possibly challenge their findings with more current information or testing methods and/or add in any other significant parameters. Here, I've printed off some of the articles for you.'

The registrar's eyes widened. So did Anna's.

How long had Luke been in here already today to search out and print off this stack of material? And this was supposed to be a day off for him. Didn't he have other places he wanted to be? Or other people he wanted to be with?

And why was the thought that he'd rather be here, having a meeting with her, a cause for a rather pleasant internal glow? Not that Anna was going to analyse her reaction. She didn't get a chance to, anyway, because her pager sounded.

The disruption earned her a sharp look from Luke and Anna sighed inwardly. 'Can I use your phone?'

'Of course.'

She found Ben Carter on the other end of the line and listened intently.

'I'm on my way,' she said a short time later. 'Luke's here as well. We'll both come.'

'What's going on?' Luke demanded as she put the phone down.

'Helicopter's due to land any minute bringing in a thirteen-year-old boy. He's hypothermic and unstable. Ectopic activity increasing so he could arrest at any time. Ben wants us on standby in case rewarming via bypass is necessary. He's put a theatre on standby as well and called in a technician.'

'You're the one on call. I'm not even supposed to be here today.'

Anna was at the door already. She turned to see the registrar looking slack-jawed at the potential case and Luke looking...good grief...wary? Or hopeful? Why?

She didn't have time to consider any personal issues. There was a child's life at stake here and if it came to trying to rewarm him by using cardiopulmonary bypass it was new territory for her. She'd read about it but never even seen it done. A flicker of something like panic had to be crushed.

She held Luke's gaze for a heartbeat despite—or perhaps because of—knowing he could probably see that flash of fear.

'But you are here,' she said quietly. The presence of

the registrar in the room ceased to matter. 'And I need you, Luke.'

They both followed her but it was Luke's tall form striding beside her that gave Anna confidence. They moved fast enough for him to be limping by the time they reached the emergency department but they were still side by side.

A team.

The main resuscitation area in Emergency was crowded. Helicopter paramedics in their bright overalls and helmets were there with the medical staff, transferring their patient with great care. There was a bustle of activity and a buzz of urgent instructions.

'Gently! Don't bump him. Cardiac function is fragile.'

'Is the Bair Hugger on?'

'Dextrose, not saline. Get some more in the microwave to get warmed.'

'Make sure that oxygen is warmed and humidified.'

'Get some more dots on. We need a twelve-lead ECG.'

'What's his temperature now?'

'Nineteen point five degrees Celsius.'

Luke whistled silently.

'The lowest ever temperature that someone's survived without neurological impairment was around thirteen degrees, wasn't it?' Anna kept her voice low. The boy's mother was on the other side of the room, looking terrified.

Ben Carter was leading the resus team and he wasn't

happy with the oxygen saturation level of the boy's blood.

'I'm going to intubate,' he decided. 'Anyone who's not directly involved step back a bit, please. It's critical we do this with minimal movement.'

One of the paramedics stepped well back, close to where Anna and Luke were watching. Standing by.

'What happened?' Anna asked.

'Kid got ice-skates for Christmas,' the paramedic said quietly. 'They live on a farm up north a bit and there's a dam. He and his brother went skating and he hit some thin ice and went through. Took his brother about thirty minutes to find a branch big enough to get him out and another half an hour to run home and raise the alarm. Probably ninety minutes before we arrived on scene and the wind chill was significant. First temperature we got was eighteen degrees.'

'Cardiac rhythm?' Luke was watching Ben and his team securing the boy's airway but he was listening to Anna's conversation with the paramedic.

'Slow atrial fibrillation. Marked J waves.'

Anything below a core temperature of thirty degrees was enough to put someone at risk of cardiac arrhythmias and arrest. This boy was dangerously cold but there was still hope. Anna remembered a lecturer at medical school talking about hypothermia.

'You're not dead until you're warm and dead,' he'd said.

The Bair Hugger was a blanket designed to force a current of hot air over the patient's skin. Intravenous fluids were warmed to try and raise blood temperature but these methods might be too slow to help someone with such severe hypothermia.

'Luke.' Ben had finally stepped back from the initial flurry of making sure their patient was as stable as possible. 'Didn't think you were on today.'

'I'm not.' Luke flicked a sideways glance at Anna and there was a hint of a smile on his lips. He was here because she wanted him to be but it seemed like he wanted her to know he was happy to be here.

'Well, I'm glad you're here. Both of you.'

'What's the plan?'

Ben looked grim. 'External exogenous rewarming is only going to achieve a rate of about a two point five degree increase per hour. He's too cold to wait that long. With full cardiopulmonary bypass we could get a rewarming rate of seven point five degrees an hour.'

'We can't justify something as invasive as bypass unless he's arrested. What about pleural lavage?'

The cardiothoracic registrar was looking bemused. Anna leaned closer. 'That's using an inter-costal catheter to pour large volumes of warmed water into the chest cavity.'

'Still pretty invasive,' Ben was saying. 'And possibly less effective. Right now we'll keep ventilator support going and monitor his rhythm. We should get results on the bloods we've drawn soon. I want to see what his acid-base status is. At least slow A fib isn't a malignant rhythm.'

'We need an arterial blood gas as well,' Anna put in. She stepped forward to retrieve the sheet of paper emerging from the twelve-lead ECG machine but she didn't get time to analyse the trace. An alarm sounded on one of the monitors at the head of the bed.

'He's in V tach,' someone warned. 'I can't find a pulse.'

'V fib now.'

'Start CPR,' Ben ordered, moving to the side of the bed. He looked back at Luke, who gave a terse nod.

'One shock. If that doesn't work, bring him up to Theatre under CPR.'

'Theatre 3's on standby. Bypass technician was paged when I called Anna.'

'Charging,' someone announced. 'Stand clear.'

Luke gave another nod and touched Anna's arm. 'Let's go. Better if we're scrubbed and ready by the time they come up if we're going to be needed.'

A cold, still heart.

This lad was technically dead and here they were thinking they could play God and bring him back to life.

Luke could see the lines of strain around Anna's eyes. He knew that her lips beneath that mask would be pressed tightly together. And, despite how subtle it was, he saw the way she flinched when her hands touched the chilled flesh in the small chest they had just opened.

'We need to work fast,' he reminded her quietly. 'Standard bypass. Arterial cannula in the ascending aorta. Right atrial cannulation with a single, two-stage cannula.'

Anna nodded. She was already placing a purse-string

suture around the major vessel that took blood from the heart to the rest of the body.

Within minutes, with both surgeons working together in a tense atmosphere, the cannulae had been positioned and the boy's blood was now being circulated through the heart-lung bypass machine instead of his frail-looking body. Circulated and being carefully warmed.

There was nothing more they needed to do surgically until it was time to take him off bypass and repair the vessels currently holding the thick tubes. Then they would—hopefully—restart his heart, close his chest and wait to see if he woke up. Wait to see whether his brain function had survived this terrible insult.

Hours later, Luke found Anna in her office. She had been pacing back and forth between the intensive care unit and the wards. Between the canteen, where she'd eaten nothing at all, and the ICU. Between her office and the ICU.

'It's taking too long,' she said when Luke appeared through the door.

'He's in a good rhythm. Body temperature is within a normal range. The hyperglycaemia has been corrected. Renal function is looking good.'

'I know, I know.' But Anna was still pacing, her arms wrapped around her body as if for comfort. 'Blood gases are fine, too, and I'm happy with cardiac pressures. But what about possible complications like thromboembolism? Or disseminated intravascular coagulation?' She dragged in a breath. 'Have you met his mum, Janet? Did you know his big brother is six years older and that she had two late miscarriages before Jamie came along? What…what if he doesn't wake up?'

'Anna…' Luke stepped in front of her, forcing her to stand still. He gripped her upper arms. She was so wrapped up in this case, so desperate for them to have succeeded, she was losing her perspective. He'd never seen her like this.

So involved.

Caring so much.

'The sedation is only being lightened slowly. It'll take time for him to start breathing on his own and he's not going to wake up before then.'

'But what if—?'

'Stop,' Luke commanded.

He was still holding her. Looking down at Anna's pale face. Those astonishing green eyes were locked on his. Hanging onto his words of reassurance. Believing what he was telling her. And then his gaze dropped to her mouth and he saw the tiny tremble of her lips and that undid something deep inside him.

'What you need, Dr Bartlett,' he said very softly, 'is distraction.'

She caught the meaning of his words as soon as he'd uttered them. Her gaze dropped to his mouth and he found himself running his tongue across his lower lip. Slowly. Deliberately.

Time came to a standstill.

'Mmm.'

The sound Anna made could have been agreement but it sounded more like need. Desire.

It was all the permission Luke needed. His hands left

her arms. He used one to cradle the back of her head and with the other he cupped her chin. Then he bent his head.

He was initiating this kiss. He was in control and he intended to make sure Anna was aware of nothing but the sensations he was going to provide with his lips. And his tongue.

This was going to be a kiss that Anna would have no chance of forgetting. Ever.

Anna kept her arms wrapped around her body even after that first touch of Luke's lips.

She'd needed to keep hold of herself in those seconds leading up to that kiss. Feeling the way his fingers splayed and claimed control of her head and her chin. Sensing the intent of this being far more significant than the last time they'd kissed.

She'd kept her eyes open as she watched his face dipping to meet hers. So slowly. And she'd held herself even more tightly with her own arms then because she'd been sure she was falling.

Desire had sucked her into some kind of vortex and she was spinning wildly. Totally out of control.

And then his lips had touched hers and moved over her mouth. Questing. Claiming. Giving. Demanding her involvement and response.

Sensations rippled through Anna and unlocked the awful tension that had been building from the moment she'd touched Jamie's small, cold heart. Her skin tingled and seemed to melt and then her muscles gave up conscious control. Her arms let go of her own body and, instead, moved to hold Luke's. She could feel the strength of his muscles and the steady thump of his heart and all the time his mouth was doing such amazing things to hers. Her bones were melting now. He could just scoop her into his arms and lay her down on the floor of this office and she'd willingly—

Luke pulled away and for a dazed moment all Anna could think of was holding on more tightly. Pulling him back.

'Phone's ringing,' he said gently.

'Oh...' Anna put her hand to her mouth and took in a shaky breath. 'I—I'd better answer it, hadn't I?'

Luke was smiling at her.

Really smiling. His eyes were crinkled and the corners of his mouth had disappeared into those deep furrows beneath his cheeks.

'Yes.' He nodded. 'I think you had.'

She actually stumbled moving towards her desk. Heaven only knew what the intensive care consultant on the other end of the line thought of her initial stammered response but the content of the call was more than enough to bring her back to the present and reality. She put the phone down a moment later.

'Jamie's breathing on his own,' she told Luke. 'He squeezed his mum's hand.'

To her horror, Anna felt tears gather in her eyes. She never cried. She most certainly never cried in front of a male colleague.

But Luke didn't seem to mind. He reached out and pulled her into his arms. Not to kiss her this time but simply to hold her. For long enough to be more than a celebratory hug. Long enough for Anna to know that he understood exactly how she was feeling. Long enough for her to take several deep breaths and get her brain working properly again.

'If we get up there soon, we might see him wake up and then we'll get an idea of what kind of neurological impairment he might be left with.'

An hour later they were part of the group around Jamie's bed in the intensive care unit as the young boy's eyes flickered open. His father and older brother were there now, too, but it was his mother who was closest. The first person Jamie saw.

He blinked a few times. Opened his mouth and moved his lips but his brow furrowed as though he couldn't find a way to make his mouth do what he wanted it to do. He stared blankly at the woman leaning so close to him, with tears running down her face.

Everybody present was holding their breath.

Luke and Anna were standing side by side. So closely their shoulders were pressed together. Unseen by anyone else in the cubicle, Luke's hand moved just enough for his fingers to tangle with Anna's.

Jamie tried again.

'Mum?' The word was croaky but clear. 'What's the matter?'

Anna felt her hand gripped so tightly it was painful but all she moved was her head. Just far enough to meet Luke's gaze.

To see the triumph at the back of his eyes.

He let go of her hand before anyone could notice but

that didn't break the link. It was still there in his gaze. A connection that had taken them way beyond being merely colleagues.

He would come home with her tonight. Or she would go home with him. It didn't matter. It wasn't even a decision that needed to be discussed because it had already been made. Back in her office. Or maybe well before that but neither of them had taken that step forward.

Now they had taken that step and they both knew there was no going back.

CHAPTER EIGHT

CRASH stayed at the farm up the road from Anna's cottage.

'He often does,' she assured Luke. 'That way I don't disturb the Turners by collecting him if I have to work late. June loves him to bits. She would have kept him except that Doug put his foot down.'

She was talking quickly, Luke noticed, as the glow of realising she had kept the name he'd suggested for her puppy wore off. Was she nervous? Unsure she was making the right choice here, a passenger in his car as they drove away from St Piran's hospital that evening?

He was feeling a bit uptight himself. Sex in an army camp was a lot easier than this. You got attracted or desperate for distraction and a tent or somewhere private was never far enough away to allow for second thoughts. No awkwardness. No pressure. No strings afterwards.

This was different.

There was danger here. For the peace of mind he was struggling to achieve. For the relationship with an important colleague that could get damaged. And for Anna…because she might get hurt. She might want something that he couldn't give her.

Like commitment.

Curious that the prospect of hurting Anna outweighed the more personal ramifications this step could represent. He wanted to protect her. To turn his vehicle round and take her back to the hospital. Let Anna drive home to her small cottage. Alone.

Luke flicked a sideways glance at his passenger as he turned onto the road that led to his beachside house. She'd pulled out whatever it was she used to restrain her hair and it tumbled to her shoulders. Her hands were clasped in her lap and she was still wearing her power-dressing clothes.

Not for long, though. Luke found he had to lick suddenly dry lips. There was still time, he told himself. He could turn round. Tell her that he'd changed his mind and maybe this wasn't such a good idea after all, given how closely they needed to keep working together.

But Anna seemed to sense that quick glance and she turned her head as well. Her eyes seemed huge in a pale face as they drove under a streetlamp. Her lips were parted a little and maybe she was experiencing the same kind of dry mouth he was because she mirrored his own action and licked her lips. The action rendered Luke helpless to act on any good intentions. Almost ashamed of himself, he cleared his throat and it came out in a kind of growl.

Anna sighed, assuming the sound was related to the conversation she was using to fill the awkward journey.

'I know, I was crazy to take on a puppy with the kind

of hours I have to work but when I am at home he's wonderful company.'

Oh, God…was she lonely?

The urge to protect this woman from being hurt morphed into something very different. He might not be able to offer commitment or any kind of a future but he could step, temporarily at least, into that void in her life and give her some companionship. The kind of closeness that would make her feel like she wasn't alone in the world. That someone cared enough to give her pleasure.

That someone cared at all.

She wasn't the only one here who needed that.

Anna was pleased that Luke didn't draw the curtains in the bedroom he led her into. His house was almost on a beach. Not one of the rocky, dangerous coves that dotted this coast but a sandy stretch with enough width for smooth waves. The kind of gem tucked amongst the rocky ones that surfers loved to try and keep secret. She could see it because it was a clear, cold night and there was enough moonlight to not only show her the view but to mean that harsh electric lighting was unnecessary inside. That pleased her, too.

She had already declined an offer for any food or drink. That could come later. Or not. They were there for one reason and that was to continue the kiss that had begun in her office. To finish what had been started.

Standing here was different, however. Anna was too nervous to look at the bed so she stood in front of the big window that had the view of the beach and stared out. Luke came to stand very close behind her. His hands brushed her arms. A slow stroke from her elbows to her shoulders and back again and there his hands lingered.

'Are you sure about this, Anna?' he asked quietly. 'It's OK if you want to change your mind.'

She turned and it was suddenly very easy. As though his body warmth was an irresistible magnet. Her breast brushed his hand as she moved and the sensation blitzed any final nerves.

'I don't want to change my mind,' she said softly. 'Do you?'

By way of response, Luke bent his head and his lips touched hers. The chill of the evening outside was coming through the uncovered glass beside them and the pale light of the moon offered no pretence of warmth, but Anna had never felt heat like this.

Scorching her lips as Luke claimed her mouth. Trickling over her body with the touch of his hands as he undid the buttons of her blouse and undressed her. Building inside as she watched him strip and stand there, bathed in moonlight. Tall and lean and powerful. Magnificently male.

She wanted him to catch her in his arms and throw her onto the bed but, instead, he came to stand in front of her. Skin to skin. Her breasts pressed into the hardness of his chest and she could feel his arousal against her belly. He wanted her. As much as she wanted him. His arms came around her then and their lips met. In a kind of slow dance, moving as one person, they somehow made their way from the window to the bed and then they were lying together. A tangle of limbs and passionate kisses and a consuming need that brooked no delay other than Luke fishing in a bedside drawer for protection.

The few seconds of watching him was like being suspended in time and space for Anna. The piercing anticipation had to be the most delicious sensation she had ever experienced and she clung to it, knowing that it would end very soon. Wanting it to end so that she could feel Luke inside her. Touching parts of her body that had never felt so hollow. Reaching places that weren't even physical.

She just knew he would be able to touch her soul.

Passion so intense had to explode and burn out in a dramatic climax and if that had been the end of it, it would have been incredibly satisfying on a physical level. Even better was that Luke smiled at Anna when they finally caught their breath.

'Now we can really get to know each other,' he promised.

And they did. A slow exploration of each other's bodies. A shaping of muscles on Anna's part with a compliment on how fit he must be. A tracing of Anna's breast with a single finger that ran across the flatness of her stomach to her belly button.

'You are beautiful,' Luke told her.

She found the scars on Luke's leg and he tried to move her hand but she resisted.

'They're part of you, Luke,' she said gently. 'Don't hide. Please.'

He went very still as she touched the misshapen muscle of his thigh and the lumpy ridges of the scars.

'Ugly, isn't it?' he ground out finally.

'No. They tell me that you have courage. That you're different.' Anna propped herself up on one elbow to look down at Luke. Even in this half-light she could see the shadows in his eyes that were part of the scars she had just been touching. What she could feel on his leg was nothing compared to the scars that had to be still hidden.

'Special,' she added in a whisper, leaning down to kiss him. She tried to put what she couldn't put into words into that kiss. To tell him that she accepted him for who he was. With scars. That she had courage too. That she could be trusted.

They made love again and this time it was slow and sweet and, in its wake, Anna fell asleep in Luke's arms, drifting off in a cloud of utter contentment. Of promise. Of a hope so compelling it was safer to go to sleep than contemplate the notion that it might be unjustified.

She woke some time later to find herself alone in a strange bed. She lay there, listening, but the house had that peculiar kind of silence that told her she was alone within these walls. Turning her head, she caught the glow of a digital, bedside clock. It was 3 a.m. Where on earth was Luke?

Taking the rumpled sheet with her to wrap around her body, Anna climbed from the bed. Instinct took her straight to the window and she stared out, the way she had when she'd first entered this room. For a long minute it was too dark to see anything. Then the moon emerged from thick cloud and she saw him. On the beach.

Running.

How could he be doing that? Not just because it was the middle of the night and it had to be well below zero out there, but how hard would it have to be to do that, in soft sand, on a leg that was damaged enough to make him limp at a fast walking pace or put him in noticeable pain when he had to stand for any length of time?

He was more driven than Anna had suspected and it was disturbing. Maybe he wasn't driving himself towards something. Maybe he was trying to run away.

He came back to the bed a while later, warm and fresh from a hot shower, and when he reached for Anna, she was happy to sacrifice further sleep to make love yet again. This time, however, there was an edge that hadn't been there before. Concern for Luke. The knowledge that she was with a deeply troubled man.

When daylight broke, Luke was absent from the bed again but Anna knew where to look. He wasn't running on the beach this time. She could see the dark shape striding into the surf. Diving into a breaking wave further out and then surfacing to swim, with a strong, steady stroke, parallel to the sand.

She had showered and dressed by the time Luke returned to the house. She saw him coming up the path in his wetsuit, carrying dripping flippers in one hand. His face registered surprise.

'You're not going to stay for breakfast?'

'I'd better not. I need to collect Crash and I've got a huge list of things I want to get done on my day off. If I can finish the painting and get the windowsills sanded and varnished, I can put my bedroom back together properly tonight.'

'Shall I come over after work and give you a hand?'

Anna hesitated. She could decline the offer and send a signal that she wanted to slow down whatever was happening between them. If she accepted, it would take them to a new level. The start of a relationship instead of a one-night stand.

Luke was pulling the zipper on his wetsuit. Peeling it away to reveal his bare torso, and Anna's body instantly reminded her of exactly what it had felt like to have those hands peeling away her own clothing. The sound of the nearby surf reminded her of watching him in the night, punishing his body by pounding over the sand. Enduring the pain in his leg because he was driven. And courageous.

And she...loved him for it?

Oh, help!

'I—I'd love a hand,' she heard herself say aloud. Good grief, what was she doing? She couldn't stop herself. 'I'll cook you some dinner. Do you realise we totally forgot to eat last night?'

Luke looked more surprised than he had on finding her dressed and ready to leave.

And then he smiled. 'Sometimes food can be over-rated. I had everything I needed.'

Anna actually blushed as she smiled back. 'Me, too.'

A day at home was important for Anna.

By throwing herself into the renovations of her

cottage and spending time playing with Crash, she could banish Dr Bartlett and let her recharge her professional batteries. Usually the door between work and home was firmly closed but today there was a wedge preventing that. She found herself wondering where Luke might be and what he might be doing.

He wouldn't be in Theatre. Although the tacit agreement that they would act as a team for surgery was still new, it was working and Anna trusted Luke not to break it. If something extraordinary happened, like Jamie's case had presented yesterday, he would call her in.

How was Jamie today? Anna peeled off her gloves and discarded the sandpaper she had been using, intending to make a call, but the phone rang as she walked towards it.

'I thought you might like an update on Jamie,' Luke said. 'We're transferring him to the ward this afternoon. He's bouncing back from his surgery remarkably well and I think we'll find he'll end up showing little effect from being virtually frozen to death.'

Anna listened to Luke's voice and absorbed the welcome news. The call ended, she went back to varnishing her windowsill. Thoughts of Luke were there as pervasively as the smell of polyurethane. Catching sight of Crash ripping her sandpaper to shreds with his tail thumping, she made a mental note to get to the supermarket so that she had something to feed Luke for dinner tonight. What did he like to eat? What would he like to do when they'd finished eating?

Oh, Lord. She could only hope that Luke wasn't in his office, struggling to concentrate on important paperwork, getting ambushed by memories of their astonishing night together. On the other hand, maybe she hoped he was. This was all as confusing as it was wonderful.

She put a roast of beef in the oven to cook slowly and fill her cottage with a welcoming aroma. She wanted Luke to feel welcome. She purchased wine, too. She wanted him to relax and feel comfortable. This was another new step. A chance to get to know each other better on more than a physical level. A chance to talk about things other than work. A chance to test these newborn feelings she was experiencing. To see if there was a chance of finding ground that might nurture them or whether they needed to be ruthlessly weeded out.

Except that turned out to be harder than Anna had anticipated. Luke seemed happy to be in her home and he clearly appreciated the meal, though he declined any alcohol. He was polite but unforthcoming when it came to any personal conversation.

'What was it like?' Anna asked at one stage. 'Working in a field hospital?'

'Basic. Fast and bloody.' His tone was detached enough to signal a lack of desire to go into details. 'These Yorkshire puddings are fantastic,' he said into the moment's silence that fell then. 'Where did you learn to cook like this?'

'My mother was adamant that a girl had to be able to cook. So was my father, come to that.'

'And you weren't.'

It was a statement, rather than a question. Delivered with a quizzical edge that made Anna think he could see right into places in her heart that even she didn't peer into too deeply any more.

'Things that boys were allowed to do were more important. I jumped through the girl hoops but it wasn't enough.' Anna looked down at her plate. 'My father wanted a son that he never got.'

She heard Luke's fork clatter as he put it down. Then she felt him touch her hand. 'He got something better, then, didn't he? They must be very proud of you.'

Anna shrugged. 'Surprised might be closer to the mark. Disappointed, maybe, that I didn't become a teacher or a nurse and shower them with grandchildren. Grandsons,' she amended with an attempt to lighten the revelation with a smile. 'What was your family like, Luke? You weren't an only child, were you?'

'No. All boys in my family but if there had been a girl she would have been expected to do the boy things. She wouldn't have had a choice, really, being dragged from one military post to another. I was the one to break the family tradition and become a doctor instead of a soldier. Even then, I was expected to aim for a career as an army medic. I rebelled.'

'You went in the end. I'm sure your parents are proud.'

'They're in New Zealand,' Luke said, as though that answered the unspoken question. And then he steered the conversation away from himself again. 'What's the next project you've got lined up for the cottage?'

He helped her clean up after the meal and then he helped her move the bedroom furniture back into place. And then, as Anna had hoped he would, he took her into her own bed and made love to her. He wouldn't stay the night, however.

'I've got so much reading to catch up on,' he excused himself in the early hours. 'You've got no idea how out of date you can get by taking a year or two off. I've got to keep up my exercise program, too, and I can't miss my early swim.'

Too many good reasons not to stay.

'Don't you ever sleep, Luke?'

'Sleep's overrated.' He bent to kiss Anna again as he took his leave. 'Life's too short to waste it.'

Maybe sleep wasn't so overrated.

Fatigue was like a form of anger. Something that simmered and bubbled occasionally to splash in unexpected directions.

'That is a surgical mask, not a damned bib. Don't come into this theatre unless you're going to wear it properly.'

The junior theatre nurse went pale and fled. Luke looked away as Anna glanced up from the meticulous stitches she was placing in preparation for a mitral valve replacement. He knew there had been no real reason to snap at the nurse. She'd been delivering some new IV fluid supplies, not planning to come and lean over the operating table.

'I've got all the anular sutures placed and tagged,' Anna said.

'Let's get the valve seated, then, and tie them off.'

'OK,' Anna said as the procedure continued. 'I'll have the aortic needle vent now, thanks.'

Luke watched as she removed more air and then re-started the heart.

'Can you elevate the apex of the left ventricle?' she asked him. 'If those adhesions are too dense, I'll go for clamping the aorta. I'd like to follow up with an echocardiograph to check.'

Would she say something when this was over? Reprimand him in some way for his irritation with the junior nurse? He probably deserved it, given that this wasn't the first time.

Ripping off his mask and the disposable hat as he left Theatre, Luke pushed his fingers through his flattened hair. What was wrong with him?

It wasn't simply fatigue. Insomnia had been a part of his life for many months now and he had coped. Maybe the difference was that he was choosing to stay awake when he craved sleep. Night after night. It had been nearly a week now. He would hold Anna in his arms after they'd made love and feel the way her body soft-ened and her breathing slowed. The blissful temptation of sleep would pull at him in those moments, too.

Taunt him.

When he needed sleep and was ready for it, it wouldn't come. If offered itself at times like this, when he couldn't accept. He just couldn't go there because he had no control over what his sleeping mind chose to do. While it could be the saving of him to have Anna to hold close in the wake of a nightmare, he had to spare her from sharing that part of his life, because then he'd have to talk about it and he wasn't going to do that with anybody.

If he could bury it, it would go away.

Eventually.

Luke fell asleep the next night Anna stayed at his house.

Maybe that was what had woken her—the change in how he was holding her. It was more like she was holding him right now. With a careful tilt of her head, she could see his face and it looked so different she was shocked. He looked so much younger. Unguarded.

Vulnerable.

Those piercing, intense eyes were shuttered. His lips were soft and slightly parted and she could hear his soft, even breaths. Even the furrows at the top of his nose had softened. Anna willed herself not to move. She didn't want to wake him. Heaven knew, he needed the sleep. Nobody could keep up the kind of pace Luke did without coming to physical harm. It was no wonder he snapped at the people around him occasionally.

So she stayed awake. Holding this man she was coming to feel more deeply for every day. Wanting to protect him and give him the healing rest that only sleep could provide. That was probably why she felt the moment the nightmare started. The way the muscles beneath her hands and arms became so tense. She could hear the way his breathing became shallow and rapid. His heart was pounding beneath his ribs and she could feel the rumble of his moan even before it reached his lips.

'No-o-o-o...'

'Luke. Wake up.' Anna held him more tightly. 'It's all right. It's just a bad dream.'

She couldn't hold him now. The strength in his body was frightening as he twisted and fought whatever demons had come in his sleep. Anna could see the sheen of sweat on his body. His breath came in choking gasps now—as though he was suffocating.

'Arghhh!' The sound was one of agony.

The covers were hurled back from the bed and Luke swung his legs over the side. He was almost crouching there and he covered his face with his hands.

Anna scrambled to her knees and across the bed. Kneeling behind Luke, she wrapped her arms around him.

'It's all right,' she said, hoping her voice wouldn't betray how shaky she was feeling. 'I'm here, Luke. You had a nightmare.' That's all, she wanted to add, but bit the words back. This wasn't something that should be belittled in any way.

His breathing was slowing now. For a moment he leaned back into Anna's embrace but then he lurched to his feet.

'I need some fresh air,' was all he said. He began dragging on clothes. Fleecy track pants. Running shoes.

She couldn't make him tell her anything about the nightmare if he didn't want to. Anna closed her eyes. Waiting. Hoping.

'You...' Luke paused as he got halfway across the room but he didn't turn round. 'You weren't... I didn't want you to see that.'

'It was a nightmare, Luke. Don't go. You don't have to run away from it.'

The huff of sound from him was angry. She knew nothing. And he wanted it to stay that way.

'Would you rather I went home?'

'Up to you. I won't come back to bed. I've got some work I may as well do now that I'm awake. After my run.'

And with that he was gone.

Anna didn't want to wait. There was no moon tonight so she wouldn't be able to see him down on the beach. She didn't want to watch either. Luke had his own way of dealing with whatever was bothering him and it didn't include her.

What was she to him? With a sinking heart Anna found her clothes and then the keys to her car. Was this just about the sex?

Distraction?

When she arrived home to her cold cottage, Anna put an electric heater on and made a pot of tea. It was nearly 4 a.m. and she was far too wound up to go to sleep again. She missed Crash.

Opening her briefcase, she got her laptop out and connected to the internet. With no emails that caught her interest, she idly clicked on a search engine and stared at the flashing cursor.

'PTSD', she tapped in on impulse.

So many sites. She opened the one that had been given first place in the queue and within minutes she was totally engrossed.

Post traumatic stress disorder was a syndrome that

could develop following any traumatic event. Things like natural disasters and car crashes, violent assaults or even medical procedures, especially for children. Top of the list, however, as she'd known quite well, was war.

Traumatic experience put the mind and body into a state of shock, she read, but most people could make some sense of what had happened, process the resulting emotions and come out of it eventually. In PTSD, the person remained in psychological shock. There was a disconnection between the memory of the event and how the victim felt about it.

Anna read on, almost feverishly, skipping a few paragraphs to the heading of 'Symptoms'.

Nightmares.

Flashbacks.

Difficulty falling or staying asleep.

Irritability or outbursts of anger.

She found herself nodding at that one. She hadn't said anything about the way Luke had snapped at that poor theatre nurse the other day but other people were talking about it. And about the way he had avoided all social invitations outside the hospital over the Christmas and New Year period. Some were keen to remember his odd behaviour at the one event he had attended and the way he'd stormed out of the canteen.

Her eyes drifted further down the list. Not that she needed any more information to confirm what she was already convinced of.

Depression was common. So was guilt. People often attempted to numb themselves through substance abuse. Luke obviously avoided drinking but wouldn't his exercise regime fit into the same category? How numb would you get, running or swimming in the middle of winter? And physical pain could override mental suffering.

The victim could also feel detached from others and emotionally numb. They would have a sense of a limited future and wouldn't expect to live a normal life span or get married and have a family. PTSD would harm relationships, the ability to function and their quality of life.

There were treatments suggested, of course, but they came with the background rider that the sufferer had to be willing to confront it and not see the admission as a sign of weakness. Luke had been brought up in a military family. Was it the kind of thing that didn't get mentioned? That he wouldn't be able to allow himself to admit? He'd denied having flashbacks. Pushed her away in the wake of that nightmare. He 'hadn't wanted her to see it'. Had he ever, in fact, gone to sleep before when she'd been in the same bed?

Maybe her intrusion into his personal life was making it worse. Removing opportunities he might have otherwise had to sleep. Putting stress on him by making him think he had to factor her into a future that might already seem too difficult.

It was so clear to her that Luke was suffering from PTSD. It was also very clear that the only way to conquer it was to confront it. Somehow he would have to learn to accept it as part of his past. Numbing it or pushing the memories away would only make it worse and it was more likely to emerge under stress.

The sound of a distant beeping finally intruded on Anna's thoughts and she realised her alarm clock was going off. Her huff of laughter was ironic. It was time to get up and get ready for work. With a heavy heart she went through the motions, but she couldn't stop thinking about the pieces that had finally fallen into place and created a picture so much darker than she had feared.

As far as she was concerned, she was a part of that picture. She was in far too deep to escape. She didn't want to.

For better or worse, she had fallen in love with Luke Davenport.

She wanted to help him.

But how?

CHAPTER NINE

'WHAT's this?' Anna had stooped to pick something up from the floor of Luke's office.

He glanced at the scalloped, gilt-edged card she was holding. Damn, he hadn't noticed he'd missed his aim.

'Nothing,' he said. 'It was supposed to go in the bin.'

'But...' Anna was reading the fancy calligraphy and then she looked up with a stunned expression on her face. 'Luke...this is an invitation to a medal ceremony, isn't it? Returning Heroes. With a ball to honour the recipients of the medals.'

'I'm not going. I hate parties.' Luke swivelled his desk chair so that he could drop a file into the cabinet behind him. 'Was there something you wanted to talk to me about?'

'Yes.'

Another file tab caught Luke's eye and he pulled it out. It took several seconds to register the silence. Anna wasn't going to talk to him until she was confident he was listening.

Fine. He swung the chair back around. 'What do you want to talk about?'

She was still holding the card and looked down at it again. 'This.'

'That's not why you came in here. You didn't know it existed.' He could feel his eyes narrowing as he sighed. 'What was the real reason you came in?'

'This isn't even an invitation. It says you're "required to attend". That sounds pretty official. Will you get into trouble if you don't go?'

Luke gave a huff of laughter. 'What can they do? Kick me out of the army? Give my medal to someone else? That's fine by me. I don't want the damn medal.'

'Why not?' Anna sank into the other chair in his office but her gaze was unwavering. Fixed on Luke. She wasn't going to let this one go.

He felt trapped. Angry. The way he had ever since he'd woken from that nightmare to find Anna in his bed. This was becoming a problem. OK, the sex was great. She was great. He loved seeing her like this, at work, in her neat clothes and with her hair all scraped back. Being completely professional in their interactions while all the time they both knew what it would be like after, away from work.

When the clothes came off and the communication came through touch and not words. When they could both escape to a place that promised only pleasure.

But maybe it had run its course. It wasn't going to work. Not long term.

She was already too close. Had seen too much. She didn't represent a rope that he could use to help him into his future any more. She was starting to resemble a roadway. With traffic in both directions. He didn't want to go back. He couldn't. Because if he did, he would be taking Anna with him and she would see who he really was and then she would be the one to go.

And that might finally destroy him.

Anna could see the play of emotion on Luke's face. The annoyance that she was pushing when he'd made it clear he wasn't interested in either going to this ceremony or talking about it. She knew perfectly well she was stepping over a boundary here. She could almost see him weighing up whether she was worth the trouble.

Would he tell her to get out? Push so hard she had no choice but to leave? He'd been holding her at a distance ever since that nightmare. They hadn't been to bed together for three days now. They hadn't even spent that much time together at work. He was avoiding her because he didn't want to talk about the nightmare. Probably didn't want to admit how often he had them. Or that they happened at all, like the flashbacks. Talking about this medal ceremony and what it had to remind him of might tip them over the edge and it would all be over, but it was a risk Anna had no choice but to take.

Maybe Luke needed a push himself to recognize that he had PTSD. He had to be willing to confront his past. She was quite prepared to help him and be with him through any rough patches but only if it was part of a healing process. Otherwise she would just be locking herself into a miserable cycle of watching the man she loved suffer. Getting pushed away and hurt herself and then crawling back for more of the same.

She wasn't going to do it. If she did, she would only

be allowing Luke to stay locked in that dark space permanently and he was worth more than that.

'Why not, Luke?' she asked again. 'Why don't you want to get the recognition you deserve? It's your name that's right at the top of that list. Does your family know about this? Will they be there, hoping to be part of the honour?'

'I don't want the damned medal.' The words burst out in an angry rush as Luke leaned forward on his desk, both hands clenched into fists. 'I haven't told my family because I don't want to celebrate what happened. Or to glorify war. To pretty it up for the media with everyone in nice, clean uniforms and rows of shiny badges. Dancing, for God's sake! That's about as meaningless as everything else in civilian life.' He lowered his voice and it became rough. Totally compelling. 'War is about blood and guts and people. People who can be terrified they're not going to get back to the ones they love. Who can die, in agony, a thousand miles away from the people who love them.'

He tipped his head back, closing his eyes. 'Yes, I survived. But what about all the others?'

Slowly, he brought his gaze back to Anna's. His eyes were dark. So shadowed they were blank of emotion. Like the rest of his face. 'I don't want a prize for being one of the lucky ones.'

Anna swallowed. Hard. She was part of his civilian life. Meaningless.

The silence stretched on. Tense and horrible. She had to say something. To try and defuse this awful distance escalating between them.

'Yes, war is about people,' she said finally. 'That's how they generally start, isn't it? You have a group of people, including innocent children, who lose their lives or have their rights as human beings threatened or taken away. Most people have to try and close their minds to the atrocities that go on because it doesn't affect their lives and they can't do anything about it, anyway.' She drew in a breath, the words coming more easily now. 'But some people are brave enough to put their hands up and say, I'll help. I'll go into horrible places and endure terrible things. Not because I might end up getting a medal for it but because it might—eventually—help to make the world a better place.'

Was he listening? Anna couldn't tell. She was talking hard and fast now, barely forming the thoughts before the words tumbled from her mouth. Desperately trying to let Luke know, somehow, that it was all right to have this as part of his past. That she accepted it. And if she talked enough, maybe by some miracle she could say something that would get through to him. Stop him from shutting her out and pushing her out of his life.

'If enough people didn't avoid even thinking about wars, maybe something could change without people having to die,' she continued. 'And maybe the publicity that comes from something like this is what makes them take notice. It's the heroes that people can't help taking notice of. That they listen to.'

Luke was staring at her now but his face was still devoid of emotion.

'Maybe the people who take the most notice are the

ones who've lost someone they love. Because they have to try and make sense of it all.'

Which was exactly what Luke needed to do himself, wasn't it?

'Or maybe it's the people who will feel lucky for the rest of their lives because someone they love has come home. Thanks to one of those heroes. I'll bet the families of all the soldiers you saved would love to give you a medal, Luke, but they don't have to, do they? The army is going to do it for them.'

Still no reaction. Anna felt a flicker of anger. 'How do you think they'll feel if you can't be bothered to show up?'

That did it. Luke's face finally moved but it was only to turn away from her. 'Are you finished?'

'No.' Anna's mouth had gone dry. This was it. She had failed. He wasn't going to let her into this part of his life. Her breath came out in a ragged sigh. She closed her eyes in defeat. 'The party wouldn't be so bad,' she said dryly. 'At least nobody would be wearing reindeer horns.'

Opening her eyes, she found Luke had turned back to face her. For a heartbeat her flippant comment hung in the air and then she saw a change in Luke's eyes. A lightening of those shadows. A vaguely incredulous expression that took her back to…

Oh, help. Back to that day when Luke had come to her cottage and discovered Anna instead of his colleague, Dr Bartlett. When she'd made that stupid joke about unlikely dogs using a staircase to become mates. So she was no good at cracking jokes? Did he have to look at her as though he was seeing someone he didn't even recognise?

Someone stupid, maybe, who said meaningless things that made him wonder why on earth he'd ever been attracted to her?

But Luke's lips were moving now.

Good grief! He was smiling. Virtually grinning.

'OK,' he said. 'I'll go. On one condition.'

'What's that?' The relief that he wasn't shouting at her or physically throwing her out of his office was enormous. It was making her feel light-headed. Ridiculously happy.

Hopeful, even.

'That you come with me.'

Anna's head cleared astonishingly quickly. An image of a military ball sprang into her head. Men in dress uniform. Luke in dress uniform. He would look impossibly gorgeous. And she would have to be dressed up and feminine. No way would she be on ground where she could feel like an equal. But they weren't equal, were they? Even here. Not on emotional grounds, anyway.

She would be so proud of him if she went. She would be getting herself in ever deeper.

But wasn't that what she wanted? Needed? Or was it that she knew she should fight it but just couldn't help herself?

Anna shook her head, trying to clear the confused jumble of her thoughts. Luke misinterpreted the gesture as reluctance.

'You think I should go,' he said. 'And you're probably correct.'

Another memory was niggling at Anna now. She'd persuaded Luke to attend the staff Christmas function by telling him that heads of departments would be expected to attend. Look what had happened there. How much more likely would a flashback be when he was surrounded by army uniforms and by people wanting to talk about why he was being honoured as a hero?

'I won't go unless you come with me,' Luke said quietly. 'Please, Anna. I…need you.'

Three little words. Possibly the only three she'd ever hear from Luke but maybe they were enough.

'All right,' she said with a catch in her voice. 'I'll come with you.'

Why had he been so determined not to attend this event?

So bad-tempered about having to put on his dress uniform 'Blues' and act like a soldier? Gritting his teeth as he'd accepted all the congratulations that came with the medal now pinned to his tunic.

Hating it all so much he'd barely spoken to Anna, even though he could see how much effort she'd put into this on his behalf. Buying a new dress and having her hair done in some fancy way. Putting up with his foul mood for the whole of their drive to London. All those long stretches when the only sound in the vehicle had been the windscreen wipers trying to cope with the sleet of the January evening.

He'd only asked her to dance because it was the last duty he had to perform tonight. The recipients of the medals and their partners had been invited to take the floor first and people were watching. Clapping.

One dance and then he could escape. Drive back to St Piran, apologise to Anna and then forget the whole excruciating business.

The lighting was softened as the orchestra began playing a waltz. Chandeliers still sparkled overhead and the reflection of the crowd present could be seen in the glass of the floor-to-ceiling windows that filled one wall and afforded a spectacular view of London beyond. Diamonds glistened on women and the buttons on dress uniforms gleamed on the men.

Holding out his hand to Anna, Luke had the sudden, awful thought that he hadn't bothered to find out if Anna knew how to dance something formal. He'd had lessons as a teenager, along with all his brothers, and the skill was automatic. Not that he'd had either the opportunity or the desire to use it for a very long time. But Anna took his hand and came into his arms willingly. The dark, emerald fabric of her long dress shimmered in this lighting and he gathered her into a formal dance hold. Stiffly at first, until the steps came more easily. It was only then that he noticed how light Anna was on her feet and how well she was able to follow his lead.

More couples came onto the dance floor but Luke didn't even notice. In his relief that he wasn't embarrassing Anna and making her evening even worse than he had already by assuming a skill she might not have, he relaxed a notch. Another notch or two got added when he remembered that the evening was almost over. He was going to get through it. And that was when he finally looked down and really noticed the woman in his arms.

Her hair had been scooped up in some clever fashion to make coils that sat sleekly against the back of her head. Little bits had been pulled free, however, so that tiny soft spirals framed her face and drew attention to the lovely length of her neck. The style was formal and precise—like Anna was at work—but it was those free tendrils that Luke really liked. They reminded him of the way Anna was when she wasn't at work. Softer. Surprising.

Pure woman.

The fabric of her dress was silky under his hands. Almost as delicious as he knew her bare skin to be. The colour was sheer brilliance. How had it taken him this long to notice how it was a shade or two darker than her eyes and made them so…luminous.

So extraordinarily beautiful.

Mesmerising.

The music altered tempo as the orchestra started something less classical. Something moody and sweet. It was the perfect opportunity to make an exit from the dance floor but Luke had lost any desire to do so. Instead, he drew Anna closer. He wasn't following any routine steps now, just moving to the music that surrounded them. Holding an amazingly beautiful woman who followed every move he made so easily it was like holding an extension to his own body.

She looked and felt so lovely. She even smelled so wonderful that Luke bent his head to get closer. Was that perfume coming from her hair or her skin? Or was it just

Anna? It was hypnotising. A new space. An escape that was better than sleep. Better than sex, even, because he could keep this up for ever.

He certainly wasn't going to be the one to suggest stopping any time soon.

Anna had been very close to tears by the time Luke asked her to dance.

Wishing she'd never agreed to accompany him. A million miles away from this would have been too close. She'd tried so hard to look the part and he'd been so closed off and angry from the moment he'd arrived at her door to collect her.

The drive had been awful. Full of silences during which she had nothing to think about except the distance between them. That she was no closer to imagining a way out of this for Luke that could offer the promise of a happy future for him.

For them both.

Watching him during the ceremonial part of the evening had been even more grim. He looked just as gorgeous as she'd expected in the crisp, dark blue uniform with its braid and insignia, but she'd been able to see how much he'd been hating it. Tension so great it seemed like he could simply snap at any moment. Luke hadn't wanted to be a part of any of this. He hadn't wanted any of it to be a part of his past.

Could no one else see what she could see? That the event that had led to him being here tonight was what had scarred him so deeply. That he was determined to escape the memories and he couldn't see that the only way to stop them haunting him to the point of ruining his life was to turn round and confront them.

The tension had been contagious. All Anna had wanted was for the evening to end. To get through that long drive home somehow and then...what?

Admit defeat and see what she could do about putting her life back together the way it had been before Luke had come back to St Piran?

It had been the thought of trying to move on without him that had been what nearly brought her to tears in public. But then Luke had held out his hand when the medal recipients had been invited to take the dance floor first. It had been the first time he'd touched her in what felt like a very, very long time, and as soon as Anna had felt that contact she'd known exactly where she really wanted to be.

Not a million miles away at all.

Right here.

In Luke's arms.

He could dance. When the initial awkwardness wore off, Anna was astonished to find he could actually dance beautifully. The music was soothing and the rhythm of the waltz easy to follow even from long-ago lessons. Glancing up, she found Luke's face still grim and turned away. He was going through the motions here, but in reality he was hunting for an escape route.

Dropping her gaze, Anna stared at the medal pinned to his tunic, awarded for an act of outstanding bravery during active operations against an enemy. It was a beautiful silver cross mounted on a wreath of laurel leaves with a crown in its centre. The ribbon had narrow stripes of dark blue on each edge and a central stripe of crimson. What would he do with it when he got home? Shut it away in its box and hide it along with the memories of why it had been bestowed?

Looking up again, Anna was startled to find Luke's gaze on her face. An intense gaze but one she was getting used to. As though he was seeing her properly for the first time. Looking…amazed.

The waltz ended and Anna knew this would be when Luke suggested they sit down or go to supper perhaps. Or just go home.

Instead, he drew her closer and she could feel some of that terrible tension leaving his body. They were so close. She could feel the length of his body against hers. Leading her. So powerful and yet it felt gentle, probably because she was so willing to follow.

And then she felt his cheek against her hair and Anna closed her eyes, sinking into the delicious knowledge that Luke wasn't just dancing now.

He was dancing with her.

Another medley of tunes began. And then another, but Luke made no move to take her away from the dance floor and Anna certainly wasn't going to be the one to break this connection.

She wanted it to last for ever.

The start of the fireworks display startled all the guests. The wall of windows provided a great view of the city lights on the other side of the Thames but nobody had noticed the grassy bank-side area until the impressive display got under way.

It began with a sound like a cannon firing. A huge silver rocket shot up into the blackness of the sky and then exploded into a shower of tiny silver spheres that drifted down slowly.

Not that Anna was watching them. At the first sound Luke had stiffened so abruptly that she had tripped on his foot. Then he moved again, so sharply Anna could swear she felt him snap. He dropped his arms from her body and turned swiftly, weaving between couples who had also stopped dancing to see what was happening. They began to move towards the windows.

Anna moved in the opposite direction. Following Luke. All the way out of the ballroom. Through the area where a buffet supper was being served. Through the vast foyer where staff were now stacking all the chairs that had been used for the initial ceremony. Down a wide flight of steps. She could feel the sting of sleet on her skin. Gathering up the folds of her dress, she raced after Luke. Around the corner of the building. As far away as he could get from where the fireworks were happening.

And there he stopped. When Anna came around the corner she saw him, his head on his arm, leaning against the stone wall. She could hear him gasping for breath in the same way he had when he'd been having that nightmare.

'Luke!'

'Go, Anna.' The plea was hoarse. 'Get out. While you can.'

She came up to be right beside him. 'I'm not going anywhere. Talk to me.'

'I can't.'

At least part of him was there and aware of her. He'd been like that in the canteen too, hadn't he? Having a flashback he couldn't control but still aware of things around him, like bumping into someone and spilling their drink. Maybe, if she tried hard enough, she could get through to him.

'Why not?' she begged. 'Why can't you talk to me, Luke?'

'My problem. If I told you, it would become your problem.' The words were staccato. Agonised. 'I won't do that to you.'

'It's already my problem.'

'No. You can go. I want you to go.'

'I can't do that, Luke.'

'Why the hell not?' His head turned and the expression on his face broke her heart.

'Because…because I love you, that's why.'

Luke buried his head again and he groaned. It was a sound of such distress but was it due to her confession or because of whatever still had him in its grip?

Fireworks were still going off, muted a little by the vast building between them but still loud. Possibly loud enough that he hadn't heard what she'd just said. Or maybe he had chosen not to hear it because he already had too much to deal with.

'It's the noise, isn't it?' She had to touch Luke. To get closer. 'Where are you, Luke? What do you see?'

A moment's silence and then Luke spoke in a low, desperate voice she barely recognised.

'We're under fire. We're on our way to a village. There's children hurt by a landmine but we don't get there.' The words were rushing out so fast it was hard to hear them clearly. 'It's an ambush. Another mine. And artillery. The truck's tipped over. Everybody's hurt. I…I felt my leg snap.'

He dragged in a breath. 'We need to get out. Danny's unconscious. His airway's blocked. There's a chopper coming. I can smell the smoke and the blood. The guys are screaming. I'm trapped. I'm trying to get them out and I can't move. I can't breathe…'

Anna was gripping his arm. 'Yes, you can, Luke. You did get them out. All of them. That's why you got the medal tonight. You saved everybody in that truck. You saved their lives.'

'But I didn't…' Luke groaned again. Or was it a sob? 'Not the life I wanted to save.' Yes, it was definitely a sob now. Torn from somewhere deep inside. 'I couldn't save Crash, Anna. I…wanted to…so much…and I… couldn't…'

Racking sobs took hold of Luke's body now. All Anna could do was to hold him as hard as she could and be there. Saying nothing. Letting him hold her so tightly it was impossible to take a deep breath and letting him rock her as he rocked himself.

And eventually, as she became aware of how damp and cold they were both going to be, Luke quietened.

'Let's go home,' she said.

Luke waited outside while she collected their coats and the car keys.

'I can drive if you'd like.'

'No. I'm all right.' Luke's voice was sombre. 'Better if I'm doing something. I'm sorry about that.'

'I'm not,' Anna said, but Luke didn't hear her. He was striding ahead to where the car was parked.

Sleet was still falling and got thicker as they left the outskirts of London but the road was still clear enough. Anna listened to the windscreen wipers. They sounded different now. Maybe because the atmosphere inside the car wasn't as charged as it had been coming in the opposite direction. The tension was gone. Luke seemed tired but calm.

'Who was Crash?' Anna asked softly. 'A friend?'

'My brother. His real name was Matthew. Mattie.'

'Oh…'

Anna was searching her memory. She'd known that name had come from something special. A kid who'd grown too fast, he'd said, and looked a bit goofy with big feet. So clumsy he'd earned the nickname of Crash. He grown into…what had Luke said? Oh, yes. The strongest, bravest guy he knew.

And then he'd given her that first smile. The one that had melted her heart.

'He was younger than you?' The question was tentative. It seemed too good to believe that Luke was finally talking to her.

Letting her in.

'Yeah.' Luke's gaze was fixed on the road ahead. He was driving a little below the speed limit. Taking it carefully.

Anna felt safe with him but did he feel the same way?

'There's an older brother, too,' Luke said after a

moment. 'The Davenport boys, we were called. A collective troop. A mini-platoon. Nobody questioned that we would do anything but take after our dad and join the army.'

'It must have been hard for you, then.'

'Yeah.' The word was heartfelt. 'I felt guilty. Especially after Crash joined up. I'd always tried to look out for him, you know? In the end, though, he was looking out for me. He was the only one who understood why I wanted to be a civilian. A doctor.'

Anna couldn't ask the obvious question but it was hanging there and Luke could sense it.

'He got killed in action in Iraq,' he said very softly. 'And it just broke me up. I owed him so much. I missed him so badly. In the end, the answer seemed easy. I joined up to honour his memory. To do what I should have done all along. I thought it would make me feel less guilty. That it would somehow help fill the horrible, empty, useless feeling I had.'

A long silence this time and then Luke sighed. 'All I really achieved was to screw up the rest of my life. I'm not fit to do my job any more. I'm not a viable proposition to be in any kind of a meaningful relationship. I meant what I said, Anna. You should get out. Relatively unscathed. While you still can.'

'And I meant what I said,' Anna whispered. She wasn't going to tell him again that she loved him. It was enough to know she had said it aloud and it was true. Instinct told her he wasn't ready to hear those particular words but she could remind him of something else she'd said. 'I'm not going anywhere. We all need courage to face the future,' she added carefully. 'It's not a sign of weakness if you have to ask for help sometimes.'

Maybe she could remind him of something he'd said, too. 'You're the strongest, bravest man I know,' she said, deliberately using the words he'd used to describe his brother. 'You'll make it.'

This wasn't the time to talk about finding the help Luke needed or how to find it. They'd made enough of a breakthrough tonight. All Anna wanted now was to get home and go to bed. With Luke.

And sleep. She was so tired. The windscreen wipers flicked in a steady rhythm. Swirls of tiny white flakes zoomed towards them in a hypnotic pattern. Anna could feel her eyes drifting closed.

She was sound asleep, Luke noticed, as they finally left the main roads behind. The snow began falling more thickly and he slowed their pace. He didn't like the deteriorating conditions but he could take his time getting them home. Funny, but he felt like he had all the time he needed now. For anything. He couldn't remember when he'd last felt this…peaceful? Maybe he never had.

He stole another glance at Anna. He would get her home safely. He knew the road and he could cope with the weather.

What he couldn't control was the other traffic on the road that night. Especially when he had no warning of what was coming around the corner. The driver of the big truck probably didn't realise how far his wheels were over the centre line of the coastal road because the snow was starting to settle in patches and the road markings were fading.

The jolt of leaving the smooth road surface and then hitting a fence post woke Anna and all Luke could hear as he fought desperately to prevent the car tipping into a roll was her scream of fear.

CHAPTER TEN

ANNA'S scream was cut off abruptly with the first impact of the rolling vehicle but the sound of metal shearing and scraping on rock was another kind of scream. Airbags deployed with a blast and shockwave that was indistinguishable from gunfire.

Luke was inside his nightmare but he knew he was awake and that made it so much worse. So confusing. His mind was being rocked and jolted as viciously as his body. One moment hanging in the straps of his safety belt, the next jarring on solid ground. A maelstrom of fear and desperation. The past, the present and things that had never been real, and never would be, existing only in his imagination.

He was in an army vehicle again but not the one in which he'd met the end of his time at war. In one that he'd never actually seen or touched. Just imagined. The one his brother, Matthew, had been driving. And each time they hit solid ground, they were hitting the mine that had destroyed the person he loved most in the world. Once, twice…three hits and he was still alive and awake.

This time, he had to save him.

Or he would die himself.

The violent churning of the landscape, vehicle and people probably lasted no more than thirty seconds but it felt like for ever. And then there was silence. A broken headlamp flickered for a second or two and then died.

It was pitch black and utterly silent.

Luke had been convinced that the worst sound he could ever hear were the screams of frightened and dying men, any one of whom could be his brother. Even the terrified sound Anna had made had become the last breath Crash had expelled.

In that instant, however, he knew the real truth.

That silence was far worse.

Crash.

Blindly, Luke reached out. His fingers caught in the limp, metallic folds of airbags that had erupted from the steering-wheel, the centre console and the dashboard.

'Can you hear me?'

A tiny sound in the silence as he strained to listen. An indrawn breath. Tentative and ragged.

'Y-yes.'

It wasn't Crash. It was Anna.

Of course it was. He'd known that all along. Hadn't he?

And she was alive, thank God. 'Are you hurt?'

'I…I'm not sure…'

He had to move. To find a source of light and then check Anna out. He had to get her out of this and make sure she would be all right. Any other course of action or result was unthinkable.

But his head swam when he tried to move. Impossible

to tell which way was supposed to be up. Had the car ended up on its roof instead of its wheels? Was it really Anna?

Luke found the catch of his safety belt and released it. His body didn't start falling so he wasn't upside down. His head started to clear.

'Take a deep breath,' he told Anna. 'As deep as you can.'

He listened to her comply with his request.

'Is it difficult? Does anything hurt?'

'N-no...'

'Can you move your arms? God, it's so dark. I can't see anything. Does your neck hurt? Don't move your head if it does.'

He could hear Anna shift position. Could see a change of shape in the darkness.

'I...I can move.'

So could Luke. He turned and began to lean sideways so that his hands could reach Anna's huddled figure on the far side of the vehicle. She was lower than he was. The car was on some kind of slope.

And then he froze.

It wasn't his head swimming this time. It was the car that was moving.

Rocking gently.

There was a scratching, scraping sound coming from somewhere beneath them. Metal on rock. And Luke became aware of another sound. He hadn't noticed it before because it could have been the rush of his own blood pulsing in his head.

Somewhere, far below, waves were rolling onto rocks.

They had been on a coastal road that often came close to clifftop. There had been a fence of some kind. A farmer's field or a barrier that was there to prevent anyone getting too close to a dangerous place? Like one that had a sheer drop to rocks that would not be survivable?

Perhaps it was just as well it was too dark to see anything outside.

Cold, damp air was coming in with the sounds of the night. Luke's door seemed to be missing or crumpled to leave an open space. Survival instinct was trying to kick in. The upward ground was on his side and he had an escape route. Even if the car was teetering on the top of a cliff, he could make a dive for it and roll free.

But that would change the weight distribution dramatically and that might be all that was needed to tip the vehicle and send it plunging over the edge.

With Anna still inside.

He would rather die himself.

The car was still rocking. Scraping.

'Luke?' Anna's whisper was terrified. 'What's... happening?'

'Don't move,' he said softly. 'Give me a sec. I need to think.'

Fear was clawing at him now. A dense cloud that contained a kaleidoscope of images and emotions that paralysed Luke for a moment. Sucking him into the place he couldn't allow himself to go.

No.

He couldn't smell blood. Or smoke. Or dust. Nobody was screaming.

They were in a car, not an armoured vehicle. This was Anna. Not Crash.

So why was it just as important that she was going to be all right? Crash was the person he had loved with all his heart. The one he would have given his own life to save.

It had taken a split second for Luke to understand the truth that silence could be more dreadful than any scream.

The truth he now learned arrived with similar, blinding clarity.

He had only been confused about the person he needed to save because of an emotion he hadn't allowed himself to entertain.

He loved Anna.

A different kind of love than he'd had for Crash but it was just as powerful. More so, even. He'd been kidding himself thinking of her as his rope. Or anchor. Or any other kind of tool to help him find his own future.

She was that future.

From that first moment when he'd found himself under her resentful glare she had entered his consciousness. His mind and—slipping somehow under a defensive radar—his heart.

'Luke…' Anna was crying. 'Talk to me. Are you hurt?'

'I'm fine.' He moved his hand carefully, just far enough to grip hers. 'As long as you are.'

'What happened?'

'We've had an accident. There was a truck. It came

around a corner on the wrong side of the road. I had to swerve and… Oh, God, I'm sorry, Anna.'

The grip on his hand tightened. 'That doesn't matter. We just need to get out.'

'We have to be careful. I'm not sure how stable the car is and I don't want it to move.'

'I'm scared.'

'I know. I am too but we'll get through this, Anna. Together.'

'Are you sure you're all right? It's not… I mean… You know…like a flashback thing?'

Oh, yes. The flashbacks he'd never admitted to. He couldn't admit to loving Anna either, could he? What did he have to offer her? He was broken.

'I want to get out. I want to get home.'

'I know. We will. I'll get you out, Anna. I'll take care of you.'

There was a light outside now. Coming closer. A powerful torch that filled the interior of this battered car in a sweeping motion. For a heartbeat Luke could see Anna's face clearly. The way she was looking at him.

She wasn't going anywhere, she'd said—way back before the accident had happened. She'd said she loved him.

He could see that love in her eyes. He could fall into it. Return it? How much courage would that take? What if he failed her, as he had failed his brother? If he lost her…

'Anna…I—'

The light got brighter. Steadier. A man's voice called out. 'Whatever you do in there, don't move. I've got a chain in the truck and I'm going to get it onto the back of your car. Help's on the way.'

Luke didn't want to move. Neither, it seemed, did Anna. The grip on his hand was tight enough to impair circulation.

'Don't let go of me,' she begged. 'Please. Not yet.'

'I won't,' he vowed. I can't, he added silently, because I love you.

The nearest hospital was St Piran's.

Ben Carter was astonished to find Anna and Luke turning up in the emergency department, dressed up to the nines, in the early hours of the morning but he was more amazed to be able to give them a medical all-clear not long afterwards.

'You're both incredibly lucky. A few bumps and bruises but nothing that a good sleep won't help.'

Anna caught Luke's wry glance. As if a good sleep was remotely likely for him even when he hadn't been through such a traumatic few hours. It was a private exchange. Ben didn't see it because he was shaking his head.

'I can't imagine what it must have felt like, seeing your car going over that cliff when the chain broke. The rescue guys are going to be talking about their good timing for years to come.'

'So will we,' Anna said. She smiled at Luke. 'Let's go and see if that taxi's here yet.'

They went to Luke's house because it was closer and Anna was still worried about the effects the accident might have had on Luke that no X-ray or examination would have picked up.

To have had this happen today, of all days, when he had been starting to open up to her about the past that haunted him so badly. No wonder he was so quiet now. And why he made no move to make love to her when they went straight to bed. They were both utterly exhausted but Anna was determined to stay awake. To be ready to hold Luke when he had the nightmare she was sure would come.

At some point, however, she fell asleep because it was impossible not to. When she awoke to find winter sunlight warming the room, she gasped in horror. Had she slept through Luke waking? Going to outrun his demons on the beach or dispel them with an arctic swim? He never missed his dawn swim.

But he was still there. Beside her. One arm draped over her body. Her gasp must have woken him because his eyes were open.

'You OK?'

Anna nodded. 'I'm sorry…'

'What for?'

'I must have slept through you getting up. I didn't mean to. I wanted…'

Luke was staring at her with an odd expression.

'What?' she breathed. 'What's wrong?'

'I didn't get up,' he said slowly. 'I didn't even wake up.'

'You slept through the whole night?'

'What was left of it, anyway.' He blinked at her, disbelief still etched on his features. 'That's hours. Hours and hours and hours.'

Anna's lips trembled as they stretched into a smile. 'How do you feel?'

'Different...' Luke's gaze dropped to Anna's lips and then dropped further. 'Hungry.'

'You want breakfast?'

'No.' He looked up again and smiled. 'I want... you.'

Anna snuggled closer, raising her face to meet Luke's kiss. 'I want you, too.'

'You're not too sore or anything?'

'A bit stiff and achy. Nothing that a walk on the beach in some sunshine won't cure.'

'Soon.' Luke's lips brushed hers gently and then came back as he sighed. 'Or maybe not that soon.'

His mouth claimed hers this time and Anna surrendered willingly. The walk could wait.

The last day of January found them walking on the beach.

A dawn walk that had become a firm habit now. Crash was with them, loping around on his big, puppy feet with a stick of driftwood clamped between his teeth.

'You're supposed to bring it back,' Luke called.

'He wants you to chase him.'

'That won't help his retrieving training.'

'No.' Besides, Anna didn't want to let go of Luke's hand. She loved this time of day with him. In the soft light and breathing the fresh, cold air. Walking so close they often leaned on each other as well as holding hands. And sometimes, as they did right now, they would stop and watch the waves rolling in for a minute or two.

'You haven't been for a swim since the accident.'

'No. I don't need to any more.'

Anna gave Luke a questioning glance but he was still staring at the waves.

'When I came back from Iraq,' he said a moment later, 'it seemed like I had no connection here any more. Or anywhere. Part of me was still over there. Caught up in the frenetic battle to save lives. To stay alive. Civilian life seemed empty. Meaningless.'

Still Anna said nothing. She couldn't. She remembered Luke saying something about that and she hadn't forgotten thinking that she had been included in the things that had no meaning. She knew that wasn't true. Maybe Luke hadn't told her as such but he was showing her. Every day. In so many ways.

'It made me numb, swimming in a freezing sea and getting tossed around by the surf,' Luke continued quietly. 'And it helped…then. I don't need to be numb now. I don't want to be, even for a moment.' He turned his head and looked down at Anna.

'Because even if it was just for the length of time it took to have that swim, it would be too long to feel numb. I don't want to give up a second of the most amazing feeling I could ever have.'

Anna's breath caught. She knew the answer but had to ask the question. To hear the words spoken aloud. 'What is it…that feeling?'

'My love for you.'

His kiss tasted of the sea and it was slow and exquisitely tender. Anna stood on tiptoe and wrapped her arms around his neck. It took the impatient bark of a large puppy to bring them back to the present moment. Luke laughed, stooped to pick up the stick that had been placed right beside his feet and threw it again. Then he took Anna's hand in his and they began walking again, a triumphant Crash making wide circles around them with the stick back in his jaws.

'I love you, Anna,' Luke said. 'You are the reason I want to get up in the mornings and the reason I can't wait to get to bed at night. I hope I never have to have a night or day without you to share it with but...' He took a deep breath and let it out in a sigh. 'I'm not going to ask you to marry me. I can't.'

Anna's feet stopped without any such instruction from her brain. Her hand tugged at Luke's a heartbeat later and he had to stop, too. She stared at him. The shadows in his eyes had begun to lift in the last week or so but the sadness she could still see in his face was heartbreaking.

'I can't offer you anything,' Luke said. 'I've lost my job.'

Anna gave her head a slow shake. 'You didn't lose it. You had the courage to go and talk to Mr White about everything and he had the good sense to persuade you to go onto the board of directors for St Piran's. You're going to be a brilliant administrator, Luke, and it's not as if you're not going to be part of the department for teaching—'

'Your department now,' Luke interrupted.

Anna looked away. It was so weird to think she had wanted to hang onto that position so badly that she would have preferred Luke to have never come back to St Piran's.

'I have PTSD,' Luke said into the silence. 'An official diagnosis from a qualified shrink.'

'An eminent psychiatrist who specialises in cognitive-behavioural therapy,' Anna corrected with a smile. 'Someone who thinks you're making amazing progress already.'

She watched a wave roll in. And then another. And then she turned to face Luke again.

'All you ever need to offer me is your love, Luke.'

He was watching her face with that intent gaze of his. Listening carefully. Waiting to hear what she would say next.

'And I don't want you to ask me to marry you,' she said.

She saw him swallow hard. Saw a flicker of doubt—fear, almost—in his eyes.

Anna smiled. 'Because I'm going to ask you.'

She took a deep breath. This shouldn't be so hard, should it? She'd been competing in a man's world for long enough to be able to tackle anything.

'I love you, Luke Davenport. With all my heart. I don't want to have a single night or day without you in it either. Will you marry me?'

He was still staring at her. One of those looks—as if he was seeing her for the very first time.

'Um… Please?' she added.

His arms came around her with such speed that

Anna squeaked as she felt herself grabbed and lifted. She was being whirled round and round and the world was spinning.

'Yes,' Luke said. 'Yes.'

He stopped whirling her but was still holding her well off the ground, his hands around her waist. Her hands were on his shoulders as he slowly lowered her enough for their lips to touch.

A new wave came in, leading the incoming tide further up the beach, and it reached far enough to swirl around Luke's ankles and splash Anna's legs with pure ice.

Luke dropped one arm to catch Anna behind her knees. He scooped her into his arms and carried her through the still foaming wave to dry sand but he didn't put her down. Crash followed as they left the beach to go home and get ready for their new day. And still Luke hadn't put Anna down.

And that was just fine by her.

She was exactly where she wanted to be. Moving into her future, cradled in the arms of the man she would always love.

ST PIRAN'S: THE
FIREMAN AND
NURSE LOVEDAY

KATE HARDY

For the St. Piran's mob—especially Caroline, Maggie and Margaret, who kept me sane!

CHAPTER ONE

THE familiar warble flooded through the fire station and the Tannoy gave a high-pitched whine.

Was it a drill, Tom wondered, at 2:00 p.m. on a Friday afternoon?

And then he heard the words, 'Turnout, vehicles 54 and 55. Fire at Penhally Bay Primary School. Query trapped children.'

Joey's school.

Fear lanced through him. Please, God, let this be a drill.

Except he knew it wasn't. Their drill was always a fire at 3 King Street, St Piran—which just so happened to be the address of the main fire station in the area. Which meant that this was real.

He headed straight for engine 54, where the rest of the crew were already stepping into their protective trousers, jackets and boots. Steve, the station manager, was in the front seat, tapping into the computer and checking the details.

'What have we got, Guv?' Tom asked as he swung into the seat next to Steve, the doors went up and the engine sped down the road towards Penhally Bay.

Steve checked the computer screen. 'Explosion and fire at Penhally Bay Primary.' He gave the driver, Gary, the map reference, even though everyone knew exactly where the school was, on the hill overlooking the bay. 'Called in by Rosemary

Bailey, the headmistress. The fire's in a corridor by a store-room and it's blocked off three rooms. Two of the classes were out, so that leaves the quiet room and the toilets. They're still checking off the kids' names, so they're not sure right now if anyone's in there or not.' He paused. 'The storeroom contains all the art stuff, so we're talking about flammable hazards and possible chemical inhalation from glue and what have you. Tom, you're lead. Roy, you're BAECO.' The breathing apparatus entry co-ordinator kept the control board with the firefighters' tallies in place so he knew who was in the building, how long they'd been in there, and when he needed to call them out because their oxygen supplies would be starting to run low.

'The rest of you, follow Tom's lead. We'll start with the tanks in the appliances, then we'll set the hydrant and check the supply.'

'Right, Guv,' the crew chorused.

'Who's our back-up?' Tom asked. Two engines were always sent out for an initial call, and then more would be called as needed, staggering their arrival.

'King Street's on standby,' Steve said. 'And the paramedics are on their way.'

All standard stuff, Tom knew.

'Nick Tremayne is going to be there, too,' Steve added.

Tom had attended fires with Nick in attendance before, and knew that the GP was unflappable and worked well in a crisis. 'That's good.' And Tom was really relieved that his crew was taking the call, so he could see for himself that his nephew was fine.

And Joey *would* be fine.

He had to be.

Joey was all Tom had left of his big sister since the car ac-cident that had claimed her life and her husband's just over a month ago, at New Year. Losing her had ripped Tom's heart to shreds; the idea of anything happening to his precious nephew, the little boy his sister had entrusted to his care...

His mind closed, refusing to even consider the idea. Joey couldn't be one of the trapped children. He just *couldn't*.

But, all the way there, Tom was horribly aware of the extra problems that small children brought to a fire. Physically, their bodies couldn't cope as well as an adult's with the heat of a raging fire. And then there was the fear factor. Everyone was scared in a fire—you couldn't see your hand in front of your face, thanks to the choking thick smoke, and the heat and noise were incredible. Children found it even harder to cope with the way their senses were overwhelmed, and sometimes got to the point where they simply couldn't follow directions because they were too frightened to listen.

Please, God, let Joey be safe, he prayed silently.

Please.

'Hello, Tommy,' Flora said as Trish Atkins, the teacher of the three-year-olds, brought the next of her charges through to the quiet room where Flora was giving the routine vaccinations. She smiled at the little boy. 'I know Mummy told you why I've come to see your class today—not with my magic measuring tape to see how tall you all are, but to give you two injections to stop you catching a bug and getting sick.'

Tommy nodded. 'Will they hurt?'

'You'll feel a bit of a scratch,' she said, 'and it's OK to say a big "Ow" and hold Trish's hand really tightly, but it'll be over really quickly and I'll need you to stay still for me. Can you do that?'

'Yes,' he lisped.

'Good boy.' She gave him the choice of which arm and where he wanted to sit; he opted to sit on Trish's lap.

'Mummy told me you're getting a kitten.' Distraction was a brilliant technique; if she could get him chatting about the new addition to their family, he wouldn't focus on the vaccination syringe and he'd feel it as the scratch she'd promised, rather than as a terrifying pain. 'What's he like?'

'He's black.'

'What are you going to call him?'

'Ow!' Tommy's lower lip wobbled when the needle went in, but then he said, 'Smudge. 'Cause he's got a big white smudge on his back.'

'That's a great name.' She smiled at him. 'What sort of toys are you going to get him?'

'A squeaky red mouse,' Tommy said. 'Ow!'

'All done—and you were so brave that I'm going to give you a sticker. Do you want to choose one?'

The distraction of a shiny rocket sticker made Tommy forget about crying, just as Flora had hoped it would. She updated his notes, and was about to put her head round the door of the quiet room to tell Trish that she was ready for the next child when she heard a huge bang and then fire alarms going off.

She left her papers where they were and headed out to the main rooms of the nursery. The children were all filing out into the garden, some of the younger ones crying and holding the hands of the class assistants. Flora could see through the large windows that Christine Galloway, the head of the nursery, was taking a roll-call of all the staff and children.

'I think everyone's out, but I'm checking nobody's been left behind,' Trish said from the far end of the room.

'Do you want me to check the toilets?' Flora asked.

'Yes, please.' Trish gave her a grateful smile.

Once they were both satisfied that everyone was out, Flora grabbed her medical kit and they joined Christine and the other teachers. Two fire engines roared up, sirens blaring and blue lights flashing, and they could see smoke coming over the fence from the primary school next door.

'I'd better get next door in case anyone's hurt and they need medical help,' Flora said, biting her lip. She knew all the children in the school, from her work as the school liaison nurse, and the idea of any of them being hurt or, even worse... *No.* It was unthinkable.

'Let us know if there's anything we can do,' Christine said. 'I'll put your notes in my office when we can go back into the building.'

'Thanks.' Flora gave her a quick smile, then hurried next door to the primary school.

The first person she saw was her boss, Nick Tremayne, the head of the surgery in the village. 'Nick, what's happened? I was next door doing the vaccinations when I heard a bang and the fire alarms went off.'

'We don't know what caused it—only that there's a fire.' Nick gestured to the firemen pumping water onto the building.

'Is anyone hurt?'

'Right now, we're not sure. The head's getting everyone out and ticking off names.'

Flora glanced at the building and saw where the flames were coming out. 'That's the corridor by the art storeroom—it's full of stuff that could go up.' And she really, really hoped that everyone was out of the block. The corridor led to the storeroom and three prefab rooms. Two of the rooms were used as Year Five classrooms and the third was used as the quiet room, where teachers took children for extra reading practice or tests.

The firefighters were already working to quell the blaze. Some had breathing apparatus on, and others were putting water on the blaze. She could hear one of the fire crew yelling instructions about a hydrant.

Before she could ask Nick anything else, two ambulances screamed up. The paramedic crew and two doctors headed towards them. Flora recognised one of them as Megan Phillips, who lived in the village, though she didn't know Megan's colleague.

'I'm Josh O'Hara, A and E consultant,' the unknown doctor introduced himself. 'And this is Megan Phillips, paediatrician.'

Josh was simply gorgeous, with black tousled hair that flopped in his indigo-blue eyes. Right now he wasn't smiling; but no doubt when he did, any woman under the age of ninety would feel her heart turning over. And that Irish brogue would definitely melt hearts.

Although Flora knew who Megan was, she didn't know the doctor well at all; Megan kept herself very much to herself in the village. So Flora was relieved when Nick stepped in and spoke for both of them. 'Nick Tremayne, head of Penhally Bay Surgery—and this is Flora, my practice nurse and school liaison. Luckily she was doing the MMR vaccinations next door and she's brilliant with kids. Flora, you know Megan, don't you? Can you work with her and I'll work with Josh?'

'Yes, of course,' Flora said.

Though she also noticed that Megan and Josh didn't glance at each other, the way that colleagues usually did. The tension between them was obvious, so either they hadn't worked together before and weren't sure of each other's skills, or they knew each other and really didn't get on. Well, whatever it was, she hoped they'd manage to put it aside and work together until everyone was safe. In this situation, the children really had to come first.

Megan gave her a slightly nervous smile. 'Shall we go and see what's going on?'

Flora nodded. 'The fire drill point's at the far end of the playground, on the other side of the building.'

'We'll start there, then, and see if anyone needs treating,' Megan said. 'As you're school liaison, you must know everyone here?'

Flora felt colour flooding into her cheeks, and sighed inwardly. If only she didn't blush so easily. She knew it made her look like a bumbling fool, and she wasn't. She was a good nurse and she was fine with the children—and the teachers, now she'd got to know them. She just found herself shy and tongue-tied with adults she didn't know very well. Stupid, at her age, she knew, but she couldn't help it. Pulling herself together, she said, 'I know all the staff and most of the children—I've either worked with their class or seen them for the usual check-ups.'

'That's good—you'll be a familiar face and that will help them feel less scared,' Megan said.

As they rounded the corner, they could see a woman leaning against the wall, her face white, nursing her arm.

'Patience, this is Megan, one of the doctors from St Piran's. Megan, this is Patience Harcourt. She teaches Year Three,' Flora introduced them swiftly. 'Patience, what's happened to your arm?'

'I'd gone to the storeroom to get some supplies. I'd just switched on the light when it went bang—I went straight for the fire extinguisher, but before I could do anything the whole thing went up. I got out of there and closed the fire door to contain it.' She grimaced. 'Thank goodness one of the Year Five classes was doing PE and the other was in the ICT suite.'

'Was anyone in the quiet room?' Flora asked.

Patience shook her head, looking white. 'I hope not, but I don't know.'

'Let's have a look at your arm,' Megan said, and sucked in a breath. 'That's a nasty burn.'

Patience made a dismissive gesture with her other arm. 'I can wait. Check the children over first.'

'Your burn needs dressing—the sooner, the better,' Megan said gently. 'Will you let Flora do it while I check the children?'

The children were shivering because it was cold outside and the teachers had taken them straight outside away from the fire, not stopping to pick up coats; some were still wearing their PE kit. Some were crying, and all were clearly frightened.

'We need to get them huddled together to conserve warmth,' Megan said. 'Under that shelter would be good. And then I can see if anyone needs treating. Flora, when you've dressed Patience's burn, do you want to come and help me?'

'Will do.' Again, Flora could feel the hated colour flood her cheeks. She was glad of the excuse to turn her face away while she delved in her medical kit; then brought out what she needed to dress the burn and make Patience more comfortable.

Tom was training one of the hoses on the flames. He didn't have a clue whether Joey was safely in the playground with the other children because he couldn't see. Although he was frantic to know that Joey was all right, he had a job to do and his colleagues were relying on him not to let them down. He had to keep doing his job and trust his colleagues to do theirs.

I swear if he's safe then I'll do better by him, he promised silently to his sister. *I'll change my job, give up firefighting and concentrate on him.*

And then the headmistress hurried over towards them.

'Is everyone safe?' Steve asked.

Rosemary Bailey looked grim. 'There's still part of one class missing. Some of the Reception children.'

Tom, overhearing her, went cold. *Joey was in the Reception year.* 'Is Joey all right?' he asked urgently.

Rosemary bit her lip. 'He's not with the others. There's a group of children who'd gone to the quiet room at the end for extra help with reading. He must be with them.'

Tom swallowed hard. 'The quiet room. Is that the room at the end of the corridor?' The room that was cut off, right now, by flames.

'Yes.'

'It's near the storeroom where the fire started. Right now, it's structurally unstable,' Steve said. 'How many children are there?'

'Five, plus Matty Roper, the teaching assistant in R2.'

R2. Definitely Joey's class, Tom knew. And he knew Matty—he'd had twice-weekly meetings with her about Joey since he'd become Joey's guardian. Joey had been struggling at school for the last month, just shutting off, so Tom and Matty had been trying to work out how they could help him settle back in.

Ice slid through his veins. The children were stranded. *Including Joey.*

CHAPTER TWO

'RIGHT, I'm going in,' Tom said. 'Gary, can you take this hose from me?'

Steve grabbed Tom's shoulder to stop him. 'You're not going anywhere.'

'My nephew's trapped in that room. No way in hell am I leaving him there!' Tom snarled back.

'Nobody's saying that you have to leave him, Tom. But nobody's going into that corridor until we've stabilised the area—otherwise the whole lot could come down. And we can't afford to let the flames reach the really flammable stuff.'

Steve was making absolute sense. As an experienced fireman and the station manager, he knew exactly what he was doing. Tom was well aware of that. And yet every nerve in his body rebelled against his boss's orders. How could he just wait outside when his nephew was trapped inside that room?

'Tom, I know you think Joey might be in there, but you can't afford to let emotion get in the way.'

Ordinarily, Tom didn't. He was able to distance himself from things and stay focused, carrying others through a crisis situation with his calm strength. But this was different. This was Joey. The last link to his elder sister. No way could he let the little boy down.

'You either keep doing your job as lead fireman and getting

the flames under control,' Steve said softly, 'or you're off duty as of now, which means you go back to the station.'

And then it would be even longer before he could find out if Joey was safe. Waiting would drive him crazy. Tom dragged in a breath. 'Right, Guv. I'm sticking to my post.'

The fire crew that had arrived as back-up started to get the supports up; Tom forced himself to concentrate on damping down the blaze. Abandoning his job wouldn't help Joey. Focus, he told himself. Just *focus*.

It felt like a lifetime, but at last the area was stabilised and they were in a position to rescue the trapped children and their teacher. Steve had already vetoed the door as the access point; although the flames were out, the corridor was still thick with smoke, and until the fire had been damped down properly it could reignite at any time. The window was the safest option, now the area was stabilised.

But there was no way Tom's muscular frame would fit through the window. His colleagues, too, were brawny and would find it an equally tight fit.

'Um, excuse me?'

Tom looked down at the woman standing next to him. She was a foot shorter than him, and her face was bright red—whether through embarrassment or the heat from the fire, he had no idea.

'I'm the school nurse,' she said. 'Look, I know I'm a bit, um, round...' her colour deepened and she looked at the floor '...and I'm not as strong as you, but the children are only little. Matty and I can lift them up between us and pass them through to you. And I can check them over while I'm in there and make sure they're all right.'

'I see where you're coming from,' he said, 'but you're a civilian. I can't let you take that risk.'

'But I know the children,' she said, her voice earnest—though she still wasn't looking at him, Tom noticed. 'It'll be less frightening for them if I go in to help.' She bit her lip. 'I know it's dangerous, but I won't do anything reckless. And we need to get the children out quickly.'

True. And, the faster they did that, the sooner he'd see Joey. That was the clincher for him. 'All right. Thank you.'

She nodded. 'I'm sorry I'm, um, a bit heavy.'

He looked at her properly then. Yes, she was curvy. Plump, if he was brutally honest. But there was a sweetness and kindness in her face, a genuine desire to help—something that he knew had been missing from the other women he'd dated. Sure, they might have been tall and leggy and jaw-droppingly gorgeous, but they would've fussed about chipping a nail. And he knew who he'd rather have beside him in this crisis. Definitely the school nurse.

And she had the sweetest, softest mouth. A mouth that made him want to...

Whatever was the *matter* with him? His nephew was missing, he had a job to do, and he was thinking about what it would be like to kiss a complete stranger? For pity's sake—he needed to concentrate!

'You're fine,' he said, and proved it by lifting her up to the window as if she weighed no more than a feather.

She scrambled through, and Tom almost forgot to breathe while he waited. Were the children all right? Was Joey safe?

And then Matty Roper and the school nurse came to the window and started lifting the children through, and there just wasn't time to ask about Joey as he took the children one by one and passed them over to the team of medics lining up behind him ready to check over the children.

Three.

Four.

He swallowed hard. The next one would be Joey.

Except the next person to come to the window was Matty Roper.

'Where's Joey?' he asked urgently. 'The head said there were five children missing—that they were in the quiet room with you.'

'Only four,' Matty said. 'And Joey wasn't one of them.'

'But he *has* to be. There were five children missing. He was one of them.'

'I'm sorry, Tom. I only took four children to the quiet room with me and they're all accounted for.'

Panic flowed through him, making every muscle feel like lead. How could Joey be missing? How?

'Please, Matty. Check again. Just in case he came in and you didn't see him.'

'Tom, I know he didn't,' Matty said gently. 'I'm sorry.'

'Then where the hell is he?' Tom burst out in desperation.

'I don't know.' She looked nervously at the supports against the wall. 'Is this going to hold?'

This was his job. He had to get Matty and the school nurse out. And then he could start to look for Joey.

Please, God, let it not be too late.

Grim-faced, he helped Matty through the window, and then the nurse.

Once they were both standing on safe ground, he leaned through the window. 'Joey! Joey, where are you?'

No answer.

Was he trapped in one of the other classrooms? 'Joey!' he bellowed.

'Do you mean Joey Barber?' the nurse asked.

'Yes.' She'd seen the other children, Tom thought, so maybe she'd seen his nephew. 'Have you seen him?'

She shook her head. 'Not today.' Again, she didn't meet his

eyes. 'He's the little boy who lost his parents just after New Year, isn't he?'

'My sister and her husband,' Tom confirmed. And it was beginning to look as if Joey might be joining his parents. No, no, no. It couldn't happen. He couldn't bear it. 'The head said there were five children missing. Now it's just Joey. Oh, hell, can't he hear me? Why isn't he answering?' He yelled Joey's name again.

The nurse squeezed his hand. 'The noise of the explosion will have scared him and probably brought back memories of the car crash. Right now, even if he can hear you, he's probably too scared to answer.'

He thought about it and realised that she was right. 'Not that he speaks much anyway, since the accident,' Tom said wryly. 'He barely strings two words together now. It's been so hard to reach him since Susie and Kevin died.' He dragged in a breath. 'If anything's happened to him, I'll never forgive myself.' He'd never be able to live with the guilt: his sister had asked him to look after her precious child, and he'd failed. Big time.

'This isn't your fault,' she said softly. 'You can't blame yourself.'

'I need to find him.' He handed over his damping-down duties to one of his colleagues and went in search of the station manager. 'Guv, Joey's still missing. I need to find him. Please.'

'All right.' Steve looked at him, grim-faced. 'But you don't take *any* risks, you hear me?'

'I won't,' Tom promised. He wouldn't put anyone in danger. But he'd take the buildings apart with his bare hands if he had to, to find his nephew.

'I, um, could help you look for him, if you like.' The nurse was by his side again. 'He knows me, and a familiar face might help.'

'Thank you.' Tom looked at her. 'I don't even know your name,' he blurted out.

'Flora. Flora Loveday.' Her face reddened again. 'And I know it's a stupid name. I'm not a delicate little flower.'

'No.' He was beginning to realise now that she was shy, like the proverbial violet—that was why she blushed and couldn't quite get her words out and found it hard to look him in the eye—but he had a feeling that there was much more to Flora Loveday than that. She'd put herself in a dangerous situation to help the children. 'No, you're like a…a peony,' Tom said, thinking of the flowers his mother had always grown in summer. 'Brave and bright and strong.'

Her blush deepened to the point where she seriously resembled the flower.

'I'm Tom. Tom Nicholson.'

She nodded but said nothing and looked away.

With Flora by his side, he checked with Rosemary Bailey and the rest of the fire crew. All the areas had been cleared, and nobody had seen Joey.

He eyed the wreckage. Fear tightened round his chest, to the point where he could barely breathe. Where was Joey? 'Maybe he's in the toilets,' he said.

Flora shook her head. 'They've been checked.'

'He has to be here. He *has* to be.' Desperately, he yelled Joey's name again.

'If he's scared already, shouting is only going to make him panic more,' she said quietly. She paused. 'When I was Joey's age, I hated going to school. I used to hide in the cloakrooms.'

Tom hardly dared hope that Joey would've done the same. But it was the best option he had right now. 'Let's have another look. I know they've been checked, but…' He glanced over to the huddled children at the far end of the playground.

'Joey's tiny. If he was sitting among the coats and didn't reply, whoever checked might have missed him.'

Together, they went over to the Reception cloakrooms.

'I'll start this end—can you start that end, Flora?' Tom asked.

'Sure.'

He'd checked under every coat at his end when he heard Flora call out, 'He's here.'

Huddled up at the far end of the cloakroom, beneath piles of coats, his nephew was white-faced. And Tom had never been so glad to see him in all his life. He dropped to his knees and hugged the little boy tightly, uncaring that he was covered in smoke and smuts and he would make Joey's clothes filthy.

Joey squirmed. 'You're hurting me,' he whispered.

The soft sound pierced Tom's heart. Of course. The little boy didn't like being touched, not since his parents had died. As a toddler, he'd adored riding on his uncle's shoulders and playing football and going down the huge slide in the playground on Tom's or his father's lap, but since the accident he'd put huge barriers round himself.

Tom let his nephew go. 'Sorry, Jojo. I didn't mean to hurt you. It's just I was very scared when I couldn't find you. I'm so glad you're all right.'

Joey stared at him and said nothing.

'I know this afternoon's been scary, but it's all going to be just fine,' Tom said softly. 'I promise. I'm going to have to stay here until the fire's completely out and everything's safe, but maybe Mrs Bailey will let you sit in her office and do some drawing until I can get in touch with the childminder and see if she can take you home.'

Joey said nothing, and Tom had absolutely no idea what the little boy was thinking. Did he feel abandoned, or could he understand that other people relied on Tom to do his job and keep them safe and he had to share Tom's time?

Flora was sitting on the low bench by the coat rack. 'Or,' she said, 'maybe you could come home with me until your uncle's finished here. I live on a farm, and I've got the nicest dog in the world.'

Tom looked at her. 'But I've only just met you.' Did she really think he'd let his precious nephew go off with a complete stranger—even if she had been brilliant and helped to rescue him?

She bit her lip. 'I know, but Joey knows me. And my boss is here—I take it you know Nick Tremayne?' At Tom's curt nod, she said, 'He'll vouch for me. And it's no trouble. I just need to pick up my paperwork from the nursery next door— the children will all have gone home by now, so I'll have to finish the clinic next week anyway.'

So she *did* think he'd let Joey go home with someone he didn't know.

Then again, Tom was usually a good judge of character and he liked what he'd seen of Flora. She was kind, she was brave, and she'd thought of the children before herself.

'Is that all right with you, Joey?' Tom asked.

Joey looked wary, and Tom was about to refuse the offer when Flora said, 'You can meet my dog and see around the farm.'

'Dog,' Joey said.

And, for the first time in a long, long time, he gave a smile. A smile that vanished the second after it started, but it was a proper smile. And it made Tom's decision suddenly easy.

'Do you want to go with Flora and see her dog, Jojo?' Tom asked.

This time, Joey nodded.

'I can borrow a car seat from the nursery—they have spares,' Flora said. She took a notepad from her pocket and scribbled quickly on it. 'That's my address, my home phone and my mobile phone.'

'Thank you.' Tom dragged in a breath. 'This is going to sound really ungrateful. My instincts tell me to trust you, but—'

'I'm a stranger,' she finished. 'You can never take risks with children. They're too precious.' She bit her lip and looked away, and Tom felt like an utter heel. She was trying to help and he'd practically thrown the offer back in her face.

'Talk to Nick,' she said. 'And then, if you're happy for Joey to come with me, I'll be next door at the nursery.'

Somehow, she'd understood that this wasn't personal—that he'd be the same even if the offer had come from a teaching assistant he didn't know. 'Thank you,' Tom said and, making sure Joey was right by his side, went to find Nick Tremayne.

At half past seven that evening, Flora heard the car tyres on the gravel and glanced across at Banjo, who was standing guard over the child asleep on the beanbag. 'All right, boy. I heard him. Shh, now. Let Joey sleep.'

She'd opened the kitchen door before Tom could ring the doorbell. 'Joey's asleep in front of the fire,' she whispered. 'Come in.'

He'd showered and changed; out of his uniform, and with his face no longer covered by a mask and soot, Tom Nicholson was breathtakingly handsome. When he smiled at her, her heart actually skipped a beat.

Which was ridiculous, because he was way, *way* out of her league. He probably had a girlfriend already; though, even if he didn't, Flora knew he wouldn't look twice at her. Looking the way he did, and doing the job he did, Tom was probably used to scores of much more attractive women falling in a heap at his feet. He wouldn't be interested in a shy, plump nurse who spent most of her time looking like a beetroot.

'He's absolutely sound asleep,' Tom whispered, looking

down at his nephew, who was lying on the beanbag with a fleecy blanket tucked round him.

'It's been a long day for him—and a scary one.' She glanced at Tom. 'Um, I've already fed him. I hope that's OK.'

'That's great. Thanks for being so kind,' Tom said.

'I could hardly let him starve.' Flora shrugged it off. 'Poor little lad. He's had a lot to cope with, losing both his parents. I know what that's like.' She'd had to face losing both her parents, the previous year, so she had an idea what he was going through—though, being twenty years older than Joey, at least she'd had an adult's perspective to help her cope. She looked more closely at Tom and saw the lines of strain around his eyes. 'You look exhausted.'

'Once the immediate danger's passed, the real work starts—making sure we keep the site damped down so the fire doesn't flare up again.' Tom grimaced. 'Sorry I've been so long. And I took time out for a shower, because if I turned up covered in smuts and stinking of smoke it might scare Joey.'

He'd put his nephew first; and no doubt the shower had been at the expense of taking time to grab a meal. It was good that he could put Joey first, but the poor man must be starving as well as tired. And if she made him something to eat, she could keep herself busy doing something practical—which was a lot easier than sitting down and having a conversation where she'd end up blushing and stumbling over her words and getting flustered. She'd learned the hard way that being practical and doing something was the best way of dealing with her hated shyness. 'He's perfectly safe and comfortable where he is, so why don't you sit down and I'll make you a hot drink and something to eat?' Flora asked.

'I can't impose on you like that.'

'You're not imposing. I made a big batch of spaghetti sauce this afternoon. It won't take long to heat it through and cook some pasta—that's what Joey and I had.'

'Thank you.'

The next thing Tom knew, he was sitting at the table with a mug of coffee in front of him and Flora was pottering round the kitchen.

The kindness of a stranger. Tom was used to women offering to cook him things—it was a standing joke at the fire station that, almost every day, someone dropped by with a tin of home-made cookies or cakes or muffins for Tom. Old ladies whose cats he'd rescued, young mums whose toddlers he'd got out of a locked bathroom—and even the hard-nosed local reporter had seen him in action, rescuing someone from a burning building, and had joined what his crew-mates teasingly called the Tom Nicholson Fan Club, turning up with a batch of cookies for him on more than one occasion.

Even though he'd explained gently that he was simply doing his job, he could hardly be rude enough to turn away things that people had spent time making personally for him. So he accepted them with a smile on behalf of the fire crew, wrote thank-you notes—again on behalf of the entire fire crew—and secretly rather enjoyed them making a fuss over him.

But Flora Loveday was different.

There was something about her—a kind of inner peace and strength that drew him. Here, on her home ground, she glowed. He'd been too frantic with worry about Joey to notice properly earlier, but she was beautiful. Soft, gentle brown eyes; her hair, too, was soft, all ruffled and curly and cute. And the warmth she exuded made him want to hold her close, feel some of that warmth seeping into him and taking the chill of the fear away…

And then he realised what he was thinking and slammed the brakes on. Yes, he found her attractive—dangerously so—but he couldn't act on it. In his job, it wasn't fair to have a serious relationship with someone. He worked crazy hours and did dangerous things; he'd seen too many friends die and leave families behind. And there was Joey to consider, too. He'd had too many changes in his young life, just recently. The last thing he needed was his uncle being distracted by a new girlfriend.

But Tom also knew that he could do with a friend. Flora was the first person who'd seemed to understand or who had managed to start to reach Joey. And he really, really needed help reaching his nephew.

'So what have you and Joey been up to?' he asked.

'I took him to see the chickens.'

'Chickens?' He hadn't expected that.

She went pink again. 'My dad started Loveday Eggs.'

He'd seen their boxes in the shops. 'So you have chickens here?'

She nodded. 'The hens are free range, so we went and collected some eggs. And then we made some brownies.' She smiled. 'There are some left. But not that many.' She placed a bowl of pasta in front of him.

'This smells amazing. Thank you.' He took a mouthful. 'Wow. And it tastes even better than it smells.'

'It's only boring old spaghetti and sauce.' She looked away.

'It's wonderful.' He ate the lot and accepted a second bowl. And then he grimaced. 'Sorry. I've just been horribly greedy.'

'You've just spent hours sorting out a fire. You must've been starving.'

'I was,' he admitted. And then he accepted her offer of helping himself to the brownies. 'Wow. These are seriously good. And you made them with Joey?'

She fished her mobile phone out of her handbag, fiddled with it and then handed it to him. There was a picture of Joey, wearing a tea-towel as a makeshift apron, stirring the chocolatey mixture in a big bowl—and there was almost as much chocolate round his face.

And he looked happy.

Tom couldn't speak for a moment. Then he gulped in a breath. 'I didn't know Joey liked cooking.'

'Most kids love messy stuff,' she explained, her colour deepening. 'And cooking's better still because they get to eat what they make.'

In one afternoon, she seemed to have got far closer to his nephew than he'd managed in a month. And he knew he needed help. Flora might be the one to help him reach Joey— and there was just something about her that made Tom sure that she wouldn't judge him harshly. 'It never even occurred to me to try doing something like that with Joey.' He raked a hand through his hair. 'Don't get me wrong, I like kids. I'm always the one sent on school visits, but I just don't seem to be able to connect with Joey—and I'm his uncle. Everything I suggest us doing, he just stares at me and says nothing. I can't reach him any more. I feel…' He shook his head, grimacing. 'Hopeless. Helpless. I don't even know where to start.'

'Give it time,' she said. 'It's only been a month since the accident—and he was one of the quieter ones in the school even before then.'

Tom blinked in surprise. 'So you work at the school? I thought you said Nick Tremayne was your boss?'

'He is, but I'm the school liaison,' she explained.

'So you visit the local schools?'

She nodded. 'I spend half my time at the local nursery and schools, and half my time at the practice. I do a health visitor clinic at the primary school for mums one morning a week, a clinic at the high school, and I do the vaccinations and preschool health checks in the nursery. Plus I take the personal development classes—I get the little ones thinking about healthy eating and exercise and how they can get five a day, and how they can look after their teeth properly.'

It was the most he'd heard her say in one go, and she looked animated; clearly she loved her job and felt comfortable talking about it. 'So I take it you like your job?'

She smiled. 'I love it.'

Just as he loved his: something else they had in common. Tom paused, remembering what she'd said when he'd first walked in. 'I'm sorry about your parents.'

'And I'm sorry about your sister.' She bit her lip, looking awkward. 'I didn't know her very well, but she seemed nice.'

'She was. My big sister.' Tom sighed. 'And I feel worse because I was meant to go to France with her, Kevin and Joey to see our parents for New Year and I bailed out. Maybe if I'd been driving the crash wouldn't have happened.'

'You don't know that,' Flora said. 'And think of it another way—if you *had* been in the crash, Joey might've been left without anyone at all.'

'Mum and Dad would've stepped in to help, but they're nearly seventy now, and it's not fair to drag them back to England and make them run around after a little one. Dad's arthritis really gives him gyp.' He rubbed his hand across his forehead, but the tight band of tension refused to shift. 'I loved spending time with Joey when Susie was alive—I used to see them most weekends. I've always tried to be a good uncle and we used to have fun—but since the accident he's just put all these barriers up and I don't know how to get them down again.'

'Give it time,' she said again, her voice kind.

'Did he talk to you this afternoon?'

'A bit. He was a little shy.' She shrugged and looked away. 'But so am I, so that's OK.'

And that was one of the reasons why Flora seemed to

understand Joey better than he did: she knew what it was like to be shy, and Tom never had. And he couldn't help wondering what Flora was like when she wasn't shy. He knew she was practical and kind—but what did she look like when she laughed?

Or when she'd just been thoroughly kissed?

Oh, for pity's sake, he really needed to keep his libido under control.

Luckily his thoughts weren't showing on his face, because Flora continued, 'I read him some stories after we'd eaten—he chose them from the box I take to clinic—and then he fell asleep on the beanbag.'

'Bless him.' Tom bit his lip. 'I think he's had a better time with you than he would've done at the childminder's.' He sighed. 'I feel bad taking him to the childminder's for breakfast and then not picking him up until after dinner for half the week, but I work shifts—it's the only thing I can do. I was trying to avoid any more change in his life, but she told me the other week I'm going to have to find someone else because she's moving.'

'Would your childminder be Carol?' she asked.

Yet again, she'd surprised him. 'How did you know?'

'I know all the local childminders, through work,' Flora explained. 'Carol loves it here in Cornwall, but her husband's been promoted to his company's head office in London so that's why she has to move.'

'So if you know all the local childminders...' Tom brightened. 'Do you happen to know anyone with spare places who'd be good with Joey and could take him from half past six in the morning until school, and then after school until a quarter past seven or so? I can hardly take him with me to the station, in case we have a shout.'

'Nobody's got any spare places right now,' Flora said. 'The

ones who did have are already booked up from taking on Carol's clients. But I can ask around again, if you like.'

Yet another example of his failure at being a stand-in parent. 'Susie would've had that sorted out on day one,' Tom said grimly. 'When Carol told me she was leaving and I'd have to find someone else to look after Joey, I was still trying to get my head around what had happened and learning to fit my life round my nephew. I didn't have room in my head for anything else. And now I *wish* I'd made more of an effort.' He blew out a breath. 'Sorry. I shouldn't be dumping on you like this.'

'Not a problem. It's not going any further than me.'

'Trust you, you're a nurse?'

'Something like that.' Flora smiled at him, and Tom realised that she had dimples. Seriously cute dimples. Dimples he wanted to touch. Dimples he wanted to kiss.

Though now wasn't the time or the place. 'Thank you. You've been really kind. Can I impose on you and ask you what's your secret? You've got through to Joey when nobody else can, not even his teachers.'

She shrugged. 'I think he likes Banjo.'

The dog wagged his tail at hearing his name. The sound of Banjo's tail thumping the floor woke Joey, and he sat up, rubbing his eyes. For a moment, he stared wildly round him, as if not knowing where he was.

'Hey, Jojo, we're at Flora's. At the farm,' Tom said, going over to him and squatting down so that he was at his nephew's level. 'You fell asleep, sweetheart. I hear you've been running about with Banjo here and seeing the chickens and making brownies.'

Joey nodded.

'Did you have fun?'

Joey nodded again.

'That's good.' Tom smiled at him. 'The fire's out now so

your school's all safe again, ready for Monday morning. And we ought to let Flora get on. Shall we go home to Uncle Tom's upstairs house?'

Joey just looked at him.

Home.

Clearly Joey didn't think of Tom's flat as home. Maybe he should've moved into his sister's house instead of taking Joey back to his place, but he simply couldn't handle it. Every second he'd been in the house, he'd expected Susie to walk into the room at any time, and it had to be even harder for Joey. Right now, Tom was caught between the devil and the deep blue sea, and he hated himself for not being able to make Joey's world right again. For being a coward and escaping to work whenever he could, losing himself in the adrenalin rush of his job.

'Shall we say goodbye to Flora and Banjo?'

Joey yawned, then made a fuss of the dog, who licked him.

'You can come back any time you like and play with him,' Flora said. 'He liked playing ball with you this afternoon.'

Joey said nothing, but there was the ghost of a smile on his face.

'Thank you for having us,' Tom said, knowing that his nephew wasn't going to say it.

'My pleasure. Come back soon, Joey,' Flora said with a smile.

Tom tried slipping his hand into Joey's as they walked to the front door, but Joey twisted his hand away. Tom was careful not to let his feelings show on his face. 'Bye, Flora. Thanks again.'

He opened the car door, and Joey climbed onto his car seat. The little boy allowed Tom to fix the seatbelt, but Tom could see by the look on his nephew's face that Joey had retreated back into his shell again. He didn't even wave to Flora.

If only he could find a way of getting through to Joey.

He was just going to have to try harder.

CHAPTER THREE

DESPITE the fact that he'd lain awake half the night, worrying about Joey, Tom's body-clock was relentless. He didn't even need to look at his alarm to know that it was six o'clock. For pity's sake, it wasn't even light. And it was the weekend. Why couldn't he just turn over, stick the pillow over his head and go back to sleep?

Ha. He knew the answer to that. Because Joey woke early, too, and Tom needed to keep the little boy safe. His life had changed completely. Nowadays, he couldn't stay up until stupid o'clock watching films or playing online with his friends on a game console, or sleep in until midday on his day off. He had responsibilities.

Coffee, first. Tom dragged himself out of bed, then pulled on his dressing gown and headed for the kitchen. He blinked in surprise when he switched on the light and saw Joey sitting at the table in the dark, all dressed and ready to go out. Joey's long-sleeved T-shirt was on back to front and he was wearing odd socks; Tom couldn't help smiling. Cute beyond words. Part of him was tempted to ruffle his nephew's hair, but he knew that the little boy would only flinch away, so there was no point.

And that hurt.

'Why were you sitting in the dark, Jojo?' he asked gently.

Joey said nothing, but glanced over to the doorway.

Of course. He couldn't quite reach the light switch. Tom's flat wasn't designed for a four-year-old.

'I'll get a light put in here you *can* reach,' Tom promised. An uplighter would be the safest. Or maybe one on a timer switch. 'You look all ready to go out.'

Joey nodded.

'Where do you want to go?' And please don't let him say 'home', Tom begged silently.

'I want to play with Banjo.'

Flora's dog had clearly made the breakthrough that none of the adults had been able to make, because this was the longest sentence that Joey had strung together since the accident.

It would be an imposition on Flora, Tom knew, but this was the most animated he'd seen Joey since the little boy had come to live with him. He couldn't afford to let the opportunity slip away. Though going to visit Flora at this time of the morning would be a little too much to ask; he needed some delaying tactics.

'OK, sweetheart, we'll go and see Banjo.' *And Flora.* Awareness prickled all the way down Tom's spine, and he squashed it ruthlessly. This wasn't about his attraction to the sweet, gentle school nurse who had the most kissable mouth he'd ever seen. This was about his nephew. 'But it's a bit early to go and visit anyone just yet; it's still dark outside. I'm not even dressed—and I don't know about you, but I really could do with some breakfast first. How about we make something to eat, then go and buy some flowers to say thank you to Flora for looking after you yesterday, and a...' What did you buy dogs? Tom's parents had always had cats rather than dogs, and he hadn't had the space in his life to look after an animal properly so he had no pets. 'A ball or something for Banjo?' he finished.

Joey nodded.

Tom put water in the kettle and switched it on. 'What do you want for breakfast?'

Joey shrugged.

'Juice? Cereals?' Flora had got through to him yesterday by baking. Tom didn't bake. He did the bare minimum when it came to cooking: stir-fries, pasta and baked potatoes were pretty much his limit. Anyway, suggesting cake for breakfast wasn't exactly healthy.

But there had to be something they could do.

'How about a bacon sandwich?' he asked. 'We can make it as a team. How about you're the chef, in charge of buttering the bread and squirting on the tomato ketchup, and I'll grill the bacon?'

Joey gave him a tiny smile, and went to the drawer where Tom kept the tea-towels. Without a word, he tucked a tea-towel round himself like an apron, the way he had in the photo Flora had shown Tom the previous evening, then fetched the butter and tomato ketchup from the fridge.

This was good, Tom thought. A positive step.

Joey buttered the bread while Tom grilled the bacon. Tom carefully laid the cooked bacon on the bread, then looked at Joey. 'Over to you, Chef.'

Joey squeezed tomato ketchup over the bacon—a bit too much for Tom's taste, but he'd wash it down with coffee and a smile because no way was he going to reject his nephew's efforts. 'Excellent teamwork. High five, Chef.' He lifted his palm, hoping that Joey would respond.

For a moment, he didn't think Joey was going to react—and then Joey smiled and touched his palm to Tom's. Only momentarily, but in Tom's view it was huge progress from the way things had been. And it gave him hope for the future.

'Can we see Banjo now?' Joey asked when they'd finished, his face eager.

'Once you've washed your face and changed your shirt—

because they're both covered in ketchup—and cleaned your teeth,' Tom said. 'And I need to wash up the breakfast things. Then we'll go to the shop on the way.'

'My singing isn't that bad, you horrible dog,' Flora said, laughing as Banjo started barking.

But then he went over to the kitchen door and barked again.

'Visitors?' Odd. She wasn't expecting anyone, and it was too early for the postman. But there was no other reason why her dog would be barking by the front door. She switched off the vacuum cleaner and went to answer the door.

'Oh—Tom and Joey! Hello.' She hadn't expected to see them today, despite telling them the previous evening that they could come round at any time. And it was incredibly early. Barely after breakfast.

'We wanted to bring you something—didn't we, Jojo?' Tom said.

Joey nodded, all wide-eyed.

'These are for you.' Tom handed her the biggest bunch of flowers she'd ever seen. 'We weren't sure what colour you like, but Joey thinks all girls like pink.'

And there was every shade of pink. Bold cerise gerberas, tiny pale pink spray carnations, even some blush-pink roses.

Flora couldn't remember anyone ever buying her flowers before—except her parents, on her birthday and when she'd qualified as a nurse—and it flustered her. 'I, um…' She felt the betraying tide of colour sweep into her cheeks. 'Um, they're lovely. I, um…' Oh, help. 'Do you want to come in?'

'This is for Banjo.' Joey was carrying what Flora recognised as a squeaky toy bone.

'Thank you. He loves those.'

Just to prove it, when Joey squeaked the bone, Banjo

bounced into the middle of the room, bowing down and wagging his tail to signal that he was ready to play.

Be practical, Flora told herself. Don't make an idiot of yourself. 'I'll put these lovely flowers in water,' she said. 'Would you like a coffee?'

'I'd love one.' Tom smiled at her, and she felt her toes curl. Which was crazy. She didn't react to people like that. Anyway, he wasn't here to see her...was he?

To cover her confusion, she turned to the little boy. 'Joey, would you like some milk or some juice?'

Joey shook his head and continued playing with the dog.

Tom glanced at the vacuum cleaner. 'Sorry, you were busy.'

'It's OK. I was only vacuuming. And you brought me those gorgeous flowers.'

'It was the least we could do. You were a total star yesterday. We wanted to say thank you.'

He'd brought her flowers to say thanks for helping with Joey. No other reason. She squished the ridiculous hope that he'd bought them for the usual reason a man bought a woman flowers. Of course not. She already knew she wasn't the kind of woman who could make men look twice; she was way too short, thirty pounds too heavy, and on the rare occasion she wore a skirt it was usually six inches below the knee rather than six inches above. Plus she spent most of her time with a red face, tongue-tied. No way would someone like Tom be interested in her.

As always when faced with a social situation involving adults, she took refuge in practicalities, gesturing to Tom to sit at the scrubbed pine table in the centre of the kitchen, then busying herself arranging the flowers in a vase. Once she'd put them on the table, she made two mugs of coffee, took the remaining brownies from the tin and put them on a plate, then sat down with Tom and slid the plate across to him. 'Help yourself.'

'Thanks…' he smiled at her '…but, lovely as those brownies are, I'd better pass. We've just had breakfast. Chef Joey there makes a mean bacon sandwich.'

She raised an eyebrow. 'I assume you grilled the bacon.'

'But he did the important bit—he buttered the bread and added the tomato sauce.'

Joey clearly wasn't paying attention to anyone else except Banjo, but then Tom lowered his voice. 'I'm sorry we turned up unannounced. He told me this morning that he wanted to come and play with Banjo—and it's the longest sentence he's said in a month. I feel bad about taking up your spare time, but this was a chance to get through to him. I just couldn't turn it down.'

'It's not a problem,' Flora said, keeping her voice equally low. 'I wasn't doing anything in particular, just the usual Saturday chores.'

'I don't want to make things awkward with your boyfriend.'

She felt the betraying colour heat her cheeks again. 'I don't have a boyfriend.' The boys at school had never looked twice at her, she'd never been the partying type as a student nurse, and she knew that she wouldn't even be on the radar of a gorgeous firefighter like Tom Nicholson. Then a really nasty thought hit her. 'Is it going to be a problem for your girlfriend, Joey coming here to play with Banjo?'

'There's nobody serious in my life—just Joey.' He smiled wryly. 'Let's just say my last girlfriend found it a bit hard to share my time. The way she saw it, I should've made my parents come back to England to look after him.'

'How selfish of h—' Flora clapped a hand to her mouth. 'Sorry, it's not my place to judge.'

'No, you got it right first time. And she told me that the day after the accident.' For a moment, he looked grim. 'Apart from the fact that we hadn't been dating for very long, it wasn't a hard choice to make. Joey comes first.'

'Well, of course he does.'

Tom gave her an approving smile that made her feel as if she were glowing from the inside.

'I've been thinking about your childminder issue. I could help out, if you like.' The words tumbled out before Flora could stop them. 'I finish at five, the same time as the after-school club—so I could meet him from there if you like. There's only me and Banjo to please ourselves, and it's as easy to cook for two as it is for one, so if you're out on a shout or something he can have his tea here with me—if you think he'd like that,' she added swiftly.

Tom looked surprised at her offer. 'That's really kind of you,' he said carefully.

Oh, no. He'd obviously taken it the wrong way. She'd better explain. 'Look, I just know what it's like to lose both parents,' she said. 'And that wasn't me trying to—well, you know.' She blushed again.

Trying to come on to him? From another woman, Tom wouldn't have been so sure. But with Flora, he knew she was genuine; he hadn't known her long, but it was obvious that she was the type to wear her heart on her sleeve. She was offering to help because she was kind, because she cared, because she'd lost her own parents and she could understand exactly how Joey felt—and she wasn't emotionally hopeless with the boy, the way he was.

'I know it was a genuine offer,' he said softly, 'and I'm not trying to come on to you, either.' Though he knew that wasn't strictly true. He couldn't put his finger on it, but something about Flora Loveday drew him. And it was completely unexpected because she was nothing like the women he usually dated. She wasn't sophisticated, fashionable or glamorous. But there really was something about her that made him—well, just *want* her.

Though, right now, he knew he couldn't think about dating anyone. His life was too complicated. He pulled himself together. 'It's always good to make a new friend. Especially one as kind as you.'

She blushed even more, and Tom couldn't help smiling. Flora was so sweet. And there was a vulnerability about her that made him feel protective. Strong.

'And it's really all right for you to help me with Joey?'

'I wouldn't have offered if I didn't mean it.'

Tom closed his eyes for a moment. It seemed as if his prayers had all been answered. 'Flora, thank you. I have no idea what I would've done if you hadn't offered to help.'

Looking embarrassed, she glanced away. 'It's not a big deal. Joey's a nice little boy. But he might not want to come here.'

Tom smiled. 'Considering that he was up before I was, this morning—and I always wake at six—and he'd got himself dressed, with odd socks and his shirt on back to front, ready to come and see you and play with Banjo…I think he's going to say yes. But you're right—we do need to ask him first.' He looked over to where his nephew was busy making a fuss of Banjo, rubbing the dog's tummy while the spaniel had his eyes closed in bliss.

'Joey—can you come here a moment, sweetheart, please?'

Joey eyed the dog, clearly torn between making a fuss of him and doing what his uncle had asked, but eventually trotted over.

'How would you feel about Flora picking you up from after-school club in future?' Tom asked.

Joey frowned. 'Carol picks me up from school.'

'I know, but Carol has to go to live in London very soon,' Tom said gently. 'It's a big change for you, I know, but I've been trying to find someone you'd like to stay with while I'm at work.'

Joey's hazel eyes turned thoughtful. 'Would Banjo come, too?'

'Banjo's normally here during the day,' Flora said. 'But he'd be here to meet you when we got back from school. You could help me take him for a walk. Would you like that?'

Joey considered it, then nodded shyly.

'And then I'll come and fetch you as soon as I've finished work,' Tom said.

'Can I play with Banjo again now?'

Tom smiled. 'Sure.'

Joey raced back to the dog and found the squeaky bone.

'When do you want me to start picking him up?' Flora asked.

Tom thought about it. 'Carol's right in the middle of packing everything now. It's pretty disruptive for Joey, and I'm trying to keep things as calm as I can.' Calm and relaxed, like it was here at the farmhouse, Tom thought. Everything was neat and tidy, though it wasn't the kind of house where you'd be scared to move a cushion out of place. It was more that everything felt *right* just where it was, warm and welcoming and organised and comfortable. Just what Joey needed.

As for what Tom himself needed...he wasn't going to examine that too closely.

'I've got a day off on Monday. I don't have anything planned, so I could start then, if you like?' Flora suggested.

'Actually, I'm off myself on Monday and Tuesday—I work four days on and then four days off,' he said. 'But if you can do Wednesday to Friday this week, that'd be brilliant.'

'What time does your shift start?'

'I work seven until seven.'

'So what happens in the mornings,' she asked, 'if you have

to be at work at seven and school doesn't start until a quarter to nine?'

'I'm still working on that,' Tom admitted. 'I've been dropping him at Carol's at half past six.'

She shrugged. 'Well—I don't start work until nine, so you can do that with me, too. I'll have plenty of time to take him to school on the days you're at work.'

Tom stared at her. 'Really?' Usually, if something was too good to be true, it usually was. It couldn't be possible to sort out his hours and Joey's so easily—could it? 'Half past six is really OK with you?'

She smiled. 'I'm used to being up with the chickens, even though I don't have to feed them myself any more. And it'll be nice to have breakfast with someone in the mornings.'

She was so calm about it, so serene. Did she know what an angel she was? Tom wanted to hug her, but he had a feeling that she'd find it as awkward as Joey did. Something told him that Flora wasn't used to people hugging her. Except maybe some of her younger patients—he'd already noticed that she had children's drawings stuck to the door of her fridge with magnets.

'I'll need your contact numbers. And you'll also need to tell the school,' Flora added.

'Sure. If you have a piece of paper and a pen, I'll write my numbers down for you.'

Flora handed him her mobile phone. 'Better still, you could put them straight in there.'

Her fingers brushed against his and a wave of awareness swept down his spine. Not that he'd dare act on that awareness. Apart from the fact that she was shy—with him, not with Joey—if he messed this up, he'd lose a friend as well as help that he badly needed right now. He needed to keep a lid on this. Trying not to think about how soft her skin was and wondering how it would feel against his mouth, he keyed in his home number, his mobile and the number of the fire station. 'I've already got your numbers. I assume if I need to get you at work I should ring the surgery?'

'Yes, or try my mobile—I don't answer if I'm driving, though, so it'll go through to voicemail,' she warned.

'Good—that's sensible. I've had to cut too many people out of cars when they've been trying to talk on the phone and drive at the same time. Why they couldn't just pull over and make the call safely, or use a headset...' He rolled his eyes. 'Sorry. Preaching to the converted. And, as a medic, you know all that already.'

Flora smiled. 'Yes.'

She went quiet and shy on him again once they'd finished with the practicalities, but Tom was aware that he was eking out his coffee, putting off the moment when he'd have to leave here. Scared of being on his own with his nephew and failing to connect with him yet again? Or something else? He didn't want to analyse that too closely. And this really wasn't fair to Flora, taking up her day. 'Come on, Joey. Remember we said we'd go and play football in the park?'

'Can Banjo come?' Joey asked.

'No, Flora has things to do,' Tom said, before Joey could suggest taking up even more of Flora's time.

'Can we come back tomorrow?'

Tom was searching for an excuse when Flora said, 'I don't mind. I don't have anything much planned.'

'Tell you what, maybe Joey and I can take you out to lunch.' The words were out before he could stop them and he could see the surprise on her face—and the wariness. Help. He needed to take this down a notch. Make it clear that he was inviting her out with both of them, not on a proper date.

Though he was horribly aware that he'd like to have lunch with Flora on her own and get to know her better—a lot better.

'I mean, you fed us on Friday so it's our turn to feed you—right, Jojo?'

Joey nodded.

'And I know a place that does a really good Sunday roast, just down the road from here.' Tom smiled at her. 'So, can we take you to lunch tomorrow?'

'That'd be lovely. Thank you.'

'Great. We'll pick you up at half past eleven.'

It wasn't a proper date, Flora told herself as she stood in the doorway, waving as Tom's car headed down the driveway. They were just acquaintances who were on their way to becoming friends. Nothing more than that.

And she'd better not let herself forget it.

CHAPTER FOUR

DESPITE her resolutions to be calm and sensible, Flora found herself changing her outfit three times the next morning. She really should've asked Tom whether she needed to dress up for lunch.

Then again, they were going out with Joey, so the restaurant was more likely to be a family-friendly place. Which meant smart-casual rather than trendy—and besides, she didn't do trendy clothes. In the end, cross with herself for minding, she opted for a pair of smart black trousers, a long-sleeved cerise T-shirt and low-heeled sensible shoes. Hopefully this would strike the right balance.

She was relieved when Tom turned up wearing black chinos and a light sweater. And she suppressed the thought that he looked utterly gorgeous, like a model. He was her *friend*. Right?

Joey's seat was in the back of the car, but she noticed that Tom included Joey in the conversation, even though the little boy barely answered much above yes, no and—from what she could see in the rear-view mirror—a shrug.

Lunch was as excellent as Tom had promised. Flora noted that Tom helped Joey cut up his meat without making a big deal about it, just a soft, 'Can I give you a hand with that, sweetheart?' Tom really was a natural father figure, even though he clearly didn't think he was good enough. And they all had fun with the ice-cream machine; Tom helped Joey make a huge mountain in his bowl, and the little boy looked really happy as he added sprinkles and sauces from the toppings bar. He decorated Flora's and Tom's ice cream, too.

'That,' Flora said, 'is the best sundae I've ever seen.' She smiled at the little boy. 'Thank you, Joey. I'm really going to enjoy this.'

'Me, too,' Tom said. 'You're really good at decorating ice cream, Jojo.'

Joey's smile said it all for him: right now, all was right with his world.

Flora exchanged a glance with Tom, and her heart did another flip. This felt like being part of a family. And the scary thing was that she liked it. A lot.

'I think,' Tom said solemnly, patting his stomach afterwards, 'we need to walk off all that ice cream. It's really sunny outside, so how about we go to the park?'

Joey nodded, and Tom drove them there. Even though it was a chilly February afternoon, there were plenty of people walking through the gardens, pushing a pram or with a toddler running on the grass beside them. At the far end of the park, there was a playground with swings, slides and climbing frames; even from this distance, Flora could see that it was busy.

'Hello, Flora! Fancy seeing you here.' Jenny Walters smiled at her; she glanced at Tom and Joey and her smile turned speculative. 'Out to the park for the afternoon?'

'I, um. Yes.' Flora felt colour bursting into her face. Oh, no. The last thing they needed was gossip. But how could she explain that she and Tom were just friends, without it sounding like a cover story? 'You, too?' she asked, hoping that it would distract Jenny.

'Just me and Rachel. Damien's at home watching the football.' Jenny glanced at her daughter, who was holding her

hand. 'Actually, I'm glad I've caught you. I know I'm probably worrying about nothing, but Rachel's got this thing on
her foot and I don't like the look of it.' She bit her lip. 'Sorry,
I can see you're out with your...' she paused '...*friend*, and I
know I shouldn't ask outside clinic or the surgery.'

But it would only take a moment and would stop her worrying. And Flora always felt more comfortable when she was
doing something practical. At work, she wasn't shy because
she knew who she was: Flora Loveday, nurse. Plus looking
at Rachel's foot might take Jenny's mind off the fact that she
was accompanying Tom and Joey. She glanced at Tom and
Joey. 'Would you mind if I took a look? I'll only be a couple
of minutes.'

'No, that's fine—isn't it, Jojo?' Tom said.

Joey nodded solemnly.

'Thanks.' Flora smiled at them. 'Jenny, would you and
Rachel like to come and sit down on that bench over there?
Then, if you don't mind taking your shoe off, Rachel, I'll have
a swift look at your foot.'

'It looks like grains of pepper on the bottom of her foot,'
Jenny said. 'I thought it was maybe a splinter but she hasn't
been running around barefoot in the garden, not at this time
of year. I've tried putting mag sulph paste on it with a plaster
on top, just in case it was a splinter, but nothing happened.'

From the description, Flora had a pretty good idea what it
was, but she needed to see it for herself, just to be sure. 'Wow,
that's a nice sock, Rachel,' she said as the little girl took her
shoe off to reveal a bright pink sock with black pawprints.
'Those are pawprints just like my Banjo makes.'

'I like dogs,' Rachel said. 'What sort is yours?'

'He's a springer spaniel, and he lives up to his name because he bounces about everywhere,' Flora said with a grin.
'Guess what colour he is?'

'Black and white?'

'Half-right. Guess again.' Flora kept the little girl distracted by chatting while she inspected her foot.

'Brown and white?'

'Absolutely. Hey, do you know a song about a farmer's dog that almost sounds like Banjo?' she asked.

Just as she'd hoped, Rachel began singing, 'There was a farmer had a dog…'

And, to her surprise, when Rachel got to the bit where a letter in the dog's name was replaced by a clap, Joey joined in.

Tom looked transfixed. And, even though she'd seen enough to have her suspicions confirmed, Flora let Rachel and Joey finish the song before she asked her next question.

'That was brilliant singing, Rachel—and brilliant clapping, Joey.'

Both children looked pleased.

'You can sing us another clapping song, if you like,' Flora said. 'But first—Rachel, does it hurt when you walk?'

'A bit,' Rachel said. 'It's prickly.'

'OK. Well, the good news is, we can do something about that. Sing me another song, and I'll have a quick word with Mummy.' She smiled at the little boy. 'Joey, can you help Rachel with the clapping bits?'

Rachel was clearly delighted to have a younger child join in and, while she explained to Joey what they needed to do, Flora explained to Jenny what the problem was.

'It's a verruca,' she said.

'But I thought that was like a single big black spot?'

'Sometimes you get a cluster together, like this one,' Flora said. 'It's actually a wart on the bottom of the foot, so you might hear it called a plantar wart. Because of where it is, it gets trodden into the foot, so that's why it looks like spots rather than a growth. It's really common and nothing to worry about; my guess is, she picked it up at swimming.'

'I had a verruca when I was a kid,' Jenny said. 'I remember my mum taking me to the hospital, and this woman put a thing on my foot that burned and really hurt—and she told me off for making a fuss.'

Flora curled her lip in disgust. 'That's awful! You can still do the freezing treatment, but you can get something at the pharmacy so you can do it at home, and it's a special liquid so it shouldn't hurt. Or you can try duct tape.'

'Duct tape?' Jenny looked surprised.

'It works fairly well, but it's a little bit more long-winded. What you need to do is cut the tape just to the size of the verruca and put it on—it stops air getting to the skin and so it dies off and lets you get to the verruca,' Flora explained. 'Keep it on for six days, then take the tape off, soak Rachel's foot in a bowl of warm water for five minutes, then dry it and rub the area with a pumice stone to get rid of the dead skin. Then you put more duct tape on, and keep following the cycle. Usually it goes in three or four weeks.'

'I'll try that,' Jenny said.

'It's really infectious, so make sure you don't share towels,' Flora warned.

'And I'd better stop taking her swimming for a while.'

'Nowadays, the advice is just to cover it with waterproof plaster when you're swimming and use flip-flops in the communal areas,' Flora said with a smile.

Just when she'd finished explaining, Rachel and Joey sang and clapped the last bit of their song.

'That was brilliant, Rachel and Joey.' Flora applauded them both. 'Rachel, I've told Mummy what she needs to do, and you'll be pleased to know it won't hurt and you can still go swimming.'

The little girl beamed. 'Yay!'

'We'd better let you get on. Sorry we interrupted.' Jenny

gave Tom an apologetic smile, then patted Flora's shoulder. 'Thanks, Flora. You're such a star.'

Absolutely right, Tom thought, though he noticed how Flora shrugged the praise aside.

'Sorry about that, Tom,' Flora said as they headed towards the playground again.

'No, you're fine. I guess that's one of the perils of being a medic—everyone always wants to stop and ask your advice instead of going to the surgery.'

'I don't mind,' she said.

No, he thought, because she was special. She made a real difference to people's lives. 'Actually, that was fascinating. I learned a lot from that.' As well as reinforcing what he'd already guessed: that Flora was patient, was instinctively brilliant with children, and was great at reassuring worried parents, too. And he'd noticed that, even though Flora clearly knew Rachel's mum, she'd been shy with the woman until she'd actually been treating the child: and then the professional nurse had taken over, pushing the shyness away. Flora clearly had confidence in herself at work, but none outside. And he really couldn't understand why. Not wanting her to go back into her shell, he kept her talking about work. 'I had no idea about verrucas. I can't remember having one as a kid.'

'You must've been about the only child who didn't get one,' she said with a grin. 'Does Joey like swimming?'

He had no idea. 'Susie used to have a paddling pool for him in the garden, but I don't know if he ever went to a proper pool or had lessons. Probably not, or the swimming teacher would've got in touch with me by now, through Carol or something.' He sighed. 'I doubt if Joey will tell me himself, so I'll have to ask Matty Roper.'

'It might help you get a routine going, if you do things together on certain days—well, obviously depending on your shift,' she said. 'Maybe your first day off after a shift, you could go swimming together. And putting stickers on a calendar will help him remember what you're doing and when—that might make him feel a bit more secure with you.'

'I would never have thought of that.' Tom said. 'You're a genius.'

She shrugged. 'I'm no genius. I work with children, so I pick things up from the teachers and childminders.'

Hiding her light under a bushel again, Tom thought. Why did she do that? Why was she so uncomfortable with praise? Had her parents been the sort who were never satisfied and kept pushing? Or was it something else?

They reached the playground, and Joey made a beeline for the swing.

'Shall I push you?' Tom asked.

Joey shook his head, and proved that he could manage on his own.

Flora was sitting on the bench near the swings where she could watch; feeling useless, Tom joined her.

'OK?' she asked.

'Sure,' he lied. Hell. He needed distraction. And Flora was really, really good at being distracting.

Not that he would ruin things by telling her that there were amber flecks in her brown eyes. Or that her mouth was a perfect rosebud.

Pushing the thoughts away, he said, 'Did you always want to be a nurse?'

'I wanted to be a vet when I was small, and I was always bandaging up the dogs and the cats,' Flora said.

He could just imagine it, and couldn't help smiling.

'But I knew I wouldn't be able to handle putting animals to sleep, and Dad said I was so soft-hearted I'd end up taking in every stray brought in for surgery and I'd have to buy a thousand acres to house them all—and he was probably right,' Flora finished with a smile.

'But the medic part of it stuck?' he asked.

She nodded. 'I was going to take my exams to be a children's nurse when I'd qualified, and work at St Piran's.'

'So why didn't you?'

She shrugged. 'I realised Mum and Dad were struggling a bit. I couldn't just leave them to it, so I came home to look after them and did some agency work. The job as school liaison nurse came through last year—ironically, not long after Mum died. She would've been so pleased.'

'Was she a nurse, too?'

Flora shook her head. 'She and Dad, their life was the farm. Loveday's Organics. Dad believed in it well before it became trendy, and he worked with the Trevelyans on sorting out a veg box scheme. Though I didn't really want to take the farm over when I left school.' She gave a wry laugh. 'Whoever heard of a farm girl being scared of chickens?'

'You're scared of chickens?' Tom asked.

'Not any more, but I was for years, even as a teen.' She blushed prettily again, and Tom had to stop himself leaning over to steal a kiss from that beautiful rosebud mouth. Did Flora really have no idea how lovely she was?

'I think they knew I was nervous and it made them nervous, too, so it made them flap more. And that in turn made me more nervous, and it just got worse. Nowadays, it's not so bad. Toby taught me how to keep them calm, and I can even go in and collect eggs now.'

Tom was surprised to feel a flicker of jealousy at the other man's name. She'd said she didn't have a boyfriend... 'Who's Toby?'

'He manages the farm for me. He's worked with us for the last four years—he was Dad's assistant, but I know he took as much as he could off Dad's shoulders. His wife's a real sweetie, too. Their little boy's a couple of years older than Joey.' She looked thoughtful. 'Actually, they live in the cottage at the bottom of the driveway. It might be nice for Max and Joey to play together.'

'Maybe.' Tom was even crosser with himself for being pleased that Toby was clearly committed elsewhere. He had no right to be jealous and no right to dictate who Flora saw. 'Though Joey doesn't make friends very easily. He keeps himself to himself.'

'Max is a nice little boy. He'd be kind. Maybe we could do a play-date in a couple of weeks, when Joey's used to me and has settled in.' As if she could sense the knot of worry in his stomach and wanted to head him off the subject, she said, 'So what about you—did you always want to be a firefighter?'

'No, I was going to be an arctic explorer or drive a racing car.'

She laughed. 'So it was always going to be something dangerous, then?'

'Sort of.' He sighed. 'I think Dad was always a bit disappointed that I didn't go to university, but I'm taking my firefighter exams and I'm ready to move up to the next level, so I've proved to him that it's a career and not just a whim.'

'So what made you decide to be a firefighter?'

He could lie and give an anodyne response, but he had a feeling that Flora would know. And she deserved better than that. He took a deep breath. 'My best friend at school died in a house fire when I was thirteen.'

She winced. 'Sorry. That must've been hard for you.'

His world had been blown wide apart. Until then, it had never occurred to him that people his own age could die. Stupid, because of course they could. But he'd never known anyone die who wasn't really, really old and really, really sick. 'Yes. I found it pretty hard to deal with. And I couldn't help thinking, if I'd been a grown-up, one of the firefighters,

I would've been able to save Ben.' He shrugged. 'I know the fire wasn't my fault, but I guess becoming a firefighter was my way of trying to make up for what happened to him.' He'd never actually told anyone that before; he risked a glance at Flora, and to his surprise she wasn't looking at him as if he was crazy. She actually seemed to understand. 'Ben's the reason why I almost never lose anyone.' Why he drove himself past every barrier, no matter how scary. 'I remember how hard it was for his parents, when he died, and I don't want anyone else to go through that.'

'It takes someone very special to be that dedicated,' she said softly.

He shrugged. 'I've done the work for long enough to have a fair idea what I'm doing when it comes to fires, even though they can be unpredictable.' He probably took more risks than others, but he didn't really have a family at home to worry about.

Until now.

And that was a real struggle. He'd been thinking about his job, whether he ought to change to something with more child-friendly hours and less danger so he could protect Joey. Yet, at the same time, being a firefighter was all he'd ever wanted to do. He couldn't imagine doing anything else. And he found it hard to be a stand-in father; work was an escape for him. Which, he thought wryly, made him a really awful person. 'But being a parent to Joey…that's something I don't think I'll ever be able to get right,' he admitted.

'Probably because you're trying too hard.'

He frowned. 'How do you mean?'

'It's impossible to be the perfect parent,' she said gently. 'I see new mums breaking their hearts because they can't get it right and everyone else seems to get their babies to sleep and eat much more easily than they can. But then they come to realise that you can't be perfect and your best really is good enough. And that takes the pressure off and stops them trying so hard, and then the babies relax too and it all works out.' She took his hand and squeezed it. 'And it's even harder when you're suddenly dropped into a parenting role—when you're expecting a baby you have a few months to get used to the idea, and your confidence grows as the baby does. Joey's four, already thinking and acting for himself, and you just need to give yourself a bit of time to catch up with him.'

He thought about it.

And, to his shock, he realised that she was right. He *was* trying too hard. Trying to make up for Susie and Kevin not being there any more, trying to be the perfect stand-in and getting frustrated with himself and Joey because the barriers between them seemed to grow every day; and then feeling guilty because he'd escaped into work to forget his problems outside.

'You're a very wise woman, Flora Loveday.'

She just smiled.

They sat in a companionable silence, watching Joey on the swings, until they heard a scream. They turned round to see a woman cradling her child on the ground by the climbing frame.

'That's Maisie Phillipson and Barney,' Flora said. 'Tom, would you mind if—?'

'Go,' he cut in softly, knowing exactly what she was going to ask. He was beginning to realise that Flora just couldn't stand by and do nothing if there was a crisis and she knew she could do something to help. And he recognised that this was her way of dealing with her shyness, too; doing practical things meant that she didn't have time to think about what was going on and to feel self-conscious.

'Maisie, what happened?' Flora asked as she reached the climbing frame.

'One minute, Barney was climbing—the next, he was on

the ground.' Maisie bit her lip. 'I should've been watching him, not chatting.'

'Even if you'd watched him for every second, you wouldn't have been able to catch him,' Flora said. 'Do you want me to take a look at him?'

'Flora, you're an angel. Yes, please,' Maisie said, giving her a grateful smile.

Flora sat on the sand next to the little boy. 'Hi, there, Barney. Mummy says you fell off the climbing frame. Does anything hurt?'

'No-o.' Barney looked torn between braving it out and showing just what a tough six-year-old he was and bursting into tears.

'That's quite a big fall, and you're being really brave,' Flora said with a smile. 'Did you hit your head at all?'

'I think so.'

'Did everything go black after you hit your head?'

'No.'

That was a good sign. 'Can I just look into your eyes with my special torch?' Flora asked.

'All right.'

She took the torch from her handbag. Both of Barney's pupils were equal and reactive, to her relief. 'Righty. And now I need you to do something else for me.' She took a thimble with a bee on it from her handbag and slipped it onto her forefinger. 'Can you follow the bee with your eyes?'

He did so, and she checked his eye movements as she moved the bee from side to side.

'That's brilliant. I haven't got a sticker on me, but I'll bring you one when I'm in school next week,' she promised.

Barney looked hopeful. 'Can it be a rocket sticker?'

'Absolutely a rocket sticker,' she said, smiling back.

'Can I go and play now?'

Maisie sighed. 'All right. But *not* on the climbing frame. And be careful!'

'He'll be fine, Maisie,' Flora reassured her. 'You can give him some infant paracetamol when you get home, if he says anything hurts, and just keep an eye on him. If he still has a headache in six hours' time, or he's sick or passes out, or he feels really dizzy or can't see properly, or goes to sleep and you can't wake him, then take him straight to hospital.' She smiled ruefully. 'I really ought to keep a bumped-head leaflet in my handbag.'

After saying goodbye to Maisie, she returned to Tom.

'Everything OK?' Tom asked, standing up as she neared the bench.

'Bumped head. He'll be fine.'

'You must see that all the time.'

'Pretty much every session at the primary school,' she agreed with a smile. 'I know the advice off by heart.'

They walked over to the swings; Joey had slowed down and was just letting the ropes rock him back and forth.

'Shall we go down the slide, Jojo?' Tom asked.

The little boy shook his head. Before Tom could ask anything else, he slid off the seat and headed for the seats on a spring. He chose the one like a frog, and sat bouncing on it with his shoulders hunched and his back turned to Tom.

'Are you OK?' Flora asked.

'Yes.'

She could see on his face that he wasn't. And she knew that male pride would get in the way of him telling her what was wrong. But he'd confided in her earlier about his best friend as a child, and something in his eyes had told her that it wasn't something that most people knew about. She was pretty sure that it was the same as whatever was upsetting him now; but he needed to get this out in the open to let him deal with it. Which meant pushing beyond her own boundaries, not letting her shyness get in the way of helping him. She took a deep breath. 'Don't fib.'

Tom sighed. 'I guess no, then.'

And now for the biggie. She forced herself to say it. 'Want to tell me about it?'

He was silent for so long that she thought she'd gone too far. And then he bit his lip. 'Joey used to love the slide. On Sunday mornings, if Susie was cooking Sunday lunch for us, Kev and I used to take Joey to the park for a kickabout with a football, and we always ended up on the slides and the swings afterwards. He used to love going down the slide, sitting on my lap or his dad's, when he was really tiny.'

And she could see on Tom's face how much he missed it. And how hurt he was that his nephew didn't want to do that any more; what he could see was Joey's rejection, not the scared little boy behind it.

'He's probably remembering that, too, and it probably makes him miss his parents, but he just doesn't know how to tell you,' Flora said softly, taking Tom's hand and squeezing it. 'It might even be that he's scared to tell you, in case you're upset too.'

'Upset with him?'

She shook her head. 'Grieving. Missing his parents the way he does. I can remember my grandmother dying when I was about four, and my mum crying, and I felt helpless because I didn't know how to make things better for her. And because I felt helpless, I hid in my room and avoided her until she'd stopped crying and she was Mum again. I wasn't rejecting her—I just didn't know how to deal with it.'

He returned the pressure of her fingers and didn't drop her hand. 'You're right, and it's stupid of me to feel rejected because he doesn't want to go on the slide with me.' He swallowed hard. 'It's just that now he hates being touched. I can't even give him a hug or ruffle his hair because he really doesn't like it—he pulls away every time. He never used to hate it. He loved playing rough-and-tumble games with me and his dad. He used to run to me and give me a huge, huge hug hello whenever he saw me. And now...' Tom shook his head. 'He's quiet and still and...I just can't reach him.'

'It's a hard situation for both of you, Tom,' she said gently. 'Give yourself a break. You're doing your best.'

'And it's not good enough. I don't know how to be a dad.'

Flora had the strongest feeling that Tom hated failing at anything, but this was even harder because he loved the little boy and wanted to make Joey's world all right again.

'You're doing better than you think you are,' she told him. 'You spend time with him, you talk to him, you take him out— that's a lot more than some kids get from their parents.'

'I guess so.' Tom looked haunted. 'I just wish...'

'Wish what?' she prompted.

He shook his head. 'Never mind.'

Obviously he felt he'd already let his guard down too much with her. But Flora also noticed that he was still holding her hand. Taking comfort from her.

Well, it was what a friend would do. Slightly less ostentatious than a public hug. And, if it made him feel better, she was perfectly happy to hold his hand.

As for the awareness flickering down her spine, the tingling in her skin—well, she'd just have to ignore it. This wasn't about them. It was about Joey.

Eventually Joey stopped bouncing on the frog seat.

'Shall we go and have a hot chocolate to warm us up?' Tom suggested.

Joey nodded. Although he didn't hold his uncle's hand, he did at least fall into step beside him; and Flora noticed that Tom shortened his stride to make it easier for the little boy to keep up. He was sensitive to the needs of others and she liked that. A lot.

When they'd finished their hot chocolates—which Tom insisted on paying for—he drove them back to the farmhouse.

'We'd better let you get on,' Tom said, before she had the chance to invite them in.

'OK. Well, thanks for lunch. I really enjoyed that—and the park.' She smiled at Joey. 'Uncle Tom has a day off on Monday and Tuesday, so he's going to pick you up from school. But I'll see you on Wednesday for breakfast, and after school we'll take Banjo for a walk and collect some eggs, yes?'

Joey nodded.

'Thanks, Flora. You're a gem,' Tom said softly. 'We'll see you on Wednesday.'

CHAPTER FIVE

'FLORA?'

Even without the caller display showing the number on her phone, she would've recognised Tom's deep voice.

'Yes?'

'Are you busy right now?'

'I was about to go out,' she admitted.

'Never mind, then. I'll catch you later.'

'Tom?' She paused. Why would he be phoning her mid-morning? 'Is everything OK? I mean, have you been called in to work? Do you need me to pick up Joey?'

'No—nothing like that. But I did want to talk to you about Joey.'

He needed her. And somehow that made it a lot easier for her to push the hated shyness away. She made a swift decision. 'I'm going to the church to put flowers on my parents' graves. I won't be long. I could meet you in the coffee shop in half an hour, if you like?'

'Are you going to the church at Penhally?'

'Yes.' She frowned. 'Why?'

He sighed. 'That's where Susie and Kevin are buried. I ought to put some flowers on their grave. I know I should take Joey with me, but I haven't been able to face going to the churchyard yet, and I don't want him to see me all choked up.'

'The first time's the hardest,' Flora said. 'Why don't you

come with me? I'm putting flowers there myself—but, if you find you could do with talking to someone, I won't be far away.'

'Are you sure? I won't be in your way or anything?'

'Of course you won't. Look, I've just picked some daffodils from the garden. I'll split them with you.'

'Really?'

The relief in his tone decided her. 'Really. See you at the church in ten minutes.'

She drove to the church and parked on the gravelled car park outside the churchyard wall. It was such a quiet, peaceful spot, overlooking the bay; her parents had enjoyed sitting on the bench on the cliffs on Sunday afternoons.

Tom was waiting for her in the little lych gate, and her heart skipped a beat as he smiled at her. 'Thanks so much for this, Flora.'

'No worries.' She handed him half the flowers.

He stared at the daffodils and swallowed hard. 'Susie used to love spring flowers. The first thing she did when she and Kevin got the house was to plant spring bulbs. I remember she was so excited at having her own garden instead of just a window-box in her old flat in St Piran. I didn't get it at all because I was happy with my flat and not having to bother with weeding or mowing the lawn, but...' He grimaced. 'I guess I still can't believe she's gone.'

'I know what you mean. I find myself talking about my parents as if they're still here,' Flora said softly.

He rested his hand on her shoulder; even though she was wearing a sweater and a coat, it was as if she could feel the warmth of his skin against hers, and it sent a ripple of pure desire all the way down her spine.

'I really appreciate the way you've been here for me,' he said.

'Hey, that's what friends are for,' she said lightly, and turned away before she did something really stupid. Like standing on tiptoe, reaching up and brushing her mouth against his. 'Have you got something to put the flowers in?'

'No.' He looked horrified. 'It didn't even occur to me.'

'If Susie and Kevin are the first people you've lost, then of course you wouldn't think about it. It's something you find out the hard way.' She'd guessed he hadn't had a chance to think about the practicalities. 'Don't be too hard on yourself.' She produced a jam jar and a plastic bottle of water from her tote bag. 'The local florist sells cone-shaped vases that you just push into the ground for fresh flowers, but this will keep the flowers nice for now.'

'Flora, thank you.' He looked surprised and relieved in equal measure. 'I can't believe you thought of that, too.'

She shrugged off his praise and patted his shoulder. 'I'll come and find you when I've finished, shall I?'

She took the previous week's flowers from her parents' grave, tidied up the area, arranged the new daffodils, and then went to join Tom. His face was set and she could see that his eyelashes were damp. She remembered the first time she'd visited her parents' grave; she'd gone alone, and ended up bawling her eyes out on her knees in front of their grave, really wishing she'd had someone to hold her. Right now, Tom needed that same strength. And this was something she could do.

'Come here,' she said softly, and slid her arms round him, holding him close.

Tom closed his eyes, wrapped his arms round Flora, and rested his face against her hair. She smelled of roses and something else he couldn't quite pin down. And something of her warmth and strength seemed to flow into him as she held him, to the point where he was able to cope again.

'Sorry about that,' he said. 'I'm not usually that weak.'

Though, for the life of him, he couldn't let her go. He needed to feel her arms round him.

'It's not weak to admit you miss someone,' Flora said.

Wasn't it? He was a firefighter. He was meant to be in control. Someone who coped brilliantly in the worst kind of emergencies. Why was he going to pieces now, after putting flowers on his sister's grave? 'It feels it.'

'It's grief,' she reminded him gently. 'And it makes you feel all kinds of weird things. You might feel angry that the ones you love have left you, you might feel as if it's your fault and you're being punished for something, you might feel numb—and it's all OK. You get through it eventually.'

'It feels never-ending,' he admitted. 'Work's easy. I know what I'm doing there. But home... I never would've believed it's so hard to be a parent. How much worry there is.'

'It's not an easy job at all, especially when you're on your own,' Flora reassured him. 'And what you're feeling right now is perfectly normal. Give yourself a break, Tom.'

'Maybe.' He dropped a kiss on the top of her head. 'Do you mind if we get out of here?'

'Sure.' She paused. 'A walk on the beach might help.'

'The sea always makes me feel grounded,' he agreed. 'I loved coming to the bay when I was a child. It didn't matter if it was summer or the middle of winter—the wind would blow my worries away and the sound of the sea would silence all the doubts.' And with her by his side, it made him feel as if he *could* do things. As if he wasn't making a total mess of his life, outside work. Her warmth and her calmness soothed him even more than the sound of the sea.

They headed down the cliff path to the beach. The tide was half-out and the sea was calm, the waves rumbling onto the shore and swishing out again. They walked in silence for a while, and eventually Tom turned to Flora.

'I've been thinking—you and Joey. Are you really sure it's all right for you to have him for so long?'

'Of course it is.'

'I feel I'm taking advantage of you. And I need to sort out paying you.'

She shook her head. 'I don't want any money, Tom.'

'But you're looking after my nephew and you're giving him breakfast and dinner. I can't expect you to do it all just out of the goodness of your heart. That's not fair.'

'I don't mind,' Flora said. 'If anything, it's going to be nice to have a bit of company.' She still found the house a bit empty in the mornings, half expecting her dad to come in from seeing to the chickens or her mum to come in from the garden with some herbs or some flowers. Not that she could tell Tom that without sounding needy, and she didn't want him worrying that she wasn't stable enough to care for Joey properly.

'Then thank you.' He bit his lip. 'Poor Joey's finding it hard to adjust to change.'

'It must be hard for you, too.'

He nodded. 'And I can't even bring myself to go over to my sister's house and sort out her stuff, even though I know I should. I did a kind of grab raid when Joey was at school, the first week. I went there with a suitcase and got his clothes and his toys from his room. I've probably missed something important, something that really matters to him, and I know I shouldn't be so selfish—but I just can't handle it. I kept waiting for Susie to walk into the room and she just didn't, and it all felt so wrong...' He shook his head, grimacing. 'Sorry, I'm being really self-indulgent and you've had it harder than me, losing both your parents.'

She took his hand and squeezed it. 'It always hurts to lose someone you love. Look, I could come with you if you like, and help you sort through the stuff. It really helped me not to be on my own when I had to sort through my parents' things—Kate Tremayne from the surgery was really kind and helped me. It made a huge difference.'

'I might take you up on that.' His fingers tightened round hers. 'Thanks.'

'I've been thinking. Something else that might help Joey—you could try inviting one or two of his friends home for tea, when you're on a day off.'

'I don't think he has any friends,' Tom said. 'He did get a couple of invites, the first week back at school, but when I tried inviting the kids back the mums made excuses, and there haven't been any invites since.' He sighed. 'I don't know whether it's because he's so quiet and hardly talks, and they find that hard to deal with; or whether the other kids see Joey as being "different" because his parents died and they don't like him.'

She nodded. 'Other children can be cruel.'

Tom raised an eyebrow. 'That sounds personal.'

'Probably,' she admitted. 'My parents were elderly—Mum was forty-three when she had me, and Dad was ten years older than her. Everyone else's parents were around twenty years younger than them, so the kids at school always wanted to know if they were my grandparents, and refused to believe me when I said they were my parents. Then they used to say I was weird because my dad had grey hair.'

'That's horrible.' And that, Tom thought, was what was really at the root of her shyness. The way the children at school had made her feel like an outsider, rejecting her and mocking her; something like that would stick and make you worry about how other people saw you. And it would make you wary of others as you grew older. 'And you're not weird. Not at all.'

'It was just childish nonsense.' She shrugged. 'It doesn't bother me now.'

He wasn't so sure about that, but held his tongue. 'Did you lose your parents very long ago?' he asked.

'Last summer. Dad had a stroke. He was the love of Mum's life and she just gave up after he died—I know physiologically there's no such thing as a broken heart, but I honestly think that's why she died. Without Dad, she couldn't carry on. I buried her the month after.' She dragged in a breath. 'I hate just having a little wooden cross and a plastic pot I stick in the ground for flowers, but the stonemason says he can't put the headstone on for another couple of months.'

'So you understand exactly how Joey's feeling right now.' Guilt flooded through Tom. 'I'm sorry, I didn't mean to rub salt in your wounds.'

'You're not. And you,' she said softly, 'I know how you're feeling now, too. What you said about your sister's house—it was like that for me at the farmhouse. I guess I could've sold up, but I didn't want to—it's my home. So in the end I painted the walls a different colour and moved the furniture around and changed the colours of the cushions, just to get it into my head that things were different now and Mum and Dad aren't coming back.' She paused. 'It's going to take a while until you get used to it, Tom, so be kind to yourself.'

He was still holding her hand and he rubbed the pad of his thumb over the back of her hand. 'Can I buy you lunch? As a friend,' he added swiftly.

Not that he needed to say that, Flora thought. It was pretty obvious Tom wasn't going to be interested in her as anything other than a friend; she was way too mousy and boring. 'That'd be nice,' she said.

'If I follow you back to your place, we can drop your car off and I'll drive us,' Tom suggested.

They ended up at the Smugglers' Rest, just up the coast; and over a leisurely lunch they discovered that they had a lot in common. They both enjoyed the same kind of music and both were fans of historical crime novels—though Flora found out that Tom preferred action movies and hated the romantic comedies she enjoyed. And she couldn't remember the last time she'd enjoyed someone's company so much. When he'd opened up to her in the churchyard, it had made her feel close to him—to the point where she'd actually stopped feeling shy with him. They'd gone past that. She felt as comfortable with Tom now as she did with the people she worked with; and the fact that he seemed to listen to what she said, was interested in her views, made her feel more confident than she'd felt outside work since...since for ever, she thought.

Eventually, Tom glanced at his watch and gave a start. 'I've got to pick Joey up from school in a quarter of an hour! I can't believe how fast time's gone. I've really enjoyed having lunch with you, Flora.'

'Me, too,' she said, meaning it.

He tipped his head slightly on one side. 'Come with me to meet Joey?'

Flora pushed away the tempting thought that Tom might want her company for a bit longer. He was simply being practical; if he dropped her home first, he'd be late for school. 'OK.'

Joey was the last one out of the classroom and, although several of the children were lingering in the playground while their mums chatted, nobody made a move to speak to him. Flora's heart went out to him; poor little mite, he was having such a tough time.

Joey was silent on the way to the car, but when Tom strapped him in he asked, 'Are we going to see Banjo?'

'I do need to drop Flora back at the farm before we go home—but, if Flora doesn't mind, we can stay for a few minutes.'

Joey's faint smile said it all for him.

Tom stayed long enough to have a cup of tea with Flora,

and Joey accepted a glass of milk and a cookie; but then Tom called his nephew over from playing with the dog. 'We need to let Flora get on, and I have to cook you something for tea. We need to go, sweetheart.'

Joey nodded, but said nothing.

Tom's eyes were sad as he glanced at his nephew, and Flora's heart contracted. If only she could wave a magic wand for them. But they were going to have to muddle through this together and learn to bond and talk to each other and trust each other.

'We'll see you on Wednesday morning, then, Flora,' Tom said, and, to her surprise, kissed her on the cheek.

She felt the betraying wash of colour flood into her cheeks. Obviously Tom was a fairly tactile person; the kiss didn't mean anything at all, and this was just friendship. Yet she could feel the touch of his lips against her skin all evening, and it sent a mixture of warmth and excitement bubbling through her.

Tuesday was busy, thanks to a cold snap. Flora was on duty at the surgery all day on the minor injuries clinic, and there was a steady stream of people coming in to see her after falling over, most of them with hands that hurt. Several of them had very obvious signs of Colles' fractures. 'I'm going to have to send you to St Piran's for an X-ray and backslab,' she explained to the first of her patients. 'Everyone puts their hands out to save themselves when they fall, and if you land awkwardly you can end up breaking your wrist. You'll be in a cast for a couple of weeks until it heals. The good news is that casts are lightweight nowadays, so it won't get too much in the way, but the bad news is that you're going to have to get someone else to do all your lifting and carrying until your arm's healed.'

It felt odd not to see Tom and Joey in the evening. Flora was cross with herself for getting too involved, too fast. For pity's sake, she knew that Tom had other demands on his time. His job was incredibly difficult, and he had to get used to being a stand-in dad to his nephew. He wasn't going to have time to keep coming over to the farm and seeing her. And, unless she was looking after Joey, he didn't really even have a reason for coming to see her. 'I'm being ridiculous about this,' she told her dog. 'Worse than a teenager with a crush—and I haven't got a crush on Tom Nicholson.'

Banjo regarded her steadily, as if he didn't believe her.

She sighed. 'All right, so I think he's gorgeous. And it's not just the way he looks. He's a nice guy and there's something about him that makes me feel more...well, confident. He listens to me, so I don't feel like a bumbling idiot when I'm with him. I like the way his mind works, I like the way he puts other people first, and I like the way he's trying so hard to fit his life round Joey, rather than making Joey fit round him.' She bit her lip. 'But I've got to be practical about this, because he's way out of my league.'

But all the same she was pleased the next morning to hear the crunch of the gravel as Tom parked outside.

'Have you had breakfast yet?' she asked as she met Tom and Joey at the door.

He shook his head. 'I'll get something at the station.'

'It's as easy to make breakfast for three as it is for two.'

'Thanks, but I need to get going or I'll be late for work.'

Of course. And she was being ridiculous, feeling disappointed that he wasn't staying. At her age, she should know better. 'See you tonight, then.' She smiled at him. 'Have a nice day.'

'You, too. Bye, Joey.' Tom ruffled his nephew's hair awkwardly, and Joey gave him a pained look. Tom was clearly careful not to react in front of the boy, but Flora saw his shoulders slump as he headed back to his car. Every time Joey rejected him, she had a feeling that it cracked Tom's heart that little bit more.

'So what would you like for breakfast, Joey? I was thinking about French toast. Have you ever had French toast?'

The little boy shook his head.

'Do you fancy playing chef?'

His face lit up and he went to fetch a tea-towel from the drawer. Flora couldn't help smiling as he tucked it round himself to keep his school uniform clean. 'Good boy—well remembered.'

Joey seemed to thoroughly enjoy helping her beat the egg with vanilla essence and dip the bread into it. While the French toast was cooking, she sliced up some fruit onto two plates, then put the cooked French toast next to it.

'Nice?' she asked after Joey had taken a bite.

He nodded.

'Score out of five?'

He thought about it, then held up his right palm with all four fingers and thumb outstretched.

'Five? Excellent.' She beamed at him. 'We make a good team, Joey Barber.'

She washed up the breakfast things, then took him to school. 'Now, Joey, I know you don't like holding people's hands very much, but there's a fair bit of traffic here and I need to know you're safe, so I need you to hold my hand from the car to the playground, OK?'

He nodded and let her hold his hand.

For one crazy moment, Flora thought, This is what it would be like to take my own child to school. Then she shook herself. How silly. She didn't even date, so marriage and children were hardly an option.

But, oh, how she missed being part of a family. How she'd love a family of her own, somewhere she'd be accepted for herself. She adored Banjo, but the dog could only listen to her, not talk back, and she wasn't quite soppy enough to believe that the dog understood every word she said to her. Right now, she was rattling around on her own in the farmhouse. Lonely. As an only child, she didn't even have nieces and nephews to spoil—not now, and not in the future. So, unless she could do something to overcome her shyness and start dating, it was pretty unlikely that she'd ever have a family of her own again.

Though where did you meet people? At work wasn't an option for her; apart from the fact that the male doctors in the practice were already married, most of her patients were children. Even if she did end up treating an adult male who happened to be single, there was no way she'd be unprofessional enough to ask him out on a date.

And she wasn't one for parties or going clubbing. Which left a dating agency—and no way would she be able to meet up with a complete stranger. She'd spend the whole evening beetroot red, fumbling for words and feeling too awkward and embarrassed to relax, wishing herself back safely at home. It wouldn't be like the other day, when she'd sat in the Smugglers', chatting to Tom. Or like this morning, when she and Joey had made French toast.

She glanced at the little boy. Joey stood apart from the other children in the playground; he'd always been one of the quiet ones, but he was really cutting himself off. Was he scared that if he let someone close, he'd lose them, the way he'd lost his parents? That would explain why he was refusing to let Tom hug him or ride on his shoulders, the way Tom had said he'd done while Susie and Kevin had still been alive.

Maybe playing with Banjo would help. Bonding with the dog might help him bond with his uncle again, and gradually he'd learn to open up to other people.

The doors opened and the classroom assistant stood there to welcome the children in. 'See you at five, sweetheart,' Flora said, and watched him walk in through the doors before she headed off to work.

She texted Tom to let him know that Joey was safely at school, and got a brief text back saying just 'Thanks'. Well, he was at work, and he was busy. She'd been an idiot to hope that he'd send a personal message back. That kiss on her cheek the other night had been completely platonic, and she was acting like a teenager. She put it firmly out of her mind, got on with her work, and then met Joey from after-school club at five.

'How was your day?' she asked.

He shrugged and said nothing.

OK. She'd try something less emotional and see if he responded to that. 'Do you like drawing?'

He nodded, to her relief.

'Great. You can draw some pictures when we get back, if you like.' She'd popped to the shops at lunchtime and bought a sketchpad and pencils; she'd also picked up some more books from the library. Joey drew pictures and played with Banjo while she prepared dinner; then she read him some stories while the veg steamed and the shepherd's pie cooked. Over dinner, he told her shyly that a policeman had come in for show-and-tell and he was the daddy of Mitchell in his class, and Flora had a lightbulb moment: this was something that might help Tom and Joey bond.

Finally, at a quarter past seven, Tom rang the doorbell.

He tried to make a fuss of Joey, but the little boy was having none of it; he turned away and concentrated on turning the pages of his book.

Seeing the hurt in Tom's face at the rejection, Flora switched on the kettle. 'How was your day?' she asked.

'Pretty eventful. I had to break into a house to rescue a family,' he said.

'Was it a fire?'

'No—it was carbon monoxide poisoning.'

'What happened?' She put a mug of coffee in front of him.

'The husband thought he had a bug or something. He felt a bit dizzy and sleepy, but he didn't have a temperature so he went in to work. He felt a bit better during the day, so he rang home—he knew his wife had been feeling a bit rough, too, and had stayed at home with the youngest because she had a vomiting bug, but then his wife didn't answer the phone or her mobile. He was worried in case she'd had to take the little one to hospital or something, so he rang their neighbour and asked him to take a look. He could see her car outside, but there was no answer when he knocked on the door. He looked through the window and saw her collapsed on the floor, so he called the emergency services.'

Flora winced. 'Lucky for them that the neighbour was there.'

'We broke in and got them out; then the ambulance arrived and the paramedics put them on oxygen.'

'Was that enough, or did they have to go to hospital?'

Tom couldn't remember talking about his job to a girlfriend before; it felt odd, chatting to someone who understood where he was coming from, but he rather liked it. 'The oxygen was enough,' he said. 'The paramedics put them on an ECG monitor and the trace was OK, so they're going to be fine. We took a look in the house and could see that the flames in the gas fire in the living room were yellow, not blue.'

'Which I take it is a problem?'

'Very much so,' Tom said. 'They called in a gas engineer to sort it out, and it turned out there was a blocked flue as well as the dodgy gas fire. It's all sorted now, and he rang us to thank us for saving his wife and youngest child's life, and to let us know what had happened.' He smiled. 'I like days like today, where I can actually fix things and make them right. How about you?'

'I was doing routine vaccinations today—back at the nursery, finishing off the ones I didn't do on Friday—and I was at the surgery this afternoon. Joey and I have had a nice evening together. We read some stories.'

Tom took the hint. 'Which was your favourite, Joey?' he asked, hoping that this time his nephew would respond.

'The one about the dog,' Joey said.

'We're going to choose the next ones together, so I don't pick ones he's already read,' Flora explained.

'I drawed Flora a picture. Me and Banjo,' Joey said.

'It's on the fridge.' Flora removed the magnet and handed the picture to Tom.

Tom suppressed the wish that his nephew had drawn him a picture, too. Flora was doing so much for him; it was churlish and ridiculous to be envious of her. Yet she seemed to be able to get through to the little boy where he couldn't, and he really wished he knew her secret.

'Can I get you something to eat?' Flora asked.

'No, you're fine. Thanks for offering, but I get a meal at work before the end of my shift.' He could see that she was taking it as a personal rejection and smiled to soften it. 'But this coffee is fabulous. Just what I need.'

There was another awkward silence while Tom wondered what he should say next to his nephew.

Flora, as if sensing his dilemma, stepped in. 'Joey had show-and-tell in class today,' she said.

'What did you see, Jojo?' Tom asked, picking up her obvious cue.

'A policeman.'

'Did you try on his hat?'

'And his handcuffs,' Joey said solemnly.

So Joey had enjoyed that, Tom thought. Would he, perhaps, like a firefighter to go in for show and tell? His gaze met Flora's, and she nodded very slightly, as if guessing what was in his mind. 'Have you ever had a firefighter in for show-and-tell?' he asked.

Joey shook his head.

'I'll have to check the schedule with my boss, but if you want me to I can maybe arrange to bring the engine and the crew out and show your class around. Obviously, provided we don't have to go off to put out a fire.'

Joey's eyes went wide.

'Would you like that, Joey?' Flora asked softly.

Joey nodded, and Tom felt the muscles of his shoulders relax. 'I'll have a chat with my boss and your teacher, then.' And maybe this would help Joey bond with him again. It would be something he could talk to his classmates about, maybe.

Tom meant to kiss Flora on the cheek again when he took Joey home, but somehow he ended up brushing his mouth against hers instead. Her mouth was soft and sweet and she tasted of vanilla. He had to resist the temptation to kiss her again; her eyes had gone wide and the amber flecks were even more obvious, and she looked utterly adorable.

And he really shouldn't be doing this.

'Flora, I—'

'It's OK.' She shook her head, clearly not wanting to discuss it. 'You'd better get Joey to bed. See you in the morning. 'Night, Joey!'

The little boy waved, and Tom mentally called himself all kinds of a fool. Flora was a lifesaver for him, right now, and he'd better not do anything to jeopardise it.

CHAPTER SIX

THE next morning, Tom looked wary when he dropped Joey off. Flora strove to be cheerful and polite and breezy so he wouldn't think she was still thrown by that kiss—even though she was, and her lips were still tingling at the memory of his mouth against hers. She knew how pathetic it was, having a crush on the most gorgeous firefighter in the crew. Of course he wouldn't be interested in boring, mousy her. They were just *friends*.

'Joey, do you like porridge, like the Three Bears had?' she asked.

He nodded.

'You can help me chop the fruit to put on top,' she said, 'and then we'll have a story while the porridge is cooking. I found a really good one where the bears get their revenge on Goldilocks; would you like to hear that one?'

He nodded again.

'Say bye-bye to Uncle Tom,' she said with a smile.

'Bye-bye.' Joey gave a tiny wave.

'See you later, Tom. Have a nice day,' she said brightly.

That was definitely a fake smile, Tom thought as he drove to work. Flora was clearly wary of him—and no wonder. He'd really messed up last night. Fancy kissing her like that. Why on earth hadn't he controlled himself? But he found her irresistible. And he hadn't been able to stop thinking about her ever since that hug outside the church.

When he'd kissed her on the cheek it had been spontaneous. Friendly. But last night's kiss—though equally chaste—had thrown him. He'd even dreamed about Flora last night. Dreams that set his pulse racing and made his body surge when he thought about it.

But she clearly didn't think the same way. So he needed to keep himself strictly under control in future.

Tonight, he'd bring flowers when he picked Joey up. He'd apologise, tell her that she had nothing to worry about—and he'd keep it platonic in future.

Thursday morning was Flora's clinic at the high school, where anyone could drop in and talk to her privately if they had any worries. She was also doing the second of the three-stage HPV vaccinations of the Year Eight girls. She could hear them chattering in the queue; one of them was talking about how her boyfriend had kissed her for the first time, and Flora thought of the way Tom had kissed her last night and how it had sent heat all the way through her body.

Oh, how juvenile. She really, *really* had to get a grip. She was twenty-four, not fourteen.

She'd just finished vaccinating one class when the school receptionist came hurrying through. 'Flora, there's been an accident. The fire brigade are on their way, but two of the Year Eight lads decided to skip lessons and go skating on the pond—they went straight through. Luckily one of the sixth formers decided to go to the library halfway through private study and heard them yelling for help; she had the sense to call the emergency services on her mobile phone and then came to tell me.'

The pond had had a reputation as a skating rink in Flora's days at the school; and, no matter how often the children were warned not to do it, there was always at least one every year willing to take the risk. As the boys had fallen through the ice and must have been there for a while, they were severely at risk of developing immersion hypothermia; they might even need hospital treatment. 'OK, I'm on my way. There are space blankets in the PE department, aren't there?' At the receptionist's nod, she said, 'Can you get someone to bring some through—and some spare clothing and towels, please?' As soon as the boys were out of the pond, the first thing she needed to do was to get them into dry clothes and start warming them up, heads and torsos first.

'I'll ring through now,' the receptionist said.

Flora took her medical bag and hurried over to the pond, pulling her coat on as she went. It was barely above freezing; why on earth had the boys been so daft? She could see the fire engine there; the crew had ladders out and one fireman was crawling along it towards the boys so he could pull them out. Her heart missed a beat. Even though she couldn't see the fireman's face and she knew that several of the fire crew were just as tall and brawny as Tom, she knew instinctively that it was him.

Please, let him be safe.

Rob Werrick, one of the PE teachers, came out with a space blanket, spare tracksuit bottoms and sweatshirts, and towels. 'It's Danny and Harry from Year Eight,' he said as he glanced at the pond. 'When I heard what had happened, I should've guessed those two would be involved.' He rolled his eyes. 'What on earth did they think they were doing?'

'In my day, there were stories about people skating on the pond. They probably thought it sounded like fun,' Flora suggested.

'Taking a huge risk, more like.' Rob sighed. 'They've all been warned to stay away from the pond. But do they ever listen?'

'Teenage boys,' Flora said ruefully. 'I think they have selective hearing.'

She could hear Tom talking to the boys, explaining how he was going to get them out and what they needed to do. He brought the first one back with him across the ladder, and kept the other one talking as he did so—no doubt, Flora thought, so he could keep a check on the boy's level of consciousness.

'Hi, Flora.' He smiled at her. 'Well, young Danny, I'm handing you over to safe hands now to get you checked over while I go and fish your mate out of the pond.' He winked at Flora, then headed back to the ladder.

'Come on, Danny, let's get you inside and get you out of those wet clothes and warmed up.' She hurried him into the nearest building.

'I can't get undressed in front of you. You're a girl,' Danny mumbled.

Usually Year Eight boys managed to make her blush or stutter; most of them were as tall as she was and it took her right back to her schooldays, when she'd been awkward and painfully shy and just hadn't fitted in. But Tom's words had bolstered her confidence: he'd treated Danny as a child and made it clear he was handing the boy over to someone whose opinion he respected. To *her*.

'You're a child,' Flora said crisply, 'and I'm a nurse. I'm not interested in your naked body. You're wet and very, very cold, and I need you to get into dry clothes before I can assess your breathing and your heart, OK?'

Danny muttered something she couldn't quite catch and didn't look her in the eye.

She rolled her eyes. 'If it makes you feel better, I'll turn my back. Dry off and get dressed, please—and don't rub your skin, pat it.'

Tom came in, a few moments later. 'What are we going to do with Harry?'

'Same as Danny. Wet clothes off, blot your skin with a towel—don't rub,' she warned, 'and then dry clothes on and a space blanket round you.'

Harry looked as embarrassed as Danny. 'I can't—'

'I've already had that conversation with Danny. I'm turning my back,' Flora said.

She could see the amusement in Tom's eyes but, to his credit, he didn't laugh.

Once the boys were dressed in dry clothes and had space blankets round them, she blotted their hair dry and then put woolly hats on them.

'Why do we have to wear hats indoors?' Harry asked, his teeth chattering.

'Because you lose the most heat from your head—the hat stops you losing the heat,' Flora explained. 'And you're both shivering, which is a good sign.' It showed that their bodies were trying to bring their temperature up again rather than just giving up.

'Is there anything else you need?' Rob Werrick asked.

'A mug of hot chocolate each would be good—not boiling hot, but warm so it helps to get their temperature back up,' Flora said.

'I'll make you both a coffee at the same time. Milk, sugar?'

'I'm fine,' Flora said.

'Just milk for me, please,' Tom said.

After the warm drink, Danny and Harry finally stopped shivering. Flora took their pulse and blood pressure, and listened to their hearts. 'You're going to be fine,' she told them. 'You were incredibly lucky this time, but for pity's sake *never* do anything like this again. It really isn't worth the risk. And nobody's going to think you're cool or clever if you end up in hospital.'

'Ice needs to be at least twelve centimetres thick to bear

your weight,' Tom said, 'and this wasn't anywhere near thick enough.'

'It looked thick enough,' Danny said, looking mutinous.

'But it wasn't. You went straight through it.'

'Dad said he skated on the pond when he was here,' Harry said.

'Your dad might have been teasing you.'

'No, he really did it.'

'Then he took a very big risk. The pond's too deep for you to haul yourself out onto the ice once you've gone through it. And you two are very lucky that someone heard you yelling for help. If you'd been stuck in that water for thirty minutes, you might not have survived,' Tom said grimly. 'Your body temperature would've dropped so low that you could've died—and think of how your families would've felt, losing you.'

Danny and Harry looked at each other, but said nothing.

'Are our parents going to have to know about this?' Danny asked eventually.

'Of course they are,' Flora said. 'Your parents need to know what happened. I'll be the one speaking to your mums and reassuring them that you're both OK and you haven't got hypothermia.'

'Mum's *so* going to ground me,' Harry said. 'And she's going to ban my games console for a month.'

'Me, too,' Danny said. 'It's not fair.'

'And it was fair of you both to skip lessons, go onto the ice to show off to your mates, and end up risking the lives of the fire crew?' Flora asked.

Harry's cheeks reddened. 'I s'pose not.'

'Danny?' she prompted.

He pulled a face. 'No.'

'Is there something you both want to say to Mr Nicholson

here, then?' Flora asked. Both boys hung their heads. 'Sorry,' they mumbled, their faces bright red with embarrassment.

'And?' she prompted.

Danny looked at her. 'What?'

'He saved your life,' she pointed out quietly. 'Which I think might be worth two little words your parents probably made you say when you were little—and you've clearly forgotten.'

They both went even redder and muttered, 'Thank you.'

'Right. Better get back to your lessons.' Flora folded her arms. 'And you might find life an awful lot easier if you stop to think things through before you act next time, OK?'

The boys nodded, looking ashamed, and shuffled out of the room.

'So you have a stern side, Flora Loveday,' Tom said, sounding amused.

'When people do really stupid things and put others at risk, then yes.' She shrugged. 'You don't need to shout or swear to get your point across.'

'No, somehow I don't think they're going to forget what you said to them.' He sighed. 'I wanted to shake the pair of them, I admit. It was a really stupid thing to do. Ice can vary in thickness across a pond—one part can be safe, but put one foot on a weak area, and you'll go straight through into the water.' He grimaced. 'It isn't the first time I've rescued someone from falling through ice, and it won't be the last.'

Flora looked at him. 'They're fine, but are you OK? You had to crawl out on the ice.'

'On a ladder. I'm fine. I'm wearing a drysuit and several layers underneath—and Rob got me that coffee, so that's warmed me up.' His eyes crinkled at the corners as he looked at her. 'I'd better get back to work. See you later.'

'See you,' she said, smiling back.

* * *

After school, Joey spent the afternoon racing round with Banjo, and he was asleep when Tom arrived to pick him up. Banjo stood next to Joey, on guard duty, and Tom ruffled the dog's fur. 'You're a good boy,' he said softly. Then he turned to Flora and handed her the flowers.

'They're lovely, Tom, but you really don't need to bring me flowers.'

'I do, today.'

She looked puzzled. 'Why?'

'Last night.' He took a deep breath. 'About that…I owe you an apology. I didn't mean to come on so strong.'

She didn't meet his eyes. 'It's not a problem. I know you didn't mean it that way.'

Something in her voice alerted Tom: Flora obviously thought she wasn't attractive enough for any man to want to kiss her. How on earth had she got that idea? He cupped her face in one hand and gently moved her chin so she was looking him straight in the eye. 'Flora, you do know you're beautiful, don't you?'

'Me? *Beautiful*?' Her face was filled with astonishment. 'You must be joking. I'm nothing like a WAG.'

Was that her definition of beauty? It wasn't his. 'I'm glad you're not. You're not caked in make-up, and you don't spend hours doing your nails and dyeing your hair. Yours is a natural beauty. And very, very real.'

She went bright pink.

'And then you have depths. You're not one of these shallow, boring women. You're kind and you're sweet and…' And he wanted her very, very badly. Too much to be able to resist. 'Flora.' He breathed her name, dipped his head and kissed her again. This time with intent. His mouth moved over hers, teasing and coaxing, until she gave a tiny sigh, slid her free arm round his neck and kissed him back.

'I'm not going to apologise for that one,' he said when he broke the kiss. 'Just so you know, I meant it.'

She blushed again and her lips parted, as if inviting him to kiss her some more.

'You taste of vanilla,' he said softly.

'It's lip salve.'

He smiled. 'Keep wearing it. I like it.'

She flushed again. 'Tom, you can't— I mean, I'm not your type.'

'No? So what do you think is my type?'

'Someone glamorous. Someone tall.' She swallowed hard. 'Someone *thin*.'

He'd begun to be bored with glamour. Height didn't matter. And he loathed dating women who nibbled on a stick of celery and refused pudding in case it made them put on a few grams; he much preferred the company of women who actually enjoyed eating out with him.

'Wrong on all counts,' he told her softly. 'And why are you putting yourself down? You have delicious curves, Flora. Curves that make me want to...' He slid both hands down her sides, moulding her curves. 'You're lovely. Luscious.'

He took the flowers from her hand, put them on the table, then scooped her up and sat down on the sofa, pulling her onto his lap. 'I know I probably shouldn't be doing this. I don't have the right to ask to start seeing you—my life is complicated, and I'm already taking way too much advantage of your good nature.' He stole a kiss. 'But I've been thinking about you all day. All week, really,' he admitted ruefully. 'I haven't been able to get you out of my head since the day I met you.'

She shook her head. 'But that's not possible.'

'Why's it so hard to believe? Flora, you're a pocket Venus. You have the most gorgeous mouth. And you taste...' he brushed his mouth against hers again '...like heaven.'

* * *

Self-consciousness washed through her. He'd just called her a pocket Venus. She knew she was just frumpy and overweight. And right now she was probably crushing his legs, and he was doing the macho firefighter thing and pretending she wasn't.

'Flora.' He kissed the tip of her nose. 'You look worried. Do you want me to back off?'

'No-o.'

'You don't sound very sure.' He twined the end of her ponytail round his finger. 'OK, let me ask you a different question. Will you go out with me?'

'I...' Heat flooded into her face. 'Look, I, um, haven't dated much.' And she certainly hadn't ever had a serious boyfriend. 'I'm not very good at this.' She bit her lip. 'And you're...'

'I'm what?' he prompted gently.

Sex on legs. Not that anything would drag that admission from her. 'You must have women falling at your feet all the time,' she said unhappily. Gorgeous women. Glamorous women who were used to dating and had all the right social skills.

'I admit, I get teased at work for having a fan club. There are a few women who insist on baking me cakes.'

She'd just bet there were.

'And some of them are in their eighties,' Tom said.

Maybe, but she was pretty sure that a good deal more of them would be around her own age.

'Some of them think of me as a surrogate grandson who rescues their cat and checks that their smoke alarms are working properly. I'm polite to everyone who makes me cakes, I thank them for their kindness but I don't make a habit of going around kissing women.'

Which wasn't the same thing as saying that they didn't kiss him.

He kissed her again. 'I guess I'm trying to say that there's something about you. I can't get you out of my head. And I really, really like kissing you.' He caught her bottom lip between his, just to prove it.

And this time she couldn't help kissing him back.

When he broke the kiss, he settled her against him, wrapping his arms round her. 'You know, this is the first time my world's felt right this year,' he said softly. 'So can I see you?'

'Tom.' She stroked his face. 'I wasn't expecting this to happen.'

'Do you mind?'

'It scares me a bit,' she admitted. 'I'm not used to this.'

'I'm not going to hurt you, Flora. I like you. A lot.'

'Are you sure this isn't—well, just gratitude?'

'Because you're helping me with Joey? Given that I was dreaming about you last night,' Tom said, 'and you'd really be blushing if I told you exactly what was happening in that dream…No. It's definitely not just gratitude.'

She blushed anyway. Tom had been having raunchy dreams about her?

'You're adorable,' he said softly. 'Actually, I love it when you go all pink and flustered. It makes me want to kiss you and fluster you some more. And your eyes are amazing. They have these little amber flecks in them. Like gold.'

That was what people always said when they knew you weren't drop-dead gorgeous and they tried to compliment you: they said you had nice eyes.

'And your ears.'

Now, that she hadn't expected. She stared at him in surprise. 'My ears?'

'Uh-huh.' He nibbled one lobe, very gently, then kissed his way down the sensitive spots at the side of her neck, making her shiver. 'And your mouth. It's a perfect rosebud. It's beautiful. Tempting. Irresistible.' He kissed her again, to make the point. 'And your curves are delicious.' He kept his arms very firmly round her. 'I like you, Flora. Very much. As a person, because you're warm and sweet and kind and you make the world seem a better place.' He paused, making eye contact. 'And as a woman. I really, *really* like you as a woman.'

'I like you, too,' she admitted shyly. 'As a— As a man.'

'So how about we see where this takes us?'

She took a deep breath. 'OK. But, as far as Joey's concerned, you and I are just friends—which keeps things stable in his world and he isn't going to worry that suddenly neither of us will have time for him.'

'That's another thing,' Tom said softly. 'You think about other people. How things affect them. You're incredibly empathetic.'

'It's my job. I'm a nurse.'

'No, Flora, it's who you are,' he corrected. 'And it's yet another thing that draws me to you.'

She still found it hard to believe that Tom was serious—how could he possibly want her, when he could have his pick of the most gorgeous women in this part of Cornwall?—and yet his dark eyes were sincere. He wasn't spinning her a line.

Joey stirred and she wriggled off Tom's lap. 'Joey,' she said softly.

Tom stole a last kiss, then went to scoop his nephew off the beanbag. 'Come on, sweetheart. You're sleepy. Let's get you home.'

To Flora's surprise and pleasure, Joey didn't wriggle out of his arms and actually let Tom carry him to the car.

'See you tomorrow, Flora,' he said softly. 'And thank you.'

Flora still couldn't quite believe what had just happened: that Tom had actually sat with her on his lap, had kissed her and told her he thought she was gorgeous.

She pinched herself. It hurt. So she wasn't dreaming, then.

And the flowers he'd brought her were still on the table. She hadn't even put them in water yet; she'd been too caught up in the way Tom had cradled her on his lap and kissed her. She smiled and put the flowers in a vase—and she was still smiling when she fell asleep that night.

On Friday evening, Tom had news. 'I'm going to do the show-and-tell at Joey's class next week.'

'That's great—he'll enjoy that.'

'And there's something else—I play football in the local emergency services league. Our team's having a "dads and sons" match on Sunday morning, when I'm off duty. I'm going to take Joey; will you come with us?'

'I've never been to a football match.'

'Because you hate football?'

She wrinkled her nose. 'Well, it's not really my sort of thing.' And she'd been utterly hopeless at sport at school—always the last to be picked for any team.

'Ah, but this is different. And Joey and I could do with someone standing on the sidelines cheering for us,' Tom said.

Put like that, how could she refuse?

Then she thought of something. 'So you're working tomorrow?' Being Saturday, Joey wouldn't have school.

'Yes.'

'Do you want to bring Joey over?'

'I can't impose on you like that.' Before she could protest that it was fine and she didn't mind, he added softly, 'Kevin's parents are coming down to see him for the day. Actually, they're coming this evening and staying overnight, so I'd better get back and sort my place out, because it's a tip.' He smiled at her. 'The match on Sunday starts at ten so we'll pick you up at half past nine, OK?'

'Half-nine it is,' she agreed.

He kissed her swiftly but very, very sweetly. 'Sorry I have to go so soon—I would rather stay with you, but Joey needs to see his grandparents.'

'Of course he does. I understand, Tom.'

'I can't believe how lucky I am to have found you.' He stole a last kiss. 'We'll see you on Sunday morning.'

CHAPTER SEVEN

ON SUNDAY, Tom picked Flora up at half past nine on the dot and drove her to the playing field. She felt ridiculously shy as she climbed out of his car. Tom seemed to know everyone; people were coming up all the time to talk to him or clap him on the back and ask how many goals he thought he'd score in the match. And she didn't know a single one of them. Nobody from Penhally was here; this was a completely different crowd to what she'd been expecting. The only person she could see that she recognised was Megan Phillips—and Megan was standing on the sidelines, shoulders hunched and hands in her pockets, her body language making it very clear that she didn't want to talk to anyone.

This was awful. Just like one or two of her mums had confided to her about the baby and toddler group, the first time they'd been—everyone else knew each other and had bonded into a little group, and they weren't part of it. Flora wasn't part of this group, either.

Her advice to her mums had been to take a deep breath and start talking to someone, and they'd soon find something in common.

What a hypocrite she was—she couldn't even follow her own advice. She didn't have a clue what to say. What did she have in common with these glamorous women in their tight jeans, fashionable boots and waxed jackets? She couldn't even go over and talk to them about children, because Joey wasn't really hers. Besides, she only recognised a couple of the children on the pitch from Penhally, and a swift scan of the sidelines told her that their mums weren't at the match—they were obviously at home looking after the younger children.

In the end, she simply stood on the sidelines, watching Tom and Joey, thinking miserably that she was never going to fit in with Tom's crowd. Maybe they ought to stop this disaster of a relationship before it had really begun.

Megan shoved her hands deeper into her pockets. What an idiot she was, turning up to the father-and-son football match. And all to catch a glimpse of Josh. Stupid, really. Josh was only there because one of the emergency department doctors had got flu and had had to drop out. He didn't even have a child with him.

Though if things had been different, he would've done. A seven-year-old boy. A boy with Josh's indigo-blue eyes and ready smile, perhaps. A boy who adored his father and had grown up knowing how much he was loved by both his parents...

The back of her throat felt tight. There was no point in wishing things were different, because they weren't. She'd lost the baby. And more. She never would have a child of her own. The nearest she could get to it was through her work, saving the lives of other people's precious babies.

And that had to be enough.

She swallowed hard. She really shouldn't have come today. Better to leave now—before Josh saw her and started asking questions.

To her surprise, Flora discovered that she enjoyed watching the game and cheering as Tom scored a goal. She had a flask of hot chocolate in her basket ready for half-time, and had also spent the Saturday afternoon making a batch of brownies and cookies. She poured a small mug of hot chocolate for Joey; Tom simply stole her mug, deliberately sipped from exactly the same spot that she had, and gave her a smile that made her knees go weak. And suddenly it didn't matter that she was on her own on the sidelines; Tom and Joey wanted her there, and that was the main thing.

'Enjoying it?' Tom asked.

She smiled. 'Yes.' It wasn't a complete fib; now he and Joey were here with her, she was definitely enjoying it.

Josh spotted Megan on the sidelines. On her own. But why would she come to a football match? Unless...

'Pay attention, Josh! That was an easy pass. You should've scored.'

'Sorry, mate.' Josh held his hands up in acknowledgement of the fault. But all the same he couldn't help looking for Megan during the match, trying to catch her eye. When the whistle blew for half-time, he caught one of the others. 'Can you substitute me for a bit? Something I really need to do.'

'What, *now*?'

'Yes, now,' Josh said, clapping his team-mate's shoulder. If Megan was here, unless she was here as the medical support— which he very much doubted—it was to see him. And he couldn't pass up the chance that she might be ready to talk to him. To start sorting things out between them.

Except, when he reached the place he'd seen her, she wasn't there. He scanned the sidelines and couldn't see her there, either. Maybe she was in the car park.

But a swift search of the car park told him that Megan had gone.

Needing a moment to himself, he leaned against the bonnet of his own car. Why had she come here in the first place? He didn't have a clue what was going on in her head. But one thing he did know: they needed to talk. Properly.

Five minutes into the second half, one of the players fell to the ground and rolled onto his back, clutching his leg. The referee stopped the match. Automatically, Flora went over; her skills were needed, and that was enough to push her shyness and feelings of awkwardness into the background. 'I'm a nurse,' she explained. 'Can I do anything to help?'

The referee gave her a grateful look. 'Yes, please. This is Ian.'

'What happened, Ian?' she asked.

'My ankle's killing me,' he groaned.

'Can I take a look?'

He nodded, his face white with pain.

'I'll need to take your boot off. Is that OK?' When he gave his consent, she crouched down, removed his football boot and drew the sock down so she could see his ankle properly, then probed his ankle gently.

'Ow. That hurts,' Ian said.

'It's a pretty nasty sprain,' Flora said. 'Looks like you've landed awkwardly—you've twisted the joint and it's damaged your ligaments. I'm afraid you're not going to be able to play for the rest of the match. Did you hear a "pop" in your ankle when it happened?'

'Yes—and then it started hurting like crazy.'

'I'm pretty sure it's not a fracture, just a simple sprain, but it's going to hurt for a couple of weeks,' she warned him. 'You'll need to rest it for the next couple of days with ice to reduce the swelling, wrapped in some kind of cloth so it doesn't burn your skin. I'd suggest fifteen minutes of ice treatment per hour, but no more than three hours in total over the next twenty-four. You also need to use an elastic bandage from your toes to the middle of your lower leg, to support the sprain. And if you can put a couple of pillows on a chair and prop your ankle up so it's higher than your heart, it'll help it heal more quickly. If you've got some ibuprofen at home, that'd be best painkiller to use because it'll help reduce the swelling.' She smiled at him. 'If it's still giving you a lot of gyp tomorrow it might be worth going to the emergency department at St Piran's and ask them to take a look, but I'm pretty sure it's only a sprain rather than a fracture.'

'I know you from somewhere, don't I?' he asked.

'I'm a nurse at the Penhally Bay Surgery,' she said. 'And I'm the school liaison nurse.'

He nodded. 'That's where I've seen you—my boy's in Year Six. He's been nagging me lately about my lunchbox not being healthy enough and telling me to swap the cake for another piece of fruit.'

She laughed. 'Glad to hear the message is getting through.'

He moved, and gritted his teeth as pain clearly shot through him. 'Thanks for looking after me. You're here with Tom, aren't you?'

'I...um...' Flora couldn't help blushing. 'Yes.'

Ian smiled. 'He's a top bloke, our Tom.'

'Absolutely,' she agreed. 'Ian, I don't have an ice pack with me, but I do have an elastic bandage. I can at least strap up your ankle and get you to elevate it until you can get a lift home.'

A couple of the other football players helped him up and supported him over to his car; Ian called his wife on his mobile phone and asked her to get a taxi to the football ground and rescue him. Flora strapped up his ankle, made sure that he was comfortable, and then went back to watch the end of the match.

'What happened to Ian?' Tom asked when he came over to her at the end of the match.

'He sprained his ankle.'

'Poor guy. It's going to make things difficult for him at work—he's a police officer.'

'He's going to be on desk duty for a few days, then,' Flora said.

'Did you enjoy the match, Joey?' Tom asked.

Joey nodded but his eyes were very dark. Tom and Flora exchanged a glance, guessing that the little boy was thinking of his dad. Tom crouched down. 'Hey. You played really well. And I bet your dad would have been really proud of you.'

Joey's bottom lip wobbled for a second, then he turned away.

Tom bit his lip, clearly thinking he'd made a mess of it.

Flora squeezed his hand and mouthed, 'You said the right thing. Don't blame yourself—just give him a moment.'

'We'd better go home and have a shower, because we're both covered in mud,' Tom said. 'And we have to be home for one, because Grandma said that's when lunch is going to be ready. She's cooking chicken, your favourite.'

'Is Flora coming?' Joey asked.

Flora hadn't been invited and had no intention of muscling in. After all, she was really just Tom's friend—acquaintance, really. She had no real connection to Kevin or to Susie.

Tom glanced at her, and she shook her head silently.

'No, we've already taken up her morning with the football. She has things to do round the farm. Come on, we'll drop her home and you can say hello to Banjo, and then we have to get going,' Tom said.

Before Flora knew it, she was home again, just her and the dog. Funny, a week ago that had been fine with her. Right now, it felt…empty.

Which was totally ridiculous.

She couldn't be falling for Tom—and Joey—that fast. Cross with herself, she made sure that she was busy for the rest of the day. Even so, the time dragged; the next morning dragged, too, because Tom was off duty and was taking Joey to school himself.

But at lunchtime she was catching up with paperwork in the surgery when her mobile phone rang.

'Hi. Are you busy tonight?' Tom asked.

'Not particularly,' Flora said. 'Why?'

'Because I'd like to invite you to dinner at my place. Joey tells me that he's enjoying cooking with you in the mornings, so he and I are going to be chefs. Is there anything you don't eat or you're allergic to?'

'No.'

'Great.' He gave her his address and directions. 'See you at six?'

'OK. Six it is.'

Flora felt ridiculously shy as she ended the call. This felt like a proper date—especially as it was Valentine's Day.

Valentine's Day.

Should she get Tom a card, or was that being a bit pushy? Was it too early in their relationship?

Oh, help. She was no good at this dating stuff. But on the way to Tom's flat, she dropped into the supermarket to buy a box of chocolates for Tom and Joey as a host gift and a huge display of cards caught her eye. She spent a while choosing one: nothing mushy, just a photograph of a simple heart-shaped box filled with chocolates. Sitting in her car, she simply wrote Tom's name inside it and signed it with two kisses; then she slipped the card into the envelope and put it in her handbag. She'd give it to him later, if she felt the moment was right.

Tom's flat was in a modern block on the first floor. She rang the doorbell, feeling ridiculously nervous.

He answered the door. 'Come in. Joey's just watching some cartoons. Can I take your coat?' He gave her a brief kiss hello as he took her coat, and her knees went weak. 'You look gorgeous,' he whispered. 'I love that colour on you.' She was wearing a black calf-length skirt and a teal-coloured top.

Colour seeped into her face. 'Thank you.' She strove for lightness. 'You don't look so bad yourself.' In dark trousers and a white shirt, he looked absolutely edible; she wanted to kiss him again, but at the same time she didn't want to seem pushy.

'Jojo, Flora's here,' he called.

Joey appeared from the living room. 'We made you dinner.'

'Thank you. And I brought you these as a gift.' She handed him the chocolates. 'Though they're for after dinner, OK?'

'Thank you.' Joey smiled at her. 'I made this at school.' He handed her an envelope.

'For me?'

He nodded.

When she opened it, there was a huge lump in her throat. The envelope contained a simple card with a heart shape cut out from red tissue paper. Inside, it said, *'To Flora from Joey'*, in very careful handwriting, and there were two kisses.

'That's lovely, Joey, and what beautiful handwriting.'

'We made cards at school.' He bit his lip, and she knew what he wasn't saying—that the children had all made them for their parents. 'I made one for Uncle Tom, too.'

She glanced at Tom and saw the sheen in his eyes; clearly the card had had a real emotional impact on him, too. She crouched down to Joey's level. 'This is the nicest card I've ever had. Can I give you a thank-you hug?'

Joey deliberated and she thought he was going to say no— then he nodded.

She hugged him. 'Thank you. And I'm going to put this on my fridge when I get home.'

'Can I watch cartoons again now?'

'Sure you can,' Tom said. 'I'm going to give Flora a guided

tour.' He showed her around the flat. 'Living room, obviously.' There were lots of photographs on the mantelpiece: an older couple that she assumed were his parents; a wedding picture that she guessed was Susie and Kevin, as there was another of the same couple with a baby; a picture of Tom with a much smaller Joey on his shoulders. There was one large bookcase crammed with books, and another crammed with films; she wasn't surprised to see a state-of-the-art games console next to his TV.

'Kitchen diner.' The kitchen was at one end and there was a table at the far end, by the window.

'Something smells nice,' she said.

'Bathroom, if you need it.' Plain, masculine and gleamingly clean, she noticed.

'And those two...' he gestured to the final two closed doors '...are my room and Joey's.'

'So where did you put Kevin's parents when they stayed?'

'My room, and I slept on the couch. It wasn't a big deal.' He glanced at his watch. 'Dinner's about ready. Would you like to go and sit down? Joey—time for dinner, sweetheart.'

Joey and Flora sat down at the kitchen table, and Tom brought in the meal.

'Chicken with cream and asparagus sauce. I'm impressed.'

'The sauce is from a packet,' Tom admitted with a smile. 'Joey, I take it you want ketchup with yours rather than my sauce?'

The little boy nodded.

Pudding turned out to be ice cream, out-of-season raspberries, and choc-chip cookies. 'Shop-bought, I'm afraid,' Tom confessed. 'I know they're not up to your standard.'

'They're still lovely, though—thank you. And I insist on doing the washing-up.'

Tom made them both a coffee, then ran a bath for Joey

while Flora made a start on the washing-up. She could hear a 'Hang on, I need to check it's not too hot before you get in—OK, safe now. Are there enough bubbles in there?' There was the sound of splashing, and then Tom reappeared, looking a bit damp.

'Joey's sense of humour,' he said.

She just laughed.

He came to stand behind her, wrapped his arms round her waist, and kissed the skin at the edge of the neckline of her top. 'You're adorable.'

'You're not so bad yourself, Tom Nicholson.' She twisted round slightly so she could kiss him. 'And that was a gorgeous meal.'

'Chicken, baked potatoes and vegetables? It wasn't exactly posh. Cooking isn't my strong point, but I'm trying.'

'It tasted good and it was a balanced meal,' she said. 'You're doing just fine.'

He kissed her again, then released her and picked up a tea-towel so he could start drying up. By the time they'd finished, Joey was ready to come out of the bath.

'Can I read you a bedtime story?' Flora asked.

Joey smiled, looking pleased, and found a story about a dog.

Tom joined them, sitting on the end of Joey's bed while Flora read. When it came to the part in the story where the dog talked, Tom did the voices and Joey's face lit up.

Flora kissed the little boy when she'd finished. 'Goodnight, sweetheart. Sleep well.'

Tom tucked his nephew in, and kissed him too. 'Goodnight, Jojo. See you in the morning.' Quietly, they left the room; she noticed that Tom left the door ajar and the landing light on.

'He gets bad dreams if it's dark,' Tom said. 'I put a night-light on when he's asleep, but he likes the light on in the landing while he's falling asleep.'

'Bless him.'

'Do you have to go yet, or will you come and sit with me for a while?' he asked.

'I'll stay,' she said.

He smiled, switched the light over from the main overhead lamp to an uplighter, and put some very quiet music on the stereo.

'I like this,' she said.

'It's good stuff to chill out to,' Tom told her. He scooped her onto his lap and kissed her; Flora, instead of worrying that she was squashing him, nestled closer, enjoying the closeness.

'I was touched that Joey made that card for me,' she said.

'He made the same one for me,' Tom said. 'When I opened it, I was so choked, I could hardly speak. And he actually let me hug him to say thank you.'

'It sounds as if he's made a decision to let you close.'

'I hope so. And he held my hand on the way to school today.' He paused. 'He said you told him he had to hold your hand between the car and school so you knew he was safe.' He swallowed hard. 'He said he wanted to know I was safe, too.'

'Oh, Tom—that's great.'

'If it hadn't been for you and Banjo I'd still be struggling. It's your warmth that's helped him open up to me,' he said. 'So I owe you.'

'You don't owe me anything.'

'Are you sure about that? I was kind of hoping to pay you in kisses.'

She smiled. 'Tom, you don't have to pay me.'

'Spoilsport,' he teased. 'Let me ask you another question.' He pulled her slightly closer and whispered in her ear, 'Will you be my Valentine, Flora Loveday?'

There was a huge lump in her throat; it was the kind of

question she'd never thought anyone would ask her, much less a man as beautiful as Tom Nicholas. 'Yes,' she whispered.

In answer, he kissed her. The kiss deepened, became more demanding, and, the next thing she knew, they were lying full length on the sofa, his body pressed against hers and leaving her in no doubt that he was aroused.

'I'm not going to push you into anything,' he said softly, his hand gliding along the curve of her bottom. 'I just wanted to lie with you in my arms.' He nudged the neckline of her top aside and rested his cheek against her shoulder. 'You smell of roses and vanilla. It makes me hungry.'

'What, after all the ice cream you ate tonight?' she teased.

He laughed. 'You make me hungry, Flora. And being with you…I don't know. You make me feel different. In a good way.'

They lay there quietly together, just holding each other and listening to the music. When the album finished, Tom went to check on Joey. 'He's asleep, bless him. I've just put his nightlight on.'

Shyness washed over Flora. 'I guess I ought to be going. Banjo needs his walk.'

'OK. Ring me when you get home, so I know you're home safely?'

It felt strange that someone was concerned about her; she was so used to just getting on and doing things by herself. It warmed her, too. 'Sure.'

'Before you go.' He handed her an envelope. 'Open it later.'

A Valentine's card? she wondered. She fished the card from her bag and handed it to him. 'For you,' she said shyly.

'Great minds think alike, hmm?' He kissed her lightly. 'Thank you, honey.'

'Open it later,' she said, not wanting him to open it in front of her.

'OK.' He paused. 'I'm doing show-and-tell with Joey tomorrow.'

'I thought you had a day off?' she asked, surprised.

'I am, but I'm still going to be there with the crew. I wouldn't miss it for the world. And I was wondering if you might be free for lunch tomorrow?'

It was a busy day, with surgery in the morning and then a postnatal class in the afternoon. 'It'd have to be a really quick one,' she said.

'Great—how about a picnic on the beach if it isn't raining?' He smiled. 'And we'll eat the picnic in my car if it's wet.'

'That'd be lovely.'

He kissed her goodbye at the door, his mouth sweet and soft and tempting. Desire and need flowed through her, and she kissed him back lingeringly.

When she got home, unable to resist any longer, she opened the envelope. The front of the card had a cartoon of a bee that had obviously flown in a heart shape, with the words 'bee my honey' written in the heart. Inside, Tom had written 'My adorable Flora' and signed it with two kisses. That was Tom all over, she thought: jokey and charming on the outside and keeping all the deep emotion inside.

She called him. 'I'm home.'

'Good. Did you open the card?'

'Yes.'

'Was it OK?'

'It was lovely, Tom.' She bit her lip. 'Sorry mine was a bit, well, drippy.'

'No. It was sweet. Like you.' His voice grew husky. 'Next time I eat a chocolate, I'm going to think about kissing you.' Heat spread through her at his words. 'See you tomorrow, honey.'

* * *

Her surgery the next morning was as she'd expected, apart from her ten-o'clock appointment, fifteen-year-old Emmy Kingston, who really should've been at school. 'Can Shelley stay with me?' Emmy asked, gesturing to her friend.

Emmy was guarding her stomach and the way she was standing made Flora think the worst. It wasn't her place to judge, but if her suspicion was right then the poor child would need all the support she could get. 'If you want her to stay with you, then that's fine.'

Emmy looked relieved, and accepted Flora's invitation to sit down.

'Tell me about it,' Flora said. 'How can I help you?'

'I've done something really stupid, and my parents are going to kill me.' Emmy bit her lip and a tear rolled down her face. 'I should've said no but I... It's so hard. And you're going to think...'

Flora reached out and squeezed her hand. 'I'm not going to think *anything*, sweetheart. I'm a nurse, and my job is to help you.'

'And you won't tell my mum and dad?'

'Your appointment is absolutely confidential,' Flora reassured her. 'It's between you and me, unless I think you're at risk of being hurt or abused. The important thing is that you're protected, OK?'

Another tear rolled down Emmy's cheek.

'Show her, Em,' Shelley said, patting her shoulder.

Gingerly, Emmy lifted up her top to reveal—not quite what Flora had expected. The girl had a pierced navel and the area around the piercing was bright red and swollen; there was a yellowish discharge from her belly button.

'That looks really painful,' Flora said. 'How long has it been like that?'

'I had it done on Saturday. Mum and Dad said I wasn't allowed to, so I didn't tell them I was doing it. I had a sleepover at Shelley's so they wouldn't see.' Emmy's voice wobbled. 'I wish I hadn't done it now.'

'It looks to me as if it's infected. It's quite common to get a bacterial infection with a piercing—have you managed to keep it dry over the last three days?'

Emmy nodded. 'That's what the piercer said, don't wash it even with salt water or it might get infected. I did everything he said.'

'You've just been a bit unlucky,' Flora said. 'I want to take your temperature—sometimes these infections can turn really nasty, and I want to be sure you're not developing septicaemia or something really scary. Is that OK?'

Emmy gave her consent, and Flora checked the girl's temperature. 'The good news is that we've caught the infection in time—your temperature's fine. You'll need some antibiotic cream to clear up the infection and stop it hurting, and if it doesn't start getting better by Friday you'll need to come back and see the doctor to get some antibiotic tablets.' She quickly tapped information into the computer. 'Try not to touch your belly button or pick at it, in the meantime.'

'It hurts too much to touch it,' Emmy said ruefully.

'Antibiotics will help with that,' Flora reassured her. 'It might be worth taking some paracetamol as well. Dr Lovak will sign the prescription for you when he's seen his next patient, if you don't mind waiting in the reception area for a few minutes?'

Emmy exhaled sharply. 'So it's going to be all right?'

'Yes.'

'See? I told you,' Shelley said, hugging her shoulders.

'And you're not going to tell my mum?'

'No,' Flora said, 'but I think you should.'

Emmy shook her head. 'I can't. Mum will go *mad*.'

'When you came in,' Flora told her gently, 'the way you were standing and holding your tummy, I thought you might be pregnant. I wouldn't mind betting your mum's thinking the same thing and she's worried sick about you—especially as my guess is that you've been avoiding her since Saturday.'

'I have,' Emmy admitted, biting her lip.

'Then talk to her tonight,' Flora advised quietly. 'Yes, she might shout at you for going against her wishes, but she'll want to know that you're all right.'

'She'll make me take it out.'

'That's not a good idea until the infection's cleared up—it needs to be able to drain and make sure that an abscess doesn't form. You can always tell her to ring me if she wants some reassurance,' Flora said.

Emmy's lower lip wobbled. 'Thank you so much.'

Flora patted her shoulder. 'A couple more days and you'll feel a lot better, I promise. But if you don't, come back and see Dr Lovak. We're here to help you, not shout at you or judge you, OK?'

'OK.' Emmy rubbed the tears away with the back of her hand, and let her friend shepherd her out to the reception area.

Flora had just seen her last patient and was finishing typing up her notes when her phone beeped. It was a text from Tom: *'Am in the car park whenever you're ready.'*

'On my way', Flora texted back, and went out to meet him.

He greeted her with a kiss.

'How did show-and-tell go?' she asked.

'Unbelievable.' Tom's eyes glittered. 'I actually saw Joey nudge the boy next to him and say, "That's my Uncle Tom." He sounded really proud.'

'That's because he *is* proud of you, Tom.' She hugged him. 'Well done, you.'

'How was your morning?' he asked.

'Busy, but good.'

He kissed her again. 'When do you need to be back?'

She glanced at her watch. 'In forty-five minutes.'

'Right—beach it is.' He drove them down to the car park by the beach; he had a picnic rug in the back of the car, along with a flask of hot chocolate and a bag from the deli containing sandwiches and fruit.

Flora enjoyed just being with him, having a leisurely lunch and then sitting on the rug with his arms wrapped round her, listening to the sea and the shrieks of the gulls.

'This is a perfect day,' he said softly, resting his cheek against her hair. 'Being with Joey this morning, and being with you right now. And you're definitely the silver lining in the school fire—I wouldn't have met you, if it hadn't happened.' He drew her closer. 'And I'm really glad I've met you, Flora.'

'I'm glad I've met you, too.' With Tom in her world, everything seemed so much brighter. Crazy—and no way would she admit that to him, not yet—but it was true. Tom made her feel special. As if she mattered.

'So when am I going to see you again?' he asked when he'd driven her back to the surgery.

'I have tomorrow off, if you want to do something.'

He looked sombre. 'Could I ask you something?'

'Sure.'

'The other day, you said you'd help if I wanted to go through Susie's things…'

'And I meant what I said. Of course I'll help.' She stroked his face. 'Are you sure you're ready for it, Tom?'

'No, and I'm not sure I'll ever be ready,' he admitted, 'but it has to be done.'

'It's better to do it with someone else,' she said softly. 'I had help and it got me through one of the hardest days ever.'

He hugged her. 'Thank you. Can I pick you up when I've taken Joey to school?'

'Absolutely.' She kissed him. 'And, Tom?'

'Yes?'

'Try not to brood about it. Yes, it'll be tough, but you won't be on your own. See you tomorrow.'

CHAPTER EIGHT

ON WEDNESDAY morning, Tom picked Flora up after he'd taken Joey to school, looking very sombre. For once, his car stereo was silent, and the grim set of his jaw told Flora that he wasn't in the mood for conversation, either.

He parked outside one of the cottages near the cliffs, and she noticed his hand was shaking as he opened the front door. He took a deep breath when he stepped inside, then leaned his head back against the wall and closed his eyes. 'I hate this. It feels so wrong.'

'I know.' She took his hand and held it, willing him to take strength from her nearness.

'Clearing out their house makes everything seem so final.' He swallowed hard. 'I suppose I was leaving it in the hope that it was all a bad dream and they'd come back—but they're not coming back, are they?'

'No, Tom, they're not,' she said, as gently as she could.

'It's such a waste. Such a bloody waste. There are people out there who hurt others, who lie and cheat and make people miserable, and they seem to swan through life without any worries. And people like my sister and her husband, people who were kind and always helped others...' He shook his head in anguish. 'It's not fair. Why did they have to die?'

There was no answer to that. All she could do was hold his hand.

A muscle worked in his jaw. 'OK. I'm pulling myself to-gether. Let's do this.' Then he looked completely lost. 'How do you go about packing up someone's life?'

This was something she could help with. Something she'd been through herself. 'You think of the good times,' she told him. 'You keep the nice memories as you go. And you have boxes. One for things to go to the charity shop, one for things you want to keep—even if you're not up to dealing with them yet, like photo albums—and one for things you're going to throw out.' She paused. 'You don't have to do it all at once, Tom. We can do just one room at a time, if it makes it easier on you.'

He shook his head. 'It needs to be done, and I've organised for the council to come and take the furniture to help families that need rehoming.' He took a deep breath. 'Part of me thinks I ought to move in here and give Joey some continuity. But I just *can't*, Flora. I can't live here with all these memories. They'll suffocate me.'

'Joey will understand when he's older,' she reassured him. 'He has a new life now and it'll be easier for him to get used to that if he lives with you away from here.'

He nodded. 'We'll do the hard stuff first. Bedroom.'

Flora helped him take the clothes out of the wardrobe and pack them into bags he was planning to take to the charity shop. 'Maybe you could to keep something for Joey—his dad's favourite sweater or his mum's favourite dress,' she suggested. 'Something personal for him, for the future.'

'Yeah, you're right.'

Tom's face was set. Grim. She knew this was ripping him to shreds inside, and yet he was trying so hard not to show any emotion.

The kitchen was next; it was easy to pack up, because there was nothing really personal there. Except for the outside of the fridge, photographs and postcards and little notes held on with magnets. Tom stripped those and put them in the 'deal with later' pile.

When they started to pack up the living room, the strain was really etched on his face. Books, music, photograph albums... She could practically see the tension radiating from his body.

And then he picked up a photograph from the mantelpiece. His hand shook, and he dropped it; she heard a crack as the glass smashed. Reaching down to deal with it, Tom sucked in a breath, and she saw red blooming over his hand.

'Kitchen. Now.' She made him stand under the light so she could check the cut for fragments of glass, then cleaned the wound and put a pad on it. 'Press on it. It'll staunch the flow,' she said. 'And I'll get rid of the broken glass.'

'I'll do it.'

'Tom, I want you to sit there for three minutes, and that's a medical order,' she said, taking an old newspaper into the living room. She wrapped the broken glass in some newspaper, then turned the frame over. She could see why he'd dropped the frame; the photograph was of Tom himself, with his sister and Joey, looking incredibly happy.

Memories.

Sometimes the good ones were the ones that hurt you most. She'd found it hard to look at her parents' photographs for the first couple of months, feeling the loss ripping through her again every time she saw them.

Gently, she removed the photograph from the broken frame and slid it inside one of the photograph albums to keep it safe. Then she wrapped up the broken frame and took the two parcels into the kitchen. 'All done,' she said quietly.

'Sorry. It just...' His voice caught.

She held him close. 'I know. I've been there myself. Come on. I think it's time we took a break. Let's go back to mine for lunch.'

Back at the farmhouse, she took a jug of home-made vegetable soup from the fridge and heated it, then set it on the table along with cheese, butter and some rolls she'd bought at the bakery the day before.

Tom pushed his plate away untouched. 'Flora, I'm sorry to be rude—I don't think I can possibly eat.'

'Yes, you can; and, yes, you will.'

'I feel too choked.'

Remembering how Kate Tremayne had chivvied her, and how she'd appreciated it later, she refused to let him give in. 'You need to keep up your strength, for Joey's sake. Listen, Tom, I didn't really know your sister, so I can't imagine what she'd say in this situation—but if she loved you as much as you loved her, I'm pretty sure she would've wanted you to remember the good times and celebrate her, not mourn her.'

Tom dragged in a breath. 'Yes, she loved me—even though I drove her crazy when I was a teenager. And I loved her. I would've done anything to spare her what happened, Flora. And Kevin—he wasn't just an in-law I had to tolerate for Susie's sake. I really liked him. You know they say you can't choose your family? Well, he was the kind of bloke I would've chosen to have as my family.'

'I know what you mean. But you still have Joey, and they'll both live on in him,' she said softly. 'You'll see them in his face as they grow up—and there will come a day, Tom, when you can talk to him about them without it hurting. You'll be able to tell him how much they loved him and how proud they'd be of how he's growing up.'

He closed his eyes. 'Right now, it doesn't feel like it.'

'Of course not, because you're not there yet. Trust me, it'll come—you'll still get days when you wake up and you know there's a big empty space in your life and you want to howl, but it gets easier to deal with as time passes.'

He opened his eyes again and looked at her. 'Is it like that for you?'

She nodded. 'Sometimes one of my dad's favourite records will come on the radio, or I'll smell my mum's perfume in a department store, and it still chokes me inside—but it's getting easier. It just takes time and you need to be a bit less hard on yourself. Let people close to you, Tom, and they'll help you.'

'I do let people close to me.'

She said nothing, just stroked his face and gave him a sad little smile.

Tom thought about it later that evening. Was Flora right? Did he let people close to him? Or did he use all the terrible jokes and puns that were his stock-in-trade at work to keep people at bay?

The more he thought about it, the more he started to realise that Flora had a point. He *didn't* let people that close. And, if he thought about it, he could trace it right back to when Ben had died. The first person he'd really lost, his best friend, and yet he'd never even visited Ben's grave. He'd withdrawn a bit after Ben had died, until his mum had talked about taking him to see the doctor; and then he'd realised that if he didn't start smiling and laughing, she really would take him to see someone. He hadn't wanted that kind of fuss. So he'd started telling silly jokes, smiled all the time, and driven Susie to distraction with practical jokes. But he'd never really let anyone close again. He'd kept everything on the surface.

Which was one of the reasons he was struggling to be a stand-in dad to his nephew, because he didn't have a clue what he was meant to do, how he was meant to feel.

And the more he thought about it, the more it worried him. Because he was starting to let Flora and Joey a lot closer than he was really comfortable with—and it scared him. Not because he was scared of being close to them, as such, more because he was scared of letting them down in the worst possible way. His job was dangerous—and he knew firefighters who hadn't made it. People who'd left grieving families behind.

Was that why he'd never let his relationships get too serious? And why he was struggling so hard to be a stand-in dad to Joey? Because he didn't want to leave a gaping hole in people's lives, and Joey had already lost so much?

He lay awake for a long, long time—and right at that moment he really could do with Flora in his arms. He needed her quiet strength, her warmth to comfort him. And that scared him even more. He'd never felt as if he'd needed a girlfriend before. He'd enjoyed female company, had fun with a carefree bachelor lifestyle...but this was different. Flora was nothing like the women he usually dated. She was quieter, more serious. She had depth.

And that made her incredibly dangerous. With her shy smile and her beautiful soft brown eyes and the sheer warmth she exuded—there was a real possibility that she could steal his heart. And break it.

Tom was still brooding about it on Thursday morning, when he dropped Joey at Flora's for breakfast. And he brooded all morning through inspection and cleaning the equipment, until the Tannoy warbled.

'Turnout, vehicle 54. Person fallen in river, Penhally Bay.'

This could be nasty, Tom thought. The cold snap had lasted a while now, so the water would be very cold and there was a real risk of the victim developing hypothermia. If the river was running swiftly, even if they managed to cling on to a branch or a rock, the current might pull them away and send them downstream,

He headed to the engine with the rest of the crew. Bazza

was in the driving seat and Steve was checking the computer. 'It was called in by mobile phone,' he said. 'So details are a bit sketchy—hopefully they'll call back with more information.'

Halfway to the village, Steve's mobile rang. 'Yup—uh-huh. Thanks.' He ended the call. 'It turns out it isn't a person in the river, it's a dog.'

Tom had come across this kind of thing before. 'Please tell me the owner hasn't tried to jump in and save the dog,' he said.

'No, the owner's an elderly man. He was walking by the river when he slipped on the ice and fell. Apparently he might have broken his hip—the ambulance is on its way. When he fell, the dog plunged down the bank and ended up in the river. The poor guy's frantic, but in too much pain to move.'

'Hopefully we can rescue the dog before the paramedics whisk him off to St Piran's,' Tom said. 'Walkway, ladder or rope, do you think?'

'We'll know as soon as we see it,' Steve said.

Even without the co-ordinates, they would've been able to see the site straight away, as the ambulance was already there. As Tom got out of the fire engine, he could see the paramedics gently lifting an elderly man onto a stretcher. The man was clearly distressed, calling, 'No, no! I can't go until Goldie's safe.'

Tom walked over to him. 'I'm Tom Nicholson—and I'm going to rescue your dog,' he said. 'Her name's Goldie?'

The elderly man was in tears. 'She fell down the bank. It's my fault. I slipped, and I caught her as I fell. She's like me, not so steady on her pins.' He choked on a sob. 'She's been in the water for ages. She's too old to cope with it. I've killed her.'

'No, you haven't,' Tom reassured him. 'Dogs are far more

resilient than you'd believe. Hang on in there, and I'll get her back for you.'

As soon he looked over the river bank, he could see that the elderly yellow Labrador was stuck against a branch and was clearly getting tired.

'Has anyone called the local vet ready to treat Goldie when I get her out?' he asked the crowd of bystanders.

'I'll go—they're just round the corner,' one man said.

'Thanks. And if someone could get a towel or a blanket to wrap her in?' He turned back to the crew. 'I'll go. It's going to be quickest if you rope me. The dog's too big for a tube—' the crew had tubes they could scoop smaller animals into and lift to safety '—so we'll get a rope round her, too, and I'll lift her.'

Slowly, knowing that his crew had the rope and could stop him falling if he slipped, he made his way down the bank to the dog.

'Goldie,' he called softly, 'hang on in there. I'll get you back to your family.' He knew the dog couldn't understand what he was saying, but he hoped the tone of his voice would reassure her and calm her.

'There's a good girl. Not long now. I'm just going to put the rope round you.' He'd just got the rope round her when there was a loud crack and the branch broke. The sound terrified the already frightened dog, who reacted by sinking her teeth into Tom's arm.

It hurt like mad, but he swallowed the yell, knowing it would panic the dog even more and earn him a second bite. 'OK, Goldie,' he said through gritted teeth. 'There's a good girl. Nearly there.'

The dog struggled in his arms, but he had her roped safely.

But, with his arms full of wet, tired, heavy dog, there was

no way he was going to be able to make it up the slippery bank on his own. 'I've got her. Haul me up,' Tom called up.

Slowly, slowly, the team hauled him up.

A flash popped in his face as he reached the top, the dog in his arms.

'Oh, for pity's sake,' he said, frowning. 'You can have your story in a minute. We need to get this dog treated, first.'

'Absolutely right,' Melinda Lovak, the local vet, said crisply. She crouched down and wrapped a towel round the shivering dog. 'Well done for bringing her out,' she said to Tom. Tenderly, she dried the dog. 'Hello, Goldie. Not the best time of year to go for a swim, is it?' she asked.

The dog looked slightly less frightened, clearly knowing the vet.

'There's a good girl,' Melinda said softly. Swiftly, she checked the animal over. 'Looks like you're going to be fine after your dip. Let's go and tell Bob, shall we?'

There was a faint wag of the tail.

'Bob, she's absolutely fine,' Melinda told the elderly man in the ambulance. 'Look, you can see her. The fireman got her out and she's wagging her tail.'

'The dog can't come in the ambulance, love,' the paramedic told her.

'What's going to happen to her?' Bob asked. 'I live on my own. I can't go to the hospital, I need to stay with Goldie.'

'Yes, you can, because you need to be treated,' Melinda said. 'Don't worry about her. I'll take her back to the surgery with me. Dragan and the boys won't mind if we have another dog for a few days—or, if Goldie decides she doesn't like it with Bramble at our place, Lizzie Chamberlain at the kennels will take her in until you're back on your feet.'

Bob was almost in tears. 'Thank you—I don't know what I'd do without her.' He looked at Tom. 'And thank you. You saved her life.'

'That's what I'm here for,' Tom said simply. 'I'm glad she's all right.'

'She'll be absolutely fine,' Melinda reassured Bob. 'Now go and get yourself fixed, OK? I'll ring the hospital later to let you know how Goldie's doing.'

The paramedic closed the door and the ambulance headed off to St Piran's.

Tom's arm was throbbing; wincing, he rolled up his sleeve to look at it.

'You need to get that looked at,' Melinda said.

Tom shrugged. 'It's not that bad. I'm fine.'

'Trust me,' she said with a smile, 'I've been bitten enough in my time. That's a puncture wound, so it could get infected—and you probably need a tetanus jab.'

He grimaced. 'Oh, great.'

She laughed, 'A big fireman like you, scared of a little needle? Don't be such a baby!' she teased. 'The doctor's surgery is just over there and it'll take ten minutes, tops.' She made a fuss of the dog. 'And I'd better get this one in the warm. Come on, girl.'

'You've had your orders,' Steve said with a grin. 'And she's a vet. She knows what she's talking about.'

'And can I interview you now?' the reporter asked.

'Look, it was just a routine rescue. No big deal,' Tom said.

The reporter smiled at him. 'But our readers love this sort of story. It's a feel-good story, perfect to lift people's spirits at a miserable time of year.'

'I...' He sighed. 'OK. As long as you put something in there about keeping your dog on a lead when you're walking by an icy river, and calling the emergency services rather than risking your own safety—in this kind of weather, you can get into difficulties really quickly and it means the emergency services have to do twice the amount of work, rescuing you as well as your pet.'

'I'll make sure I put that in,' the reporter said. She glanced down at his left hand and clearly saw that he wasn't wearing a wedding ring. 'Actually, maybe I can take you for a coffee? You must be freezing.'

'He's going to the doctor's to get his arm seen to, love,' Steve put in.

'I can interview you while you're waiting to be seen,' the reporter said with a smile, 'and then maybe we can go for a coffee afterwards.'

Tom didn't want to go for coffee with anyone except Flora; though they were keeping things to themselves, right now, and he wasn't going to make life awkward for her by giving a declaration in front of half of Penhally. 'Mmm,' he said noncommittally.

He had no idea if Flora was in surgery this morning or if she was working at one of the schools, and suppressed the hope that she might be the one to patch him up. And he still had to give the reporter a story. Feeling embarrassed, he went up to the reception desk, explained what had happened, and asked if someone could fit him in.

'Sit down, and we'll call you as soon as the nurse is free,' the receptionist said with a smile.

The reporter wasn't budging. 'So how did you feel when you saw the dog?'

'The same as the rest of the crew—we wanted to get her back safely on dry land, and reassure her owner so that he'd let the paramedics treat him,' Tom said. 'Look, there isn't much of a story. We simply responded to an emergency call.'

'But the dog was heavy. And it bit you.'

'The dog was cold, tired and frightened. She didn't mean to hurt me.'

'And the bite won't put you off rescuing the next dog?'

'Of course not. It's my job,' Tom said firmly.

'OK.' She finished scribbling notes on her pad. 'Shall we go for that coffee anyway?'

'Sorry, I have to get back to work,' Tom said.

She took a business card from her handbag. 'If you think of anything else, give me a call. Actually, it'd be nice to run a few features on the local emergency services. Maybe I can come and shadow you for a day.'

Something in her eyes told Tom that she didn't have just business in mind. And his suspicion was confirmed when she added, 'And, since you can't make that coffee, maybe I can take you out for a drink to say thanks for your help.'

The reporter was pretty; three months ago, Tom might've accepted the invitation. But things were very different now. 'That'd be nice. I'll have to check when my partner's free,' he said.

'Your partner?'

Three months ago, those words might've made him run a mile. But now...now, it was different. 'I assume the invitation extends to her, too?' Tom said, knowing full well that it wouldn't.

'I, um, sure. Of course.'

His name flashed up on the board above the reception desk. 'Sorry, I need to go.'

'Sure. Catch you later,' she said, and Tom had a pretty fair idea that she wouldn't call him at all.

To his mingled pleasure and embarrassment, it turned out that the nurse on duty was Flora.

She looked worried when he walked into her treatment room. 'What's happened? Are you all right?'

'I rescued a dog from the river, and she bit me.'

'Right, let me take a look—whose dog was it?'

'I didn't catch his last name. His first name's Bob. He's quite elderly, and the dog's a yellow Labrador called Goldie.'

'I know who you mean. Bob Thurston. Is he all right?'

'He slipped on the ice—the paramedics were worried enough to take him to St Piran's, so my guess is that he's probably broken something. Goldie slid down the bank and into the river. Luckily she was swept against a branch and stuck there, otherwise who knows how far she could've ended up downstream.'

'And she bit you? But Goldie's really gentle.'

'She was scared. It's not a big deal.'

'Does it hurt?'

'A bit,' he admitted. 'It throbs more than anything.'

'OK. Let me take a look—I want to make sure there isn't any damage to the structures beneath the bite, tendons and what have you. Is Goldie OK?'

'The vet's taken her back to the surgery. She says she'll look after her.'

Flora smiled. 'That's Melinda all over—she's lovely like that. She helped me find some homes when one of the feral farm cats had a litter. Jess Carmichael at the hospital—well, Jess Corezzi now she's married—took a couple, too.' She finished examining his arm. 'That looks fine,' she said. 'Tom, is your tetanus up to date?'

'I think so.'

'Mind if I check?' She looked up his record. 'It is. So you're safe from having a big fat needle in your arm.'

'Pity,' Tom said. 'I could've asked you to kiss it better.'

'You wish.'

'So how about it?' he asked.

'That depends on how brave you are while I sort this out.' She gave him a local anaesthetic, cleaned the wound, making sure there were no foreign bodies in it, and debrided some of tissue. 'I'm not going to stitch this,' she said, 'because it's a puncture wound, and you're more likely to get an infection if

I close it. And you do need antibiotics to be on the safe side, so I'll ask the doctor to write you a prescription.'

'OK. Do I get my kiss for being brave now?'

'Tom, I'm at work and so are you. I have patients waiting,' she protested. But she gave him a swift kiss.

'Would that be on account?' he asked hopefully.

She rolled her eyes. 'Yes. Go and rescue someone.'

'I'd rather scoop you up in a fireman's lift and take you somewhere quiet,' Tom said. He stole another kiss. 'But I'll do that later. Thanks for patching me up.'

'It's what I do,' she said with a smile.

When Tom had finished his shift, he drove to Flora's farm-house to pick up Joey.

'How's your arm?' she asked.

'Sore,' he admitted, 'but it's OK.'

Joey looked worried. 'What's wrong with your arm?'

'I rescued a dog today—she fell in the river and got stuck. She was a bit worried when I rescued her,' Tom explained, 'and dogs can't tell you in words that they're scared, so she bit me. She didn't mean to hurt me, she was just frightened.'

'I know the dog,' Flora said. 'She's really quiet and soft, normally—she's quite old, too. She's a yellow Labrador called Goldie.'

'And she's doing absolutely fine,' Tom added. 'I rang the vet before the surgery closed, to see how she was. I'm fine, too, Jojo. Flora cleaned me up and put a dressing on, and I've got some special tablets so I don't get an infection in the wound.'

'So you rescued Uncle Tom,' Joey said to Flora.

'I was just doing my job—like he was doing his,' Flora said with a smile. 'Actually, I had to do a rescue myself today. This cold snap really seems to be knocking everyone for six. Young Jane Hallet in Year Four fell over in the playground at lunchtime and broke her arm, poor thing. I was there so

I could give her a painkiller and put her arm in a sling to make her more comfortable, but her mum had to take her to the emergency department in St Piran's. Luckily it happened just after her mum Marina finished her shift in the kitchen, so Marina was able to take her. I'll drop in to see them tomorrow on my way back from lunch and see how she is.'

'So what were you doing today?' Tom asked.

'Healthy eating with the Year Sixes—one of the girls has just been diagnosed as a diabetic, so we were talking about sugar and how the body processes it. I have a quiz so they can guess how many teaspoons of sugar are in each item.' She smiled at him. 'Guess how many teaspoons of sugar there are in a can of fizzy drink?'

'The non-diet sort, I assume?' Tom asked.

'Uh-huh.'

He thought about it. 'Five?' he guessed.

'Too low. Joey?' she prompted.

'Seven?' the little boy suggested.

'Closer—but still too low. Believe it or not, it's nine,' she told them. 'That's why they're really bad for teeth. We did some experiments with eggshells in different sorts of drink so the children could see what effect the drinks would have on their teeth.'

'Eggshells being made of the same sort of stuff as teeth?' Tom asked.

'Exactly. Anyway, when they saw which ones dissolved, it's made a few of them think that maybe water's the best drink you can have.' She smiled at Joey. 'I'll do that with your class when you're in Year Six. But I'm going to be doing germs and super-soap with your class after half-term. And we might do the eggshell thing too, if you think it sounds like fun.'

Joey nodded enthusiastically.

'Ah, so you like science? Excellent. We can do some kitchen experiments,' Flora said. 'I know how to make a volcano.'

Joey beamed. 'That's cool.'

'Hey, can I be in on this?' Tom asked. 'And I know an experiment about how to make a plastic bottle into a rocket.'

'This sounds like a very half-term kind of thing to do,' Flora said. 'And I've heard the mums at school talking about that new science museum just up the coast. They say it's really good.'

'I think we need to go,' Tom said. 'What do you think, Joey?'

The little boy nodded.

'Then it's a date. Flora, is there any chance you can have a day off, next week, and come with us?' Tom asked.

'I'll check at work tomorrow to see if I can swap a shift with someone,' Flora said. 'Given that I won't be doing my usual school sessions, I should be able to get a day off.'

'Cool,' Joey said, smiling at both of them.

CHAPTER NINE

ON FRIDAY, Flora dropped Joey at school and spent the morning working at the high school, doing a couple of talks about healthy eating and one about sexual health. During her lunch break, she drove out to Chyandour Farm on the outskirts of Penhally to see how Lizzie was doing.

As she reached the end of the drive, she saw the fire engines there; water was being sprayed onto one of the barns.

Tom came over to her as she climbed out of the car. 'Just the woman we could do with.'

'What's happened?'

'The lower barn caught fire. John rang us, then tried to beat out the flames, but he burned his arm. Can you take a look?'

'Sure.' She grabbed her medical kit from the car, then followed Tom to where John Hallet was standing. She persuaded him to go and sit down in the kitchen so she could take a look at his injuries properly and treat him.

'I only popped in to see how Lizzie was doing—I wasn't expecting to treat you, too,' she said wryly.

'They say things come in threes,' John said. 'Let's just hope they don't!'

She looked at his arm. 'I'm relieved to say the burns are pretty superficial. If it had been your hands, I would have sent you to St Piran's, but I can dress this for you. Have you taken anything for the pain?'

'Not yet.'

She gave him a painkiller, then cleaned and dressed the burn. 'So how's Lizzie doing?'

'She wants to be back at school, but Marina had to take her to St Piran's to have her cast on today. She'll be fine,' John said. 'Nicola's home with a headache. I'll get her to come down and put the kettle on and make tea for everyone.'

Nicola Hallet was the quiet one in the family, Flora remembered, the only one who wasn't sporty or glamorous. Her older sisters Stacey and Keeley were both model-thin and stunning, popular with all the girls in the village and drooled over by the boys; young Lizzie was into tap-dancing and gymnastics and athletics, and was always talking about how her older brother Jonathan was the captain of the football team at the primary school last year and had a purple belt in kick-boxing. And she had a feeling that Nicola had a pretty hard time fitting in.

'If she's got a headache, she's probably better resting. I can make the tea,' she offered.

'No, she'll do it. She's been that mardy, lately.' John called up to her, and a minute or so later Nicola came downstairs into the kitchen.

'We need some tea for the firefighters, love,' John said.

Nicola nodded and filled the kettle with water.

'How's your headache?' Flora asked.

Nicola shrugged. 'It'll go.'

'Have you taken anything for it?'

Nicola shrugged again. 'I will in a bit.'

Flora looked at the girl, wondering. Nicola had always been a bit on the plump side, but she'd definitely put on weight since Flora had last seen her—and she was trying to hide it with baggy clothes. Remembering her own teenage years, how she'd felt she didn't fit in and had cheered herself up with chocolate biscuits, Flora wondered if Nicola might be worried about something and comfort-eating as a way of dealing with it. Not that she'd ask the girl in front of her dad.

'Let me give you a hand with the tea, Nicola,' she offered. 'John, if you can do us a favour and find out who takes sugar?'

'Will do,' he said.

As soon as he'd closed the door, Flora asked gently, 'Is everything all right, Nicola?'

'I'm fine. Just fine,' Nicola said. 'It's only a headache.'

Flora was pretty sure it was more than just a headache making the girl miserable. 'You're not having any problems at school?'

'Why should I be?'

'No reason,' Flora said quietly. 'I just remember that it's hard being a teenager, that's all. And sometimes people make it harder for you.'

Nicola just shrugged, and concentrated on putting tea leaves in the pot.

'If you ever need anyone to talk to, you know you can always come and see me at the drop-in clinic at school. Or at the surgery. Anything you say will be just between you and me, OK?'

For a moment, Flora thought that the girl was going to say something—but then the kitchen door opened and John walked back in. Any chance that Nicola would confide in her vanished instantly.

She didn't get a chance to talk to Nicola when the tea had been handed round, either, because the girl had disappeared back to her room. And Flora was due back in the surgery for the afternoon, so she had to get on. 'If you're in pain or you see any sign of infection, John, don't be stubborn about it—come and see us at the surgery.'

'I'll be fine.'

John was of the old school—and that meant he'd only see the doctor if he was in so much pain that he couldn't sleep. 'As long as you know that the sooner we look at a problem, the quicker it is to fix it,' she said gently. 'Don't be too proud or too stubborn.'

'All right, love,' he said.

After surgery that afternoon, Flora picked Joey up from school as usual, and made dinner with him. When Tom arrived after his shift, he gave her a hello hug and ruffled Joey's hair; Flora was pleased that the little boy didn't pull away.

While Joey played with Banjo, Flora made coffee for herself and Tom.

'Flora, are you busy next weekend?' Tom asked.

She was never busy. Not that she wanted him to think she was completely desperate. 'I'm not doing anything important. Why?'

'It's the football league dinner—kind of a late Valentine's ball sort of thing. We have it every year. It's the local emergency services league, so all the teams have a table—fire crews, the police and the medics—and we take our partners with us. The fire crew team has a huge rivalry thing going on with the medics, but it's all in good fun and—well, I know it's a bit late notice, but I wasn't even sure if I was going to go this year, the way things were. But my parents are going to be here next weekend and they're more than happy to babysit for us, if you'd like to come to the dinner with me?'

He wanted her to go to a posh do with him? Help. She never got invited to posh dos like this. She didn't have a thing to wear, or a clue where to find something suitable. And if it was the same crowd as the football lot, who were incredibly cliquey, she wasn't sure she wanted to be there. 'Um, can I think about it?'

He looked slightly hurt, but shrugged. 'Sure. Can I ask you something else?'

She spread her hands. 'Of course.'

'My parents are coming over from France for a week or so. They're staying for a long weekend, then visiting Mum's brother, and then they're coming back next weekend. So I was wondering…will you come to dinner at my place tomorrow night to meet them?'

Asking her to a formal dinner as his date was one thing, but now he was asking her to meet his parents. As his friend—or as his girlfriend?

'I…um…' Oh, help. This situation was way outside what she was used to.

'They're nice, my parents. And they said they'd like to meet you.'

His parents knew about her? What had he said? Had he told them that she was Joey's babysitter, or that he was seeing her?

'Please?' he added.

How could she resist the appeal in his gorgeous dark eyes? 'All right.'

'Great. It'll be a proper home-cooked dinner. About six?'

Which meant it'd be early enough for Joey to be eating with them, she guessed. 'Sure. I'll be there.'

'I'd better get back,' he said. 'They'll be here in an hour or so.' He looked at Joey. 'Want a fireman's lift to the car?'

Joey's eyes brightened. 'Cool,' he said.

Tom looked delighted that Joey was finally opening up to him again, returning to their old rough-and-tumble relationship, and hoisted his nephew over his shoulder. But Flora noticed his wince of pain. She slipped her coat on and followed them out to the car. When Tom had strapped Joey into the car seat and closed the door, she said, 'Is your arm hurting you?'

'No.' But he didn't meet her eye.

'Tom?'

He shook his head. 'It's nothing. Just a bruise.'

Not his arm, then. And the fact he wasn't telling her straight made her suspicious. 'Where?'

'My back.'

'And you did that rescuing Goldie?'

He flapped a dismissive hand. 'Look, I'm fine.'

'Tom,' she said warningly.

He rolled his eyes. 'OK. There was another fire this afternoon. A little girl was stuck in her bedroom. Just as I got her out, the roof collapsed and a beam caught my shoulder. I'm fine.'

Flora's eyes narrowed. 'The roof collapsed.'

'Yes, but it missed me. Well, most of it missed me. And the little girl's absolutely fine.'

There was something he wasn't telling her. He was an experienced firefighter. He would've known if the structure was dangerous and the roof was likely to cave in—and yet he'd gone in anyway. And she remembered what he'd told her when he'd spoken about Ben. *I almost never lose anyone. I remember how it was for his parents...I don't want anyone else to go through that.*

And so he took risks. More risks, she thought, than anyone else on his crew would take. Reckless, even, because he didn't think of his own safety.

'Was anyone else with you?' she asked.

'No, they were putting out the fire.'

'So you went into a burning building, on your own, to rescue someone. You could've been killed.'

He frowned. 'Flora, it's my job. What was I meant to do, let her burn?'

'She was stuck in her bedroom. You could've put a ladder at the window or something, so you didn't have to go through the dangerous bit of the building to rescue her.'

'What I did was quicker.'

Maybe—but it was also something else. Something that really worried her. And it had to be said. 'And r-reckless.'

Tom lifted his chin. 'It's my job, Flora. I rescue people from fires.'

'I know, but you go above and beyond. You don't protect yourself enough.' She dragged in a breath. 'You could've been killed. And what would've happened to Joey, then?'

Tom stared at her. 'So what are you saying? That I should give up being a firefighter? It's who I *am*.'

'I know that.' It was like that for her, too, with her job. 'I'm not saying this right.' And she'd started to stumble over her words. 'I just don't want you to take stupid risks, Tom. It's not going to bring Ben back. It's not going to b-bring your sister back. And if you die, what about Joey?' She was shaking now, so worried and angry when she thought about what could have happened that the words spilled out before she could stop them. 'What about me?'

Tom looked utterly shocked. 'Flora, I...'

She shook her head. 'You could've been really badly hurt. If you'd been trapped under that beam, you could've been killed, or so badly burned that...' She choked the words back. 'That little girl could've died.'

'She's fine. And so am I. It's just a bit of a bruise.'

A huge bruise, she'd bet, though she couldn't make him show her. Not outside, on a chilly February night, while Joey was sitting in the car, his face white with anxiety as he looked at them.

'Joey's waiting. You'd better go.'

Tom took a step towards her, as if he was going to kiss her, and she took a step back. Not now. She was still so angry with him for taking a stupid risk, for not thinking before he acted, that she didn't want to kiss him. She wanted to shake him—shake some sense into him.

'Flora—'

'Joey's waiting,' she said again, taking another step back.

Tom's face tightened, and he got into the car without another word.

She waved as he drove off—more for Joey's sake than for Tom's—and then headed back inside.

It was the first time she could ever remember shouting at anyone. The first time she'd ever had a real fight with anyone. And it felt horrible. But what else could she have done? If Tom was taking risks like that at work...

She was miserable for the rest of the evening. When the phone rang, much later that night, she didn't answer it. The answering machine clicked in, and she heard Tom's deep voice leaving a message.

'Flora, it's me. I've been thinking about what you said, and...well, you have a point. It never occurred to me. When I'm at work, everything else is excluded. I don't think of anything except my job. And you're right, I do need to think about other things. About Joey.' He paused. 'About *you*. I'll call you tomorrow morning, OK? Bye, honey. And I'm s—'

The answering machine beeped and cut him off.

Had he just been about to apologise?

But words were easy. Actions were harder. If he wasn't prepared to put Joey first and take more care of himself, this wasn't going to work.

At practically the crack of dawn, the phone rang again. Flora answered it automatically.

'Sorry, did I wake you?' Tom asked.

'Sort of.' She hadn't slept too well.

'I apologise. But I needed to talk to you. About last night.'

'I'm sorry I shouted at you.'

'You were right,' he said softly. 'My life's different now—if

I take risks, it impacts on more than just me. I need to think about that. Properly.' He paused. 'I'm sorry for worrying you.'

'OK.' Flora had no idea what to say next. Never having had a huge row with someone, she didn't have a clue how to make up, either.

'Will you still come for dinner tonight?' he asked.

He still wanted to see her? Or—a nasty thought crept in—was it that he was worried about losing a babysitter?

'Please? And then I can apologise properly, in person.' He sighed. 'I don't want to fight with you, Flora.'

'I don't want to fight with you, either.'

'Then will you still come for dinner? Please?'

'I... OK.'

'Good. See you tonight. And I am sorry.'

'Me, too.'

She thought about it all day. What did you wear when you met your partner's parents for the first time? In the end, she decided to wear the black skirt and teal top she knew Tom liked. She left her hair loose, but put an Alice band in it to keep it off her face. She'd forgotten to ask him if she should bring red or white wine, so she played it safe and bought a decent bottle of each, plus chocolates and a magnetic fishing game for Joey. If it all went pear-shaped, she could play a game or two with Joey, then claim a headache and leave early.

Tom answered the door to her. 'Hi. You look lovely.'

'Thanks.' She felt the betraying colour seep into her face and wished she'd worn make-up, except she was hopeless at anything other than lipstick; her parents had always told her she didn't need to wear it, so she'd never joined the other girls at school in experimenting with eye-shadow and blusher. Ha. Blusher. She blushed way too much as it was.

He drew her into his arms and rested his cheek against her

hair. 'I really am sorry, honey. And you've given me a lot to think about.'

'I'm sorry, too. I was pushy.'

'You,' he said softly, 'were absolutely right.' He kissed her lightly. 'Come in.'

She handed the wine over.

'You really didn't need to bring anything,' he said, 'but thank you. That's really sweet of you.'

Joey rushed over to greet her and gave her a hug. 'For me?' he asked when she handed him the bag.

'For you,' she said with a smile.

He peeked inside. 'Oh, wow! Will you play with me, Flora?'

'If Uncle Tom says there's time before tea, of course I will. Otherwise we'll have a game afterwards,' she promised.

'Cool.' He beamed at her.

'Flora, these are my parents, Thomas and Lisa—Mum and Dad, this is Flora.' Tom introduced them swiftly.

Tom looked very like his father, Flora thought, and Thomas Nicholson was just as tall as his son; though he had hazel eyes, like Joey's. Tom had clearly inherited Lisa's eyes. 'I'm pleased to meet you both,' Flora said shyly, shaking their hands.

'I hope you like roast chicken,' Lisa said. 'It's Joey's favourite.'

'I promised you a proper home-cooked dinner tonight, so you knew I wasn't going to have anything to do with it,' Tom said with a grin, resting his hand on Flora's shoulder.

She smiled, and his parents laughed.

'Can I do anything to help?' Flora asked.

'No, love, you're fine,' Lisa said. 'Go and sit down. You've got time to play that game with Joey if you want to.'

Within five minutes, Flora had Tom and his father sitting on the floor with her and Joey, and Joey was clearly thrilled to have everyone playing with him. As well as pleasing the little boy, the game broke the ice for her, so she found it easy to answer Tom's parents' questions about herself over dinner, about her job and where she lived.

'Flora's got a farm but she used to be scared of the chickens,' Joey said. 'And she's got a way cool dog. He's called Banjo and he's a springer spaniel.'

Tom stared at his nephew, clearly dumbstruck by the fact that he was talking so much.

'She's got a picture of him on her phone,' Joey added. 'Can I show Nanna Lisa, Flora?'

'Sure.' Flora delved into her handbag, retrieved her phone and let Joey show the photo of the dog to his grandmother.

'Very cute,' Lisa said.

'He's an old softie,' Flora said with a smile.

After she'd told Joey a bedtime story and promised him another game of fishing later in the week, Flora helped Lisa wash up.

'You've been really good for Joey,' Lisa said quietly. 'And for Tom. I was so worried about the pair of them. Thomas and I were going to come back from France and help out, but Tom said it wouldn't be fair to any of us. Thomas's arthritis is bad and I'm not as young as I was; I just can't do all the things that a young lad needs people to do with him.' She sighed. 'And Joey went so quiet after the accident. He'd hardly speak; and I can see you've made a huge difference to him. You've really helped bring him back out of his shell.'

'He's a lovely boy,' Flora said, 'a real pleasure to have around.'

'And Tom—you've changed him, too,' Lisa said thoughtfully. 'He's less guarded. He doesn't use those awful jokes as a wall as much as he did.'

'He told me about Ben,' Flora said softly.

Lisa nodded. 'It changed him, when Ben died. He'd never show any emotion after that; he turned everything into a big

joke and never let anyone talk to him about serious things.'
She bit her lip. 'And he adored his big sister. Losing Susie hit
him hard, but he just wouldn't talk about it to anyone—he
clammed up or changed the subject.' She paused, looking
hopeful. 'Has he talked to you about her?' Lisa looked worried sick about her son.

'He has,' Flora reassured her gently. 'It was probably easier
for him to talk to me because he knew I'd been there myself—
I lost both my parents last year.'

'Oh, my dear, I'm so sorry.'

'I don't have any regrets about the past,' Flora said. 'My
parents knew I loved them and I knew they loved me. I
would've liked a bit more time with them, but it just wasn't
to be.' She shrugged. 'I miss them but, the way I see it, I'm
really lucky that I had them for twenty-three years.'

Lisa hugged her. 'Tom's right, you're special.'

Tom—who, on his own mother's admission, wouldn't talk
about serious things—had told his parents that she was special... There was a lump in Flora's throat as she hugged Lisa
back.

She enjoyed the rest of the evening, chatting to Tom's parents over coffee and chocolates, and then realised with a shock
that it was almost ten o'clock. 'I'd better get back,' she said.

'It was lovely to meet you,' Lisa said. 'And Thomas and I
were thinking, you both deserve a night out, so we've booked
a table for you both for tomorrow night at a little place down
the road that's meant to do excellent food. It's our treat, and
we've already paid the bill, so don't argue.' She smiled. 'We're
going to take Joey to the pictures in St Piran's in the afternoon
and have something to eat out afterwards, so you don't have
to worry—we'll have a wonderful time.'

'Thank you,' Tom said, looking stunned. 'That's really nice
of you, Mum.'

'I don't know what to say,' Flora said, 'except thank you. That's so kind.'

'Just enjoy it,' Lisa said, hugging them both.

CHAPTER TEN

THE meal was perfect. Beautifully cooked, beautifully presented...and Flora, for once, found it hard to eat. Because this was the first time that she and Tom had been out on a proper date, on their own. It wasn't like their fun impromptu lunches on the beach or playing in the park with Joey; this suddenly felt very serious and very grown-up. And her shyness was back to hobble her.

Then she caught Tom's eye and realised that he was as nervous as she was.

'You've gone shy on me again, and I don't have a clue why I'm so nervous,' Tom said. 'This is crazy. We talk for hours over lunch and when we're with Joey.'

'But this is different.' She swallowed hard. 'It's a proper date.'

'Our other dates were proper dates,' Tom said. 'But I know what you mean. This feels...' He paused. 'Different.'

With each course, Flora felt more and more awkward.

And then a band started playing.

'Dance with me?' Tom asked.

This was where she really ought to tell him she wasn't good at dancing. She'd never been one for the school discos, and her parents had never played the kind of music that her schoolfriends' parents had played.

'I have two left feet,' she said quietly as he led her onto

the dance floor. 'So I apologise in advance if I tread on your toes.'

'You won't,' Tom said confidently. 'My parents made Susie and I have lessons when we were teenagers. Follow my lead, and this is going to be just fine.'

To her surprise, he was right. Instead of feeling clumsy and gawky, she found herself actually dancing with him—it felt effortless, and as if she were floating. She'd never, ever experienced this before, and she loved it.

'OK?' he asked.

'Much better than OK,' she said. 'I've never been able to do this sort of thing before.'

'All you need is confidence,' Tom said softly. 'And I didn't tell you, you look lovely tonight. Your hair looks amazing.'

Flora felt as if she was glowing.

And when the music slowed down, Tom kissed her.

In public.

And although her knees had gone weak, he was holding her, supporting her, and she didn't fall flat on her face.

The evening went by way too quickly, and Flora wasn't quite ready for it to end when Tom dropped her at home.

'Would you like to come in for a coffee?' she asked.

'I'd like that. Very much.' He smiled at her.

When she switched the kettle on, he stood behind her and wrapped his arms round her waist, drawing her back against him. His mouth traced a path down the sensitive cord at the side of her neck, and she sighed with pleasure.

'Flora.'

She wriggled round in his arms and reached up to touch his cheek, rubbed her thumb along his lower lip.

Tom sighed and drew her thumb into his mouth, sucking hard; a wave of heat slid through her. When he released her thumb, he kept his hand curved round hers; he kissed the centre of her palm and folded her fingers over it, and then traced a path down to where a pulse beat rapidly in her wrist. He touched the tip of his tongue to it, and she shivered. 'Tom.'

Everything seemed to blur, and then she was in his arms, and he was kissing her properly, his mouth demanding and yet enticing at the same time, making her want more. Her arms were wrapped round his neck; his fingertips slipped under the hem of her top and he stroked her skin, the pads of his fingers moving in tiny circles.

His hands settled for a moment at the curve of her waist, then moved round to her midriff. Her heart began to beat faster as his hand moved upwards, so very slowly; she could feel her breasts tightening and her nipples hardening.

And then she panicked.

He sensed it and pulled back. 'What's wrong?'

'I...' She bit her lip, feeling a fool. How could she tell him? 'I'm not good at—at *this*,' she whispered miserably.

'Usually, when a man says that to a woman, he's the one at fault and he's trying to boost his ego at her expense,' Tom said drily. 'Just so you know, I don't think you're bad at this at all.' He stole a kiss. 'You make me feel... I don't know. I'm not good at the verbal stuff. Wonderful.' He took her hand and placed it against his chest. 'Feel that?'

His heart. Beating. Hard. Fast.

'Yes,' she whispered.

'That's what you do to me, my adorable Flora.'

She swallowed hard. He was under a real misapprehension here, and she was going to have to tell him the truth. 'Nobody actually said I was bad at it.'

'You just assumed it?' he guessed.

She shook her head. 'I...um...' Oh, why was it so hard to say?

'Tell me,' he said softly.

She felt colour shoot into her face. 'Did I just say that out loud?'

''Fraid so.' He squeezed her hand. 'What is it? Am I pushing you too fast?'

'It's not that,' she said miserably. She wanted him, all right. He made her feel the way that nobody else had ever done. 'I've always had a quiet life. I never did all the partying as a student. I was too busy studying.' Unable to face the scorn she knew she'd see in his face when he learned the truth, she closed her eyes. 'I'm still a virgin.'

Tom said nothing, and she knew she'd blown it.

'I know. It's pathetic. Twenty-four and never been touched.'

'It's not pathetic in the slightest.' To her surprise, she found herself lifted off her feet and carried over to the sofa. Tom sat down and settled her on his lap. 'You're not pathetic at all,' he said fiercely. 'You're a lot of things, but you're definitely not pathetic.' He traced her lower lip with the pad of his thumb. 'You're beautiful. You're sweet. You make me feel as if I could conquer the world.'

'But?' She could see it in his eyes. A huge, enormous, horrible *but*.

'But,' he said, 'I want to behave honourably towards you.' He grimaced. 'Actually, no, I don't. I want to carry you upstairs and kiss you and touch you until you feel as if you're dissolving. I want to make you feel as amazing as you make me feel.'

She swallowed hard. 'But my virginity's in the way.'

'It's something precious,' he said. 'Not something you should throw away. You should hold out for the right person.'

'So I'll be a virgin on my wedding night? That's...' She shook her head. 'That's so old-fashioned, Tom. I'm twenty-four years old and this is the twenty-first century.' She bit her lip.

'When I was at school, all the cool girls used to laugh at me. Fat, frumpy Flora, they called me. They always said I was so old-fashioned. And I hated it, Tom. I wanted to be cool, just like them.'

'No.' He wrapped his arms round her, pulling her closer. 'You're better than cool. You're real. Genuine. And, just for the record, you're not fat. You're deliciously curvy. And you're not frumpy—you're natural, rather than being caked in gunk.'

'But you're going to leave and go home now. And you're not going to touch me again.' And the knowledge made her feel as if her heart had cracked right down the middle.

'Because I'm trying very hard to do the right thing,' Tom said. 'To be honourable.'

'What if,' she said slowly, 'I don't want you to be honourable?'

His eyes darkened. 'What are you saying?'

'What if…?' she said. 'What if I want to go to bed with you? It's not as if I don't know the theory—I'm a nurse. I just…haven't done the practical side of things before, that's all.'

Colour slashed along his cheekbones. 'Are you sure about this, Flora?'

She was as nervous as hell, and her voice was shaking, but she said the words and meant them. 'I'm sure.'

'Absolutely sure?' he checked.

In answer, she kissed him. Hard.

'No pressure,' he said softly, and kissed her again. 'My beautiful, adorable Flora. Do you have any idea how precious the gift you're giving me is?'

'I want you, Tom,' she whispered.

'I'm with you all the way, honey,' he said, his voice husky. He scooped her up in his arms again and carried her up the stairs.

'What about your back? You were hurt on Friday.'

'I'm fine. Nothing that a hot bath couldn't sort out. And, right now, all I can think of is how much I want to make love with you.' He kissed her, his mouth hot and arousing. 'Which one's your bedroom?'

'On the left.'

He opened the door, then gradually let her down until her feet were touching the floor, keeping her body pressed close to his all the way so that she was left in no doubt of his arousal.

Doubts flickered through her again. A man as gorgeous as Tom had no doubt dated plenty of girls. Girls who knew what they were doing.

'What's the matter?' he asked softly.

'Just...I don't want to disappoint you.'

He switched on the bedside light, then got her to sit down on the edge of the bed and knelt down in front of her. He took both her hands in his. 'Look me in the eye, Flora Loveday.'

She did so.

'Now listen to what I'm telling you. You're not going to disappoint me. *Ever*,' he emphasised. 'And I'm going to do my best to make sure this is good for you. If I do anything that makes you feel uncomfortable, just tell me and I'll stop.' He drew her hands to his mouth. 'You have no idea how much self-control I'm having to use, right now. But I'm going to take this slowly, because I want to enjoy every single second of this. And I want you to enjoy it even more.'

Excitement rippled through her.

'Flora,' he said, his voice low and sensual, 'I'd like to see you.'

She felt incredibly self-conscious, but lifted her arms and let him peel her top up and over her head.

Then she remembered that she was wearing a very plain, functional bra. How she wished she'd bought something frivolous and lacy. She crossed her hands automatically over her breasts, not wanting him to see the boring, frumpy garment.

'You want me to stop?' he asked.

She bit her lip and shook her head. 'It's not that.'

'What, then?' His voice was very, very gentle.

'My bra's horrible. It's embarrassing.'

He smiled at her. 'I have an idea. Let's get it out of the way, so it doesn't spoil this for you. How about I close my eyes and undo your bra without looking?' His smile went all the way up into his eyes and she knew that he was laughing with her, not at her.

'I'm being silly, aren't I?'

'No, you're not—and I want the first time to be good for you,' he said. 'You're beautiful.' He kissed her lightly. 'And now I'm closing my eyes.' He deftly removed her bra and dropped it on the floor.

And then he opened his eyes and sucked in a breath. 'Wow. *Flora*. I don't know what I want to do first—touch you or taste you or just look at you. You're *gorgeous*.'

The expression on his face told her that he was completely sincere; Flora blushed again, but this time from pleasure rather than embarrassment.

He was still kneeling in front of her; he cupped her breasts in his hands, lifting them up and together and teasing her nipples with the pads of his thumbs. 'Seriously, seriously gorgeous. And your skin's so soft.' He swallowed hard. 'Flora, I really need to...'

'Yes,' she whispered, and he dipped his head, closing his mouth round one nipple.

She knew the theory.

But she hadn't been prepared at all for the way Tom made her feel. The surge of desire that ran through her entire body; the hot, wet, tight feeling between her thighs; the need for *more*. More of what, exactly, she wasn't sure, but she needed it. She slid her hands into his hair and drew him closer.

He paid attention to her other nipple, and she arched against him. 'Tom,' she whispered.

He stopped and looked up at her; and she noticed just how wide his pupils were. Huge with desire. 'Yes, honey?'

'I want to see you, too.'

He smiled. 'OK.' He removed his tie and dropped it on the floor, then undid the top button of his shirt and spread his arms. 'I'm in your hands. Do what you want with me.'

All hers.

Wow.

She unbuttoned his shirt, revealing strong pectoral muscles and a sprinkling of hair on his chest. 'You're beautiful, Tom.'

She slid the soft cotton from his shoulders and enjoyed stroking his bare skin, feeling his musculature tightening under her touch.

'My turn now?' he asked. At her nod, he said, 'Stand up.' He unzipped her skirt and let it slide to the floor; her slip went the same way, and then he slowly peeled her tights down, stroking her skin as he moved lower. 'Gorgeous. And all mine,' he said, pressing a kiss against her navel.

Flora sucked in her stomach, feeling self-conscious, and he stood up, too.

'We need to even this up a bit.'

She knew what he meant. Her hands were shaking as she undid the button of his trousers and then lowered his zip; she eased the material down over his hips and he stepped out of his trousers, heeling off his shoes and his socks as he did so. His underpants outlined his arousal, and he was bigger than she'd expected. Help. This was going to be the very first time; she wasn't sure whether she felt more nervous or excited.

Maybe it showed in her face, she thought, when Tom said

softly, 'Let me tell you how this is going to be. I'm going to touch you, and kiss you, all over. You can do whatever you like to me. And then...' his breath hitched '...then I'm going to make you completely mine.'

Gently, he lifted her up and laid her against the pillows, then climbed onto the bed beside her. He kissed and stroked his way down her body, clearly taking notice of what made her react more strongly because he lingered in some places and skated over others. He took his time exploring her with his mouth and hands, from the hollows of her collarbones down to the soft undersides of her breasts, her navel, her hipbones.

And then, just when she thought he was going to cup her sex with his hand and deal with the ache inside her, he shifted and started from her feet, stroking her insteps and kissing the hollows of her ankles. She discovered that the backs of her knees was definitely an erogenous zone; her sex felt hot and wet and tight, and it was as if her body was slowly being wound up to a pitch.

Finally, he slid his fingertips under the waistband of her knickers and drew the material down.

'You're so beautiful,' he whispered, 'absolutely gorgeous—and I need to touch you, Flora. I really, really need to touch you.'

'Yes.' She barely recognised her voice, it was so low and husky.

He kept his eyes locked with hers as he stroked her inner thigh. Anticipation made her breath hitch; she had no idea how this was going to be, how it was going to make her feel.

And then, at last, he let one finger glide across her sex, and she found out.

Like nothing on earth.

A shiver of pure desire went through her. 'Oh, Tom,' she whispered.

He wasn't going to...?

Her cheeks flamed as he knelt between her thighs.

And then she stopped thinking at all as his tongue flicked lightly over her clitoris. She slid her hands into his hair, sighing his name—not really knowing what she was asking for, but knowing that he was driving her crazy.

He teased her with his mouth and his fingers. Her body tensed even further, to the point where she didn't think she was going to be able to handle any more, and then suddenly the pressure peaked and released, shocking her with the depths of pleasure. She cried out his name.

He shifted up to hold her close. 'OK?'

'I think so.' She felt the colour in her face deepen. 'I didn't realise it would be like that. It was incredible, Tom.'

He stroked her face. 'Do you know how it makes me feel, knowing I'm the first person who's been able to make you feel like this? As if I'm king of the world,' he said softly.

'I feel pretty good myself,' she said, her voice shaking.

'This is just the start, honey,' he promised.

She wasn't sure when he'd removed his underpants, but when he climbed off the bed she was left in no doubt of just how big and how strong Tom Nicholson was. Though she knew he'd be gentle with her; he'd already given her pleasure she'd never dreamed existed, and he was planning more.

He found his wallet in his pocket and removed a condom.

'OK?' he asked. 'If you want to wait, that's fine.'

'No—I want you, Tom.' I want you to love me, she thought—and realised in that moment that she loved him, absolutely. It didn't matter that she hadn't known him that long; he was kind, gorgeous and strong, and she trusted him to keep her safe.

He rolled the condom on and knelt between her thighs, nudging them apart, then bent to kiss her. 'You're beautiful,

Flora. You take my breath away. And I've wanted this almost since the first moment I met you.'

A thrill went through her at his words. 'You're beautiful, too.'

Slowly, slowly, he eased into her. She felt a sharp twinge and he must've realised it too, because he paused, giving her time to get used to his weight and the feel of him.

'OK, honey?' he asked.

She nodded. 'Very OK.'

'You're sure I'm not hurting you?'

'Not any more.'

He kissed her, then lifted her hips so he could push deeper into her. And then Flora discovered that he'd been telling the truth, that the first climax was just the start. Pleasure started to build and build again; warmth spread through her, coiling and pulling tight, and then the release hit her.

She felt his body tighten inside hers; she looked into his eyes and saw them go wide with pleasure as his own climax hit.

He held her tightly afterwards. 'My adorable Flora,' he said softly.

Finally, he gently withdrew from her. 'I'll be back in a moment, honey.' He was completely unselfconscious as he left the bed, but Flora wriggled in embarrassment. She couldn't just lie there, naked, waiting for him to come back. Should she get dressed, or would he expect her to stay in bed? Unsure, and feeling ridiculously shy, she grabbed the duvet to cover herself.

When Tom came back, he was smiling. 'You, Flora Loveday, are a wonderful woman, and I feel incredibly privileged.'

He climbed into bed beside her and pulled her into his arms. 'Right now, I just want to hold you; it feels wonderful to have you in my arms, your skin against mine.' He brushed a kiss over her temples. 'What I'd really like to do is fall asleep with you in my arms and wake up with you in the morning, but I can't do that—it's not fair to Mum and Dad.'

'What's the time?' She glanced at her bedside clock. 'They'll already be worried about you.'

'It's almost midnight. They won't be expecting me back just yet—they knew when they booked the table that there was a band as well, and they'll guess that I'll have coffee with you.'

She bit her lip. 'I didn't actually make you any coffee.'

He smiled. 'You can remedy that some other time. I'm not going anywhere and you sure as hell aren't moving from my arms right now.'

Gradually her tension eased, and it felt good to lie in his arms like this, with her head against his shoulder. Little by little, her eyes closed, and Flora finally fell asleep, warm and comfortable.

CHAPTER ELEVEN

Tom wished he could stay in bed beside Flora all night—but he couldn't. His carefree bachelor life was gone now; and, even though he knew that his nephew would be perfectly safe with his grandparents, he also knew that it wouldn't be fair to them if he stayed here with Flora. They'd worry that something had happened to him, and the car crash that had taken Susie and Kevin from them would be uppermost in their minds. He couldn't put them through that kind of torment. And it wouldn't be fair to Joey, either; the little boy needed security, and seeing Tom there in the morning would help.

Reluctantly, and careful not to wake Flora as he did so, Tom wriggled out of the bed and dressed swiftly. She looked so peaceful that he couldn't bear to wake her. But he also wasn't just going to walk out and abandon her. Not when she'd given him something so very precious.

He tiptoed downstairs, and Banjo was instantly alert.

'Shh, she's asleep. Don't bark,' Tom said softly.

He went over to the memo pad by her phone and scribbled a quick note.

You look adorable, asleep—couldn't bring myself to wake you! Have to get back to Joey, but will call you in the morning. T x

He left the note propped against the kettle, where she'd be bound to find it in the morning, made a brief fuss of Banjo and persuaded the dog back to his basket, then quietly let himself out of the house.

Driving back to his flat, he thought about Flora. The way she'd responded to him. The wonder in her eyes.

And then it hit him.

He'd felt that exact same sense of wonder. And not just because he'd known that this was a big deal for her—it had been a big deal for him, too. He'd never really let himself connect with anyone in the past: but tonight he'd connected with Flora. Heart and soul. It was like nothing he'd ever experienced before.

Oh, hell.

He'd always promised himself that he'd never let his relationships get serious. It wasn't fair to expect someone else to face the burden of the risks he took every day in his job.

And yet he'd done it. Fallen for her completely. Her warmth, her kindness, the sweetness in her smile—everything about her drew him. And, at some point over the last couple of weeks, he'd stopped guarding his heart. More than that, he'd actually given his heart to her. Freely and completely.

Oh, double hell.

What did he do now?

Because now the whole world was different. Two months ago, he'd been a carefree bachelor, enjoying life as a single man. Now he was a stand-in father to someone who'd lost almost his whole world—and he couldn't risk letting Joey lose the bits he had left. And he wasn't a carefree bachelor any more: he was involved with Flora. Really involved with her, from the centre of his heart.

Letting Joey down wasn't an option.

Un-falling in love with Flora also wasn't an option; being with her had shown him that, before, he'd only been living part of a life. There was much more to it than working hard, and playing just as hard. Football was fun, but teaching Joey how to dribble and score goals was even better. And as for parties with loud music…maybe he'd suddenly grown up overnight, but he discovered that he'd rather have a walk on the beach and a soundtrack of laughter.

With Flora and Joey, he could have a real family. The same kind of love his parents had. The same kind of happiness his sister had had.

But Flora had made him think, the other night, and now he knew that the happiness and love were bitter-sweet: at any time a fire could turn rogue and take him from them. He'd be forced to let them down in the most fundamental way, unable to fight his way back to them.

On paper, it was easy. All he had to do was take the danger out of his life so they wouldn't have to shoulder the risk of losing him.

Change his job.

In real life it wasn't quite as simple as that. As he'd told her the other night, fighting fires and rescuing people wasn't just his job, it was who he *was*. He'd joined the fire brigade at eighteen, straight after his A levels, and had never looked back. How could he walk away from the job he loved, from what'd he'd done for almost half his life and the whole of his adult life?

Without that, he didn't have a clue what he'd do.

But maybe the small hours of the morning wasn't the best time to make decisions. He needed to sit down and work out what all his options were. Make a rational decision. Do the right thing.

When he let himself quietly into the flat, he discovered that his mother was waiting up for him. 'Did you have a nice time?'

'Wonderful, thanks,' he said as he sat next to her on the sofa.

'Sure? You look a bit worried,' Lisa said.

'I'm fine. I just realised I'm a bit late back,' he fibbed, 'and I didn't want you to be worrying about me.'

'It doesn't matter that you're six feet four and thirty-two years old. You're still my baby and always will be, so I'll always worry about you,' Lisa said with a smile, ruffling his hair.

'Is Joey all right?'

'Yes, and we all ate far too much ice cream, was lovely—just like taking you and Susie to the cinema when you were little.'

'Mmm, I remember.' He gave her a wistful smile. 'I had a really happy childhood, Mum.'

'Good. That's what we wanted.'

'That's what I want for Joey, too.' He sighed. 'And I'm not making a very good job of it. Flora's helped a huge amount, but…I'm never going to be good enough, Mum.'

'Don't do yourself down, love. Joey's been through a lot. But he knows you're there for him and he knows you love him, and that's going to help him through,' Lisa said. 'Don't worry. It's all going to be fine. You're doing your best, and that's all anyone can ask.' She kissed the top of his head. 'I'd better let you get some sleep. See you in the morning.'

Tom lay awake for much of the night, trying to work out what he ought to do. But he still hadn't come to a decent compromise the next morning. He showered, dressed and made himself a mug of tea, then Joey appeared.

'I hear you ate lots of ice cream yesterday,' Tom said as he poured his nephew a glass of milk.

Joey nodded.

'How was the film?'

'Good. Can we play fishing?'

Tom smiled. 'Sure we can.'

They were in the middle of their third game when his mother emerged from the bedroom, wrapped in a towelling robe and yawning.'

'The kettle's hot, Mum. Do you want some tea?' Tom asked.

'Thank you, darling.'

When Joey went to get dressed, Tom asked quietly, 'Mum, would you mind very much if I sneaked over and had breakfast with Flora this morning?'

Lisa raised an eyebrow. 'She's really important to you, isn't she?'

He smiled. 'I'm not answering that one.'

'Well, she's the first girl you've actually let us meet—and that tells me a lot. She's lovely,' Lisa said. 'I like her very much, and I think she'll make you happy.'

'Mmm, but it's whether I'll be able to make her happy.' He bit his lip. 'I'm a firefighter.'

'And she's a nurse, so she's going to understand the demands of your job a lot more than someone who doesn't work in the emergency services.'

'Maybe.'

'Are you thinking about giving it up, love?'

'I don't know.' He sighed. 'Mum, being a firefighter. It's who I am. I can't see myself as anything else—the world wouldn't feel right. But…I've got Joey to think of now, and Flora, and… It's a lot for them to have to put up with. All that worry.' He shook his head. 'I can't work this out.'

'And I'm not the person you should be talking it over with,' Lisa said softly. 'Find out what Flora thinks.'

He already knew what she thought. That his job was dangerous and he took reckless risks that could mean Joey was left alone.

'Talk it over with her. But don't rush into anything.'

He smiled wryly. 'Yes, you're right. It's too fast. I've only known her for a few days.'

'That's not what I meant—when you meet the right one, you'll know.' Lisa smiled. 'And I think you might just have met your "the one", in Flora. I've never seen you like this about anyone else. No, I meant you need to talk things through and weigh up all your options, not just rush in and do what you think is the right thing. Now go and have breakfast with your girl. We'll see you later.'

'Where are you going?' Joey asked when he came back from his room, fully dressed and wearing odd socks.

'To see Flora,' Tom told him.

'Can I come?'

'Another time,' Lisa said, 'because I want you to teach me how to make that lovely French toast you say Flora makes. How about being Chef Joey and taking Grandpa some breakfast in bed?'

Tom gave his mother a grateful look, and kissed both her and Joey goodbye. 'I'll be back soon. Flora has to be at work at half past eight.'

He called in at the out-of-town supermarket on the way to the farm and bought flowers and croissants. When he rang the doorbell, Flora took a while to answer, and she was wearing her dressing gown, so he'd clearly woken her.

'Perfect timing,' he said with a grin. 'This means I can have breakfast with you and then I can have a shower with you.'

'Tom Nicholson, that's shocking!' But she was smiling. 'I wasn't expecting to see you this morning.'

'Mum and Dad are with Joey and I wanted to see you for breakfast.' He handed her the flowers. 'These, because you're beautiful.'

She sniffed them. 'Thank you, they're lovely.'

'And these, because... Oh, wait. Forget about the healthy

eating stuff you do with your classes. These, because they're the nicest breakfast ever.'

She peered into the bag and laughed. 'I love croissants, too. And I have posh strawberry jam from the farm shop.'

'Brilliant.' He paused. 'Did you find my note this morning?'

She smiled. 'Yes. I have to admit, I felt a bit strange when I woke up and you weren't there, but I knew you had to get back for Joey.'

'I wish I'd woken with you.' He stroked her face. 'You look so cute when you're asleep. Like a little dormouse.'

'A dormouse?' She raised an eyebrow. 'Thanks. I think.' But her eyes were sparkling.

She made them both coffee, put the flowers in water, and Tom thoroughly enjoyed feeding her croissants and licking jam from her fingers. Not to mention having a shower with her after breakfast.

'Tom, I'm going to be late!' she said, sounding shocked, when they finally made it back to her bedroom and she glanced at her clock.

'No, you won't. I'll drop you at the surgery. Do you need your car this afternoon?'

'Only to get home.'

'That's easy, then. I'll pick you up,' Tom said. 'I thought maybe we could take Joey out ten-pin bowling and then eat out at that new burger place.'

'That'd be lovely. Provided you let it be my treat,' she added. 'And I insist on that.'

Flora made it to the surgery with three minutes to spare. Kate Tremayne smiled at Flora as she walked in. 'I'm not going to ask,' Kate said, 'but it's lovely to see you sparkling like this.'

Was what she'd just done with Tom so obvious? Flora felt herself blush to the roots of her hair. 'Um…'

Kate laughed. 'It couldn't happen to a nicer couple. And Tom's a sweetie.'

Flora was gobsmacked. 'How did you know?'

Kate raised an eyebrow. 'Penhally's not exactly a huge place—and when you're holding hands on the beach with someone, you can expect someone to spot you.' She paused. 'And Nick took me out to dinner last night. The food's good at The Mackerel, isn't it?'

'You were there?' Flora looked at her, aghast. 'I'm so sorry I was rude and didn't say anything to you. I just didn't see you.'

Kate smiled. 'I know, love. You two only had eyes for each other.'

Flora felt her blush deepen. 'I guess so.'

She discovered during her surgery that morning, while doing a blood-pressure check for one of her patients, that Kate hadn't been the only person to see her and Tom at the restaurant.

Worse still, Mrs Evans, whose venous ulcer she was dressing, had seen Tom kissing her goodbye in the surgery car park that morning.

'Your young man's a lovely boy. He rescued my neighbour's dog from the river last week, and he never made a fuss when Goldie bit him—he's a smashing young lad,' Mrs Evans said. 'He's a keeper, you mark my words.'

By lunchtime, Flora realised that quite a few people in Penhally had already got her and Tom married off, and her protests that it was still very early days were just ignored.

'You make a lovely couple, dear,' was the standard response.

She just hoped that Tom wasn't getting the same kind of comments, or he might start avoiding her.

But he was there with Joey to meet her from work, and Joey greeted her with a hug. They made a quick stop back at the farmhouse to let Banjo out and feed him, then went off ten-pin bowling. Tom put the bumper bars up on their lane and got Joey to use the ramp, and Joey was thrilled to get a strike.

This, Flora thought, was what it felt like to be a family.
And she loved it.

Josh scanned the hospital canteen as he walked in: force of habit. Most of the time, Megan wasn't there. It was as if she had some kind of radar system that told her when he was having a break so she could avoid him.

But then he saw her at a table in a quiet corner. On her own.

It was too good a chance to miss. He headed straight over to her table. 'Megan.'

Her eyes widened. 'I'm about to go.'

'Don't go,' he said softly. 'Stay and talk to me. I'm just going to get myself a sandwich. Can I get you a coffee?'

'I…'

She was wavering; hope bloomed within him. 'I saw you at the football match, the other week.' And she'd avoided him at the hospital ever since.

'I was just passing.'

That might've been true, because the football pitch was halfway between St Piran's and Penhally, where Megan lived. But she wouldn't be 'just passing' after her shift at that time of the morning. Not that he was going to call her on it. He didn't want her to bolt. 'Stay and have coffee with me?'

Hell, she was beautiful. Even with her hair pulled back for work, she was beautiful. And he knew exactly what her hair looked like when it was tumbled over her shoulders. Tumbled over his pillow. Soft and silky and…

He dragged in a breath. Not now. He needed to take this slowly. Get her to talk to him again. 'Please, Megan?'

She looked wary, but she nodded. 'OK.'

Josh wanted to punch the air. 'Back in a second, OK?'

Even though he grabbed the first sandwich he could see from the chiller, by the time he'd paid for them and two coffees, he could see that Megan had changed her mind.

'Sorry. My bleep just went.'

She might've been using it as an excuse; then again, it might not be. Her department was busy.

But this felt just a little too convenient.

'Sorry,' she said again, and fled.

Tom and Joey met Flora at the surgery on Tuesday with a picnic basket; although it was cold, it was dry and for once not windy. They ate sandwiches on the beach, then went for a walk to collect shells.

'So have you thought any more about going to the football dinner with me?' Tom asked.

'I'm still thinking about it,' she admitted.

'Sure. I don't want to rush you.'

Which made her feel even worse, because he was being so patient with her. The dinner was less than a week away, and there would be a cut-off point for getting tickets.

But she still couldn't help thinking that someone as popular as Tom could have absolutely anyone he wanted. Was he only spending time with her for Joey's sake? And besides, despite what they'd shared on Sunday night, he hadn't actually said he loved her—just that she made him feel amazing.

Was she expecting too much? All she'd ever wanted was someone who loved her for herself. Could Tom be that man?

And why couldn't she shake the feeling that this was all going to go horribly wrong?

Flora was miserable all evening; and, at the surgery the next morning, Kate Tremayne came in to the treatment room and closed the door behind her.

'Are you OK, Flora?'

Flora summoned a smile. 'Of course I am,' she lied.

'Don't fib.' Kate put her hands on her hips. 'You've got five minutes before your first patient. Now talk.'

Flora opened her mouth to say that nothing was wrong—but ended up spilling all her doubts. She finished miserably, 'He's asked me to go to the football league dinner with him, and I don't have a clue what to wear—I don't exactly go to posh dinners. And, if I do go, he's going to be surrounded with people all night and I won't know anyone there.'

Kate squeezed her hand. 'Love, first of all, Tom sees you exactly as you are—and you're lovely. You probably will know people there, because there are a few medics who play in the league. So I think you should say yes. Go to St Piran on Saturday morning, buy yourself a fabulous dress, and knock his socks off.'

Flora was none too sure that she'd be able to do that, but she knew that Kate meant well. 'Thanks, Kate. I will,' she said.

On Thursday, Flora went to the science museum with Tom and Joey. Not having children of her own, she'd never visited it before, and she loved it as much as Joey did.

Tom and Joey insisted on trying every single one of the interactive exhibits—from Joey standing inside a giant bubble, through to doing a duet on the giant keyboard where you pressed the notes with your feet, and making a tornado inside a bottle. The bubble show—where the woman on stage actually managed to set bubbles on fire—and the planetarium shows were also a huge hit with Joey. And Flora discovered a whole heap of leaflets they could take home to make their own experiments. 'We're definitely going to have to try making our own slime—what colour d'you reckon, Joey?'

'Green,' Joey said enthusiastically.

She laughed. 'Good call.'

She took photographs of Tom and his nephew together, having fun.

'Excuse me, love.' A middle-aged woman smiled at her. 'Would you like me to take a picture of the three of you? I know how it is when you're always the one behind the camera.'

The three of them.

Like a family.

'That'd be wonderful,' Flora said warmly, and returned the compliment by taking a picture of the woman with her grandchildren.

Tom had reverted completely to being a child, and Flora found his enthusiasm adorable. Over lunch, he looked through Flora's leaflets.

'Making a plastic out of milk? Oh, now, we have to do that. Hey, Joey, did you know this is how they used to make windows for aeroplanes in the Second World War?'

'Really?' Joey asked, wide-eyed.

'That's what it says here.'

'Wow.' Then Joey smiled. 'This is the best day ever.'

Flora, seeing the look of relief mingled with delight on Tom's face, had a lump in her throat.

Tom hugged his nephew, and then Flora. 'I'm having a brilliant day here, too, and I wouldn't have wanted to share this with anyone else except you two.'

'Snap,' Flora said. 'I never knew this sort of place could be so much fun.'

'It's just the best,' Joey said.

* * *

That evening, when Joey was in bed, Tom said, 'So what do you want to do on Saturday?'

She frowned. 'I thought you were going to the football dinner?'

'Not without you,' he said. 'And you've been avoiding the subject, so I know you don't really want to go.'

She sighed. 'Tom, they're your friends and it's something you all look forward to at the end of the season, isn't it?'

'Absolutely,' he agreed, 'but if it's the choice of going to the dinner or spending time with you, it's a no-brainer.'

He'd really give up something he was looking forward to, for her? She remembered what Kate had said. *Tom sees you exactly as you are...I think you should say yes.*

She stroked his face. 'Tom, I'm not going to stop you going.'

'I don't want to go without you. Come with me, honey.' He stole a kiss. 'I know you're probably worrying that you won't know anyone there, but they're a nice bunch and they won't shut you out.'

They had at the football match, Flora thought.

Although she didn't say it aloud, her reservations must have shown on her face because Tom said softly, 'You'll be part of the crowd because you're with me—you're my girl.'

And this time he'd be with her instead of running around on a pitch, so it might be different. She took a deep breath. It was time to be brave about this. 'What's the dress code?'

'Black tie.'

Which meant a cocktail dress—and she didn't possess one. 'I'd better go shopping, then.'

'You'll really come with me?'

She nodded.

He hugged her. 'I'm so glad. I'll go shopping with you, if you like.'

'No. Joey would hate being dragged round dress shops.' She

smiled. 'And anyway, I'd like to surprise you.' She thought again about what Kate said. *Knock his socks off.* Maybe, just maybe, it was time to stop being shy, frumpy Flora and show Tom that she was a woman who was worthy of him.

CHAPTER TWELVE

On Saturday afternoon, Flora drove to St Piran. She couldn't see any dresses that would suit her in the first three shops she went into, and the assistants in the fourth turned out to be really snooty; she didn't even approach them, because she could see them mentally sizing her and wondering what on earth she thought she was doing in their shop when they were so clearly in the market for people five dress sizes smaller.

But then she saw a beautiful floaty dress in the window of a little boutique. It probably wasn't right for her, but maybe there was something else that would catch her eye.

'Can I help you?' the assistant asked.

'I'm just looking,' Flora said.

'For anything special?'

The assistant looked genuinely interested and didn't give the impression that she would only be interested in selling size-eight clothes. 'I'm going to a black-tie dinner. I need a cocktail dress, and I don't have a clue what will suit me.'

The assistant's eyes lit up. 'Would you trust me to pick something for you?'

'I… Well, sure.'

To her surprise, the assistant didn't even ask her size. She looked through the racks and picked out several dresses in very bright colours—the kind of colours that Flora never wore.

'Should I have a black dress?' Flora asked.

The assistant smiled. 'Your colouring's gorgeous, so don't hide yourself in black.'

Help, Flora thought. I don't want to stand out from the crowd.

The assistant put a gentle hand on her shoulder. 'Is he special?'

'Yes.'

'Then you'll stand out from the crowd for him anyway, so you might as well do it properly.'

Flora was beginning to agree until the assistant handed her a bright turquoise dress. It had a wrap front with a V-neck and wide shoulder straps, plus layers of silk georgette in the skirt, and it was much shorter than the kind of thing she normally wore, finishing just at the knee. She looked dubiously at it. 'I don't think I'm thin enough to wear this.'

'This shape will look fantastic on you. Just try it on and see what you think,' the assistant coaxed. 'If you hate it we'll try something else.'

Flora looked at a dress with a much higher neck. 'Something like that.'

'That's absolutely wrong for you—you need to be tall and a stick insect to suit that style,' the assistant said. 'You're much better off with something that flatters you, like this, or maybe an Empire-line dress.'

Flora knew when she was beaten and tried the dress on. To her surprise, it looked amazing.

'Just what I thought. Hang on, you need accessories.' A couple of moments later, the assistant returned with a turquoise and silver pendant, and a pair of silver strappy shoes with medium kitten heels. 'Try these. And if you wear your hair up with just a couple of curls tumbling down to soften your face...' She demonstrated, and Flora stared at herself in the mirror, barely recognising herself.

'And you're so lucky—you have fabulous skin. All you need

is a touch of eyeliner, mascara and lipstick—you're going to look amazing, and he's going to think he's the luckiest man on earth,' the assistant finished with a smile.

'Thank you—you've been really kind.'

The assistant smiled. 'My pleasure. It's lovely to be asked for advice instead of having someone come in with set ideas who refuses to try something that'd really suit them.' She paused. 'Forgive me for being rude, but you know the other way of giving yourself loads of confidence?'

'No.' Flora knew she needed all the help she could get on that front.

'Really, *really* nice underwear.'

Flora loved the silk and lace confections that the assistant showed her, and couldn't resist a buying matching set. The whole outfit came to quite a bit more than she'd intended to pay, but she didn't care. In this underwear and this dress, she was going to feel fantastic—and she was going to knock Tom's socks off.

On impulse, she texted Kate when she got home. *'Thanks for your advice. Found really lovely dress.'*

Two minutes later, her phone rang. 'That's great. What about your hair and make-up?' Kate asked.

'The shop assistant said I should wear my hair up. I was going to see if Maureen could fit me in this afternoon at the salon.'

'On a Saturday afternoon in half-term, you'll be lucky.' Kate paused. 'Let me come over and do your hair and make-up, then I can see the dress as well.'

'Kate, I can't ask you to do that.'

'You're not asking, I'm telling you,' Kate retorted.

It was the work of only a few minutes. When Flora looked in the mirror, she could hardly believe it was her. Kate hadn't caked her with make-up, and yet her eyes looked huge and luminous, and her mouth was a perfect rosebud.

'You're going to have an amazing time.' Kate hugged her. 'Let yourself be happy with Tom, Flora. You deserve each other.'

Tom arrived at seven to pick her up. When she opened the door, he didn't say a word, and Flora's heart plummeted. She'd thought she looked good. Had she got it so wrong? And then Tom blew out a breath. 'Flora. You— I— You…' He shook his head. 'I'm gibbering. Sorry. You look so fantastic, I can't remember how to speak. That dress… God, I want to carry you upstairs to bed right now and forget about the dinner dance.'

Flora was lost for words.

'But I'm not going to,' Tom continued, 'because I want to show you off.' He smiled at her. 'You always look lovely to me, but tonight…tonight, you're *glowing*.'

Confidence, she thought. Confidence that Tom had given her.

When they arrived at the dance, as Flora expected, Tom was in demand; but he kept his arm round her the whole time and introduced her to everyone on his table. A couple of them knew her anyway from the village, but to her pleasure everyone seemed to accept her.

'Weren't you at the football match, the other week?' one of them asked.

Flora bit her lip. 'Um, yes.'

'I didn't realise you were with Tom or I'd have asked you to come over and join us,' she said. 'You must've thought we were all so snooty.'

'I did feel a bit out of place,' Flora admitted.

'I'm so sorry. Tom never brings his girlfriends to anything, so I just assumed you were with another crowd. Well, I'm Cindy, and it's lovely to meet you.' She beamed at Flora. 'And it's especially lovely seeing our Tom so happy.'

Over the next few minutes, Flora discovered that, actually,

she *was* a part of Tom's crowd. She was included in the general teasing about how the wives forced the men to hold the league dinner to make up for all those weekend afternoons spent freezing on the sidelines of a football pitch and the amount of scrubbing they had to do to get the mud out of their kit. She discovered that people were interested in what she did, and interested in her opinion. It wasn't just the champagne that made her feel heady: it was Tom, because he made sure that he was sitting next to her with his arm round her shoulders, more or less telling the whole world that she was his.

Megan was really beginning to regret accepting the invitation to the football league dinner. If she'd known that Josh would be there, she wouldn't have come.

Oh, who was she kidding? Seeing him was torture—and yet not seeing him was just as bad.

This whole thing was a mess. No way was she a home wrecker, the sort of woman who destroyed someone else's marriage on a whim. Her feelings for Josh—despite the fact she'd tried to bury them for all those years—were still the same. But she knew it wasn't going to lead anywhere. How could it? Too much had happened.

And there was Rebecca.

Beautiful, fragile Rebecca.

No, she couldn't be the one to destroy Josh's marriage. To hurt another woman the way that she'd been hurt.

When Tom was dancing with Flora, a tall, glamorous, slinky blonde came up to them. 'Tom. Make sure you save a dance for me, yes?'

Tom simply smiled. 'Sorry. Tonight I'm dancing with my girl, and only my girl—and anyone who wants to dance with her is just going to be disappointed, too.'

'Tom, I'm not that insecure,' Flora said. Not any more. 'If you want to dance with your friends, that's fine.'

'That's the point.' Tom stole a kiss and drew her closer. 'There's only one person I want to dance with tonight. She's in my arms, right now—and that's how it's staying.'

'Dance with me?'

No. Tell him no. Tell him you don't dance.

And yet Megan found herself on the dance floor with Josh.

And he *would* choose to show off with a waltz. Typical Josh.

'I've missed you,' he said. 'You've been avoiding me.'

'You know why.'

'How would I know, when you never talk to me, Megan?'

A muscle flickered in her jaw. 'There's nothing to talk about, Josh.'

Josh's eyes became pleading. 'Megan.'

'You have a wife,' she said crisply, taking a step back that forced him to drop his hands from the dance hold. 'Maybe you should be talking to her. Go home, Josh.' And, just to make sure that he couldn't follow her, she headed for the ladies' toilets.

Josh stared after her. Hell, he hadn't meant to upset her. He just wanted to... No, he wanted *her*. And he realised yet again what a huge mistake he'd made, all those years back. He should never have married Rebecca; he'd tried to anaesthetise his feelings and in the end he'd been unfair to all of them. Himself included.

So what now? He and Rebecca didn't want the same things any more. They'd agreed before they'd married that there would be no children; and now Rebecca had changed her mind, was desperate for a baby; but Josh knew that having a baby wouldn't repair their broken marriage. If anything, their marriage would crack even further under the strain. And Josh had lived in a family fractured by the pressure of children. He'd been forced to take the place of his excuse of a father—of course he couldn't have stood by and watched his mother struggle on her own—and no way did he want to go back to that. One generation of that was enough.

Frustrated, hurt and completely confused, Josh headed for the bar.

'Are you all right?'

Megan didn't even look at the woman who had just walked into the toilets. 'Yes,' she fibbed.

'You don't look it. Can I get you a glass of water or something?'

'No, but thanks for offering.' She looked up, this time, and recognised the concerned-looking woman in front of her. Flora Loveday, the school nurse. 'I'll be fine. Just a bit of a headache.' And a whole lot of heartache, otherwise known as Dr Josh O'Hara. Megan forced a smile to her face. 'Are you having a nice time tonight?'

Flora simply glowed. 'Yes. Tom's danced with me all night.'

'Tom the firefighter? He's lovely.' Megan had worked with him a couple of times. He reminded her of Josh—everybody's friend, full of good humour and charm—except she didn't think that Tom was the type to lie, the way Josh had lied to her.

'Yes. I still can't believe how lucky I am. I never expected to find...' Flora paused, looking dismayed. 'Megan? What's wrong?'

Megan scrubbed the tear away. 'I'm fine.' There wasn't a cure for heartache. Unless she could excise Josh from her heart—and she hadn't managed to do that in eight years of trying. 'I think I'll get a taxi home.'

'Let me call it for you, and I'll sit with you while you're waiting,' Flora offered. 'Have you taken anything for your headache yet?' She rummaged in her handbag. 'I've got some paracetamol, if you need it.'

'No, I just need some fresh air and some sleep. You know how busy things get at a hospital.'

'True,' Flora agreed.

Megan splashed water on her face, then called a taxi on her mobile phone.

Flora went out to the reception area with her; on the way, she caught Tom's eye and gestured that she'd be a few minutes. She saw Megan into the taxi, then went back to Tom, who was sitting back at their table, chatting to his friends.

'Everything all right?' he asked as she joined him.

'Megan—you know, the paediatrician from St Piran's?— had a bit of a headache. I waited with her until her taxi arrived.'

'That's my Flora,' Tom said softly, stealing a kiss. 'Looking after everyone.'

'Do you mind?'

'It's one of the things I adore about you,' Tom said, stroking her face. 'My adorable Flora.'

They danced together for the rest of the evening; and Flora found herself disappointed when the band finally stopped playing.

'Come on. I'll drive you home,' Tom said.

Flora was still high on dancing with him all evening. Enough to take a risk when she'd unlocked the front door. She hadn't quite finished knocking his socks off, yet. 'Tom, your parents are with Joey tonight, aren't they?'

'Yes.'

'Are they expecting you home?'

He went very still. 'What are you asking, Flora?'

'I'm asking you to stay the night with me.' She lifted her chin. 'To sleep with me. And wake up with me.'

He moistened his lower lip. 'Are you sure about that?'

'Very sure.'

He smiled. 'Give me two minutes to make a phone call.'

'And I'll let Banjo out while you're doing that.'

By the time she'd called the dog back in and locked the front door, Tom had finished his call.

'OK?' she asked.

He nodded.

She smiled. 'Good. And now I'm taking you to bed.' She took his hand and led him up the stairs to her room. The curtains were already drawn but she didn't put the overhead light on; instead, she switched on a string of fairy lights that she'd draped above the bed earlier.

'Wow. This is like a princess's boudoir,' Tom said.

'Which makes you Prince Charming, yes?'

'Me, I'm just a humble firefighter,' he said with a grin.

'No, you're gorgeous. And you're all mine.'

He laughed. 'If this is what champagne does to you, remind me to keep a bottle in the fridge at all times.'

'It's not the champagne,' she said. 'It's you.' He'd given her the confidence that made her feel as if she could do anything.

Slowly, she undressed him; she untied his bow-tie first, then removed his jacket.

Tom tried to undo the zip at the back of her dress but she wagged a finger at him. 'Uh-uh. I'm in charge.'

Her face was very serious; Tom hid his amusement, not wanting to hurt her. Flora couldn't be bossy if she tried. But he liked the surge of confidence; tonight, she simply sparkled. 'In that case, honey, I'm completely in your hands—do what you want with me.'

'Good.' She plugged her MP3 player into a set of speakers by her bed, and soft jazz filled the room. She stood on tiptoe and kissed him, then finished undoing the buttons of his shirt, sliding the material off his shoulders.

He waited for her to hang it over the back of a chair, knowing that she was the tidy sort.

As if she'd guessed what he was thinking, she gave a grin and tossed it over her shoulder, just to prove that she didn't always run to type. She explored his chest with her fingertips, moving in tiny circles across his skin; he caught his breath as her hands moved lower, to his abdomen.

'Nice six-pack, Mr Nicholson,' she said.

And then his mouth went dry as she undid the button and zip of his formal trousers.

'Gorgeous,' she breathed.

'Flora.' He had to stop himself grabbing her; he knew she wanted to be in charge and he had to be patient—even though right then he really wanted to pick her up and lay her back against the pillows before easing into her.

Slowly, slowly, she eased the material of his trousers over his hips.

He helped her then, kicking his shoes off and stepping out of his trousers, pulling his socks off at the same time.

'Turn round,' she said.

He did so, in a slow pirouette.

'Just gorgeous,' she said. 'Tom, you're perfect.'

'That's pretty much what I think about you,' he said. 'And, pretty as your dress is, I really want to take it off.'

She shook her head. 'You'll have to wait. I have other plans.'

He had no idea what she had in mind, but he was definitely playing by her rules tonight. 'I'm in your hands,' he told her.

She pulled the duvet aside and patted the pillows. 'Lie down.'

He did so, and she stood at the end of the bed, swaying to the music. His mouth went dry as she slowly, slowly peeled off her dress.

'Oh, wow. That lace stuff…it's gorgeous.' And he was desperate to take it off her.

She gave him a shy smile. 'You like it?'

'Very much. You're beautiful, Flora.'

She finished peeling off everything except her knickers, then sashayed over towards him.

'I need to touch you, Flora.' His voice was hoarse with need.

She glanced down at his underpants, which were hiding absolutely nothing. 'Mmm. I can see that.'

His breath hissed. 'Flora.'

She held up a finger. 'Wait.' She went to the drawer of the cabinet by her bed, opened it, and withdrew a condom. 'I think we might need this.'

Flora had bought condoms?

He must have spoken aloud, because she looked hurt. 'I'm not that staid and boring, Tom.'

'No, of course you're not.' He leaned forward and kissed her lightly. 'Just that it's my job to take care of you.'

'This is the twenty-first century. And I'm not fat, frumpy Flora any more.'

'You're gorgeous, curvy, incredibly sensual Flora,' he said. 'And I really, really need to touch you.' He dragged in a breath. 'I really, really need you to touch me. Before I implode.' He took her hand and tugged her towards him.

To his pleasure, she climbed onto the bed and straddled him. She manoeuvred him so she could remove his underpants, and then the only thing between them was the lace of her incredibly pretty knickers. He could feel the heat of her sex against his skin, and it sent him dizzy. 'Flora. I'm begging. Please?'

She ripped open the foil packet and slid the condom over his penis. Her hand was shaking slightly, but she was completely in control—and he was happy to let her take the lead, loving the new confidence she was showing.

She lifted herself slightly, drew the material of her knickers to one side, positioned him at her entrance and then slowly, slowly lowered herself onto him.

She leaned forward and touched her mouth to his before rising and lowering herself back on to him. As her arousal grew, she tipped her head back; Tom shifted so he could kiss her throat. He could feel the pulse beating hard there, just like his own heart was racing with desire and need and...*love*.

He felt her start to ripple round him, and he was lost.

'My adorable Flora. I love you,' he whispered, and kissed her hard as his climax shuddered through him.

She looked completely stunned.

'Are you OK?' he asked, wrapping his arms round her and holding her close.

'Yes.' She frowned. 'Did you just say what I think you said?'

He nodded. 'I'm sorry. I know it's fast. I know it's crazy. But my mum said something last weekend, something I know now is just so true. She said when you meet the right one, you *know*. And I do.'

'You love me,' she said in wonder.

'I love all of you, from those beautiful soft curls down to your pearl-pink toenails and everything in between. All that you are, I love,' he said softly.

Her eyes filled with tears. 'Oh, Tom. I love you, too.'

'Good.' He smiled. 'I was hoping you'd say that.'

Tom dealt with the condom, then switched off the music and the lights. Flora cuddled into him, resting her head on his shoulder; and he drifted off to sleep with his arms wrapped round her, feeling warmer and more at peace than he could ever remember.

CHAPTER THIRTEEN

FLORA woke the next morning in Tom's arms. He was already awake, and smiled down at her. 'Good morning, sleepyhead. How's the hangover?'

'What hangover?'

'The champagne you drank, last night,' he reminded her.

'I didn't drink that much,' she said with a smile. 'It wasn't champagne that made me all giddy. That was you.'

'I know the feeling—that's what you do to me.' He stole a kiss. 'I love you, Flora.'

She'd never get tired of hearing this. Never. 'I love you, too,' she said softly.

'So what are we doing today?'

'Much as I'd like to stay here with you all day, that's not an option.' She paused. 'Aren't your parents going back to France this evening?'

'Yes.'

'Then how about I cook us all Sunday lunch,' she said, 'and we spend the afternoon on the beach making sandcastles with Joey until they have to go?'

Tom held her close. A day with all the people he loved. *His family.* 'That,' he said, 'sounds absolutely perfect.'

'Turnout, vehicles 54 and 55. RTC.' There was a pause. 'Cutting gear needed.'

Road traffic collision.

Given the cold snaps they'd had over the winter, Tom had had to face several car accidents since he'd lost his sister to one. But this was the first time since then that they'd been told up front that they'd need cutting gear.

Please, God, let them be able to free the trapped and get everyone safely to hospital. Don't let another family have to go what his had gone through.

It turned out to be only one vehicle involved, wrapped round a tree. It looked as if the driver had hit black ice and spun off the road.

'The ambulance is on its way but we need to check out the driver now. Tom, you've got the ALS training,' Steve said.

'OK, Guv. I'm on it.' The passenger's side of the car was bent round the tree; Tom tried the driver's door, but it was jammed. He tried the rear passenger door, and to his relief it opened.

There wasn't a huge amount he could do before the ambulance arrived, but he could do the basics. ABCDE—airway, breathing, circulation, disability, exposure.

'I'm Tom, one of the fire crew,' he said, leaning in through the back door. 'The ambulance is on its way and we're going to get you out, mate. What's your name?'

'Ethan.'

The driver could speak, which meant his airway was clear. His breathing seemed a bit shallow, but Tom couldn't get a proper look to see if Ethan was losing any blood. ABC. D: disability. There were no immediate neurological problems, he thought, because Ethan had been able to answer a question. But as for exposure, checking the extent of his injuries—that would have to wait until they'd cut him out.

'Do you have any pain anywhere, Ethan?' Tom asked.

'My neck,' Ethan said.

Could be whiplash; could be a spinal injury. 'As soon as

the ambulance is here, we'll get a collar on you and get you out. Anywhere else?'

'My legs. My foot's stuck.'

The front of the car had crumpled, so Ethan's foot was probably caught between the pedals. They'd need the cutters to get him out—and they'd have to take the roof off the car to move him.

'We'll get you out of here soon. Can you remember what happened?'

'I was late for a meeting—then the car fishtailed and I was heading straight for the tree.'

Which sounded like a classic case of black ice. Given that he was running late, Ethan probably hadn't been giving his full concentration to the road; black ice was tough to spot at the best of times, but when you weren't looking for it you didn't stand a chance. Tom glanced into the car's interior. He couldn't see any passengers, but he needed to check. 'Were you on your own in the car?' he asked.

'Yes,' Ethan said.

'OK. I'm going to talk to my station manager about the best way to get you out. I'll be back in two minutes.' Steve was already assessing the car when Tom went to talk to him. 'Possible spinal injury, and his foot's stuck.'

'We're going to have to open the car for the ambo crew so they can get a board in, then,' Steve said. 'And probably cut the pedals to free him. Right. Let's stabilise the car.'

'I'll tell him what we're doing.' Tom leaned into the back of the car again. 'Ethan, we're going to make the car safe so it won't move, and then the paramedics are going to get you out, OK?'

'Uh-huh.'

The first emergency vehicle to arrive wasn't the ambulance, as Tom had expected, but the rapid response unit car. Josh O'Hara climbed out of the front seat.

'Hey, Tom. Looks nasty. What have we got?'

'Just the driver—his name's Ethan. He's talking, but th front's jammed so I can't tell if he's bleeding or how badly he's injured. His neck hurts and his foot's trapped.'

'If I get a collar on him, can you cut him out?'

'Sure.'

While Josh sorted out the collar, Tom and the rest of the fire crew sorted the rams and spreaders.

'Can you sit with him while we cut him out?' Tom asked.

'Course I will.'

Tom handed him the blue tear-shaped plastic shield and leaned into the back. 'Ethan, we're going to cut you out so the doctor can take a proper look at you. It's going to be noisy in here, but don't worry—Josh is going to stay with you. We have to cut through the windscreen, so Josh is going to hold a shield in front of you to make sure you don't get any glass in your face.'

'Uh-hmm.' Ethan's voice sounded slurred and Tom exchanged a concerned glance with Josh.

'Ten minutes and you'll be out of here,' Tom said.

By the time they'd cut him out, the ambulance crew had the trolley next to the car, ready to take Ethan in, and Josh had got a line into him so the all-essential fluids could go in. Tom put a shield over Ethan's legs to protect him, then used the cutter to snap the pedal trapping his legs. After that, the paramedics took over, getting a spinal board on Ethan, then taking him off to St Piran's.

Josh looked at Tom. 'You OK?'

'Yeah.' Just. And he knew why Josh had asked. 'I admit, it's making me think of my sister. And I just wish…' But wishing couldn't make things right. Couldn't bring her back.

Josh laid a hand on Tom's shoulder. 'I'm sorry, mate. There's nothing anyone can do or say to fix it.'

'No.' Tom looked at Josh. 'You don't look so good yourself. this bringing back memories for you, too?'

'No. It's just that life can be so… Have you ever done something you really, really regret later?'

Josh was usually the life and soul of the football match, joking and laughing afterwards. And Tom had the strongest feeling that his friend was doing exactly the same as Tom himself had always done: using laughter as a shield to hide his emotions. It looked to him as if Josh needed to talk to someone. And it might as well be him. 'Look, it's practically lunchtime,' he said. 'You must be due a break, too.'

'Well, yeah.'

'Fancy grabbing a sandwich?'

Josh shook his head. 'A sandwich won't do. Even if it comes with chunky fries.'

'If it's a serious carb fix you need, how about pizza?'

'That,' Josh said, 'would definitely work for me.'

'OK. See you at Luigi's in twenty minutes?'

'You're on.'

Twenty minutes later Josh walked into the pizza parlour to see Josh already there. Josh ordered a pizza loaded with absolutely everything, and wisecracked his way through the whole meal. Tom waited until their coffees had arrived, then said gently, 'OK. You do the same as I do—tell enough jokes and it'll all go away. Except it doesn't.' He paused. 'So what's happened?'

Josh sighed. 'It's messy.'

'I'm not going to spill to anyone. Tell me,' Tom encouraged him.

'Years ago, I fell for someone. It went wrong—and it was my fault.' A muscle flickered in Josh's jaw. 'I never forgot her, but there was no way we were going to be together.'

'And you got married on the rebound?' Tom asked. He'd heard the rumours that Josh's marriage was in trouble, and his

wife never appeared at the football matches nowaday
had met Rebecca a couple of times; she was nice enoug.
maybe a little too picture-perfect.

Josh sighed. 'No. I loved Rebecca, thought I did, but
I'm honest I know I never felt the same connection with he.
as I did with my ex. We've been drifting apart for years.' He
looked grim. 'I don't think our marriage can be saved and I
don't think either of us really wants to try saving it.'

'So you're looking at divorce?'

'I guess so. We want different things out of life. She wants
a baby above all else.'

'And I take it you don't?'

Josh grimaced. 'I've never wanted kids—never—and she
knows that. We had a deal.' He blew out a breath. 'And now
I've done something really stupid. I got drunk at the dinner
on Saturday night. And...you know how it is. You're tired,
you're not thinking about what you're doing. She was warm,
she was there—and, God help me.' He raked a hand through
his hair. 'I shouldn't have done it. It wasn't fair to her. I didn't
use a condom—and she didn't stop me.'

Tom looked at him in sympathy. 'Have you talked to her
about it since?'

'No. She's pretending it never happened, but we both know
it did. And we both know why it happened, too.' Josh sighed.
'This is crazy. I don't love her any more, and she doesn't love
me. I ought to let her go, find someone who'll give her what
she wants.'

'And you're still thinking about the girl you lost?' Tom
guessed.

'It would help,' Josh said drily, 'if I didn't have to work
with her.'

Tom blew out a breath. 'Tricky one. Does she know you
still have feelings for her?'

'I'm not sure. She won't discuss it with me. On Saturday,

me to go home to my wife. And, like an idiot, I did.
.' He sighed. 'Rebecca knew I was drunk, that I wasn't
king straight. And I'll never forgive myself if we've made
aby.'

'She's not on the Pill?'

'She was,' Josh said, but his tone made it clear he didn't think she was any more.

'It doesn't always happen first time,' Tom said. 'You're a doctor. You know the odds.'

'Yeah.' Josh drained his coffee. 'Well, enough of my problems. How are things with Joey?'

'He's really started to open up to me,' Tom said. 'Funny, I used to be like you. I never thought I wanted kids. But now I'm Joey's stand-in dad…and I'm getting used to it. More than that, I'm actually enjoying it.'

'And you have Flora. She's a sweetheart.'

'A definite keeper,' Tom said.

'I hope it works out for you,' Josh said. He glanced at his watch. 'And we'd better get back on shift. See you at the game on Sunday?'

'Absolutely. And we're going to beat you four-nil,' Tom said with a grin.

'In your dreams.' Josh clapped him on the shoulder. 'Thanks, mate.'

'I didn't do a lot.'

'You listened. It helped.'

Though, seeing the shadows in his friend's eyes, Tom wasn't so sure.

'Good day?' Flora asked as Tom walked in.

'Sort of.' He ruffled Joey's hair, made a fuss of Banjo, then came to steal a kiss from Flora. 'I had to cut someone out of a car today.'

Joey went very still.

'He skidded on the ice,' Tom said gently, 'but he was all right. He wasn't very well when he got to hospital, but they made him better. He's got a sore shoulder and a broken ankle, but the doctors told me he's going to be fine.'

'That's good.' Flora put a mug of tea in front of him.

'I've been thinking,' he said. 'I'm going to resign from the fire service.'

'What?' She stared at him. 'Why? You love your job. It's who you are.'

'I know.' He wrinkled his nose. 'But I think it's the only way.'

'The only way to do what, Tom?'

'I know what I want out of life. I want to be a family with you both,' Tom said. 'And my job's dangerous. It's not fair to make you take on that burden.'

'Tom, we love you for who you are—and you've always been a firefighter. It's what you've always wanted to do. You'd be miserable doing anything else.'

'Maybe.' He looked at Flora and Joey. 'But you're worth it.'

'Don't we get a say in this?' Flora asked.

Tom frowned. 'How do you mean?'

'We know what you do is dangerous but it's an important job. Provided you don't take stupid risks—and you know exactly what I mean by that—I can handle it,' she told him. 'Joey?'

Joey frowned. Then he said, 'I love you, Tom.'

Tom stared at him, completely unable to speak. A month ago, Joey had barely been stringing two words together and had hated being touched; he never, but never spoke about anything emotional. And now, unless his hearing had suddenly gone skewy...

He glanced at Flora, and knew that he'd definitely heard Joey say it.

I love you.

'I love you too, sweetheart,' he whispered.

'If your fire engine had gone to rescue my mum and dad, they'd still be here instead of going to heaven,' Joey said.

Tom felt as if his soul had just been flayed. The little boy had that much confidence in him? And yet, even though Tom knew he was incredibly committed to his job, he wasn't sure that he could've saved Susie and Kevin. Nobody could've been pulled out of a collision like that. 'Joey, sweetheart, I don't know if anyone could've saved them,' he said softly.

'But if anyone could, you could,' Joey said. 'And I don't want someone else to lose their mum and dad because you're not on the team any more.'

'Out of the mouths of babes,' Flora said. 'He's got a point. You're good at what you do. No, you're amazing at what you do.'

'But wouldn't you both be happier if I had a less dangerous job—something that didn't risk my life?' he asked.

Flora and Joey looked at each other, clearly considering it, then shook their heads in unison.

'I'd still be worrying about you,' Flora said, 'but I'd be worrying that you were unhappy, not that you were in danger.'

'So you'd be OK if I stayed as a firefighter?' He could really have it all—a family *and* his career? It was really that easy? He'd spent days and days trying to work out what he should do, ever since Flora had made him realise that he had to consider Joey before he took the more dangerous risks. And he'd come to the conclusion that there wasn't a middle way—that he'd have to give up who he was.

And now, it seemed, he didn't.

Joey nodded. 'You're really cool, Uncle Tom.'

'I second that,' Flora said.

Banjo barked, as if to third it, and Flora and Joey laughed.

'If we're a family,' Joey said, 'does that mean we'll all live here with Banjo?'

'Would you like that?' Tom asked.

Joey nodded. 'You'd be like my dad and Flora would be like my mum. That'd be cool. And then you'd have a baby.'

'A baby?' Flora asked, looking surprised.

'Because that's what people do when they get married. Have babies. And I'd be a big brother.' He beamed. 'That'd be cool, too.'

Tom thought of Flora, pregnant with his child, and sheer desire surged through him. 'Sounds good to me. Flora?'

She coughed. 'Is that a proposal, Tom Nicholson?'

He smacked his forehead. 'I'm meant to be down on one knee, and there should be champagne and diamonds and—'

'And none of that's important,' Flora interrupted. 'What's important is exactly what Joey said.'

'So how about it? Would you marry us and be a family with us?'

'Would you?' Joey said. 'And can we live here?'

Flora smiled at them. 'I can't think of anything in the world I'd rather do. Yes.'

Tom picked her up and swung her round, Joey whooped with glee, and Banjo barked madly. And when he set her back down on her feet, he enfolded Joey in a hug along with Flora. 'My family,' he said. 'My perfect dream come true.'

LET'S TALK
Romance

For exclusive extracts, competitions
and special offers, find us online:

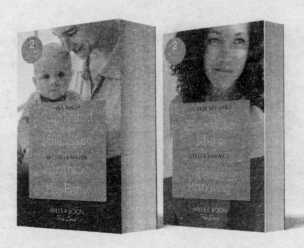